LITTLE HATCHET

ALSO BY PHIL OAKLEY

LITTLE HATCHET

Book One in The Oakleys Series

PHIL OAKLEY

Stoney Creek Publishing

A Member of the Texas Book Consortium

Published by

Stoney Creek Publishing Group

StoneyCreekPublishing.com

ISBN: 979-8-9879002-5-3
ISBN (ebook): 979-8-9879002-6-0
Library of Congress Control Number: 2023922041

Cover design by Market Your Industry, marketyourindustry.com

Originally published as Telegraph © *2000 by Phil Oakley*

For my granddaughter, Sophia Grace Oakley
You bring love, joy and hope always

CONTENTS

AUTHOR'S NOTE

Little Hatchet is an origin story. It's about an American family who set roots in the frontier, first in New Mexico and later in the Texas Hill Country. Their hard work to build a peaceful life alongside the bubbling waters of Little Hatchet Creek and the South Llano River began after the Civil War. Their challenges were formidable, but the newcomers learned to get along with the old residents of their new neighborhoods: the Mescalero Apaches, the Comanches and the Tejanos.

The family built for themselves and for their new America, but they were horrified as the violent storms of Texas washed away their hard work in furious, boiling floodwater. Their children were beautiful and smart, but the third generation faced eradication from the decadence, drunkenness, and violence of Prohibition and the Jazz Age.

The family in Little Hatchet, the Oakleys, is loosely based on my own, but the book is very much a work of fiction. Some of these things happened, but not in the same way or in the same locations described in the book.

I have always wondered how my life might have been in an earlier time. Could I have met the challenges of the frontier? Would I have been tough enough to do what my great grandparents did? Would I have had the internal strength to endure the heartbreak my grandparents suffered when their own children were beset by one tragedy after another, in what must have seemed like an endless sequence of misery, sorrow and disappointment? Could I have ever been as wise as my grandparents? Could I have kept the faith? How do I measure up to the high bar they set?

In creating what would become this series of three books, I started with some family stories, handed down through the generations, but as I developed the characters, the story took on a life of its own. I hope you enjoy the journey as much as I did.

CHAPTER ONE

Little Puma sat statue like overlooking a prosperous farm spread along Little Hatchet Creek, evaluating his target. Turning his head slightly, he studied the mounted Mescalero horsemen forming a line to his left, poised and ready to strike. Little Puma moved his eyes along the row and stopped, focusing on Peyote, the oldest of the braves.

Great God! What can I do with this crazy cousin of mine? If he were here, facing this dilemma, what would my grandfather do? Little Puma dismissed the comparison, certain that the revered supreme elder of the Mescalero had never been as unsure of himself as Little Puma was. Nothing like this could ever have happened to the legendary warrior chief, who had put Little Puma in charge of this foray.

Little Puma's cousin had been called Peyote since the age of four, after his father and mother had died of cholera. Peyote's elderly grandmother was the favorite sister of Little Puma's grandfather. She had taken in the boy, who, even at that young age, had been thought of as bizarre.

"We will call him Peyote," Little Puma's grandfather had proclaimed.

"He sees things others do not, and he acts like an entranced warrior dancing by the firelight," the chief had explained.

That was only half of Peyote's troubles. Not only did he see visions; but at the worst possible time, Peyote's hallucinations led him to do things that were clearly and completely crazy, often endangering the lives of the other young members of the tribe. And each time, when the catastrophe was over, no one could make Peyote understand how insane and dangerous his actions had been. Little Puma had reached the point of total frustration with his cousin.

If I sent him home, my aunt would die from disgrace, Little Puma believed.

If I sent him back to the stronghold, he might refuse to go. Little Puma knew that if his cousin did not leave when ordered, there would almost certainly be a fight, a contest that Little Puma might not win. Not only was Peyote bigger and stronger, but he was possessed by a spirit that did not seem to be of this world.

But if I don't send him home, we will fail here, just as we did at Tularosa, Little Puma concluded. One more failure would mean certain disgrace for Little Puma. As he struggled to wipe these negative images from his mind, the young chief could not erase the picture of himself standing in utter humiliation before the entire tribe.

In the valley below, it had been a frustrating day for the Oakleys, as well. James' still saddled horse, a big gelding, stood in front of the ranch house. Alongside it, the paint Walter rode also remained saddled with her reins resting atop the hitching rail, as she waited patiently. Upstairs, Rebecca lay with a fever that had not let up for five days. Little Matt, the baby of the family, had seemingly been forgotten, left on the front porch by his older sister Katie, while she struggled in the kitchen inside the house, attempting to prepare the midday meal for the entire Oakley family. The task was clearly too challenging for an eleven-year-old.

James, the family patriarch, was out of Little Puma's sight in the farthest hog pen, where he was attempting to free one of his boar hogs that had become stuck between two posts. Walter was inside the barn, arguing with a mule.

CHAPTER TWO

As Little Puma stared down intently at the activity on the Oakley farm from above, the young brave's mind wandered back thirteen days to Tularosa. For the thousandth time, he went over what had gone wrong on that earlier night. He'd left Peyote with the horses a hundred yards downwind of the ranch hands. Little Puma had planned the attack carefully. Even though the Mescalero had ridden up on the herd just before sundown, the band of raiders had waited in silence with perfect discipline, until long after the ranchers were asleep.

All the young men, except for Peyote, had slipped quietly up to the cowboys' horses. They were taking the hobbles off noiselessly. No sign of stirring came from any of the ranch hands. Two more horses stood within easy reach of the native hunters. Just two more horses to gather, and the raiding party could slip away from the camp. The braves' eyes and ears were alert to any sign of danger.

Across the ravine, Peyote watched in complete terror. His brothers were all about to be killed! Peyote's entire body became taut, poised for action as his eyes tracked the bright blue, green, and yellow monster that danced between his position and the raiding party.

Peyote had first spotted the menacing devil, just about the time his companions had reached the cowboys' corral. The hideous giant was threatening and spewing fire from its mouth, but initially did not attack.

His fellow tribesmen are brave, but very foolish, Peyote thought, as he readied an arrow and kept careful watch on the demon. He would protect his friends, with his own life, if necessary. No one had ever questioned Peyote's bravery. The same could be said of the strange one's devotion to his friends and kin.

At times, the bright vision would charge directly at Peyote, but would pull up just short of him. Then it would dash back toward the other members of the raiding party. Each time, just before it attacked, the spirit would laugh, billow smoke from its head, then turn away—a demonic feint, Peyote was sure.

While Peyote had not figured out how the band would get past the taunting monster and bring the horses across the ravine, he had complete faith in Little Puma. When the fiery devil jumped directly on top of Little Puma, Peyote could wait no longer.

"Watch out!" he screamed and released the arrow he had held ready.

"Damn!" Peyote cursed, as the arrow went wide.

Instead of striking the evil spirit, the arrow stuck in the eye of one of the cowboys' horses Little Puma was holding. The horse reared and screamed at the top of its lungs. Warning the other braves, Peyote began shouting as loudly as he could.

"Run for it! Come on! I'll cover you!"

Total chaos. The braves dropped the reins to the captured horses and sprinted for the ravine. Just as Peyote got his second arrow ready, the ranch hands opened fire with their rifles. One of the first bullets must have struck the devil. Because as Peyote looked up to aim, the terrifying monster had vanished from sight. Peyote quickly removed the arrow from his bow and replaced it in his quiver. He scurried to line all the horses up as the young braves charged toward the ravine. Little Puma reached his horse first and sprang onto her, while shouting to the others.

"Let's get out of here! Come on! Let's go!" he commanded.

Only seconds after the braves started to ride, the ranch hands' guns exploded into frantic, constant, deadly fire. In an instant, the young natives heard the thunder of hoof beats and bullets whizzing close to their heads.

The cowboys were charging breakneck after the braves, shooting as they rode.

In the initial chaos, each of the braves seemed to head in a different direction. If Little Puma had not jerked on Peyote's horse's reins, Little Puma's cousin would have ridden directly into ranchers' barrage and immediate death. After reining in Peyote, Little Puma headed each of his other charges west.

Even though the night was pitch dark, Little Puma could see the faint shape of hills in the distance, where he hoped to hide his raiding party. The horses ridden by the young tribesmen were fast and their feet were sure, but the Mescalero led the race against the cowboys by only a half mile.

The confusion in the first moments of the escape had cost Little Puma's hunters dearly. The youngsters lurched through the darkness at full speed, as bullets zinged past. Sometimes the bullets came so close, the young men could feel the air move as the projectiles passed.

The braves covered the distance to the first hill in thirty-six minutes, but it seemed like a lifetime to the adrenaline-charged tribesmen. As the horses moved over a ridge between two small hills on the eastern edge of the range, each of the braves was ready to scream with joy and relief. Instead, they kept silent, remained disciplined and fell in, single file, behind Little Puma, who would lead the climb up the first hill.

When the shooting stopped, Little Puma did not pause. He moved the braves onward into the darkness. The unshod feet of the tribesmen's horses were almost silent on the limestone of the creek bed they were following. As the youth rose further into the hills, they could hear the unmistakable sound of horseshoes clicking against the rocks, still not far behind.

Suddenly, Little Puma's horse lurched, almost leaving him behind. He pulled the horse's head back, but it was no use. The animal charged on and the others followed. In minutes, the native horses were standing in a small pool of water, drinking.

Little Puma led his group straight through the night. Thirty minutes before the sun rose to the top of the hills, the braves started down the rocky slope, sparsely dotted with mesquite and cactus, heading toward the big sand. Those blinding white sands stretched thirty miles to the rocky San Andres Mountains, then west for another twenty miles.

At daylight, the cattlemen and their horses drank some water that had risen out of the mud at the bottom of a creek bed and filled their canteens with what was left. They trailed west along the mostly dry creek.

The older men knew their quarries had cut north through the hills, but that was slow going. In less than an hour, the creek bed had led them to the white sands. They turned north along the western slope of the ridge for about two and a half miles, where the dry stream passed seamlessly into the sand.

"Them boys turned west as soon as they could. We'll have 'em in an hour or two," one cowboy predicted.

It was past noon when another rancher pointed at a black dot, two miles north and three miles west.

"That's them," he announced.

That was when the men made their only mistake of the chase, a misstep which probably saved the young Mescalero from dying on the white sands.

"They got another ten miles of sand before they get to the San Andres. They'll never make it. Good chance we won't either."

The cowboy who had spoken earlier pulled his horse to a stop.

"They'll die out there," he asserted, pointing to the barely visible speck at the very edge of the horizon, the dot that the ranch hands believed to be the disappearing warriors.

"No point in us dying chasing 'em," he concluded.

Little Puma had spotted the pursuing cowboys just before they turned around. He knew the ranch hands were leaving the young men to die in the desert.

CHAPTER THREE

In a legend Mescalero tell by the fire, a young chief like Little Puma would still be sitting erect and alert in the saddle, leading his band to safety. In truth, like the rest of the braves, Little Puma had fallen asleep from exhaustion and dehydration. The horses were doing only a little better, but they had kept moving, perhaps to find water or maybe because they were only dumb animals.

About a quarter mile into the rocky hills, the horses stumbled onto some soil beside the bed of a dry creek. There was no water, but clusters of dried grass were scattered about. As Little Puma's horse lowered her head to graze, the young chief fell from the pony onto the rocky ground.

He was still alert enough to remember he was leading other braves. Little Puma rose unsteadily to his feet. He pulled the others and their blankets from their horses. He got his own blanket from his horse, lay on the ground, and fell deeply asleep.

An intense dream enveloped him. His braves were all being tugged toward death. Little Puma sought desperately to wake up and rescue the young men under his command. As hard as he struggled, Little Puma couldn't break away from the incapacitating sleep, could not force himself awake.

The young Mescalero slept through the thunder and lightning that had moved into the hills from the south. It had been raining hard for almost five hours when Little Puma finally woke. The horses were soaked and huddled together near the stream bed, where water several inches deep rushed past toward the white sand.

Little Puma sprang to his feet and ran into the rushing water. He put his face directly in the cold water and began sucking it in. When his thirst was quenched, he rose and began waking his charges. Each of the young braves went to the water just as Little Puma had done. By sunup, the young men sat close together a few feet from their horses. The braves were soaked and freezing, but they were alive.

Just as the light became full, Peyote, lying on the ground, rose at lightning speed to a full upright stance, skillfully gripping a rock in his hand. In a single motion, the eldest brave hurled the stone, instantly killing a large jackrabbit that had been drinking from the stream. Within an hour, the experienced young hunters had also killed an armadillo, a rat snake, and a second rabbit. They topped their meal with ripe prickly pear from a patch of cactus growing close to the surging desert wash.

Little Puma's band had narrowly and miraculously survived. They drank all the water they could hold, then rode west. Two nights later, Little Puma's group camped beside the Rio Grande. They killed a deer, rested and regained their strength.

Having been tested by such fire, the rest of the young braves' mission should have seemed easy. But, as Little Puma's band rode further south and west, nothing went right. They raided several ranches, but came away with nothing more impressive than chickens.

No matter how dark or how late, the ranchers seemed ready for the braves. The young men were tormented by dogs, rifles, and discouragement. Two more weeks passed, and the Mescalero still had captured no horses to take back to the tribe. As disappointing as their raids had turned out, it was astounding that none of the braves had been shot or savaged by angry hounds.

Little Puma was a natural leader and a careful planner. His sneak attack on the herd near Tularosa had seemed flawless. He had the horses in hand. The cowboys had slept on. The braves were all set to ride home as heroes with the captured horses. But Peyote's hallucinatory battle against the devil spirit had immediately destroyed success, plunging the raiders into chaotic failure.

At each of the succeeding raids, Little Puma had planned carefully, and the youngsters had followed his orders, but the loot was paltry, embarrassing. The band was discouraged and ashamed.

As they sat on their horses overlooking the Little Hatchet, Little Puma knew it was time for bold action. He saw the horses in the corral beside the barn and the two prize animals tethered to the porch. He also calculated that James was too far away from his horses to intervene.

Without hesitating, Little Puma led the braves down the hillside toward the ranch, ordering everyone but Peyote to go with him to the corral. The raiders slipped in quietly, careful not to alert James. When they were almost to the barn and still unnoticed, Little Puma's group eased noiselessly into the pen with the horses, while Peyote crept stealthily toward the two saddled horses close to the house.

Inside the barn and out of the site of the raiders, the mule had Walter cornered in a stall. He was shoving a hayfork in the animal's face trying to get past him when Walter heard the horses' noises. Little Puma's braves had leads on all the Oakleys' horses and had passed them successfully out of the corral. Peyote had the reins of the big gelding in his hands, but Walter's horse had backed away from the porch and trotted out of reach. Peyote circled around behind Walter's horse, but the prize mare was cunningly eluding her would-be thief.

Walter hurriedly shut the gate to the stall and trotted quickly to the barn door. Walter wondered if a wolf or mountain lion could be stalking the remuda in broad daylight. Was a stray grizzly bear prowling?

What Walter saw was even more shocking. Just as the eldest Oakley child reached the door, Little Puma's party had brought the ranch horses and their own mounts to a trot as they hurried past the edge of the house.

Next, a horrified Walter spotted Peyote astride an Apache pony with no saddle only a few feet from the Oakleys' porch. Peyote had stolen James' horse, but Walter's mare taunted the intense young warrior from ten feet away.

Peyote had lost sight of Walter's horse for only a second or two. But then, the stout young warrior fixed on another tiny horse lying on the porch, wrapped in a baby blanket. As rapidly as he had killed the jackrabbit and shot at the devil attacking Little Puma, Peyote slid from his horse to the porch. With lightning quickness, he swooped up the creature wrapped in the blanket and jumped back on his own horse, holding the new captive in his arms.

Walter stood frozen in the barn door as the big Apache whisked little Matt Oakley, Walter's youngest sibling, off the front porch. He tried to scream, but Walter couldn't force out any sound at all. He attempted to run, but his legs were locked in place and would not budge. Walter was paralyzed and silenced by his disbelief, by the horror he had just experienced, the kidnapping of his infant brother.

Peyote kicked his horse, galloping after the rest of the Mescalero. Walter attempted again to summon a scream, but still was frustrated by a silent void. He lunged forward, calling up every last particle of strength and determination. And this time, his legs finally came back to life. Walter ran for all he was worth. As he hit the front door of the house, he screamed to Katie.

"Run! Get Papa! Indians have stolen Matt!"

Now it was Katie who was immobilized by terror. The words she had just heard were beyond comprehension.

"Get Papa!" Walter commanded his sister.

Katie dropped the wooden spoon and raced from the house. Walter flew into action, reaching above the fireplace to grab his father's new Winchester. In a second, he was out the door and into the front yard. He raised the rifle toward the raiders, who were halfway up the bluff. Peyote was in his sights and Walter began slowly expelling breath, preparing to squeeze the trigger.

But an instant before the metal moved, he saw Little Matt's blanket. Walter jerked the gun toward the sky and let the round discharge into the air. He could not risk killing his little brother.

Walter dropped the rifle in the dirt and ran full out for his horse. Leaping into the saddle, he tore toward the fleeing Mescalero at dead speed, mercilessly digging his heels into his horse's flanks.

Katie had almost reached the hog pens when she heard the shot. She tried with everything inside herself to holler to her father, but she was too winded from the run. James looked up and saw his son running for his horse. He dropped the timber he had been using to free the hog and vaulted over the top rail of his hog pen. In seconds, he was standing beside Katie with both hands on her shoulders.

"What happened, daughter?"

Katie, gasping for air, managed to get out three words.

"Indians got Matt!"

James ran full speed for the house, scooping up the Winchester Walter had dropped. Frantically, James wiped dirt from the gun with his handkerchief as he trotted into the house. He grabbed bacon, biscuits, and cornmeal, stuffing them into a saddlebag. He shoved two boxes of shells into the bag, swooped up two canteens and all the blankets in sight, then burst out the door. A second later, Katie reached the porch.

"Where's my horse, Katie?"

"Indians got him, Papa," the girl answered, breathlessly.

"Go upstairs and tell your mother I'm going to get Little Matt back," James commanded as he charged toward the barn.

James jerked down a dusty old saddle that had belonged to his father and slung a blanket and the saddle over the mule. He stuffed a bit into the animal's mouth. The mule wasn't finished with the tantrum he had earlier been inflicting on Walter, but the stubborn animal knew not to mess with James. Walter and Matt's severely determined father swung himself onto the giant draft animal. In seconds, James was out of the barn, and the rescue of his two sons was on.

Walter had never ridden so fast or so well. As he topped the ridge overlooking the Little Hatchet, he spotted the warring natives moving away. Walter dug his heels into his horse, but the little mare was already at full speed. She kept her intensity and Walter gained on the Mescalero braves, whose pace slowed slightly because they were leading the horses they had taken from the Oakleys.

Little Puma looked back for the first time as his band topped the bluff. He thought his raid had been a complete success until he his eyes stopped on Peyote. Why had Peyote taken the child? What could have possessed him?

Little Puma had known Peyote all his life. He knew there were no answers to his questions. His instincts told him to stop, take the child away from Peyote, and leave the baby where the ranchers would find him. Before he slowed his horse to act on his instinct, another thought struck.

He remembered all the crazy things he had seen Peyote do. If stealing this child was one of those insane things, Little Puma might have to kill his childhood friend to get the baby away from him. While they fought, the white men would likely catch up. Then they would have to choose whether to leave the horses or fight the white men. He knew these ranchers had guns.

He knew something else about Peyote. He was the biggest and strongest of the young raiders. No brave had ever beaten Peyote in a fight. Little Puma had never wrestled with his cousin, but he recalled his earlier doubts. If Peyote was being controlled by his schizophrenia, Little Puma might well be the brave who would die in a fight.

Little Puma kept riding at full speed. When he looked over his shoulder a second time, he spotted the rancher, who was pursuing the Mescalero for all he and his horse were worth. Walter was far enough behind that he only appeared as a figure on a horse. Little Puma, age sixteen, did not realize that he was being chased by a twelve-year-old. It seemed that white men had been malevolently coming after him, ever since he had left home. They all had guns and all of them wanted him dead. At that moment, Little Puma categorized Walter as another angry white man with a gun.

Little Puma motioned to Swift Deer. The brave responded instinctively and instantly. Swift Deer moved closer to Little Puma and handed over the reins to the horses he was leading. As Little Puma took the leather straps controlling the horses, Swift Deer's own mount cut an arc to the right, then fell in behind the other braves. He would keep an eye on Walter from that vantage point, just as his leader had ordered.

Walter's pursuit was intense. He noticed that the Apache carrying Little Matt was no longer at the rear of the band. Walter recalculated, deciding to ride past the warrior who had become the new rear guard.

Walter focused fully on the raider holding the youngest Oakley child. When he caught up with the big brave who had his brother, Walter intended to spring from his horse and pull the stout rider and Matt to the ground. Then, he would scoop up his infant brother and stomp on the head of the Mescalero who had taken Matt. If everything worked just right, Walter would disable the kidnapper, quickly remount his own horse, and dash back toward the ranch.

Walter could not figure why the band had taken Matt, but he was certain the raiders wanted the Oakleys' horses more than they wanted the white baby.

Walter never once looked at the smaller brave who had become rear guard, so he didn't see Swift Deer load an arrow into his bow. Neither did Walter see the arrow as it whizzed directly at him, knocking Walter to the ground.

CHAPTER FOUR

James topped a ridge and saw his son's horse grazing, but there was no sign of Walter. James fought back tears and panic. He was almost certain that somewhere ahead, he would find two of his sons dead. James Oakley was a man who had seen too much death. The memories of the scores of dead bodies he had encountered could never be erased from his mind. James had been haunted by images of blood, gore, maiming and death, long after his service in the army of the Confederate States of America ended.

As an officer, James Oakley had been entitled to keep his horse and sword. He had lost the useless sword early in the fighting, and his horse had been killed eight months before Lee surrendered. That's when James began riding an old mule named Anderson, the same cantankerous beast he was astride, when he spotted Walter's riderless horse. For the first time since he had settled in New Mexico, all those horrible images surged back into James' thoughts. And in this moment, he was in dreadful fear that the sight of two dead sons was about to be added to his catalogue of unbearable memories.

The former soldier from Arkansas dismounted from the mule and slid onto Walter's horse, trailing the mule behind him. He spurred the little mare. When the mule had balked at running, James had slapped it sternly in the face with the lead rope. If the animal had not broken into a gallop, James would have shot him on the spot. Life was getting too far out of his control.

After a seemingly endless search that, in fact, consumed only thirty minutes of real time, James was kneeling beside Walter.

"Thank you, God!" James prayed, instantly, joyful and relieved to find his son alive.

But the extremely grateful father knew there was an urgent task lying on the ground in front of him. Proper prayers and contemplation could come later. First, James must determine how seriously Walter had been hurt. Quickly, he noted the big knot on his son's head and the Apache arrow in his left arm. The arrow had only cut through an inch or so of the skin on the inside of his arm. By the time his father arrived, Walter's bleeding had stopped of its own accord.

James poured some water from one of the canteens onto a big blue handkerchief and began washing Walter's face. In a minute or so, the boy moaned. Then he jerked his head up, apparently intending to spring to his feet. James gently restrained his son, who only then seemed to recognize his father kneeling beside him.

"Papa, the Indians took Little Matt," Walter gasped.

"I know," his father answered evenly, seeking to calm his wounded son.

"Come on. Let's get going. I had almost caught them when I fell off my horse," Walter urged, feeling he had made all the case for an instant pursuit that was needed and thinking there was no time to waste on further explanation.

Then Walter looked down at his arm. Seeing the arrow sticking out, he realized for the first time that the Apaches had shot him. Walter instinctively reached to pull the arrow out of his arm, but his father stopped him.

"That needs some attention, son. We'll take care of it as soon as we get you home," James said calmly, in a low, soothing voice.

Walter looked at his father. He was not an impetuous boy, but strong willed and determined. If not a grown man, at least he was a big brother, one with serious responsibilities. A few moments earlier, Walter's little brother had been almost within his reach, and Walter did not intend to give up his quest because an Apache arrow was piercing his arm.

"We can't go back home. We have to go get Little Matt," Walter pleaded with conviction, his iron will on full display.

James could have confessed his fear for Walter's safety to his very determined and almost foolishly brave son, but he didn't. Nor did James admit how emotionally charged his own state of mind was. He could have revealed to Walter, for example, that less than an hour had passed since James had been prepared to shoot his own mule, had it defied him. James summoned up every bit of self-control available, so that his face would not betray the relief he felt, knowing that his eldest son was not dead.

"All right," James conceded after a long period of silence he had used to consider Walter's brave but less than cautious proposal.

"We won't go back. I'll fix your arm here, and we'll resume our rescue of Matt in the morning."

Walter badly wished to convince his father to wait until after they had Little Matt back in their care, before using precious time to treat his arm. Walter strongly believed that he and his father should mount up at once. However, he restrained himself, saying nothing and deciding to accept his father's decision.

Up to the northeast, Little Puma was glumly and silently speculating about what was happening behind him. Would the rancher stop to bury the cowboy who had been chasing him? Would he take the body back to the ranch, then come looking for Peyote after he had grieved? One way or another, Little Puma knew the rancher would come. Peyote had seen to that by whisking the baby from the rancher's porch.

As soon as the sun had set, Little Puma slowed the horses. They couldn't run all night, but they could walk until daylight. Little Puma knew he had to put as much distance between his band of braves and that hapless ranch as possible. The young leader's concentration was broken by the sound of a crying baby. Little Puma handed the reins of the horses he was leading to the tribal member closest to him, then rode to the rear of the small column.

The young chief couldn't help being struck by the wonder in Peyote's eyes. It was obvious that Peyote had no idea how a fussing baby had gotten into his arms. The big, powerful Mescalero youth looked at the child like a bewildered new father. Little Puma reached out his arms and Peyote handed over the child.

Little Matt wouldn't stop crying. Who knows what the baby had thought during the kidnapping and the mad flight away from the Little Hatchet? But now, Matt was determined that everyone know his thoughts. It was past his suppertime and Little Matt was hungry. If hunger went unattended, Little Matt knew just what to do: cry as loudly as possible.

The Mescalero rode on for another hour with Little Matt screaming at the top of his volume range. Finally, off in the distance, Little Puma spotted the adobe hovel of a poor Hispanic family. The young leader realized at once that these people were far too poor to own any kind of firearm.

There was no hope of sneaking up on the adobe with Little Matt screaming. So the band, except for Peyote, charged the house at full speed. On Little Puma's signal, the young braves surrounded the house and readied their weapons. Little Puma called, and the herdsman walked out of his adobe to face the warriors.

Little Puma had never heard a language other than his own Apache dialect. So when the Spanish-speaking goat herder looked at him, Little Puma forcefully spoke the Mescalero word for woman. The herdsman did not understand, but Little Puma held up the screaming baby to emphasize his point and its urgency.

"*Uno momento, por favor?*" the man requested.

He went into the house and quickly returned with his wife, who took the child from the young chief. Little Puma was tempted to leave the baby with the *familia*, but he stared up the hill, where Peyote waited with the horses.

Once again, the young leader was forced to consider how Peyote might react if Little Puma actually followed through and rid the war party of this serious threat to their mission and to the tribe's safety. The probability of a catastrophic reaction by Peyote was just too great.

Inside the adobe, Little Matt had stopped crying. In a few minutes, the herdsman brought out some corn tortillas. The frightened little man did his best to put the threats posed by the warriors out of his mind as he doled out the splendid bread his wife had lovingly cooked for their family.

The young men had eaten the corn bread before the herdsman reached his door with the empty plate. The next time the owner came out of his house, he offered dried goat meat to the young Mescalero men at arms.

The roasted goat was tough and stringy and lacked the pungent taste of the wild game the hunters would have preferred. Still, they gulped the meat just as they had done with the tortillas.

The goat herder also brought a jar of warm goat's milk, pausing while each of the braves took his turn drinking from the clay urn. When the braves had devoured the milk, Little Puma spoke again.

"Woman," he repeated in his Apache tongue.

"*Momento señor?*" the farmer responded.

The little man entered the house once more and was inside much longer. When he came out, his wife was with him. She carried Little Matt, but she had wrapped him in a fresh blanket. The woman motioned for Little Puma to get down from his horse.

After he had dismounted, she looped the blanket over his shoulder so that Little Matt could ride on the Mescalero's chest, leaving the brave's hands free. After Little Puma had climbed back on his horse, the woman handed him a skin filled with goat's milk. She pointed toward Little Matt to indicate the milk in the skin was for the baby.

Finally, she took Little Matt's blanket from her husband, who had been holding it, and handed it to the brave. The herdsman's wife had filled the blanket with more tortillas and meat. Little Puma took the blanket from the woman, but kept staring directly into the goat herder's eyes.

"Let's go!" Little Puma commanded his braves.

The warriors on the other side of the house brought their horses to a trot. Those near Little Puma backed their horses away from the adobe house, then turned and galloped up the hill.

Little Puma told the braves to tie the spare horses together in three groups so they could lead the animals more easily. He handed a stained rag filled with tortillas and dried goat meat to Peyote. As soon as the braves had rearranged the horses, Little Puma led the braves and their animals off to the northeast.

Back toward the Little Hatchet, James had built a mesquite fire. When it burned down, he laid his Bowie knife on the glowing coals. Walter had been resting on a saddle blanket.

His father wet a small piece of rag and secured it around Walter's head using the big blue handkerchief. James broke off the front end of the arrow and gave it to Walter, who examined it, admiring the skill with which the arrowhead had been chipped from stone.

James didn't carry whiskey in his saddlebag, but he kept a small quantity of tobacco for medical emergencies. He put some of the leaf in his mouth and worked it around. James picked up a small mesquite stick and handed it to Walter.

"Bite down on this, son. What I'm about to do is going to hurt," he cautioned.

"No use for me to pretend it won't."

With that, James walked behind his son, grabbed the large part of the wooden arrow shaft, and pulled it through Walter's arm.

Walter cried out despite his best effort not to. Giant tears flowed down his cheeks. James pressed his lips to the back of his son's arm and squirted the tobacco juice as far into the wound as he could. Walter's pain was unbearable.

When the arrow had struck Walter, he had not felt it. While Walter concentrated on the pain in the back of his arm, his father moved in front of Walter and repeated the spitting procedure in the front opening of the wound.

"Wait," the boy called.

James looked up. Walter had bitten completely through the mesquite stick. So his father handed him another. Without interrupting his motion, James took the red-hot knife from the coals. He seared the back of the wound with the knife.

This time, the pain was so intense that Walter fell back on James, fainting as the knife seared his flesh. Young Walter was dead weight resting against his father.

James had to hold the knife carefully while he removed the stick from his son's mouth. Then James positioned Walter so that James could touch the knife on just the right spot on the front of his son's arm. When the knife burned skin a second time, the boy did not move.

James tossed the knife aside and picked up the sleeve he had cut from Walter's shirt. James took half the tobacco from his mouth and placed it on the rear of the wound. He held that in place with one hand, then took the other half of the tobacco and placed it on the front of his son's arm.

Next, he put the cleanest part of the shirt sleeve against the wound and wrapped it as a bandage around his son's arm. When he had secured the bandage, he rested Walter's head on the saddlebag, which had now taken on an additional function, serving as a pillow.

James located his knife, wiped it on his pants and slid it back into its sheath. James removed the blanket from the back of his mule and covered his son as snugly as the size of the small, coarse, crystalized sweat-encrusted wool blanket would permit.

Walter's father piled enough desert dried mesquite on the fire to keep it burning all night. Seated on the ground beside his resting son, James removed a slice of bacon and a biscuit from the saddlebag and savored the stale morsels as slowly as he could.

As he ate the camp food, James' thoughts drifted back in time to Tennessee, where he had fought in battle against his own countrymen. How many of his friends and fellow soldiers had he bandaged during those long three years? How many of those men had he watched die? With each death, James' joy at being alive had diminished. Some who had died had been total strangers, but others had been boyhood friends.

James looked at his sleeping son and realized what he was experiencing with Walter differed completely from James' war memories. The young man who lay wounded beside him was his child.

James had never been so afraid before. He pulled a small stone from his pocket and began honing his knife. After a few moments, he felt the blade, decided it was sharp enough, and put the knife back in the scabbard before returning the stone to his pocket.

James stood, walked over to the animals, rested his forearms on the back of his son's horse, and prayed.

As the sun rose, the braves steadily moved farther from the Little Hatchet, their horses almost at a trot. Little Matt had slept soundly all night. However, he was stirring, an act accompanied by grumpy vocal protests that had become audible and seemed to transition into an insistent crescendo.

Not since his early childhood in the women's tents had Little Puma seen a baby up close. At first, the odor rising from his chest was a mystery.

But as Little Matt's noises became full-blown screams, what had happened became suddenly obvious.

Little Puma ordered the Mescalero raiding party to stop and dismount. One by one, the sleepy braves slid from their horses and stretched while Little Puma struggled with the noisy infant.

The young chief placed Little Matt on a flat rock and unrolled the blanket, trying to etch an image in his memory. If his effort was successful, Little Puma thought he might have a chance to fold the blanket against itself to match the way the herdsman's wife had done it at the goat farm. As Little Puma tried to cope with the diaper, he felt someone's eyes looking over his shoulder. Turning his head, revealed a surreal scene. Peyote stood behind his cousin, smiling at Little Matt.

Little Puma backed away from the child. In a moment, the older brave had removed Little Matt's diaper, shaken it out on the ground and was rubbing the cloth against a flat rock to clean it. Little Matt had stopped crying and grinned as he looked up at Peyote.

Peyote turned the diaper inside out and wrapped the clean side against the baby. He took the skin of goat's milk from Little Puma's horse and held it carefully, allowing just enough to trickle out so that Little Matt could suck the milk into his mouth.

With Peyote in charge of Little Matt, Little Puma removed the other blanket from his horse and began distributing tortillas and meat to his comrades. The Mescalero ate while the horses grazed on dry prairie grass that had grown in the shadows of the big rocks.

When Little Matt finished his breakfast, Peyote resealed the milk skin. Neither Little Puma nor Peyote could fix the blanket back the way the señora had, but Peyote took some deerskin strips and bound both ends of the blanket. He made an opening in the blanket around Little Matt's face and slung the device containing the child over his head. This permitted his shoulder to support the strap and the blanket to rest against Peyote's chest. Little Matt looked up into Peyote's face, smiled again, and drifted off to sleep.

The hunting party mounted and trotted off to the northeast, headed home.

CHAPTER FIVE

J ames had risen two hours before the Mescalero stopped for Little Matt's diapering. He checked Walter for fever and found none. A few moments later, Walter woke to the smell of Little Hatchet bacon cooking and saw James kneeling by the fire.

"Good morning, son," James called.

"Good morning, Papa. My arm hurts," Walter replied.

"Well, let's have a look," James said, removing the bacon from the fire.

"Turn your arm toward the light so I can see," he directed.

Walter did as he had been told and his father unwrapped the shirtsleeve he had used for a bandage the night before.

"It looks like the tobacco did its job," James observed.

"See this?" James quizzed, as he pointed to the drainage on the bandage.

"The tobacco drew that infection right out of the wound. During the war, I saw doctors use all kinds of things, but few remedies work better against an infection than chewing tobacco," he asserted.

Walter had never heard his father mention the war before, not even once. The only reason he knew his father had been a soldier was that he had seen a photograph of him wearing a uniform. His mother had told him that his father had been a Confederate officer, but Walter was never to ask about it. Perhaps these circumstances permitted an exception to Rebecca's rule, Walter thought.

"Was it bad in the war, Papa?" Walter asked.

"Yep," his father confirmed, concluding the only conversation the two would ever have about the Civil War.

"Come on, let's put a fresh bandage on your arm," James said.

If Walter learned nothing about the war from his father, he had long known of the miraculous medical properties of tobacco juice. It made cuts heal. It fixed bee stings. And on the Oakley ranch, rumor had it that tobacco juice would even cure the bite of the feared diamondback rattlesnake. James rarely chewed tobacco. He just kept it handy for doctoring.

"Maybe before we put a fresh bandage on your arm we should have a look at that bump on your head, too," James said, altering course slightly before removing the bandage from his son's head.

Walter still had a large knot on his forehead. The discoloration was mostly red, but some of the injury had turned purple.

"I believe we better keep some padding on it," James suggested.

"That bump still looks pretty bad. Does it hurt?" he inquired.

"It hurts, but only a little," Walter admitted.

James stood and pulled his shirttail out of his pants. With his knife, James carefully cut part of the tail off the shirt, then ripped the cloth to make two fresh bandages. He used some water to clean the wounds, then tied the new dressings over Walter's arm and forehead. He threw the old bandages onto the fire.

"Let's eat some breakfast," James suggested as he took three biscuits from his saddlebag.

He handed two to Walter and kept one for himself. Next, James held up the stick he had been cooking the bacon on and Walter accepted a strip of the meat.

"Take two," his father directed.

"No, one's enough," Walter responded, shaking his head to indicate his refusal as his father pushed the stick back at him.

"Take two. You've lost some blood and the meat will help build it back up."

Walter did as his father said.

"I wish we had some coffee, but I figured we needed to travel light," James mused.

After they had eaten, James passed a canteen to his son. Both drank some of the water and then hastily began preparing to leave the camp. Walter had slept on the ground many times when he and his father hauled bacon and ham from their farm to El Paso, so the work the two did was a familiar routine. This time, however, there was an added urgency to get moving with haste.

Walter spread the fire and covered it with dirt. When Walter turned to saddle his horse, he saw his father had already secured the saddle on the mare. James was sitting on his mule, waiting. Even though it was still very dark, James' keen eyes had no difficulty following the large number of animal tracks that led off to the east.

This would be a deliberate journey. There was no way to overtake the Apaches before they reached their destination. The mule set the pace for the trip. As the Oakleys rode, James monitored Walter to make sure his son was all right. But clearly, the young man was strong, and his arm was not severely infected. Walter had a headache and a sore arm, but they were minor distractions. The younger Oakley alternately watched the tracks in front of him and looked ahead, hoping to see Little Matt's blanket.

About two hours after sunrise, the Oakleys came to the spot where some tracks moved off to the north. James' eyes glanced to the north and saw the adobe house the Mescalero had visited the night before.

"Let's go see what they did," James instructed his son.

Expecting someone to come looking for the baby, the goat herder and his wife had stayed close to home. The herdsman spoke no English and James knew only a few Spanish words. Even so, the two managed to communicate. James learned that eight braves had surrounded the adobe dwelling the night before, while one man had stood watch with several horses on the hill above. Walter and James ascertained the band of Apaches had Little Matt and that he was safe and being cared for. The herdsman indicated his spouse had sent along goat's milk for the child.

As James and Walter turned to ride away, the goat herder's wife came out of the house with tortillas and dried goat meat for their journey. James took out a twenty-dollar gold piece to pay for the food and to thank the family for taking care of Little Matt.

"*Gracias, no, por favor señor?*" the diminutive man told James.

Even though it was more money than he had ever had at one time in his life, the herdsman could not accept money for doing what God expected. James understood. He would find another way to repay the family for looking after his son.

Walter continued to hold up well. He didn't want to stop for lunch, but James felt he should take another look at the wounds. Walter was still free of fever. The pair rode until midnight, then rose at four and continued until they reached the Rio Grande. James made a fire, boiled water and cleaned Walter's wounds. They ate lunch, refilled their canteens, and allowed the animals to drink and graze. James suspected there might not be any water for the animals for the next two days.

The Oakleys camped on a small creek near Tularosa. It was no more than a trickle, but it was the only trace of water they had seen since the Rio Grande. The little paint pony and the mule were tired, thirsty, and hungry. Walter's arm had healed significantly and the bump on his head was almost gone, though he still wore the handkerchief around his head.

James and Walter were also tired. And while confident Little Matt was all right, the child's father and brother spent their long hours in the saddle thinking of how to get the infant back.

The raiders had ridden a mostly straight course since leaving the adobe ranch house. Twice, the Oakleys followed the tracks to two other adobes. Both times, the story had been the same. Two young Apache men had come on horseback with a goatskin sack. Using sign language, they had requested and received goat's milk. They had asked for nothing else. The braves hadn't drawn weapons, and they had taken no animals.

The Oakleys' campsite by the Rio Grande was the same spot the natives had used two nights before. James had discovered the bones of a freshly killed deer at the camp. James deduced that the Mescalero, who had stolen his son and his horses, were now mostly living off the land. The only item the hunters were taking from the herders was milk for a captured baby.

The sun was about to drop beneath the horizon when Little Puma's band completed their climb into the mountains and rode through the pass that led to the Mescalero stronghold. They had left as boys and they were riding home proudly as men. They had proved that they could help support the tribe.

Almost everyone in the village watched as their returning sons rode past with the fine horses from the Little Hatchet. Little Puma led James' big gelding at the front of the small procession. In the herd kept by the tribe, no other horse was so fine. The gelding would be a present for the chief, Little Puma's grandfather.

But even James' magnificent horse did not provide as much excitement among the onlookers as Peyote. Mouths dropped open when the tribe saw the largest brave in the procession carrying Little Matt strapped to his chest. Other warriors in earlier times had come back to the tribe with an occasional captive, but they had usually been women. No one who gathered to receive the returning warriors could remember ever hearing of anything like this.

CHAPTER SIX

A s the chief moved to the center of the encampment to greet the braves, he appeared composed and stoic. However, Little Puma could sense uneasiness in his grandfather. He wanted to blurt out an explanation; instead, he kept silent. After the horses had stopped and the tribe gathered, the chief spoke.

"Welcome home, brave sons. You have brought us many fine horses. Truly, you have passed the test. Now, you are Mescalero warriors."

As he spoke, the old chief could not help but wonder what kind of trouble the little white baby would bring to his people. Unlike the Comanches in Texas, Mescalero did not steal white children. In their stronghold, high in the Sacramento Mountains, the clan had all they needed. What they did not need in their peaceful land were the white and black soldiers in the blue coats. These were his thoughts, but the chief kept his concerns to himself. He walked over to his grandson and called his name.

"Little Puma," spoke the great leader, before pausing dramatically for effect.

"You have led your people to a great triumph. Surely, this is a good sign that you shall become a great chief of the Mescalero people, when the time is yours," the chief proclaimed to the tribe.

Little Puma had never heard such praise from his grandfather, who was about to be stunned by his grandson's words, which began at a level that was barely audible.

"Great chief of the Mescalero, this horse is for you," the grandson managed to respond.

The chief took the reins of the horse and looked at him with proud admiration.

"Well done, Little Puma."

Then, turning his face toward the rest of the newly proven warriors, the chief repeated his praise.

"Well done," pronounced the old man, stating a fact without bombast or embellishment.

Little Puma and his band had done what scores of generations of his people had done before. They had performed as expected. Other braves, a year or so older, led the horses away. And all but one of the returning sons went to see his mother.

Peyote, whose mother and father were long dead, walked over to his grandmother, the chief's sister. Carefully, he unwrapped the blanket from Little Matt and handed the infant to the elderly lady.

Little Matt, who had been silent through the whole ceremony, cried loudly. As Peyote turned to walk away, the baby shrieked. Just as his big brother and father had felt so helpless a week ago, now Little Matt sensed his life had spun completely out of control.

While the women bathed and dressed him, the crying continued. A young Mescalero mother with a recently born infant of her own sought to nurse him, but Little Matt cried louder. He refused to suckle this strange woman's milk. Instead of taking nourishment, he screamed and kicked. After three hours of frustration, a girl was sent as a messenger to bring back Peyote.

He came to his grandmother's tent, held the baby, and offered some goat's milk. Little Matt ate heartily, belched, then fell asleep on his friend's chest. Peyote left the tent to rejoin the other braves.

The other young men, sitting by the fire after their feast, would have laughed at anyone else. But the look on Peyote's face made it clear to the Mescalero braves that this was no time for any of them to snicker.

The next night, James and Walter reached the mountains surrounding the Apache stronghold. James decided to camp in a gully away from the trail at the foot of the mountains. The two Oakleys made no fire that night so guards from the tribe would not spot them. For the last day and a half, they rode while James and Walter thought only of how they best could rescue Little Matt from the mighty force, their Mescalero neighbors.

James knew that there would be no way to get into the camp without being seen. Walter believed that if they scouted the camp for a day or so, they would learn where Little Matt was. Then, if they used the darkness properly, they could sneak in, get Little Matt and sneak out. Walter decided to tell his father his plan the next morning.

The fall night was frigid. With no fire, father and son put their blankets close together to stay as warm as possible. The ravine kept the wind away, but the two Oakleys were frozen down to their inner souls.

Walter wished to be home in a warm bed. The young man tossed and turned, worrying about the next day. James forced himself to lie still so Walter could get as much sleep as possible.

As tough as the journey had been, the Oakleys would face the test of their lives the next day. If James didn't do everything perfectly, it was likely he and Walter would be killed; and Matt would grow up, not as an Oakley, but as a Mescalero warrior.

James went over and over his plan. He had rejected the idea of scouting the camp and sneaking Little Matt out for two reasons. First, he believed they could not watch undetected for long enough to learn where the baby was. Second, even if they did, they could never grab Little Matt and get away without being caught.

James knew if the Mescalero caught them, they would be considered thieves and death would almost certainly be their punishment.

James knew to succeed, he and Walter had to prove to the chiefs and tribe that they were fearless. They also had to be in a position to trade. So James decided to ride in openly. They must appear strong and demonstrate they had something more important to offer their neighbors than the white baby they held, an act that could well lead to an all out war between the Mescalero and the blue-coated soldiers at Fort Bliss.

When they were intercepted, they would ask to see the chief, saying they wanted to trade. He reasoned that the first Apaches they met would know who they were and why they came. James was counting on being able to gain the respect of the outer guards with this bold action.

Because of the danger ahead of them, James had wanted to ride into the mountains alone, but he knew Walter would not stay behind, no matter what his father said.

At four in the morning, James woke Walter. They ate the last of the bacon and some corn bread James had cooked two nights before.

As they rode into the mountains, James explained to Walter why he decided to ride into the stronghold openly. The father did not go through his own discarded plan to sneak Matt away from the Mescalero, but he had explained why he had rejected that approach.

"We must not show fear," James told Walter, speaking with unarguable authority.

"If we show even a hint of fear, the Apaches won't respect us. And if they don't kill us on the spot, they'll tie us up and carry us into camp as captives," the father warned.

James left no doubt in his son's mind that he, James, had led men in war and faced these kinds of decisions many times before. Walter understood, but he still felt they had a better chance of getting Little Matt if they attempted to grab him in the dark. Walter kept quiet because he knew his father had made up his mind.

It had been many years since James had fired a rifle at another man. He considered wounding the first Mescalero he saw, but immediately dismissed the idea. James concluded that if he shot first, there would be a fight. Half an hour before the sun rose, he took the Winchester out of his blanket and rode with the gun conspicuously across his lap. By the time the sun began to appear, the Oakleys were several miles into the mountains and climbing steadily.

Just as the light became full, Walter spoke.

"Papa, look up there."

James expected to see warriors, but saw no one.

"What, son?" he asked.

"There's a cave up there," Walter explained.

James acknowledged his son's discovery and waited for Walter to continue.

"We could hide in that cave until dark, then sneak into their camp at night," the younger Oakley suggested.

As the two rode in silence, Walter felt that his suggestion was having some effect.

"No, son," James responded after a period of silence.

"Even if we were to get Little Matt away from the Mescalero without being seen, we could not get him out of these mountains. We must make them respect us, or we have no chance of rescuing your brother," James reasoned.

Walter knew there was no point arguing, but he felt his father was making a mistake. They rode on in silence and both kept alert, watching for the Apaches to swoop down. The farther they rode without being detected, the edgier they became. Hour after hour, they progressed toward the stronghold, stopping only to water the horses. Now they were high into the mountains. An hour before noon, clouds grew together quickly, and the sun's warmth faded. An icy wind blustered.

The Oakleys stopped, unrolled their blankets and used them to wrap themselves against the growing chill. Walter, who was without a hat, pulled his blanket over his head. James pulled his hat down on his head as far as it would go, but carefully kept the rifle ready outside the blanket.

With each thousand yards they rode up into the clouds, the biting of the cold intensified. Soon the temperature was near freezing. By twelve-thirty, big wet snowflakes began falling. Walter only saw snow a couple of times a year on the Little Hatchet. He had never seen it fall in October and he worried about what kind of strange place he was entering.

The snow was cold, but it melted as it struck them and the animals. In half an hour, father and son were both soaked and freezing. They were still looking out for outlying guards, but found it harder to concentrate. The numbness of the cold and wet all but overwhelmed them.

Father and son rode on for another hour and a half. The snowflakes became smaller and then stopped. In twenty more minutes, the clouds had passed east out of the mountains and the sun was shining again. The air was still cold, and the wind was brisk and whistling down from the higher mountains to the north, but when the sun peaked out, it brought a few scattered moments of relief.

"Look," Walter spoke again.

Smoke was rising between the two mountains in front of them. The sign that natives were so close brought Walter and James back to full alert. The trail forked in front of them. The left trail seemed to lead toward the largest concentration of smoke. They followed along the mountain that had been on their left for about half a mile. The trail took the pair into a small pass which James expected would be guarded. It was not.

Cautiously, they rode on, emerging onto a ridge that looked down on the Apache stronghold. Apparently, during the snow, the braves guarding the pass had taken shelter in their tents in the valley.

Walter and James observed hundreds of tents below. All had flaps at the top and smoke from fires inside appeared to be coming from every tent. A few women were moving about the encampment, but most people appeared to be inside.

James could not believe his good fortune. He had come right to the edge of the stronghold, without seeing a single warrior. Quickly, he made an adjustment. He would ride into the village just as planned; but because there were no guards, he could leave Walter up on the ridge. James handed the rifle to Walter.

"See those rocks?" he asked, pointing up and to the left.

"Take your horse up that face, put her behind the rocks and take a position where you can see the village, but not be seen. If I signal, shoot into the ground one foot in front of my boots. Don't shoot anyone!"

"No, I'm going with you," Walter asserted.

James was not used to people refusing to follow his directives. Had they been at home or on the road to El Paso, he would not have tolerated his son's defiance. Thinking quickly, James appreciated Walter felt responsible for Little Matt's kidnapping, and he knew the guards would storm up the ridge at any moment.

"All right, hide the rifle in those rocks and we'll go down together," James agreed.

Walter tapped the mare on the flanks with his heels, and she climbed swiftly up the slope. He hastened to hide the rifle and the little mare steadily took him back to where his father waited.

CHAPTER SEVEN

As the Oakleys started down the mountain trail into the Apache village, they could see people emerging from the tents and beginning to move around. The ground had been too warm for the snow to stick, but the Mescalero seemed cautious and moved slowly.

When the Oakleys were still fifteen-hundred feet above the village, Little Puma spotted the two riders on the mountainside. The young chief called to several braves near him. The warriors ran to their horses, mounted and rushed up the slope.

"When they get here, stay calm," James coaxed.

"They are less likely to hurt us if we don't show fear," he reminded his son.

Walter nodded.

"Just follow my lead," his father instructed.

Within a couple of minutes, the raiding party had surrounded James and Walter. Little Puma immediately recognized the mare Walter was riding and was shocked. The rider was younger than Little Puma. He had assumed that a man had been chasing him.

Little Puma quickly scanned for the rifle that had been fired at the fleeing braves back at the Oakley ranch, but it was nowhere in sight.

One brave grabbed a rein on Walter's horse. Without looking at the

Apache rider, Walter continued edging his mare forward. Before the brave jerked the rein to stop the animal, the sentry looked to his young chief for guidance. Little Puma's facial expression indicated he wanted the Oakleys to be allowed to proceed. The brave dropped the rein.

As they moved down the trail toward the village, the Mescalero kept a tight circle around the Oakleys but made no further effort to stop them.

Below, elders and braves gathered in the center of the village. Last out of his tent was the chief. He had known something like this would happen and had been thinking about what to do when the white men arrived. The chief began evaluating possible strategies the first moment he had seen the baby.

Little Puma had told his grandfather the story of how Peyote had shot the horse on the first raid and how he had swooped Little Matt off the front porch at the last house, the one where this man and boy lived.

The chief was relieved the white men had not brought soldiers, and he was surprised to see there were only two ranchers, one only a boy.

Little Puma was courageous and restrained. As always, his grandfather was very pleased with his performance. There was no scuffling with the intruders and no risk of starting trouble the young braves could not handle on their own. Little Puma was focused, calm, and in control.

The braves stopped about ten feet in front of the elders. Before the young tribesmen could move to escort the invaders to the chief, James and Walter had dismounted and walked between the horses toward the old leader.

As he had ridden toward the stronghold, James had considered attempting to speak to the Apaches in Spanish and had tried to put together enough words in his mind to explain that he wanted his son back. He had reasoned that the Mescalero were far more likely to know some Spanish than English. But as he stood before the elderly chief, the words he spoke were in English.

"I am James Oakley from Little Hatchet Creek. I have come to get my son," he said firmly, but with no tone of aggression in his speech or manner.

As James spoke, he could see that the chief did not understand his words.

To avoid any chance of being misunderstood, James elaborated.

"I have come for my son," he explained, holding his arms together in front of him to mime cradling a baby.

This time, the chief nodded slightly, but did not speak.

There was total silence, and no one moved for well over a minute. James decided it was time to offer the proud warriors something in trade for his son.

He turned, walked between the braves and led Walter's mare to the chief. The chief looked at another man standing near him. The man came forward and took the reins of Walter's horse.

Again, there was silence and total stillness.

James walked back to the mule, grabbed his reins and started toward the chief. As he turned to face the tribe's senior elder, James observed the chief move his head slightly from side to side.

This was trouble. James looked at the chief and the expression on the old man's face could have been on the head of a statue. It was a complete blank, without emotion or movement.

As he pondered the actions taking place in front of him, the elderly leader was concerned. He could not accept only one horse for the child, and he certainly had no use for a mule.

Silently to himself, the chief cursed his responsibility. While he had always been fond of his sister's insane grandson, the chief knew that Peyote had been nothing but trouble. The chief longed to rush to his sister's tent, get the baby, and hand him to the white man. Of course, that was totally impossible.

The aged Mescalero warrior waited for what seemed like an hour, as James considered what else he might have to trade.

James was reaching into his pocket for the gold piece he had offered to the family at the first adobe, but hesitated. If he offered the gold now, and it was not enough, James would have no place to fall back. The gold had to be a last resort. If the elder refused it, all could be lost. It was unthinkable that James could leave the stronghold without Little Matt. His offer had to be right. As he thought, James' eyes stayed fixed on the chief. He turned his head toward Walter.

"Son, go and get the rifle," James directed his eldest child.

"When you ride in with it, hold it way above your head and move slowly, so they can see you mean no harm," the father instructed.

Walter had watched this drama unfold directly in front of him. When his father gave away his horse, the young man had clinched his teeth tightly to contain the tension he felt rumbling inside. He had wanted to rage or even cry, but Walter had stood still and silent.

When the chief refused the mule from his father, Walter had ached to explain how important Little Matt was to the family. Surely, the chief had a family. Surely, he understood.

When Walter heard his father's instruction, he was relieved. At last, Walter had been assigned a role that would help get Little Matt back. His heart was pounding so loudly that Walter felt everyone in the gathering could hear it.

He ran for the mare but held back. She was not his anymore. She belonged to this stone-faced old Mescalero in front of him. The thought slowed Walter's movement.

James saw his son hesitate and was about to speak firmly to Walter. However before he could talk, James watched Walter walk toward the mule. The young warriors let him pass between them. Walter looked up at the enormous mule.

How was he going to get into the saddle? Walter asked himself. His father was too far away; and anyway, he could not ask James for help. Certainly, the braves would not help him get up into the saddle. He would have to jump for the stirrup.

But what if he missed? Would they laugh at him? Or would they grab him and drag him away? Walter had been waiting for that to happen ever since the Apaches approached them as father and son rode down the mountain.

Thank God his foot hit firmly in the stirrup when he jumped; but disaster still loomed. As he swung his right leg over the animal, his shin struck the back rim of the saddle, shooting intolerable pain up his leg. Somehow, Walter successfully moved his leg over the top of the saddle on his second effort, saving embarrassment and loss of face. The young man's eyes watered slightly from the pain in his shin, but Walter kept up a good front.

Two additional problems remained. The first, he was trying to ride a mule. What if the stubborn beast wouldn't move? Walter held his breath and laid the left rein on the mule's neck to turn its head. He clicked his tongue and nudged the animal with his boots. It turned, took a step, paused, then began to walk. The mule's enormous shoulders bumped the horses ridden by two of the braves guarding James and Walter.

The young warriors looked toward the chief, while struggling to push their horses to block the mule. For the first time during the encounter, the chief spoke. His voice was loud and clear. The braves ceased their attempts to resist.

The mule, which was used to pulling heavy wagon loads of bacon, had paid no attention to the Mescalero horses. He had almost walked completely through the two straining animals by the time the chief voiced his order.

Walter tapped his heels into the mule's ribs to speed him up. But even for James, the seemingly ageless mule had only one speed. Walter expected at least one of the Apaches would follow him, but none did. After a time, Walter's blood flow returned to normal. Walter tried desperately to concentrate solely on reaching the rifle and focus on what he would do after he picked it up. But his efforts were repeatedly interrupted by the mule's excruciating slowness.

Walter reached the spot where he had concealed the rifle after a journey that had seemingly taken hours. Walter jumped from the mule, scampered up the rocks, and retrieved the Winchester. In less than a minute, he was back atop the mule, plodding toward the crowd waiting in the center of the village. Despite his intense concentration, Walter forgot to hold the rifle up. A hundred feet or so down the mountain, he remembered and jerked the weapon above his head to show the Mescalero that he meant no harm.

During his return trip, Walter had two things to concentrate on: the interminable pace of the mule and his arms which ached horribly from holding the gun in the air. Every few minutes, he switched the rifle to an alternate arm, but both of his arms throbbed. It seemed Walter would never get back to where his father waited. Walter repeatedly felt that he would faint and fall off the mule. The cold wind blowing against his face revived him several times.

Below, the waiting was just as agonizing. All watched frustrated while the mule plodded up the hill. They saw Walter return to the mule. They took notice when he hoisted the Winchester, as the sunlight reflected off its barrel. They waited for him to change the rifle from one extended arm to the other. Witnessing Walter's torment was painful for everyone.

A very long time had passed when the mule walked back into the enclosure of Mescalero braves. Walter held the rifle as high as he could, trying with all the will he possessed to ignore the pain in his arms. He still held it above his head as he jumped from the stirrup to the ground. Somehow, Walter precariously maintained his balance during the dismount. Walter resisted a strong urge to race to his father with the gun. He walked toward James carefully and deliberately instead. The villagers parted, allowing Walter to pass through their circle of protection.

James had decided to speak. He wanted to instruct Walter on how to hand him the rifle without alarming the Mescalero. Every eye piercingly focused on Walter. No weapons were drawn, but Walter could intensely feel the anxious collective attention. One quick move, and the Apaches would be all over him and his father. Walter gingerly brought the Winchester out of the air. He pointed the barrel toward the ground and pushed the butt of the gun to his father ever so slowly.

James had taught his son well. With deliberate moves, Walter's and Matt's father accepted control of the rifle and kept the weapon pointed at the earth. He took several slow steps toward the chief. James raised the Winchester up in both hands, keeping it parallel to the ground directly between himself and the chief.

The chief had been stoically inspecting the gun from a distance since Walter had returned to the camp with it. When James pushed it slowly toward him, the chief held out his arms with the palms of his hands facing up and took possession of the prized firearm. Slowly, but in a single motion, he turned to a brave standing about ten feet to his right and slightly behind him. The chief spoke two words, or what sounded like two words to James and Walter. He faced James, then turned his body a bit to the left and placed the rifle in the hands of a tribal elder standing next to him.

Soon, the brave, who had walked away immediately after the chief had spoken the two words, returned, leading a woman who carried Little Matt in her arms.

Both Oakleys thought they would collapse. There Matt was, right in front of them, healthy and well cared for. It seemed to Walter and James that their legs would give way. Their hearts pounded and the roar from that pounding reverberated like thunder in their ears.

The brave and the woman walked past the great chief and the woman handed the baby to James, who was holding out his arms to receive his son. Neither James nor Walter screamed out the joy they felt inside, but both wanted to.

"Thank you for taking care of my son," James told the woman.

She did not speak, but passed an animal skin filled with mare's milk to Matt's father. The Mescalero kept neither cows nor goats.

James accepted the skin.

"Thank you," he said again, before turning toward the chief so he could address the leader directly.

"Thank you for returning my son. I am in your debt. Your people will always be welcome on the Little Hatchet. We are friends now and forever," James concluded.

The chief nodded. Of course, he did not comprehend the English words James spoke; but intuitively, he understood the man who was speaking, and could make a good guess about the rush of emotions James was experiencing.

The chief paused as he remembered how he had felt years before, when he learned Comanches had killed his own sons in a surprise attack by Comanches. He remembered how he had grieved, how his wife had died from her sorrow. The great chief looked over at his grandson, Little Puma.

After a few seconds of contemplation, he turned back to James, made a sweeping gesture with his arms and spoke a single word, which James interpreted as "go."

CHAPTER EIGHT

James turned to walk toward the mule and Walter followed close behind. Just as they moved into the circle of braves, Walter suddenly pivoted, a move James saw out of the corner of his eye. In a flash, Walter stood, poised beside his mare. Every eye was locked on Walter. James was terrified, praying that he would not lose both his sons in a few seconds because of some foolish impulse tormenting Walter.

In an instant, Walter had passed within an inch or two of the stunned young Apaches holding Walter's horse. In two quick motions, the twelve-year-old loosened the straps that held his bedroll to the saddle and jerked his blankets off the animal's back. As he spun abruptly to return to his father, the chief looked directly at Walter and spoke.

Walter did not understand what the chief said, but he saw the chief motion for him to come. Walter knew he could not have his mare back, but he was prepared to fight to the death for his blankets. Enough was enough.

To Walter's amazement, for the first time since the ordeal had begun, the stern expression on the chief's face appeared to relax. He looked like the kindly old grandfather he was. The thoughts of his sons had made the elderly man sentimental and had him wishing for circumstances that would permit him to give the boy's horse back.

Knowing that was impossible, the chief chose an alternative. He decided to reward Walter's bravery, a characteristic Mescalero admired.

The chief called to Little Puma. Again, Walter could not understand the words, but he could sense the change in the chief's tone.

Little Puma left the gathering at a trot. He returned shortly, carrying a skin filled with something, and a small lance. The spear had a flint tip and an eagle feather secured to it with a fine leather strap. The skin contained about a pound of dried venison.

"Thank you," Walter said to the chief, then looked at Little Puma and nodded to express his appreciation for the gifts. Carrying the blankets, the lance, and the deer meat, Walter walked through the circle a second time and back to his father.

"Hold Matt while I get into the saddle," James told Walter, the father successfully concealing his intense relief that Little Matt and Walter were still alive and safe.

Walter reached out his arms and held his little brother for the first time since the long ordeal had begun. James, several inches taller than Walter, swung easily into the saddle. First, Walter passed the lance to his father, then the blankets, then the venison. James secured these items in front of the saddle. Finally, James leaned over, and Walter handed Little Matt up to his father. James shifted Little Matt into his right arm and extended his left arm to help Walter onto the mule.

Little Matt had ridden most of the way to the Mescalero stronghold wrapped in a blanket and tied to his carrier. He would ride all the way home to the Little Hatchet in his father's arms.

Without waiting for instructions, the big mule headed up the trail toward the mountains. Little Matt was safe, and the Oakleys were going home.

Along the Little Hatchet, the waiting had drained everyone. Rebecca's fever had lasted for the first five days Little Matt had been missing. She had wanted to get up and bring the family back together, but she was too weak and could not.

It had fallen on Katie, who had struggled continuously with overwhelming guilt associated with Little Matt's kidnapping, to keep things going on the farm. Katie fed, clothed, and comforted the younger children until Rebecca was well enough to lead the family.

Try as she might, Rebecca could not convince her eldest daughter that Katie was not responsible for Little Matt's abduction. It was ironic. For the entire ride from the Little Hatchet to the Mescalero stronghold and back, Walter blamed himself for Little Matt's kidnapping. While at home, Katie was convinced her negligence had gotten her little brother stolen.

Rebecca guided the prayers of the family members still at the ranch, each morning before breakfast and each night by the fire before the Bible reading. The Oakleys prayed for the safe return of James, Walter, and Little Matt. Dozens of times each day, Rebecca assured one child or another that their father and brothers would come home safely.

James had been to war. He had moved the family from Arkansas to New Mexico. He had built a thriving ranch and prosperous business in their desert valley. He had faced every imaginable hardship. He had met every challenge of his life and Rebecca promised James' children that their father would overcome these unthinkably awful circumstances, as well. The mother's confident belief appeared to be a matter of unshakable faith.

However, at night alone in her bed, doubt haunted Rebecca. No matter how hard she tried, she could not stop the worrying. Repeatedly, she dreamed the Apaches had slaughtered her two children and her husband. In the light of day, she would not allow her fear to show. But in the dark, there was no escape from the nightmares.

What would she do if James did not come back? What if only James came back? What if only Walter came back? The fears bounced off one another from the time she got the last child to sleep until she saw the first light of morning. Walter was too young to be on a mission like this. What had James been thinking? Why hadn't he brought Walter home? Had they all been murdered on the night of the raid?

Each night, Rebecca would conclude that the following morning, she would have to find out. Tossing and turning restlessly alone in her bed during those dark, scary hours, Rebecca always returned to the same strategy.

In her plan, after breakfast each coming day, the anxiety-ridden mother would hitch up a wagon and drive over the hill to find out for herself whether the murdered bodies of her children and husband were lying abandoned on the desert ground. That was the only way Rebecca could know with certainty. It was the not knowing that was killing Rebecca.

But instead of acting on her plan, after each morning's breakfast, Rebecca's confidence in her husband returned. She understood Walter would not come home without Little Matt, no matter what his father said. During the light of day, Rebecca knew that James' iron will would prevail. When the sun was out, she was certain that one day, the three of them would ride off the ridge and back down to their family home.

Day after day, night after night, Rebecca lived through the same cycle: total confidence in the light, followed by doubts in the dark that nagged at her, until the doubts became abject fear. When would her ordeal end?

What about James? How was he bearing up under the strain?

He was drained. As the mule reached the edge of the first mountain, he felt he could not sit in the saddle five more minutes. He had ridden all this way, agonized over what to do when he found his son and triumphed.

James had one son in his arms and another riding behind him. Everyone was safe and free. Against incalculable odds, he had done what he had come to do. He should have been giddy, elated. Instead, he felt he was crumbling underneath numbing exhaustion.

James was grateful to God and to the Mescalero for the outcome but could not focus on his gratitude. There was no way to stop and enjoy the reunion. He couldn't focus on the long journey ahead, couldn't formulate a plan for a safe trip home. On that afternoon, James Oakley needed every ounce of will he possessed just to continue riding that mule.

The three Oakleys were aboard the same mule which had worked through much of the Civil War on James' father's farm until James had sent word that he needed the animal. Somehow, his father had delivered the mule to his son just in time. Later, this would be the mule that would pull the wagon carrying the Oakleys' belongings from Arkansas to New Mexico, where the mighty animal had skidded the logs down the mountain to build the Oakleys' home on the Little Hatchet. He was the same cantankerous beast that had hauled the bacon from the Little Hatchet to El Paso for twelve years, then had carried James to the Mescalero stronghold. That brutish animal was now solely in charge of the Oakleys' fate. Their lives were in his control as he made one patient, confident step after another up the rocky mountainside away from the Mescalero.

James sat. Walter nodded and dozed, restlessly. Matt slept soundly in his father's arms, and no one spoke. Just as it had done for Walter that morning, the cold mountain wind kept James awake. And when the sun set, the air grew even colder. The Mescalero had taken good care of Little Matt. He was still securely wrapped in blankets, and his father made sure the covers stayed snugly around him, leaving only enough space for the baby to breathe.

At last, the mule reached the top of the mountain range guarding the stronghold and plodded on down the winding trail toward the desert. James knew he could not stop until they were out of the mountains. The temperature was already at the freezing mark, and it would be far too cold for them in the mountains that night.

In three more hours, the Oakleys returned to the spot where James and Walter had slept the night before. The sky was clear and a bright moon was rising over the mountains. It was cold, even in the desert; but the winds lessened as the norther moved on into Texas. James found the ravine where they had camped the night before, dismounted and placed Little Matt on the ground in a sheltered place where he would be out of what wind remained.

James walked back to the mule where Walter slept, leaning forward. He smiled as he noted that Walter, who had charged after the Apaches as a man, was once again a boy.

His father gathered him from the mule and carried him to a spot near Matt. Walter, like his younger brother, continued to sleep. The mule wandered a few steps for some grass and began grazing. The toughest of the lot, the animal made it clear by his demeanor that he was prepared to walk all the way back to the Little Hatchet that very night, if anyone dared think he couldn't do so.

In minutes, James had a fire going and enough wood stocked to maintain it for the night. He stretched a blanket for Walter, picked him up and lay him on it, then wrapped his son warmly in the other blanket. He placed Matt next to Walter, then spread his own blanket on the ground on the opposite side of the soundly sleeping infant.

James unsaddled the mule and used the saddle blanket as additional cover for Walter. James rolled his own blanket, climbed in and disappeared into sleep beneath its cover. The sun was two hours high when he woke. James could not remember ever having slept past sunup. He was sorry there was no coffee to break the morning cold, but he did not dwell on it.

James stoked the fire to ease Walter's chill, when it would be time for the youngster to crawl out of his blankets.

James looked up to see that the mule had wandered a quarter of a mile away for a drink of water and for grass that he liked better than the sparse weeds near the ravine.

By noon, after the Oakley trio had been on the trail for a little more than four hours, Walter sensed that someone else was traveling with them. He turned around several times, trying to find the eyes he was convinced were staring at his back.

Walter considered telling his father what he believed so strongly to be true, but kept quiet. He would have felt foolish, informing his father they were being followed, when he couldn't see their pursuer.

That night, as they made camp, Walter continued to feel uneasy. He was certain someone was tracking them.

James had decided on the first day of their return trip that he would simply retrace his steps back to the Little Hatchet, but he subsequently adjusted his decision.

The night of the fifth day, the three Oakleys on a mule stopped on a hill overlooking El Paso. James and Walter concluded that the toughest parts of their ordeal were past and they had prevailed.

CHAPTER NINE

The mule carrying the Oakleys ambled automatically to the livery stable they always used when they brought bacon into the small city. James turned the mule over to the stable keeper and the Oakleys walked down the street to the Texas Hotel. All three had baths. A woman stayed in the room with Matt, while James and Walter went to the hotel's dining room for a proper meal, their second in three weeks.

Walter had slept in a bed the previous night. He didn't wake up when his father left the room at daybreak or when the woman brought Little Matt back to the room. He had slept until after ten o'clock, when the sound of wagons creaking and bouncing down the street outside his window finally woke him. The night before, he had eaten until the kitchen ran out of food. However, this morning, he was starving again. It was too early for lunch. James talked to the owner of the hotel. Reluctantly, the cranky Chinese cook agreed to fix breakfast for Walter: eggs, potatoes, sweet milk, coffee, a plate of biscuits with honey and, best of all, six slices of Little Hatchet bacon.

"Do you think that will hold you until lunch, son?" James laughed.

Walter didn't laugh. He could hardly move with all that food inside.

"Come on, son. Let's walk off some of that breakfast," James said.

They had walked the six blocks from the hotel to the train depot before Walter began feeling normal. He had lost weight on the trip and he seemed taller. His pants were right at the top of his boots. At the depot, James turned south toward the river.

"Where are we going, Papa?" Walter asked.

"You'll see. We're almost there," James replied, his facial muscles revealing no hint of the surprise waiting around the next corner.

The two stopped in front of a collection of huge stock pens.

"Pick the one you want," James directed his son in a barely audible voice.

Walter was silent, thinking that he had imagined his father's words. He looked into a pen holding forty horses.

"What did you say?" Walter exclaimed in disbelief.

"Pick the horse you want," James repeated, displaying a broad smile on his face.

Walter's proud father was just barely able to repress an urge to explode into laughter.

"Why?" was all Walter could think to ask.

"Because you can't walk all the way back to the Little Hatchet and I'm getting real tired of you riding with me," James responded with a sparkle in his eyes.

Walter didn't wait any longer. He vaulted over the rail of the corral and began moving among the horses. They were all prime ranch animals. Some were trained cutting horses. Cowboys had lost a lot of the stock in card games. Some had been sold to Wallace Peterson by cowboys down on their luck. And more than a few had wandered across the river from Mexico, led by men who carried side arms on their hips and weren't regular with baths and shaves.

Mr. Peterson did not require papers on horses without brands. Sometimes when owners came to claim animals, he turned them over. He made his judgment on whether the claimant was a good customer or a good friend of the sheriff. Other factors he might consider included the phase of the moon, the amount of whiskey remaining in his bottle and Mr. Peterson's reckoning of how likely he was to be shot by an irate rancher if he refused to turn over the horse. Sometimes when he felt good, Mr. Peterson resolved disputed claims with the toss of a coin.

In a bad mood, Mr. Peterson settled the issue by running the pretender off using the sawed-off shotgun he kept leaning next to his door. The shotgun resolution was his most reliable method. If the rancher was making a bad claim, he stopped by the saloon for a couple of shots of whiskey before leaving town. If his claim was strong, he always went to the sheriff. In fact, Mr. Peterson was a mostly honest man who employed common sense in carrying out his business. He had never been sued, and no one had ever been shot over a horse in his keeping.

Walter struggled to contain his excitement, to be logical. At first, he had charged around selecting the candidates; but his flurry of movement had caused the horses to run, slowing the process. Walter paused to catch his breath, then walked over to a paint quarter horse.

She looked very much like the pony he had left at the stronghold, but it was obvious she had been trained to work cattle. She was very sure-footed and confident. Walter patted her neck, then began walking around her slowly. When he had completed his circle, he stopped and raised her left front leg. She had nearly new shoes and her hooves were well cared for.

"That's a fine cow pony, son," Mr. Peterson called out from the spot by the fence rail, where he had joined James.

The livestock dealer punctuated his sentence with a big downwind spit of tobacco juice.

"Cowboy brought her in from New Mexico less than a week ago," Mr. Peterson said, turning his comments toward James.

"Said he was going to work for the railroad and wouldn't need a cutting horse anymore. Lots of 'em doing that now, quitting cowboying to work on the railroad."

James made no response but offered Mr. Peterson a sideways glance. The horse trading had begun.

Walter was busy with his decision. He was comparing the mare with four or five other animals, carefully walking around each of the other horses. He was evaluating the horses' physical condition thoughtfully, but his attraction for the mare was too obvious and he recognized his mistake. James had seen the pull of the horse on the boy at once. So had Mr. Peterson, even before he had spoken the first time. This was going to make the trading tougher for James.

Walter wasn't thinking of the price, only of a horse he planned to spend much of his life with. Walter didn't know that his father and Mr. Peterson had been through this exercise twice before, earlier in the day. James' two new horses were already over at the livery stable getting fresh shoes.

While the two men waited by the fence, Walter compared the horse he had selected with the little mare now in the possession of the Mescalero chief. Twenty minutes passed before Walter decided. He looked up from the latest horse he had been evaluating, scanned the herd, and located the quarter horse. He walked gently to her, clicking his tongue.

"Here girl, let's give Papa a look at you," Walter said to the mare as he patted her once on the neck, indicating that she should come with him.

The little quarter horse followed without hesitation.

"What do you think of this one, Papa?" Walter called to his father as he and the horse came within about thirty feet of the two men.

"Bring her over here and let's have a look," James replied.

"She's a fine pony, Papa," Walter volunteered, bringing a broad smile to Mr. Peterson's face.

"Bring her through the gate," James said sternly, and Walter noted the change in his father's tone.

Father and son knew each other well. Walter had watched carefully when James had bargained with people in times past. Usually, after the trade was made and the two were alone, James would explain to his son what had happened at various points during the discussion. James never bragged, but Walter guessed his father was as good at horse trading as anyone in El Paso. Everyone in town treated James with respect and deference.

Walter focused carefully on all of his father's signals. He really wanted the mare and didn't want to make a mistake that would keep him from getting her. He didn't know how much a horse should cost, but he guessed this one would not be cheap. As Walter ushered the paint through the gate and closed it behind her, his father stepped in front of her. He opened the horse's mouth, turned her head from side to side, and took a long look at her teeth. James raised her left front leg. Not only did he look at the shoe and the hoof, but he carefully worked her joints as well.

Peterson was right. The horse had been well cared for. As James circled the horse, he lifted each of her legs. When he moved to her far side, he poked his outstretched fingers into her flank. The mare was pregnant.

Finally, James pulled her head down and looked in her right ear. Walter bit his tongue.

"I think you need a bigger horse, son," James declared.

Peterson felt words headed down his tongue, but he too kept silent, hoping the boy would speak. With little hesitation, James walked away from the mare and began scanning the herd. Peterson could wait no longer.

"Now, Mr. Oakley, there's not a finer cow horse on this lot than that little mare your boy picked out," Peterson pitched.

"That may be true, but we raise pigs and my boy is growing like a weed. Just look at his britches. They're halfway up to his knee and all that has happened in the three weeks since we left home," James responded.

Walter laughed. His father knew how to play this old horse trader.

"Your boy wants that mare. Anyone can see that," Peterson countered.

Walter was feeling confident. Now it was time for him to play, too.

"You may be right, Papa. That black gelding I was looking at may be more my size," Walter announced.

"That's a Mexican horse, son. You don't want him," Peterson protested.

Walter opened the gate and headed toward the gelding.

"Come back, son," Peterson called,

"I can tell I'm not going to make any money off you two."

Walter stopped and faced the two men but did not return to the fence.

"That's a four-hundred-dollar pony you got there, Mr. Oakley, but I'll let you have her for two," Peterson said.

"Hundred and a quarter," James countered.

"Two hundred," Peterson said, and this time there was a tone of finality in his voice.

Walter's optimism was gone, but he wasn't going to panic. He turned and started walking toward the gelding.

"Maybe," James' voice started, then trailed off as he thought.

"Maybe, hundred and fifty?"

"Hundred and seventy-five. I won't sell a horse for less than I paid for it," Peterson said.

Walter kept walking, but he was listening closely.

"Deal," his father said softly, and Walter turned and ran back to the mare.

Walter wanted to hug his father, but he hurdled the gate and hugged the mare instead.

"You don't mind taking this to the bank? We want to get out of town before sundown," James explained.

James and Mr. Peterson stepped into the office to fill out the bank draft Walter's father had held up a few seconds earlier. When the two men came outside again, Mr. Peterson carried a rope lead for Walter to slip over the mare's head.

"Take good care of her, son. That's a fine horse you got there," Mr. Peterson told the young man.

CHAPTER TEN

All was well with Walter. As the horses clopped toward home, he whistled, whistled every tune he had ever heard. With the sun beginning to set, Walter pulled the brim of his new hat down to shade his eyes. Little Matt, now an experienced horseman, slept in his father's arms as they bumped along the dusty trail.

Just as the last rays of light squeezed through the mountains, Walter turned around. He realized he was again feeling the gaze of a tracker's eyes on his back. He scanned behind them but saw nothing. But he couldn't shake the feeling that they were being followed. Walter wondered if his father had the same sensation. He wanted to ask, but he wouldn't, not now. In an hour, they stopped to change and feed Little Matt and to get some dried meat from their packs. They ate in the saddle as they rode late into the night. When they made camp, Walter was sure the eyes were still there.

Sleeping on the ground felt more normal than sleeping in a hotel bed. Walter and James slept soundly with Little Matt snuggled safely between them. They rose at four o'clock, as they had on their journey to the Mescalero camp. They enjoyed at least one pleasant difference. When James stoked the fire in the predawn cold, he had coffee to brew and some of his own bacon to fry. The trip home seemed much like a regular journey from El Paso, just like the ones Walter had been making with his father since he turned eleven. The biggest differences? They had no wagons and Walter kept feeling those eyes staring at his back. The whole ride home, they never went away. About five miles before the trio reached the Little Hatchet, Walter decided it was time to speak up.

"Papa, someone's following us," he announced calmly.

"I know. I'm pretty sure it's one of the Apaches," James agreed with equal composure.

"How do you know? Have you seen him?" Walter asked.

"No, I've looked, but I haven't been able to spot him," James responded.

"Then how do you know it's a Mescalero?" Walter followed.

"I think that, because I felt we were being shadowed right after we started to climb into the mountains outside their camp. In fact, I stopped several times and could hear the hoof beats for a few seconds after halting. Whoever he is, he's real good at staying out of sight," James concluded.

Every day for weeks, Katie had gone to the porch at sundown. She looked up onto the ridge, hoping to see her father and brothers. Each night, when she saw nothing, she shed a few quiet tears, wiped her eyes and nose on her apron, put a smile on her face and went inside for dinner.

Now, it was November. With each passing sunset, it seemed less likely she would ever see her father and brothers again. However, every evening, Katie stood on the porch, looking into the hills, praying.

That night, she had finished her prayer and began crying. As the tears flooded her cheeks, Katie kept looking up at the ridge. The crying distorted her sight, but it seemed to Katie that something in front of her was moving. The motion was strangely real. It seemed as if she saw men on horses.

At first, Katie thought she was dreaming. Then she decided she must be going crazy from the worry and guilt.

She rubbed her eyes with her apron and looked again. She could see something, but the images were so blurry. She rubbed some more, but the tears wouldn't go away and the figures on the horses were a blur and did not seem real. As they started down the ridge toward the house, Katie thought she could see one of the men waving at her. She stomped her foot on the porch and began talking to herself. Actually, it was more like a command.

"Stop crying!" Katie heard herself demand.

She rubbed her eyes a third time and took a deep breath, still trying to stop the tears. Katie looked up once more. Someone was waving at her, waving for all he was worth! It was Walter! Positively! No doubt!

"Thank God!" Katie screamed and waved back as broadly as she could.

Walter could wait no longer. He spurred the mare, and she took the last two-thirds of the steep drop into the valley with quick, sure steps.

Katie screamed as loudly as she had ever screamed in her life, screamed until it seemed her lungs had collapsed!

"Thank God! They're all right!" she cried, as tears gushed from her eyes.

In seconds, Katie was blinded by her own tears again, but that didn't stop her from charging off the porch toward the rider who now rode at a full gallop in her direction. Rebecca knew of her daughter's nightly vigil. At first, she had tried to stop her, but after a while, Rebecca had become used to the routine. However, the massive stomp on the porch had been the first variation Rebecca had heard from her daughter in weeks.

That perked up her ears. When Katie said, "stop crying," the words had been too soft for her mother to make out; but Rebecca had understood "thank God!" And by the time Katie shouted, "they're all right," Rebecca was running toward the porch. The kids had never seen Rebecca run through the house before. So when she ran, all the other children in the house chased after her. By the time Rebecca reached the front door, Katie was already two hundred yards away. Rebecca looked past her daughter and saw Walter galloping toward his sister. Up on the ridge, Rebecca could see her husband working his way down the trail toward the valley. She had to grab the post anchoring the porch rail to keep from collapsing.

"Thank God!" Rebecca said aloud and began dabbing the corner of her apron on her watering eyes.

"Thank God," she repeated, but her words were drowned out by the screams of children, who had burst through the door in a gaggle and were all running as fast as they could toward Katie and Walter. The pack of wild kids was whooping and screaming as loudly as their vocal cords would support.

In another second, Rebecca was running behind them. Like Katie, her eyes were blinded by tears. She was gasping for air and there did not seem to be enough oxygen on the entire farm for Rebecca to catch her breath. As Katie reached Walter, she too was out of breath and nearly hysterical, but she managed to get out a few coherent words.

"Is Matt all right?" she gasped.

"Yes!" Walter boomed with joy.

"He's fine," Katie's big brother added.

Katie had never been so relieved. All the guilt she had carried for what, to her, had been an eternity, had been misplaced. Thank God her family was safely home. She had prayed so hard and wanted so much; and now Katie's prayers were answered. Walter realized everyone wanted to know the answer to Katie's question. So the next time he spoke, he made his voice as loud as his breathless state allowed.

"Matt's all right!" Walter shouted.

And a second time as reassurance, "Matt is fine."

Rebecca could not believe what she was hearing. All three of her boys had come home to her.

"Thank God!" she proclaimed again.

But she could not actually hear her own words. Rebecca was completely out of breath and there was too much confusion in every direction. After his second announcement, Walter reached his arm down to Katie and pulled his sister up on to the horse. She landed on the saddle horn. It hurt a lot, but she didn't care. Her big brother was home. Matt was home and her father was home.

"They're home! Papa's home!" the younger children all shouted, as a chorus that kids repeated several times.

Everyone was completely wild with excitement. James beamed with joy at the reunion of his family that was taking place below him in the valley. He wanted to spur his new horse into a gallop and grab up Rebecca as Walter had done with his sister, but little Matt was still sleeping in his arms. So he kept watching the celebration as he safely progressed down the hill.

He saw his son and daughter riding to their mother. He saw Walter climb down and Rebecca hug him. He saw Katie hug Walter. He saw the younger children grab their big brother, and he felt certain tears were streaming down Rebecca's face, even though he was too far away to see them. James drank in the joyful sounds of screaming.

Perhaps he had been this happy the day he and Rebecca were married, or when Walter was born, but he was not sure. James felt a deep joy just for being alive. It was as if a long nightmare had ended and he was waking from the worst dream he would ever have. Before he had faced them, James could not have imagined defeating such difficulties. Now that he had done so, the life that lay ahead appeared wonderful and exciting. Finally, the big gelding stopped beside his wife. At that instant, he could see the actual tears on her face, tears that were proof of relief, gratitude, and joy.

"Thank God, James!" she sobbed.

"You have brought my boys home and God has brought you home," Rebecca added.

"I love you," James told his wife as he handed their baby son down to her.

He allowed Rebecca a minute with Matt, a moment like she'd had with Walter earlier. Then James stepped off his horse to hold his wife and son together. He kissed Rebecca on the forehead, then turned to Katie.

"I'm sorry, Papa," Katie confessed, with tears streaming down her cheeks.

"I didn't mean to let them take him," Katie was attempting to apologize, but a flood of tears choked her, and she could not continue.

"Now, now, daughter. There's nothing to worry about. It wasn't your fault, and you can see that everything is just fine," James reassured Katie, holding her with one arm and smoothing her hair with his opposite hand.

"See, look at your brother. He got a new hat out of the deal and some pants that fit," James teased.

Katie laughed. Her father was back, and he made her feel good again.

"I love you, Papa," she managed.

"I love you, too, Katie," James replied, pulling his daughter into a tighter hug.

"Now take this baby, so I can give your mother a kiss," he instructed.

Katie reached toward her mother and took little Matt into her arms.

James put his arms around Rebecca and kissed her right on the lips. None of the children could ever remember having seen anything like that.

Then, one by one, James hugged and kissed each of his children: Harry, Sam, Charlie, Hattie, Lottie, and Ike. Next, his father catapulted little Ike through the air. When he landed, his legs straddled James' neck, and he rode into the house on his father's shoulders.

Little Ike whooped for joy. Good times had returned to the Little Hatchet.

Always precise and consistent, James was even more predictable during hog killing time. However, on the morning after his return, Rebecca was shocked to find her husband in the kitchen when she went down to prepare breakfast.

James was frying bacon and fixing biscuits. Rebecca had seen him make breakfast before, but always on a Sunday and never when there was work to do making bacon out in the smokehouse. Here it was a weekday, and the slaughter was already three weeks behind. And there stood her husband, in the middle of Rebecca's kitchen, happily cooking breakfast, as if he had nothing else to do.

"And what do you think you're doing, James Oakley?" she fussed.

"Well, I think it's obvious. I'm baking biscuits and cooking bacon," her husband replied with a mischievous smile lighting his face.

"And do you expect those hogs to kill and cure themselves?" Rebecca asked sternly.

"Well, if they want to die today, I guess they'll have to make their own arrangements, because I intend to take my children fishing," James announced, leaving Rebecca speechless.

James roared with laughter.

"You know, in all the years we've been together, this is the first time I've ever seen you without something to say," James told his wife, as his laughter echoed through their home.

James had a spatula in his hands, and Rebecca grabbed it and shoved him.

"Get out of my kitchen," she commanded.

"But the biscuits are going to burn," James protested.

"Its all right if they do," Rebecca impatiently retorted.

"You can't just march into my kitchen and take over."

Sure enough, as Rebecca continued talking, the smell of burning biscuits began filling the room. The harder James laughed, the madder Rebecca got. To be on the safe side, James retreated into the parlor. Just as he entered, he spotted little Lottie coming down the stairs, rubbing her eyes and carrying a rag doll. Lottie looked up and saw her father. She dropped her doll on the stairs, jumped down the last three steps, leaping into her father's arms. James lifted his daughter into the air, paused for a good look at his precious girl, and twirled her above his head.

"And how are you on this spectacular morning?" James asked Lottie.

"Fine," the little girl answered shyly.

"How would you like to go fishing today?" James asked.

"Fishing!" Lottie screamed.

"I guess that means yes," James decided.

"Well, that's just what we'll do. Right after breakfast, we'll all head down to the creek and catch some fish for supper," James pronounced, as he put Lottie, who was shrieking with excitement, down on the floor.

In minutes, the rest of the household was stirring, and the commotion intensified to an uproar. When breakfast was over and his wife stood to clear the table, James threw caution to the wind.

"I don't suppose you would consider joining us for fishing, mother?" James taunted.

At first the children giggled, then Katie gasped. Rebecca had raised the wooden honey spreader and for a minute it looked as if she were going to hurl it at James. But for once, Rebecca's sternness cracked.

"Well, I suppose, if everyone else here has gone completely mad, then I'll just go crazy, too. Not crazy enough to go fishing, you understand. But I will fry some chicken and bring it down for a picnic lunch," Rebecca announced, keenly aware of how shocking her break away from the unfailingly consistent and reliable routine Rebecca demanded from herself and everyone else would be for her family.

The Oakley family reunion was absolutely perfect. That night everyone went to bed feeling all was right in their world again.

CHAPTER ELEVEN

James was up early the next morning. He had hogs to process and three fewer weeks than usual to get his work completed. As he was getting his tools ready before breakfast, he made an important decision. He determined he would kill half the hogs and make half the bacon and sausage as soon as he could. When that meat was cured, he would take it to El Paso, then make a second trip in January with the rest of the bacon.

So, three weeks before Christmas, James and Walter loaded the wagons for El Paso. After they had finished packing the second wagon and returned from the barn with the canvas and rope, Walter spoke up.

"I think I saw that Apache, Papa," he reported.

"When?" his father asked.

"Two days ago," Walter replied.

"He was sitting, hidden in some rocks on the ridge right through those trees," Walter reported, pointing over the corner of the barn toward the ridge line.

"Have you said anything to anyone else?" James asked.

"No, I've been waiting to tell you," Walter responded.

"Have you seen him, Papa?" Walter asked.

"No, but I've seen signs that he's been in the barn. I think maybe he's slept in there a couple of times," James said.

"What does he want?" Walter asked.

"I don't know," James answered.

"Do you think maybe he's waiting for us to leave to do something?" asked Walter, clearly concerned.

"I don't know," James replied in a tone that indicated to Walter that it wasn't the first time his father had pondered that very question.

The conversation stopped and James spread the canvas he would tie over the wagon. It was an intricate procedure, and he worked without talking. The fifteen minutes or so that it took to secure the tarp gave James the time he needed to think.

"I'm going to get up at three o'clock to feed the mules," James began.

"After I get that done, I'll wake you. You may need to stay here and watch out for the family."

"How will you get the second wagon to El Paso?" Walter asked.

"Harry will have to drive it," James answered.

"He's too young," Walter said, surprised by what his father was considering.

"He's almost as old as you were when you started going with me," James countered.

"But the first time I went, I didn't try to drive a team," Walter reminded his father.

"I know. I'm going to sleep on it and decide in the morning," said James.

"I don't think I can sleep," Walter admitted.

"What will I do if the Apache tries something? What if Harry can't handle the team?" he asked.

"You'll do whatever you need to do," his father pronounced.

"You proved that when little Matt was taken."

"I still don't think I can sleep," Walter responded.

"Well, get to bed anyway," his father told him.

"Tomorrow's going to be a long day. And you need to be alert and at your best."

James closed the door to the barn, and the two headed back to the house. It was cold, and they could see their breath in the moonlight as they walked. James and Walter went inside and said goodnight at the foot of the stairs.

Walter tossed and turned for a while, but eventually fell asleep. He had been sleeping soundly for about two hours when he felt his father touching his shoulder. Walter jumped.

"Shhh," his father cautioned.

"Get your boots on quickly and come with me. The Mescalero is in the barn."

"Be quiet," James added.

"I don't want to wake anyone else up."

Within seconds, Walter was going down the stairs with James. He was still mostly asleep, but he was wondering why his father had asked him to be quiet. Surely, the terrible pounding he was hearing had awakened everyone else. It sounded as if someone were beating on the bottom of a metal washtub with a stick of firewood. The sound repeated every two seconds or so.

"What's that noise?" Walter asked James.

"I'm not sure, but I think it's one of the mules," his father speculated.

"What's he doing?" Walter asked.

"Sounds like he's kicking the side of the barn," James answered.

As they walked past the table, James picked up a lantern that he had already lit. He handed it to Walter, then grabbed his rifle.

"Don't make any sudden moves," his father cautioned.

"When we get inside the barn, try to hold the light where I can see and keep the light from shining on me. If anyone's in there, it's best if they can't see me. If someone tries to run, let them go."

"All right," Walter whispered.

With each step they took toward the barn, the pounding sound grew louder. As they reached the barn door, James motioned for Walter to stand slightly to the left of where the doors came together. James opened the door and looked inside. He moved his head carefully, squinting through the darkness, mindful that someone who might want to hurt him was probably inside.

James stared into the dark barn for about thirty seconds before he distinguished a shape inside. When he was confident about what he saw, James called to his son in a normal speaking voice.

"Give me the light," he directed.

James took the light and walked slowly into the barn, then spoke again.

"Come on in, Walter," he called in a firm voice.

Cautiously, Walter poked his head around the open door. Near the middle of the big barn was one of the craziest sights Walter had ever witnessed. He saw Peyote clutching the inside wall of the building with his fingers and nails. His face was against the wood siding. His left foot was on the top of a stall rail. His right foot was in a hole in the barn's wall that the mule had apparently kicked out. About once a second, the giant animal would kick at Peyote, causing him to jerk his leg away, while trying to keep his very tenuous balance.

Walter almost wanted to laugh at the absurdity of this situation, but he could see that Peyote was hurt badly. He was covered with blood. His right leg had a large gash that went from the bottom of his foot to the Mescalero's knee. Blood poured from cuts in Peyote's head.

"Son, we need to get him down from there. I'm going to slip a halter over the mule, then pass the lead out to you," James explained to Walter.

James opened the gate to the pen as the mule continued to kick at Peyote. He slipped a rope halter over the animal's head and snapped it in place. He held the lantern high above the mule's head and kept his eyes fixed on the injured brave. Once the halter was secure, James took the lead in his hand and began coaxing the mule.

"Come on Anderson, let's get you out of here," he said.

The mule kicked at Peyote and did not respond. James jerked sharply on the rope and spoke sternly to the mule.

"Anderson!" he barked.

This time, the mule took a step forward, but kicked again. James tugged the rope once more and made a clicking sound. The mule stepped away from Peyote cautiously.

James handed the lead to Walter, who led Anderson across the barn to a hayrack. Walter draped the rope over the rail to another pen, took a fork, and slung some hay into the rack for the mule. Anderson stuck his nose in the hay and began munching, as if what had been going on happened every night.

Peyote remained glued to the wall of the barn. James wondered how to tell the young warrior that he meant him no harm. If he were to step forward, that might appear threatening. Were he to step back too rapidly, that could seem like the prelude to an attack. James took one easy step toward Peyote, then dropped slowly to his knees. He pointed to some hay on the floor of the stall with his finger, indicating to the brave that he should drop into the soft hay.

Peyote's eyes met James's. Perhaps he was too weak to jump.

James rose slowly and inched toward the stranded Mescalero. He knew that Peyote could not understand his words, so he tried to make the tone of his voice soothing.

"Here, I'll help you," James urged, speaking gently.

Easily, James wrapped his arms around the brave's legs.

"Turn lose. I've got you," he instructed.

Peyote looked into James' eyes again to make certain he could trust the white man. Reassured that James meant him no harm, Peyote relaxed his grip on the wall of the barn. James allowed Peyote's legs to slip through his arms for about six inches, then pulled his arms tight. The weight of Peyote's torso fell over on James' broad shoulder. James steadied himself, then slowly dropped to one knee. Carefully, he let Peyote fall backward, using his left arm to cushion Peyote's slight drop into the soft hay.

When Peyote's head was resting on the straw, James released his grip on the brave's legs and stretched them out. Peyote moaned, then exhaled deeply, relieved that his ordeal with the mule was over. Whatever was ahead for Peyote could be no worse than the terrible kicking Anderson had given him. Walter was still standing with the mule when his father called to him.

"Get some water and rags," James told his son.

Walter trotted out of the barn toward the house. He bolted through the door, then jerked to a halt. His mother was standing about six feet inside the door.

"What's happening?" Rebecca asked.

"There's an Apache in the barn and Anderson has kicked him real bad," Walter answered.

None of this made any sense to Rebecca, who had been waiting in the parlor for about ten minutes. She had thought a wolf might have gotten into the barn and had noted that the rifle was not in its usual place above the mantel.

"An Indian? What's an Indian doing around here?" she exclaimed.

"I don't know, mother, but I need some rags. He's hurt real bad," Walter replied.

Rebecca turned. In seconds, she was back from the kitchen with a pile of rags about a foot high.

"These should do," she offered.

Walter took the rags from his mother, turned and dashed through the door into the barn. A few steps from the stall, he stopped running. He walked to his father and gave him the rags.

Walter turned around, walked a few steps, then ran across the yard to the well. Working quickly, he primed the pump and filled a bucket two-thirds from the top with water. In a moment, he was kneeling beside his father with the bucket of water.

For the next hour, James worked with the water and rags and with some turpentine he kept in the barn. He preferred turpentine to tobacco juice when he had it. After he had cleaned the cuts thoroughly, he turned to Walter.

"This cut on his leg is too long and too deep to heal the way it is. Go into the house and get a needle, thread, matches, and a candle from your mother," James directed.

In a moment, Walter was back with the items. Rebecca was extremely curious about what was going on in the barn, but she would wait until the crisis passed. Walter handed the thread and needle to his father.

"Light the candle," James directed his son.

While Walter lit the candle, James threaded the needle.

"Hold the candle over here," James instructed.

James held the needle in the flame until the heat burned his fingers, then he started suturing the gash on Peyote's leg. The brave was out cold. However, as the needle pierced the tender flesh on the edge of the wound, Peyote's leg jerked reflexively.

When James finished sewing the wound, he blotted some more turpentine on the injured tissue, then wrapped one of the rags loosely around Peyote's leg.

Ninety minutes after he had started, James turned to the bucket of water, washed his hands, then splashed some water on his face and finally stood.

"I think we had better put off our trip to El Paso," he told Walter.

The young man was relieved. However, Walter felt he was close to lapsing into a state of shock as his father walked past him. He jolted back to reality when he felt James put the rifle in his hand.

"I don't think he's going anywhere but keep an eye on him while I go tell your mother what happened," James said.

Walter moved toward the stall as his father walked by a second time with a couple of saddle blankets in his arms. He gently covered Peyote with the blankets, then headed toward the house.

It was after daybreak when James returned to the barn, carrying a cup of steaming coffee for his son. The weather had gotten much colder, and Walter had found another saddle blanket to warm himself while his father had been in the house.

"Has he moved yet?" James asked.

"No sir," Walter replied.

"Well, go on inside. Your mother has some breakfast for you. When you get through, wash up and come back here. I want you to ride over and get Miguel."

Miguel Velasquez was the patriarch of a small sheep ranch just south of the Little Hatchet. Miguel presided over an assortment of adobe ranch houses that were occupied by Miguel and his wife, two of his sisters, one sister-in-law, and four of his daughters. There were also grandchildren.

Two of the women's husbands had been killed in mining accidents. Two others worked for the army at Fort Bliss, and the rest had run off. It was the women from the Velasquez ranch who helped make the bacon and sausage on the Little Hatchet. Miguel did not own a horse. So as Walter rode to get him, he led his father's gelding.

The children on the ranch spotted Walter when he was still a mile away. By the time he rode up to Miguel's house, most of the family had gathered outside. As Walter dismounted, one of Miguel's daughters went inside the house to summon her father.

Miguel was the only member of his family who spoke English, but he used Spanish when he gave directions to his daughter.

"Teresa, bring our guest some water. He has had a dusty ride," the elderly man said.

Then Miguel turned to Walter.

"Good morning, Walter. And what may I do for you today? I thought this was the day that your father was taking the meat into El Paso."

"Yes sir. We were," Walter confirmed.

"But early this morning we found a Mescalero in our barn. He is badly hurt, and Papa needs you to come watch after him while we take the bacon to El Paso. He knows this is a bad time for you, but he said to tell you he would pay you two dollars a day if you could come."

"Well, of course I will come, young Walter," Miguel replied.

"You rest for a few minutes while I get some things together."

Miguel was nearly eighty years old, but he worked on his ranch every day. Until the army said that he was too old, he had worked at Fort Bliss. When they told him he had to leave, Miguel returned to the spot south of the Little Hatchet where he had been born and lived as a boy.

He made the move, because Miguel believed it was the best place for him to care for his family. Despite the harshness of the land, no one had ever gone hungry. Since the women had begun processing sausage and bacon, the Velasquez family had attained a measure of prosperity, at least by local standards.

The old man said goodbye to each member of his family and picked up every one of the smaller grandchildren to hug and kiss them.

"I should be back the night before Christmas," he told his family in Spanish.

They said their farewells, and Miguel mounted the big gelding. Walter climbed into the saddle of his mare and the two rode off toward the Little Hatchet. As they rode, Walter told Miguel the story of how Anderson had attacked the brave. He also explained that the Apache had followed them all the way from the Mescalero stronghold.

Miguel had dealt with the Mescalero all his life, and he knew most of the chiefs. He thought for a long time, saying nothing.

"I'm not sure," Miguel said finally.

"But from the way you describe this brave, he could be the one they call Peyote.

"You say he is very big and strong?" Miguel asked Walter.

"Yes sir," Walter answered.

"He's bigger than any of the braves we saw in the Mescalero camp."

Of course, Walter had not known that Peyote's grandmother had kept him in her tent, while James and Walter were talking with the chief. Walter also did not know about the attachment the brave felt for his little brother, Matt. When they reached the Oakley place, Miguel continued discussing his theory with James.

"If it is Peyote, he could be trouble," Miguel explained.

"He is the grandson of the chief's favorite sister. They call him Peyote, because sometimes he acts like a cow who has eaten the loco weed," Miguel continued.

"Well, I suppose you can ask him his name when he wakes up. If Walter and I leave right now, we might still get back home before Christmas," James hoped.

There was another round of goodbyes on the Little Hatchet. Then James and his son drove the heavily loaded wagons up the ridge and out of the valley.

Rebecca and the children stood on the porch and watched until the wagons disappeared out of sight. In the barn, Miguel settled in for a long stretch of guarding the injured Peyote.

CHAPTER TWELVE

The entire trip was uneventful, both on the Little Hatchet and along the trail. Peyote had awakened the night James and Walter had driven off. Miguel nourished him back to health with chicken soup that Rebecca made. In a few days, Peyote could walk again. The cut on his leg became seriously infected, but James had sutured it skillfully, leaving an opening for the infection to drain out.

In two weeks, Peyote was as good as new, but he did not try to escape from Miguel and never tried to harm him. In fact, during the last week that James and Walter were on the road, Miguel began teaching Peyote how to tend the hogs. Both men slept in the barn. And except for the extra food Rebecca fixed for them every day, the Oakley family would not have known they were on the ranch at all. Miguel talked to Peyote, mostly in sign language. And by Christmas Eve, Miguel felt he had pieced the Mescalero's story together.

All that day inside the house, the children had been excited. They knew it was Christmas Eve, and they expected their father would return from El Paso with presents. Every few minutes, they had run out onto the porch or peeked from the windows, looking for Papa and their big brother.

Finally, just after the last light from the sunny winter day was gone, they heard the sounds of the wagons outside. The children, bubbling over with Christmas anticipation and uncontainable excitement, darted out of the house. James and Walter, bone tired, were climbing down from the wagons to the music of the smaller children's delighted squeals.

"What did you bring us, Papa? What do we get for Christmas?"

"And why do you think I brought you Christmas presents? Didn't your mother make everyone a new dress this fall?" James teased.

"Please, Papa! Please tell us!" they shouted.

"Well, maybe there are some presents somewhere. I'm not sure. But first, we have to take care of the mules, and we have to get Miguel on his way back to his family. Now go into the house and I'll be in there, directly," James told his children.

Walter was already leading the first wagon toward the barn. He was far too tired to be excited about Christmas. Walter and his father had driven late every night to get home in time for the holiday.

As Walter reached the barn, Miguel came out to help with the mules. Peyote had come to the door of the barn; but when he saw the mules, he ducked back inside. He was taking no more chances with those fierce animals.

"And how did things go, Miguel?" James asked.

"Fine sir. Our Peyote has his strength back, and he is even learning how to care for the hogs, sir," Miguel announced, a proud smile beaming across his face.

"So, it is the crazy one that you were concerned about, then?" James asked.

"Yes sir. It's him. But he hasn't made any trouble at all," Miguel reported.

"Did you find out why he followed us?" James continued

"Yes sir. I think so. I am pretty sure he wanted to make certain that you were taking good care of Little Matt. I think he believes the boy is his. Maybe he thinks the spirits gave Matt to him, but I'm not completely sure about that part," Miguel replied.

James pondered all this strange information for a moment, then put another question to his friend and neighbor, revealing that James was significantly concerned.

"But to be clear, the Apache hasn't tried to hurt anyone or to run away?" James asked, seeking reassurance.

"No sir. I don't think I could make him leave. And he's as gentle as a lamb. He hasn't gone near any member of the family," Miguel said.

"What if I left him in the barn by himself? Would he do all right with that? Would Walter or I have to guard him for the family to be safe tonight?" James questioned.

"Sir, I'm sure he would be just fine in the barn, and you wouldn't have to guard him to keep your family safe. Like I said, I don't think you can make him leave. He seems determined to look after Little Matt," Miguel explained.

"I don't know how to thank you for taking care of everything for us. I know it's a bad time of the year to be away, but I had to get that bacon to market before Christmas," James said.

"I know, sir," Miguel agreed.

"It was nothing," he added in Spanish.

"Oh no Miguel, it was vital. This is not enough, but I want you to know I appreciate everything you did while I was gone," James asserted, handing his neighbor a fifty-dollar gold piece.

"It is far too much, sir," Miguel protested.

"No sir, it is not enough. There are a lot of mouths to feed at your place. And your sons-in-law will be home for Christmas," James added.

"Oh, and Miguel," James remembered, as he handed the old man a large sack.

"These are toys for your grandchildren. Walter and I counted as carefully as we could, then we threw in a couple of extras just in case there were some new arrivals we didn't know about.

"It has been such a crazy fall that almost anything could have happened around here and I wouldn't have known about it, even the birth of children."

"Yes sir," Miguel agreed.

"It has been very crazy this fall, but there are no new grandchildren."

"Well, maybe there will be some this spring then," James suggested, laughing.

"Now you take a horse and get on home to your family. After Christmas, I would like to find out more about Peyote. This is not going to sit well with Mrs. Oakley. I know that much.

"Merry Christmas," James said to his neighbor in Spanish.

"Merry Christmas," Miguel responded in English.

Miguel walked into the barn to speak with Peyote, before the old man began his journey home. He explained to the Mescalero warrior that the owner of the ranch was home and that Peyote was to stay inside the barn until he (Miguel) returned in two days. Peyote nodded that he understood, but he made some signs and pointed toward the mules. Miguel nodded and walked outside.

"Sir, Peyote has agreed to stay inside the barn, but he is very much afraid of the mules. Can we move him to a stall where the mules cannot get close to him?" Miguel suggested.

"Well, I guess that makes sense," James responded with a knowing chuckle.

"Anderson almost killed him. I expect he's smart to be afraid of mules. I suppose I'd be afraid of 'em too, if I had any sense," James concluded with another little laugh at his observation about mules.

Within a few minutes, Miguel had moved Peyote to the far end of the barn, saddled a horse, and was on his way home for Christmas. Before James and Walter began leading mules into the barn, James walked back to the stall where Peyote was.

"Good evening," he said to his mysterious guest.

"I'm glad that you are feeling better."

Peyote nodded.

Then James and Walter resumed their work. When they finished watering and feeding the mules and storing their trail gear, the two gathered the children's presents and went into the house. After the presents were opened and the excitement died down, James took Rebecca, Walter, and Harry into James and Rebecca's room.

"Miguel says that our uninvited guest has been well behaved," James said.

"Yes," Rebecca responded.

"If I had not seen him when I took out the food, I would not have known that he was there for the first two weeks. For the last couple of days, Miguel had him help with the hogs, but he hasn't come near the house."

"Well, I don't think there is anything to worry about," James announced.

"But I think just to make sure, we should move Matt back in our room with us for the night. And I want Harry to put his mattress in front of the door to the boy's room. And Walter, you should do the same thing. Please put your mattress in front of the girls' room."

"And boys, let's make sure none of the kids wanders around by themselves in the morning before the whole household is awake and stirring," James directed.

"Yes sir," they both concurred, emphasizing their understanding with nods.

James took one more precaution that night. After everyone settled in, he quietly removed the Winchester from its rack over the mantel and brought it into his bedroom.

The next morning, after Christmas breakfast, James and Walter walked out to the barn with some biscuits and honey for Peyote. In honor of the holiday, Rebecca even included some sausage in the bucket. Peyote was awake and standing when they walked in.

"Good morning," James announced cheerfully as he approached Peyote. "We brought you some breakfast."

Peyote nodded and smiled faintly as he accepted the bucket with the food. He knew the white man could not understand his speech, so he made no effort to express himself with words. In fact, Peyote seldom spoke when he was around his own people. Silence was normal for him.

"We're going to feed the mules," James told Peyote.

"Ordinarily, we would only feed them once a day. But when we come back from a trip like this, we feed them twice a day for a spell to build their strength back up," James explained, even though he knew Peyote had no idea what he was saying.

James and Walter finished with the animals, collected the empty breakfast container from Peyote, and went inside to relax. Later, they brought Peyote some of the same chicken and dumplings the family had for Christmas dinner. It seemed like strange fare to him, but all the food the people on the Little Hatchet ate was difficult for Peyote to comprehend.

That afternoon, when James, Walter, and Harry came to feed the hogs, James stepped into the barn again. He carried two of the buckets they used to feed the hogs over toward Peyote.

"Miguel tells me you've been helping with the hogs," James said, holding the buckets up for Peyote.

Peyote nodded, took the buckets and followed James out toward the hog pens. He filled the buckets as Miguel had shown him and helped slop the hogs. This was a strange place. At home, the women tended the animals. Here, the women seemed to do little work.

Almost any other Mescalero brave in Peyote's circumstances would have been consumed with worry about when the white men might kill him, but Peyote never thought he faced danger from the Oakleys. Peyote was homesick as he worked with the hogs, but he knew his duty. He must stay and look after the little boy.

An hour or so after they had finished with the animals, Walter and Harry brought Peyote some more food: cornbread and milk. The cornbread tasted somewhat familiar, but the cow's milk was sweet, not strong like the goat's milk that he had drunk a few times before. Strange food, he thought. And they eat so much.

The next morning, Miguel rode up to the barn an hour after the sun had risen. Peyote was glad to see the old man again. It took about forty-five minutes for James and Peyote to have their talk, aided by Miguel's sign language.

Peyote explained that he must stay and look after the child. He did not understand why the question was asked, but he assured James that he would never hurt Matt. James told Peyote that all the people on the Little Hatchet were important to Matt and they must not be hurt, either. He said that the Oakleys also were supposed to look after Matt. God said so.

Peyote thought for a moment. That was all right. Maybe they could help him protect the child. He did not think that they were strong enough, but James seemed wise, like the chief, Peyote's great uncle. Maybe if there were real trouble, he could help.

He thought some more. Even after he had been shot, Walter had followed the braves all the way back to the stronghold. Perhaps he could prove useful in a crisis. This was a strange place, and these were strange people, but they had helped Peyote, after the giant horse had attacked him. They were kind.

"Are these people your friends?" Peyote asked Miguel in sign language.

"Yes, they are my best friends. They have helped me and all of my little children," Miguel replied.

Well, that was it then. If they helped the old man's small children, then they could help his little child, too, Peyote decided.

"And the white chief says you will have to follow his rules," Miguel said in sign language.

"Yes, he is chief here and I will follow him in his village just as I follow my chief in my village," Peyote answered.

James was satisfied. He carefully explained the ground rules for Peyote's stay on the Little Hatchet. Miguel told Peyote that in this village, when two men reached an agreement, it was customary to shake hands; and Miguel demonstrated how that was done.

After the lesson, Peyote reached to shake James' hand. That too went well, except that Peyote nearly pulled James' arm out of its socket.

When the handshake was finished, Peyote turned to Miguel and asked a question using sign language.

"Sir, he wants to know when he can see Little Matt," Miguel explained to James.

"Tell him to wait here," James answered.

CHAPTER THIRTEEN

James walked to the house and asked Rebecca for her permission to allow Peyote to have a carefully supervised visit with Little Matt, knowing in advance that his wife would be opposed. Rebecca never wanted Peyote to have another chance to hurt Matt. James knew his wife was about to dig her heels in, opposing any contact, ever.

"It boils down to this. Either we can make an agreement with him that says he can help us keep Little Matt safe, or I have to kill him. There's no middle ground here," James told his stunned wife.

"James, you're talking crazy," Rebecca burst out.

"You could send Miguel to Silver City for the marshal. Or you and Miguel could tie him up and take him to Fort Bliss and let the army deal with him," Rebecca suggested, hoping that she had come up with a solution her husband would accept.

"And what would the marshal do with him?" James asked quietly.

"Put him in jail, I suppose," Rebecca answered.

"No. He would hang him. He kidnapped a white boy," James said, still speaking softly.

"Well, what about the army? Would they hang him, too?" Rebecca asked.

"Perhaps. And maybe they would just put him in the stockade," he continued.

"But if they put him in the stockade, he will escape. And when he escapes, he'll come straight here. And then we will be right back where we are now. Except when he comes back, he won't trust us and he will likely attempt to kill all of us, so that he can take Little Matt back to his tribe.

"This Apache is a strong and brave warrior. He's also crazy and the chief's nephew. And he believes some kind of powerful and holy spirit gave Matt to him to guard and care for. That means Peyote believes he must be willing to die, if necessary, to keep Little Matt safe.

"Either we will have to come to terms with him, or Peyote must die.

"Is that what you want?" James asked, continuing in his calm tone, hoping that he was conveying reason to his wife, whom James knew was every bit his intellectual equal.

"I don't want him to hurt Matt. That's what I absolutely don't want," Rebecca replied quietly and with conviction equal to her husband's.

"That greatly overgrown Apache boy took Matt from our front porch to the Mescalero camp, nearly three hundred miles from here. And Matt never got a scratch or missed a meal. Why would he hurt him now?" James offered.

There was a long silence. James was the most thoughtful and persuasive man Rebecca had ever met. He was probably right, even though the whole idea of keeping a crazy person who had kidnapped their son on their farm just seemed insane.

She thought some more. Rebecca did not want her son hurt, but she did not wish for Peyote to be killed, either. Finally, she reluctantly agreed.

"All right, James. I agree to let you try this crazy business. But I don't want Peyote alone with Matt. You or Walter should always be with Matt if this overgrown child is anywhere near him. And when you and Walter go to El Paso, either the Apache must go with you, or Miguel must come watch Peyote.

"Promise me?" Rebecca concluded.

"I promise," James answered firmly.

After a minute had passed, James walked up the stairs, got little Matt and took him out to the barn. As soon as he saw Peyote, he began giggling and wiggling and reached for his friend's arms. As Peyote moved forward to take the child, a smile bright as sunshine came to the Mescalero warrior's lips.

Peyote was totally happy. He had missed his best friend. Matt was happy, but not nearly as happy as Peyote. Everyone in Matt's world wanted to hold him. For Peyote, there was only one person on earth, whom he could hold, this incredible child the spirits had left especially for him on a front porch many days' ride from his home.

Seeing the two together could not erase all of James' fear. Matt was his son. However, had James been capable of analyzing the circumstances from the point of view of an observer, who was not Matt's father, such a person would almost certainly have felt confident making a substantial wager that the oversized and mentally underdeveloped warrior would do anything to keep Little Matt from harm.

The four of them stood in the barn for fifteen minutes, while Matt and Peyote renewed their acquaintance. Then James gently took his son back into his arms.

That evening, Peyote was feeding the hogs before James and the boys came out. The next morning, Peyote was up, watering the stock, when James appeared at the barn. The Apache was skillful with the horses, and James noticed.

Over the next six weeks, Peyote became a dedicated farm hand. He enjoyed working with the horses and kept a watchful eye out for the dreaded mules. He did not complain about taking care of hogs and chickens, chores he considered woman's work. Peyote began hunting regularly and was always pleased when the plate he received at night contained venison or rabbit, instead of sausage, beans, or cornbread.

At least every other day, James or Walter brought Little Matt for a visit. Peyote lived for those times.

After six weeks, Walter rode over, leading an extra horse to bring back Miguel.

"Thank you for coming, Miguel," James said to his neighbor after the old man was seated in the Oakley's parlor.

"We are going to El Paso Monday, and I would like for you to help me explain to Peyote that he needs to come with us," James requested.

"Sir, you do not have to explain," Miguel told his neighbor.

"What do you mean?" James asked.

"You are chief of this village. Peyote will do as you say," Miguel responded.

"But wouldn't it be better to ask him to come or to explain why he needs to come with us?" James asked Miguel.

"No sir, not to Peyote. Being chief is the only reason he expects. It's like the army, sir," Miguel explained.

Both men understood the army. James could not make himself comfortable with the concept that someone would prefer to be told to do something without a reason, but he trusted the old man's judgment.

"Fine," James conceded.

"Would you please tell him that he is to come with us on Monday?" James asked.

"Yes sir, I will tell him. And what is he to do while you and Walter go into town?" Miguel inquired.

"I hadn't thought about that," James admitted.

"I don't suppose he can stay at the hotel with us?"

"No sir, he cannot," Miguel agreed, suppressing a smile at his neighbor and friend's naiveté where cultural and racial mores were involved.

"Then tell him that when we get to El Paso, he is to stand watch for us outside of town, as he did before," James said. "Does that make sense?"

"Yes sir, I think he will see that as wise," Miguel responded.

On Monday, when the Oakleys rolled out for El Paso at four in the morning, the procession looked strange. Not only was the Mescalero brave riding guard on the wagons, but tied behind the back wagon were three of James' prize hogs: a boar and two sows.

Rebecca was relieved that Peyote would not be on the ranch with James away. Peyote was also relieved. At last, he was doing work suitable for a brave, instead of women's chores. He rode proudly in front of James' lead wagon, poised to act decisively against any threat.

Each day as they rode, Peyote kept a keen eye for game. Each night, James, Walter, and the Mescalero warrior enjoyed the freshly roasted meat that Peyote had killed.

When the wagons reached the hills overlooking El Paso, Peyote fell back to watch over his charges, just as Miguel had instructed. Two mornings later, as Walter and James rode out of the city, he fell in ahead of them at the same spot, ready to lead them safely back to the Little Hatchet. When they reached the ford, James called to Peyote.

"This way, Peyote," he said, pointing north along the Rio Grande.

Peyote was confused, but pulled his horse back out of the water and resumed north along the trail that followed the river. Four days later, they reached the hills overlooking the goat ranch of the Mexican family that had provided food for little Matt and later for James and Walter. James motioned for Peyote to wait on the trail with his wagon. The elder Oakley climbed onto Walter's wagon with him and took the reins. In a few minutes, they had driven through the hills to the ranch house. This time, their approach went without notice. When they pulled up to the house, James called out.

"*Señor*, may we step down?"

The lady cracked the front door slightly. Then she cautiously stepped out. When she recognized James and Walter, a big smile came to her face. She rushed out into the yard, speaking rapidly.

James could not understand her Spanish, but he could deduce that she was glad to see Walter and him. After a few minutes, James learned that the woman's husband had the goats in a far pasture and would not be home until sundown. She urged them to come inside, to wait and to join them for supper.

"No, we can't stay," James said in English

"But I want to say thank you," he told her before pausing.

"*Gracias*," he repeated in Spanish, then gestured with his arms, as if he were holding a baby.

The words just weren't working. So, James stepped down from the wagon and untied the pigs he had been trailing behind the wagon.

"*Por ustedes*," he tried again.

"*No, no, no, señor*," she objected.

James walked the hogs over to the post where visitors tied their horses. He secured the animals to the hitching post.

"Thank you, again," he said and climbed back on the wagon.

"*No, señor*," the woman repeated, but now tears had come to her eyes.

As James turned the team to head back to the trail, the herder's wife spoke strongly through her tears.

"*Vaya con Dios*," she called.

"God bless you, kind woman," James replied and clicked his tongue, signaling to the mules that it was time to move along.

James and Walter rode back to the trail in silence. When they reached Peyote and the second wagon, Peyote noticed that the hogs were gone.

Good riddance, he thought. That would be three fewer animals for him to feed.

In the fall, Matt took his first steps. By June, he was running all over the yard. As she had done with all her children, Rebecca used a fresh switch on Matt's bare legs to teach him to stay away from the barn, the hog pens, and the creek, but the lessons were not learned all at once.

Matt spent as much time as he could with Peyote, and Harry joined the list of acceptable guardians.

There were lots of new animals on the Little Hatchet, just as every spring. But this season was special. Walter's mare had a foal. All the kids had fun playing with the little animal, but she belonged to Walter.

After a couple of weeks, Walter told his father he had an idea about what to do with the colt.

"I think when she is weaned, we should give her to Miguel," he suggested to James.

"That's a great idea," James agreed.

"But she won't be of any use to Miguel for at least two years. He's getting on in age. If he's going to have a horse he can ride, we need to act a little sooner, don't you think?"

"But Papa, this is the only horse I have to give Miguel," Walter protested, clearly disappointed.

"We could swap, and you could give the horse I trade you to Miguel, and I could give the colt to Harry to raise. What do you think?" James asked his generous son.

Miguel was the happiest man in Southern New Mexico. Peyote helped Harry begin the colt's training. When the Oakleys hauled the first load of bacon to El Paso in the fall, James went to Mr. Peterson's horse yard to purchase a new saddle horse to replace the animal Walter gave Miguel. But James never talked about that transaction as being in any way connected to Walter's colt.

A new hand rolled out from the farm along Little Hatchet Creek on the first trip of that fall to El Paso. Harry traveled with Peyote, Walter, and their father. Walter was slightly uncomfortable having his little brother with them on the journey. Something that had been Walter's sole province was now being shared. Walter was not angry. He had just preferred it the other way. That winter, there were four trips to El Paso and Peyote became used to the routine. He enjoyed the hunting, and he enjoyed getting away from the chores related to providing for the pigs, but he missed Little Matt.

Matt had become extremely active. Despite everyone's, including Peyote's best efforts, Matt was into everything from sunup to sundown. When Matt was not with his friend Peyote, he was trying to find Harry or Walter to take him down to the barn for a visit.

Rebecca had gone through what seemed like an orchard of peach switches to prevent Matt from running off to the barn, but keeping up with him was a full-time job. He was the youngest and fast becoming the most precocious of Rebecca's and James' children.

When Matt took off for the barn on his own, it posed a problem for Peyote. Peyote knew that the chief expected Walter or Harry to be around when Matt came to visit. Peyote also knew that the chief's wife did not like him. So when Matt came to the barn alone, Peyote was reluctant to pick him up and carry him back to the house.

Instead, he would walk in between the house and the barn, hoping to catch the attention of Walter or Harry, so that one of them could see Matt safely back to the Oakleys' house. Peyote did not want to break the chief's rule, and he especially did not want to make the chief's wife angry.

CHAPTER FOURTEEN

The Thursday after Easter, a sparkling New Mexico sun was warming the Little Hatchet ranch. Just a few weeks earlier, ice had still coated the animal troughs and the wet spots by the barn. Now, with rising temperatures, the earth was waking for a new spring. Breakfast concluded, and Rebecca and the girls were clearing the dishes, while the older boys prepared to head outside for the day's work.

Peyote first spotted Matt headed for the barn as the the young Mescalero warrior was finishing his chores. Peyote quickened his walking pace toward the barn but hoped that one of the boys would bolt through the door of the house to bring Matt back before Peyote reached the overly active child.

Matt's eyes had fixed on something at the corner formed by the wall of the barn and the railing of the corral. Matt was scurrying toward the spot that had captured his interest. Peyote could not tell what Matt was intrigued with, but he suspected trouble. The brave broke into a trot. A hundred yards from the barn, Peyote stopped abruptly when he heard Rebecca screaming to Matt from the porch of the Oakley home.

"Matt, you get back in this house," his mother called sternly.

Matt paused for a moment, then ran toward his mother. However, after five or six steps in Rebecca's direction, the youngster circled and headed back toward the barn, giggling as he ran. He took several steps in that direction, encountered a slick spot of mud, and fell flat on his face.

"I'm getting a switch, Matt," Rebecca warned her son.

With those words, Rebecca started off the porch. Peyote stopped, transfixed on Matt's predicament. Rebecca intended to grab her son, but after a few steps, she halted curtly, emitting a panicked, deathly, blood-curdling scream. Peyote had never heard a sound so terrifying. Instantly, he too was seized by the sight of seemingly inescapable death.

Just five feet from Matt was an enormous rattlesnake, coiled with his rattle in motion. The snake raised its monstrous head high, poised for a lethal strike. Matt was obliviously struggling to get to his feet.

"Matt, don't move," Rebecca commanded with a force only a mother can muster.

Peyote sprang to action, charging headlong for the barn as fast as he had ever run. He also screamed at the top of his voice, hoping Matt would look at him instead of moving closer to the snake.

The sunshine had apparently brought the giant rattler out for its first foray of the spring. The serpent had been hibernating in a hole in the creek bank. The rattler's journey up to the barn had been at a lazy crawl. The serpent's eyes were still covered with a milky layer of skin from his hibernation, so there was no way the reptile could be certain about what kind of animal was stupidly lunging at the cold-blooded creature. What-ever it was, the rattler felt that, at the very least, a stern warning was in order.

A milky layer of skin from his hibernation still covered the rattlesnake's eyes, so there was no way the reptile could be certain about what kind of animal was stupidly lunging at the cold-blooded creature. Whatever it was, the rattler felt that, at the very least, a stern warning was in order.

This was the first day of the deadly predator's new season, when the monster was most vulnerable. The nearly blind rattlesnake had lost sight of the threatening creature. Was that good or bad? There was no sense taking a chance with such an enormous animal. It was time to kill.

Matt had become frozen and was no longer moving toward the snake, but Peyote could see that the giant predator was not giving any ground.

Peyote had learned about rattlers when he had been only slightly older than Matt. He knew that the early spring was when the serpents posed the most danger.

These thoughts flashed through the warrior's mind. Even though his feet were moving faster than at any time in his life, Peyote's lunges forward could not keep pace with his thoughts. He needed to grab Little Matt and move him out of the snake's striking range. But Peyote was just too late. He could see the rattlesnake's head set to jerk back. The imminent strike would be lightning fast.

Peyote appeared to be twenty or thirty feet from the child, but Matt's guardian had to make a desperate attempt to save the boy he loved with all his being. Focusing his entire strength into his legs, Peyote leapt toward his little friend with such intense effort that the warrior appeared to be in actual flight, much like that of a falcon attacking a prairie dog or rabbit.

Peyote landed six feet short, but his lurch broke the snake's instinctive concentration and its lethal strike fell just short of the boy. Supercharged with adrenaline, Peyote summoned even more strength for a second effort. As the snake recoiled for another attack, the Mescalero's leap exploded just before the snake lunged at Matt a second time.

In his hyper-charged state, Peyote was faster and stronger than the snake. He landed his body on the ground in front of the boy. Peyote's belief was absolute. He knew Little Matt was his God-given child. In his all-out effort to save his child, the big Mescalero arrived at the point of attack a fraction of a second ahead of the rattlesnake. The reptile's fangs plunged completely through the flesh on his cheek and into Peyote's bone. They went so deep that when the snake tried to pull his head back, his body was dragged toward Peyote's head before the fangs finally dislodged from the Mescalero's cheekbone.

Rebecca grabbed Matt and rolled out of the way with him. Peyote clutched the snake with both hands directly behind its head and held on for dear life, choking all substance from the writhing animal.

Rebecca rose to her feet with her baby, and in one continuous, fluid motion, raced toward her front porch. James dodged away from a collision with his wife and son as they passed each other. In a second, James burst through the barn door. In five seconds, he was back outside with a razor sharp ax. Ten seconds later, he had chopped the snake's body almost in two.

James grabbed the front part of the rattler just below Peyote's hands and pulled with all the force his muscles could generate. Peyote's whole body was being dragged across the muddy earth by James' incredible, adrenaline filled strength. But the brave Mescalero warrior would not release his iron tight grip on the giant rattlesnake, unaware that Little Matt had been rescued and was far from the spot where the attack had occurred.

James picked up his ax. With the skill of a surgeon, he made a second cut just below Peyote's hands, leaving him holding only about ten inches of the snake and taking away any leverage the rattler might have had left.

James looked down at Peyote. He was out cold, in the mud, looking up toward the sky. His eyes were closed. James glanced at the house and saw Walter staring from the front porch. James shouted to his son.

"Walter, bring my knife!"

In a flash, Walter was standing over the two men, offering James his razor-edged skinning knife.

"Carefully hold Peyote's hands away from us, in case that snake's got any bite left in it," James directed.

"But pass the knife to me first," the father added.

James quickly X'd the two fang marks on Peyote's cheek. The entry wounds were almost an inch and a half apart, indicating how huge the snake had been. James worked as quickly as he could, sucking the blood and poison from Peyote's face.

The young man's head and neck already were swelling badly and beginning to discolor. There was little hope, but Peyote had saved James' son from certain death. James would not give up until he had halted the migration of the poison, or until the patient died.

The bite Peyote had suffered had been to his head, which was bad for two reasons. There was no way to apply a tourniquet to stop the spread of the venom, without also choking off the brave's air supply. And because the poison had entered Peyote so close to his brain, there was very little hope of getting the venom out in time to prevent death.

James' efforts were frantic. The ground next to Peyote's head was quickly growing red from all the blood James had spat out. He worked so furiously that he choked on Peyote's blood, as he gasped for air between sucks.

James continued the effort for about fifteen minutes, then sat back on his knees to assess the brave's condition. Peyote was still breathing, and he still had a pulse. The area of his head from about three inches below the fang marks up to his hairline was turning blue. Peyote already had a fever that James could detect with only the touch of his hand.

James had not stopped the poison, but maybe he had removed enough of it from the young man's bloodstream to give him a chance at life. They should know in a few hours.

Drained from the effort, James stood, but felt that his knees were going to give way. He took about thirty seconds to steady himself before trying to walk to the well. Once he got there, he pulled up the bucket filled with cool, fresh water, scooped out a dipper full, and began washing Peyote's blood from his mouth. It took about six mouthfuls before James was satisfied.

He took several large swallows of the water and paused to get his bearings. It had seemed hours before that James had been sitting at his table eating biscuits and eggs. In fact, less than thirty minutes had elapsed since Little Matt had bolted from the house. James walked back to where Peyote lay in the mud. The courageous Mescalero was still breathing.

"Walter, Harry, we need to fix a clean, warm place for Peyote in the barn," James called.

"We'll put him in the parlor," Rebecca interrupted.

If everyone had not already been in shock, Rebecca's decision would have put them there. From the beginning, Matt's mother had made it clear that she did not want the Mescalero anywhere near her house; but that had been before Peyote had offered his own life to make certain that Rebecca's son would live. Whatever the reason, and no matter how muddled Peyote's brain might have been, the young Mescalero had acted bravely and in superhuman fashion to protect Little Matt, when no one else could have.

Rebecca had Walter and Harry carry a mattress to the parlor. In a few minutes, she had it neatly made up with clean sheets. She also spread some more clean sheets on the porch, and she had the boys bring two buckets of clean water to the porch. When her preparations were complete, Rebecca walked back to the barnyard, where James kneeled over Peyote.

"James, let's get him to the porch where we can clean him up," she suggested.

James stood and walked to the barn. In a short time, he returned with a tailgate he had removed from one of the wagons and laid it on the ground next to Peyote.

James instructed Walter and Harry on how to place their arms under Peyote's hips and legs to help lift the brave onto the tailgate that would serve as a litter.

Once Peyote was securely on the board, James showed the boys where he wanted them to place their hands to help raise the young man off the ground. Everyone got set and lifted. Slowly the Oakleys carried Peyote to their house and situated him on the porch next to the sheets.

James held Peyote up, while Rebecca washed the mud from him. When they had finished, they spread clean sheets under the brave on the tailgate and covered him with another clean sheet. James and the boys carried Peyote into the parlor and rested him on the mattress Rebecca had prepared. She dried him with the sheets from the tailgate, then covered him with another clean, dry sheet. She added several blankets on top of the sheets to keep Peyote warm.

In a few minutes, Rebecca returned from the kitchen with an herb poultice she had prepared, hoping it would draw more of the poison from his blood. She placed the poultice on Peyote's wounds and secured it with a bandage.

Rebecca battled Peyote's fever with wet towels. For hours, she nursed the young brave, just as if she were caring for one of her own children. As night fell, Rebecca continued to sit with and work over Peyote.

Several times, James came to Rebecca and offered to take her place, so that she could get a little sleep, but she refused each time. Finally, at sunrise, Rebecca allowed Katie to take her place, while Rebecca fed break-fast to her family. After the dishes were done, Rebecca resumed her vigil.

Twenty-four hours passed from the time Peyote was bitten. He remained unconscious, and his fever was blistering. If there was any chance the young man could recover, Rebecca was determined to see that he got it.

Rebecca's efforts continued for six days, until Peyote died, never having regained consciousness. Exhausted, Rebecca went upstairs and sat in the rocking chair by the window, where she sewed and sobbed, heartbroken that the young man, who had saved her baby from the giant rattlesnake, had died, before Rebecca could thank him for his brave and selfless act.

For several days, James and Walter had been preparing for a trip. The day Peyote was bitten, James had decided that if the brave died, he would take him home for burial. So, at four the next morning, James and Walter rode away from the Little Hatchet, toward the Mescalero stronghold, for the second time.

Peyote's body was transported home by Anderson, the giant mule that had nearly killed him. James had built a strong wooden pallet, which he lashed to a packsaddle. Before strapping Peyote's body to the pallet, James had wrapped him in several blankets, then in three separate layers of canvas to keep down the odor. Peyote's horse trailed behind Walter's.

The trip was an ordeal few men would have undertaken a second time. However, because Peyote had saved his son's life, James felt obligated to honor the brave sacrifice the young man had made. Returning Peyote's body to his grandmother and uncle was the only repayment James could think of.

James and Walter bypassed El Paso coming and going. The route would save a couple of days' travel time and help avoid other people. Peyote had brought major change to the Oakleys' lives from the very moment he had swooped Little Matt from the front porch. Living with him had been an experience they would never forget. Living without him would be an adjustment for everyone on the Little Hatchet.

On the ride home, James' thoughts revisited his meeting with the chief. Had the old man understood what James had tried to communicate to him? He had certainly been cordial. James had carefully planned the sign language he had used to explain how Peyote had looked after his son and lived with the Oakleys on their ranch.

The chief had nodded that he understood, but the old man's gaze had been so blank. James had always felt that he could read the thoughts behind any man's face, no matter how expressionless. This time, James had been stumped; he could not tell what the chief was thinking. When James had gone through his sign language description of how Peyote had given up his life, taking a bite from a giant rattlesnake intended for Little Matt, the chief had again nodded that he understood. However, he had shown no emotion.

Had they been able to use a common spoken language, Walter would have told the chief that Peyote's act was very brave and selfless.

Unfortunately, James had not known how to make these words with signs and the chief had offered him no help. Still, it seemed the old man had understood. Before they left the stronghold, the chief had led them to the tent of his sister, Peyote's grandmother.

The woman was composed, but she obviously was deeply hurt by the loss of her special grandson. She faced each of the Oakleys, nodding her head in thanks and making a sign with her arms.

Then she turned and picked up two blankets she had woven. She gave one to Walter and the second to James. After she handed James his blanket, Peyote's grandmother again nodded and made her gesture of thanks with her arms. She looked at James for what seemed a long time before stepping back. James nodded to show his gratitude and left her tent.

The first time they approached the stronghold, Walter was frightened. He knew the likelihood that he and his father could be killed. However, when the braves intercepted them coming into the camp on the second trip, Walter had no fear.

The braves immediately recognized Peyote's horse and surmised that his body was on that strange contraption atop the mule's back. They led James and Walter into the village with no apparent tension.

Walter, too, was puzzled by the chief's stern, blank stares. He and James had discussed these expressions on the ride home, but they could not reach any conclusion about the old man's emotions.

They were mostly certain that he had appreciated the gesture the Oakleys had made by returning the body of the nephew the chief had treated as his grandson, but they could not penetrate his unspoken thoughts. James and Walter remained unsure about how much of their message the chief had understood.

Both Oakleys had questions that remained unanswered, as father and son rode back to Little Hatchet Creek. Walter missed Peyote. He had gotten used to having him around. Peyote had represented protection from fear of unseen threats. The Oakleys had gained from his protection, but the young warrior's vigilant, heroic service had been used up saving the boy he loved.

Now that they were back to where they had been before Peyote had burst into their lives, what remained were the memories of the courageous Mescalero that the members of the Oakley family would carry for the rest of their lives.

CHAPTER FIFTEEN

After a week of adjustment, reflection, and the passage of time, the sadness the Oakleys felt faded. Spring was the busiest time along the Little Hatchet. It was the season for building and putting everything on course. Setting the direction properly in the spring meant a good harvest of bacon, sausage, and ham in the fall.

However, before the Oakleys could devote themselves totally to raising hogs and putting their ranch in order for the growing season, they had one more trip to make to El Paso to deliver the last of the winter's bacon. Not only would this be the first trip in a while without Peyote; but as preparation for the journey concluded, the Oakley family believed that this would almost certainly be Walter's last trip.

James wanted his son to have the chance to accomplish something the Civil War had robbed James of. He wanted his son to go to college and become an engineer. Because Walter's only education had come from his parents, James did not feel that Walter was ready to send east to college. James had not had time to teach his son enough math to prepare him to study engineering. He also believed Walter needed to know more about life than what he had learned living along the Little Hatchet.

The previous spring, James had met a man named William Easterly in

El Paso. Easterly was the chief surveyor for the Galveston, Harrisburg & San Antonio Railway, part of the Southern Pacific system.

Easterly had heard, as everyone in El Paso had, of the young man who had ridden with his father into the camp of the Mescalero to rescue his little brother. The railroad executive, who was laying out the route for the Southern Pacific tracks, had agreed to take Walter on as an apprentice on his survey crew.

Rebecca did not know what to say to her son. She had risen in time to see her men off to El Paso. Actually, she had not slept at all. Her life had been extremely busy, and she had done so much for her family, but she felt as if she had spent no time at all with Walter. Her eldest son had seemed to become an adult before he reached his teens. Rebecca felt that Walter had spent most of his time working with his father. And except for Katie, who was close to Walter's age, the children had thought of Walter more as an extension of their father than as their big brother.

This morning he was leaving home, a young man about to make his own way. To Rebecca, it seemed only a few days before that Walter had ridden into the Little Hatchet valley, a newborn wrapped in baby blankets. So much had happened so fast. Where had the time gone? Surely Walter could not be ready to go out on his own. But Rebecca could not deny what her eyes told her. The proof that her son had already entered adulthood stood in front of her.

Walter was three inches taller than his mother, almost as tall as his father, and still growing. He had the same broad shoulders as his father. Walter was rock solid muscle from his neck to his toes, just like James. The little boy who had guided his father's saw and helped James build their cabin ten years earlier was gone. A young man fully grown was standing before his mother. Gathered before Walter were brothers and sisters spreading across a wide range of ages.

Rebecca felt a sense of rage welling inside her. She wanted to beat her fist against life and shout, "Stop! It's not supposed to happen this way!"

Despite these emotions, Rebecca remained mostly controlled, sobbing only slightly and softly.

"Walter, you have had a good upbringing. Remember it," she reminded her son.

"Whatever Mr. Easterly tells you to do, you do it. Every week you are in El Paso, I expect you to be at the Methodist church for Sunday school and church. I also want you to write every week, even though we only get mail when your father goes to El Paso."

Walter could not speak, fearing he would burst into tears. Rebecca could not stop her own soft crying. She quickly hugged her husband, then Harry, and finally Walter.

"I love you," she told Walter.

"Take good care of my little boy."

Rebecca turned and ran into her house, where she sat in the parlor sobbing until the sun came up. She had not noticed that the other children, still sleepy, had gone back to bed.

The wagons rolled away from the house and up the ridge, then turned east toward Walter's new life.

When Katie came back downstairs, she found her mother fixing breakfast as she did every morning. Rebecca's eyes were red, and she did not speak. Otherwise, things went on just as they had every other morning.

In El Paso, life was businesslike. James took Walter to the bank so he could have his own account. Walter would have a place to put the money he earned from the railroad and a way to get money for his living expenses.

James introduced Walter to the Methodist minister and his wife. There was no Presbyterian church in El Paso. Walter assured the pastor that he would be a regular for church every Sunday he was in El Paso and the minister's wife promised James that she would look after Walter.

James arranged to board Walter's horse at the livery stable and to have the feed bill paid directly by the bank. He also got a room for Walter at the boarding house run by the widow Elvira Smith.

Walter would stay there when he was not out on a survey trip and Mrs. Smith would see to Walter's meals, laundry and mending. She would also make sure that Walter stayed away from the trouble an unsupervised young man could find in a frontier city like El Paso.

These arrangements were well intended; but as it would turn out, they would be unnecessary. The survey crew worked so long and hard that they did not return to El Paso until late fall.

James turned Walter over to Mr. Easterly on Saturday afternoon. Sunday after church, the crew, and their equipment were loaded onto two rail cars. There were two wagons: one to carry the crew, the other to carry food, supplies, and the survey equipment. The wagons were loaded onto a flatcar. The livestock and the young men in the crew rode in a cattle car. Mr. Easterly and his assistant had seats with the paying customers in a passenger coach, included as part of the train.

At three o'clock, the eastbound train steamed out of El Paso. Five and a half hours later, it pulled into Sierra Blanca, which was hardly a town at all, mostly just a railroad camp where the Southern Pacific met the Texas & Pacific Railway.

Trainmen from the T&P shoved the two cars Easterly's crew was in onto a siding, replenished the locomotive with water and coal and headed for Fort Worth. The Southern Pacific was racing to complete its tracks between San Antonio and El Paso. A year earlier, the T&P had finished laying rails into Sierra Blanca, connecting El Paso with Fort Worth. Easterly faced intense pressure from his superiors to get the Southern Pacific on an even footing with its northern rival.

After the wagons were unloaded, the crew set up camp along the tracks. Following a meal of cold corn bread and molasses, the railroaders bedded down.

At first light Monday morning, the survey crew assembled and rode east into the desert. Most of the young men in the crew rode in one of the wagons, but Mr. Easterly had hired Walter and his horse as well. So Walter rode alongside Mr. Easterly and the other engineer, irritating the young men on the survey gang who had to endure a brutal beating from the bumpy wagon ride.

Walter rode confidently with the two grown men as he had done with his father so many times before. Mr. Easterly was in his early fifties and had little to say. Bryan Whittaker was only twenty-eight and a graduate of Cornell University. Walter had never known anyone like him before. As a matter of fact, Walter was realizing that he had hardly known anyone outside his family.

He had lived his whole life along the Little Hatchet with his parents, brothers, and sisters. Except for the people who came to help with the hogs and the people he met when he went to El Paso, Walter knew no one who was not a close relative.

He had seldom been with anyone his own age. Walter had been in a few minor scraps with Harry, who was several years younger. Those sibling tussles were the closest he had come to fighting. It was not because Walter was too well behaved; he had just never had an occasion to fight.

That changed Walter's first night on the trail with the railroad crew. All day, he had watched the young men staring at him from the wagon and he knew something was wrong. As soon as they made camp and started a fire, the young men went to the stream to wash while the cook started dinner. When the boys reached the creek, a young man of twenty spoke up.

"I suppose you're too good to ride in the wagon with us?" he growled at Walter.

Walter stood silent. Even though he had never been in a fight, he could sense what was coming. The young man was three inches taller than Walter and he was missing two front teeth on top. Walter guessed that he probably had lost those teeth brawling.

"I'm talking to you," the young man barked, appearing to become more agitated.

Walter was silent, but looked directly at his accuser. He could feel the palms of his hands were wet and noticed that he had clinched his hands into fists.

"I guess you're too good to talk to us, too," the young man pronounced in an even louder voice, pushing on Walter's chest with his hand.

Walter did not move. When the young man pushed against Walter, he could not move him. Walter's strength surprised the young man. He paused for a moment but decided to go through with what he had started.

Walter had never fought, but he had been swinging an ax skillfully since before he was six. He had been lifting heavy timbers and loading wagons all his life. He was as stout as the Hill Country cedars he would learn to cut through later in life.

The other young men gathered around the two, clamoring for Walter to fight. Easterly and Whittaker heard the commotion and headed for the creek. They arrived just as the young man attacked.

He had backed up four steps and charged Walter, putting his shoulder squarely in Walter's abdomen. Walter gave one step, then used his arms to stand the young man upright. Next, Walter swept his right leg behind the young man's calves, taking his attacker off his feet. The young man hit the ground face first. He was shocked and determined to jump to his feet and teach Walter a lesson.

Easterly intended to separate the boys, but neither Easterly nor Bryan was fast enough. Even though Walter had never fought another human, he had wrestled two-hundred-pound boars on the Little Hatchet.

He had learned never to fool with one of those animals when it was angry. Experience had taught Walter how to deal with the animals that were much bigger than he was. Walter had learned to apply all his strength to a critical point on the animal. He handled the young man the same way.

As soon as his attacker hit the ground, Walter landed on his back with both knees. He grabbed each of his opponent's arms at the wrist and jerked them back, pulling his arms up as if they were wings, and holding them out stiffly. The young man could not move. In fact, for a minute, he thought he might be dead, because he could not breathe at all. Walter felt a gentle touch on his shoulder.

"Get up, Walter," Mr. Easterly coaxed.

At first, Walter did not let go. Then he heard Mr. Easterly's voice again.

"Get off him, Walter. You've got him whipped," he ordered.

That sounded strange to Walter. He had reacted so quickly he had not realized that he had been in a fight. As he had been told, Walter released the young man's arms. Walter raised himself off the ground and the young man's back by doing what amounted to a pushup, even though Walter didn't know what a pushup was. He also had no idea that men trained to fight and often used regimented exercise programs as part of such preparation.

When he was back on his feet, Walter looked at the young man who had attacked him.

"Is he all right?" Walter asked.

"I think so," Mr. Easterly answered.

"I think you just knocked the wind out of him."

A couple of the other young men rolled Walter's adversary over.

"Are you all right, young man?" Mr. Easterly asked the fellow who had attacked Walter.

The young man pointed to his mouth to indicate that he could not breathe.

"You've just had the wind knocked out of you. You'll be better in a minute," Mr. Easterly told him.

The young man continued to lie on the ground for what, in his mind, seemed like an hour. He waited about thirty seconds before attempting to breathe again. This time, his lungs worked. After two or three deep breaths, the young man, still shaky, was able to sit up.

He had a notion that he would jump to his feet, but all he could do was sit. Another minute passed before he could stand. Even then, his balance was unsteady, and his eyes would not focus. He wanted to ask what had happened. But he knew the answer. It was the stocky kid he had shoved earlier. Before the young man had completely regained his senses, he heard Mr. Easterly's voice.

"Have you two met?" he asked.

"Ezra Johnson, I'd like to introduce Walter Oakley," Mr. Easterly said.

Walter extended his right hand. After a brief pause, the young man sheepishly shook Walter's hand.

"Now that you two have gotten acquainted, I assume there will be no further cause for fighting," Mr. Easterly continued.

"But if there is, the one who initiates the fight will be fired. Is that clear?" Mr. Easterly asked.

"Yes sir," both boys said at once.

Mr. Easterly looked at the other young men.

"Does everyone else understand that there is to be no fighting around here?" Mr. Easterly asked.

All the young men nodded and answered yes.

No one spoke to Walter for the rest of the night, but no one else pushed him, either.

CHAPTER SIXTEEN

The camp was awakened at 4:30 for breakfast. The bedrolls were put up and the kitchen packed away. At first light, the surveyors were ready to roll. Except for some muted sounds the animals made, the early morning desert was virtually silent, until Mr. Easterly's voice boomed, calling Walter's name, then pausing slightly for impact.

"I would like you to ride up front with us, so Mr. Whittaker can begin teaching you how to scout terrain."

Just as he would have done, had he been with his father, Walter acted without speaking. He pulled his horse up to the front, in line with Mr. Easterly's and Bryan's. When he was in place, the group moved out. As the sun rose, Walter rode easily for about thirty minutes, until he heard Mr. Easterly's voice again.

"Bryan, would you and Walter veer about thirty degrees to the east and see if you can find the top of that sand hill formation we spotted near Mica? But don't get more than about fifteen miles away from us, because I want you back with the wagons at sunset."

"Yes sir," Bryan acknowledged as he set a more easterly course.

When he and Walter had ridden about a mile away from the main group, Bryan spoke.

"That was quite a show you put on at the creek last night," he remarked.

"Sir?" Walter responded, somewhat sheepishly.

"You don't need to call me sir and you don't need to pretend with me, either," Bryan chided.

If his father had not already been Walter's first hero, Bryan would certainly have been a candidate for that honor. Walter was awestruck riding next to Bryan. Walter had never been boastful and had no way of understanding that, to others, his behavior had conveyed deep shyness.

"I wasn't pretending, sir," Walter stumbled, forgetting that he had just been told not to call Bryan sir. Walter was flustered.

"Is it true you were shot by an Apache who kidnapped your brother?" Bryan continued.

"No, the brave who kidnapped my little brother was my friend. I don't know which one of the Apaches shot me."

While Walter's answer baffled Bryan, the younger man was grateful he had answered Bryan's question coherently, in spite of the nervousness that possessed Walter whenever he attempted to talk with his new friend.

"Your friend kidnapped your little brother?" a clearly puzzled Bryan asked.

Oh, this conversation is a mess, Walter realized. He was not making himself understood at all.

"No, I'm sorry. He was not my friend at the time he kidnapped my brother. He became my friend later, and he saved my little brother's life. My father and I took his body back to his family after he died," Walter added.

"Kid, I'm lost here," Bryan chuckled.

Walter was trying hard, but he was not accustomed to long conversations like this one. He and his father understood almost everything about each other, so they seldom spoke more than a few words at a time. Walter had assumed that all men were like his father. But it was slowly dawning on Walter, that James Oakley was a truly exceptional man. Walter also was discovering that people he did not know seemed to be fascinated by him. It had never occurred to Walter that chasing the Mescalero braves who had kidnapped his little brother and stole his family's horses was unusual.

"I'm sorry, sir," Walter apologized.

"Let's start over," Bryan smiled.

"When did the Apache who stole your brother become your friend?" Bryan asked.

"After he came to live with us," Walter answered.

"And when was that?" Bryan asked, concluding that he would have to pull this story from Walter word by word.

"After we got back to the ranch with Little Matt," Walter answered, providing no context to go along with this single, sparse fact.

Bryan was ready to give up.

"Maybe you just don't want to talk about it. And that's okay."

"No, it's not that at all," Walter said, hoping he was concealing the exasperation that was tying his tongue and tangling his thoughts.

"What is it then?" Bryan asked.

"I'm just not sure what you want to know, and I'm not used to talking about things so much. I want to answer your questions, but I suppose I just have to get used to talking this way."

"How is the way I talk unusual?" Bryan asked, smiling again.

"I suppose I am just used to talking with people I have always known, people in my family, people I don't have to explain things to, because they already know all there is to know about me," Walter responded.

"Ah, so you haven't been away from home much?" Bryan suggested.

"No. I've been away from home quite a bit, but I guess I have always gone with my father, and I suppose he's done most of the talking with other people," Walter explained.

"So do you mind talking about your dealings with the Apaches?" Bryan asked.

"No, I guess you just kind of caught me off guard."

"So, how did you get to be friends with the one who kidnapped your brother?" Bryan inquired, returning to his previous line of questioning.

"Did he just ride up and introduce himself or what?" Bryan teased, adding another smile.

"No, he tracked us. We thought there was someone following us, but we didn't actually see him for a couple of weeks after we got back to our ranch on the Little Hatchet. Then the mule got after him in the barn," Walter said.

When Walter told Bryan about Anderson pinning Peyote against the wall in the barn, both laughed so hard they almost fell out of their saddles. Walter had wanted to laugh about the incident ever since the morning it had happened, but he had never done so. It had been funny; but because Peyote had been seriously hurt, neither Walter nor James had laughed when the mule attacked Peyote. Telling Bryan the story about Peyote and the mule, plus the laughter that the account produced, put Walter at ease. That made it easier for Walter to tell the rest of the story about the contacts between the Oakleys and the Mescalero. When Walter finished his narration, he realized he had become more confident talking with his new friend, so much so that he surprised himself, allowing a personal question to escape through his mouth, a question that might seem rude or offensive.

"Why do you talk that way?" Walter gushed.

Bryan briefly considered that he would have some fun with Walter by pretending that he didn't know what Walter was asking. Instead, the older of the young men laughed. Walter's question was one Bryan had heard regularly since his arrival in Texas.

"I'm from the Hudson River Valley in New York, a place called Hyde Park," Bryan explained.

"Up there everyone talks with an accent like mine, except the Dutch people, and they talk even funnier," Bryan chuckled.

"I'm sorry. I forgot my manners," Walter apologized, realizing that he should not have asked such a personal question.

"That's all right. I'm used to people asking questions about the way I talk. Some people have even laughed when they heard me speak."

Bryan was smiling, making Walter feel better about his gaffe. Walter's education on the Little Hatchet had skipped geography, except for the Biblical lands. Walter knew his parents were from Arkansas and Arkansas was a long way from New Mexico. He knew there was a place called California. He knew Mexico was another country and that there was a Pacific Ocean. However, James had concentrated on teaching Walter math, something an engineer had to know.

Walter could solve life situation problems using trigonometry and algebra, but he did not know where the Hudson River was or New York or Virginia. Rebecca had taught her son to recite the Psalms, how to spell and even how to break a sentence down into its parts. But except for a reading or two about the American Revolution; history, government, and geography had been left for another time. Bryan guessed that his young friend might not know where the Hudson River was.

"New York state is in the northeastern part of the United States between Pennsylvania and New England, and it's the largest state in the country," Bryan explained.

"I thought Texas was," Walter let slip, without thinking.

Walter considered the Little Hatchet his home, but he knew he was the only member of his family who had been born in Texas.

"Texas has the most land, but New York has the most people," Bryan said with a laugh.

"So which one is bigger?" Walter asked.

"I guess they both are, each in its own way," Bryan grinned.

"At any rate, do you know where New York is now?" Bryan tested.

"Not really," Walter admitted.

"Well, I have a book of maps back on the wagon. It's called an atlas and I'll be happy to loan it to you, if you like," Bryan offered.

"That would be terrific!" a grateful Walter exclaimed, his face lighting up, knowing he would devour the book and memorize everything in it.

Walter's lessons continued at a fast pace the next morning as Bryan taught his eager pupil the skills of surveying: how to use a windup tape measure, estimate distant heights, sketch terrain onto a contour map, and how to use the advanced math Walter had learned from his father to make the calculations and estimates for the maps and charts that would be used to determine the Southern Pacific's path from Sierra Blanca to San Antonio.

Each night, after most of the other workers had gone to bed, Bryan would get a lantern from the wagon and work with Walter on the symbols, perspective, and scale used in the drawings in sessions that would last about two hours. In less than two weeks, Walter was drawing simple maps with Bryan's help. After six weeks, Walter was riding out on his own to map sectors being considered by the railroad.

CHAPTER SEVENTEEN

Walter did not see his father until James brought bacon to El Paso in the fall. By then, Walter was not only drawing maps, but could use the complicated survey equipment on his own. James was extremely proud of the young man he had sent off as an apprentice six months earlier. As the Oakleys began their return home to the Little Hatchet, Walter listed the things he had done and what he had learned from Bryan. James spoke softly after Walter had talked nonstop for fifteen minutes.

"That's a good start, my son. There will be a lot more to learn when you go back with the survey crew in the spring," James pronounced, congratulating Walter.

No more words were spoken until noon, when James, Walter, and Harry stopped to eat.

In the spring, when the three returned to El Paso with the last load of the winter bacon, Walter was set to rejoin the survey crew, but he was too late. The survey was complete, and the last few miles of track were being laid east of Sierra Blanca.

Walter's heart sank. He heard the news before they reached the hotel. People in El Paso buzzed with excitement as they anticipated the first Southern Pacific train from San Antonio. Everyone was sure it would steam in any day. Walter didn't complain, but his father could see his son's deep disappointment. When the Oakleys went to the hotel to check in, there was hope: a letter to James from Mr. Easterly. Ordinarily, James would have waited to open a letter until he had reached their room. But sensing Walter's anxiety, James opened the letter as the trio stood at the registration desk and began reading.

Dear Mr. Oakley:

I hope by the time you receive this Southern Pacific trains from San Antonio will be in El Paso. I am sorry for Walter that we completed our survey work in West Texas before he could return to the crew.

However, there is still much work to be done around San Antonio and the counties to the northwest. I have enclosed a rail pass to transport Walter and his horse to San Antonio in hopes that he can join us here for the spring and summer.

In San Antonio, anyone at the Southern Pacific depot can tell him how to reach my office and I will arrange for his boarding with a Christian woman for the time he remains in the city.

Be assured we will look after his safety and well-being.

The letter was dated two weeks earlier and was signed, William Easterly, Divisional Vice-President, Southern Pacific Railroad.

Walter was jubilant and clutched the rail pass in his hands. He could not imagine life in a city as big as San Antonio. However, he had to wait for two weeks for the tracks to be completed, two weeks he spent restlessly at Mrs. Smith's boarding house. When the first train pulled out of El Paso, Walter was on it. This time, he was riding in a passenger coach. Mrs. Smith had packed biscuits, bacon, and cornbread for Walter to eat on his journey. The whole time there was daylight, Walter sat with his face glued to the window as West Texas flew by at twenty miles per hour.

Walter had ridden the train the previous spring and fall, but it had been dark and he had been in a stock car, so there had been nothing to see. This time, with all the exciting sights in clear view, Walter didn't want to miss a thing.

LITTLE HATCHET · 105

When the sun rose on the second day, the train was passing through the Hill Country and Walter was in love. The hills were a lush green from the spring rains. With the exceptions of the Little Hatchet valley and the mountains surrounding the Mescalero stronghold, this marked the first time Walter had seen a green landscape. The desert around El Paso had appeared almost completely brown during all of Walter's prior travels.

The train crossed crystal-clear streams bubbling with runoff from rainfall. The fresh green of live oaks and mountain cedar dotted the hills, interrupted by beautiful flowering redbud and dogwood. Even the cactuses sported bright yellow flowers. The hills gave way to open meadows awash in seas of bluebonnets and Indian paintbrush.

The names of the towns had magical rings to them: Uvalde, Sabinal, and Hondo. Each sounded so exotic to Walter as he read their names off the water towers. So far, only Uvalde had an actual depot, but each of the towns was neat and well-ordered, with a square in the center. There were big new courthouses in Uvalde and Hondo and horses and wagons were everywhere. Walter could clearly see that Texas was a booming place.

San Antonio was by far the best. It had big broad avenues, some paved with brick. There was the military palace built for the Spanish governors: enormous houses lined the avenues and a beautiful little green river flowed through downtown lined with trees, grass, and flowers.

Near the station was a giant cathedral and marketplace where all kinds of fresh fruits, vegetables, meats, wool, cloth, and leather were for sale. There was also a ruined mission: the Alamo, which had been part of Walter's experience from the first time he could remember.

All these sights filled Walter with excitement as his train chugged into the station. The streets were bursting with activity. Hundreds and hundreds of people were about, and horses and wagons clopped and rumbled everywhere. What a place! Walter's thoughts raced to the stories Bryan had told him about New York. Surely it could not be busier or grander than San Antonio, Walter decided.

When he reached the depot, Walter was told by the conductor to wait on the train until everyone else was off. When the train was empty, the conductor led Walter to an office with the word *Stationmaster* painted on the glass door. Walter was ushered in and invited to have a seat. In a few minutes, the stationmaster emerged from an inner office. As Walter stood, the man extended his right hand to greet Walter.

"I'm Newton Grantham," he announced, as Walter accepted the stationmaster's handshake.

"Mr. Easterly asked us to keep a lookout for you. We're going to have your horse unloaded and boarded in the stable that the railroad keeps a few blocks from here. I think I better have one of the telegram delivery boys walk you over to Mr. Easterly's office, so you don't get lost."

"Thank you," Walter managed, his mouth too dry to produce more words.

Quickly, Mr. Grantham and the conductor were gone, and the delivery boy appeared.

"It's a busy day around here. You must be somebody special to rate a seat on the first train from El Paso," the young man suggested.

As strange as the words sounded, Walter had been thinking the same thing all the way across West Texas. It had been great, sitting in one of the passenger coaches with the dignitaries from El Paso and San Antonio and the paying customers. No one had ever done anything like that for Walter before.

Walter realized he had been standing around in a trance.

"I'm sorry," he fumbled, extending his right hand to his guide, who appeared to be about the same age as Walter.

"I'm Walter Oakley from Little Hatchet Creek in New Mexico."

"Sam," the young man in a hurry responded.

"Sam Winder. We need to get going. I've got a bunch of telegrams to deliver."

Walter picked up the canvas bag containing his extra clothes and chased after Sam, who had raced out of the building and onto the street. In less than five minutes, the two were standing in front of a big limestone building.

"He's in there," Sam informed Walter.

"Thanks," Walter acknowledged, as Sam disappeared down the street.

Walter went inside to discover that there were offices on both sides of the lobby of the building, stairs on the right behind the first set of offices and a hallway in the center of the far end of the lobby, which seemed to indicate that there were more offices in the rear of the structure.

This was the largest building Walter had ever been in, but he had passed even grander buildings on his walk from the train station. At the bank in El Paso there were people right up front to ask if you didn't know where something was.

However, in San Antonio, it seemed that you were expected to know where you were going. Walter was standing, looking at the names on the doors, trying to figure out which one to knock on, when he detected a familiar voice echoing off the stone floor.

"Walter, is that you?" he heard.

Walter looked up and saw Bryan coming down the stairs. He had a big grin on his face as he charged down the last four steps and across the lobby toward his friend.

"How are you?" Bryan called out, lingering on the middle word for about two and a half steps.

"I'm lost," Walter confessed in a voice barely above a whisper.

Bryan's laughter thundered through the cavernous foyer.

"It's a little bigger than El Paso, huh?" Bryan teased.

Walter just nodded his head.

Walter had been so excited when the train rolled into San Antonio. Now he was just scared, wondering whether he was up to all the challenges of such a large city. He was very glad to see his old friend, but even that didn't make him comfortable in these strange surroundings. Bryan put his hand behind Walter's elbow.

"Come on," he invited, with generous enthusiasm.

"I'll take you to Easterly's office. You got here just in time. I'm leaving tonight for a surveying trip up toward Kerrville. I want you to come with me."

It was a whirlwind for Walter. Before he could get his bearings, Walter had been upstairs, said hello to Mr. Easterly, gotten a new rail pass and was following Bryan out the door and back into the street.

"Where's your horse?" Bryan asked.

"I don't know," Walter admitted.

"Are you going to start that again?" Bryan teased.

Walter was exasperated.

"I don't know," he repeated.

"I had just barely gotten off the train when I ran into you."

"When did you eat last?" Bryan asked, noticing that Walter had very little color in his face.

"I'm not sure. This morning, I guess. There was so much to see on the train, I suppose I just forgot," Walter explained.

"Well, we've got to catch another train, but we better get you some food before you pass out," Bryan suggested.

Then Walter felt another tug on his elbow as Bryan pulled him into the lobby of a huge hotel. There was a dining room to the left and Bryan grabbed Walter's other arm and guided him through the door into the restaurant.

In similar fashion to the hotel in El Paso, Walter observed that tables with cloths and silverware were arranged neatly around the big room. Each table had a complete set of dishes and several glasses at each place. The effect was elegant.

To Walter's surprise, Bryan swept him past the tables to a bar in the back of the room. At least it looked like a bar at first. However, the bar was only waist high and short stools were attached to the floor along the length of the bar. The room was empty except for Bryan, Walter, and a man who approached the pair walking behind what Walter would later learn to call a lunch counter. When he was still three or four steps away, Bryan called out to the man.

"Chili, please. Two bowls with some cornbread and buttermilk, please," Bryan requested.

The man turned away, almost as if Bryan had insulted him. But in less than two minutes, he was back with two steaming bowls of red stew, placing one in front of Bryan and setting the second in front of Walter.

"I'm sorry for the rush, but we have to catch a train," Bryan explained.

"Happens all the time," the man remarked, before walking away again.

In a moment, he was back with a large plate of steaming cornbread and two glasses of buttermilk. The buttermilk arrived just in time to save Walter's life. The chili had his mouth on fire.

Walter had lived on the Mexican border all his life, but his mother was from Arkansas. He thought she was the best cook in the world, but none of the food she fixed had the fiery spices the Tejanos in San Antonio liked in their food. He downed half a glass of buttermilk in a single gulp.

"Chili hot?" Bryan laughed.

Walter did not answer but stuffed some cornbread in his mouth, trying to absorb the rest of the hot pepper. When Walter finished half a cake of cornbread, he could finally answer.

"What is that?" he gasped.

Bryan was laughing so hard he could barely sit on his stool.

"Haven't you ever had chili before?" he asked.

"No," Walter answered.

"I thought the place you live is just a few miles from the Mexican border?" Bryan said, still trying to control his laughter.

"It is," Walter confirmed, downing the rest of the buttermilk.

"But my mother is from Arkansas, and she never cooked anything like this."

Bryan convulsed in another wave of laughter. He could not speak for about two minutes. As soon as he regained his composure, he asked the waiter to bring Walter another glass of buttermilk. Walter finished the cornbread and the second glass of buttermilk but gave up on the stew.

Bryan shoveled the rest of his chili into his mouth, paid the bill, grabbed Walter's elbow and hustled him onto the street, headed toward the depot.

"We've got to hurry and get someone to load your horse," Bryan informed Walter.

"I'd like to see her. I haven't checked on her since last night, when they stopped the train for coal and water," Walter said, hoping the visit would meet with Bryan's approval.

Before he had stopped speaking, he felt Bryan's hand behind his elbow again. They had made a right turn and were charging down another unfamiliar street. The pair walked for two blocks, turned left and walked another half block to a huge stable.

A Tejano named Martín was standing just inside the door. Bryan greeted him in Spanish and Martín returned his greeting, a big smile lighting the stable hand's face.

"Martín, this is Walter. He owns that beautiful paint mare that came in on the train from El Paso," Bryan said, switching to English.

"*Momento?*" Martín replied.

In a couple of minutes, the man was back, leading Walter's mare. She balked when she saw Walter. The horse was unhappy about her unpleasant ride on the train, and she wanted Walter to know how she felt.

Walter walked over to his mare and stroked her face. She sniffed in his pocket for an apple or carrot. When she saw there was nothing there, she pulled her head back and tried to jerk away.

"Come on, girl," Walter urged, tugging her halter to let her know he meant business.

"We don't have time for that now."

"Your saddle, *señor?*" Martín called, as he emerged with Walter's saddle, blanket, and bridle.

"Thank you," Walter responded, and quickly saddled the mare, ending her rebellion.

Bryan, Walter, and the mare walked to the station. The work train they were to catch was on a siding by the water tower. It comprised several flat cars loaded with equipment and supplies, a stock car, and a caboose. Walter and Bryan loaded the mare onto the stock car, leaving her saddled. Workers huddled into one end of the stock car, attempting to make themselves comfortable by leaning against hay bales.

Walter and Bryan boarded the caboose for the ride to Cypress Creek, where a bridge was under construction. The trip to the site took less than an hour. Walter, exhausted from all the excitement and his tour of San Antonio, fell asleep before the train had pulled past the station.

"Huh?" Walter mumbled, as he felt Bryan nudge him.

"We're here," said Bryan.

"Where?" Walter responded, groggily.

"The end of the line. Time to get off the train," Bryan answered.

Walter stumbled to his feet as Bryan led him out of the caboose. Walter stood beside the train, stretching and yawning.

"It's beautiful," Walter noted, looking at the rushing stream in front of him.

"That's Cypress Creek. Wait until you see the Guadalupe River. We're going to ride along the river for part of our trip. You won't believe how pretty it is until you've seen it," Bryan suggested.

Walter and Bryan walked over to the stock car to unload their horses. Bryan had a second horse packed high with equipment and supplies.

"We'll be camping. There are no hotels where we're going," Bryan informed Walter.

"That's good. I've been cooped up in Widow Smith's boarding house in El Paso for two weeks. It will be good to get outside," Walter informed his friend.

"Why don't we ride for a couple of hours before we make camp?" Bryan proposed.

"Sounds fine," Walter agreed, as the two headed their horses about a hundred yards downstream to a ford, where they crossed.

"This is the Fredericksburg road," Bryan told Walter.

"Didn't you say we would be heading toward Kerrville?" Walter responded.

"You take the same road to both towns. At the Guadalupe River, a place called Comfort, the road splits. The west fork goes to Kerrville, and the north fork goes to Fredericksburg," Bryan explained.

"The people are mostly Germans, here and up there, too," Bryan added.

"Up where?" Walter asked.

"Fredericksburg," Bryan answered, then traced the history of how Germans began coming to Texas in the early part of the century and how they continued expanding their colony near Fredericksburg.

"When times are bad in Europe, when there is war, more people immigrate. When times aren't so tough, fewer settlers come, but there's been a stream of Germans coming here for fifty years," Bryan told Walter.

As they rode, the two friends caught up on the events of the winter. Walter told Bryan about what had happened back on the Little Hatchet. Bryan told Walter how busy he had been and how much effort had gone into getting the track finished between the Pecos River and Sierra Blanca.

In what seemed like only a few minutes, two hours had passed. The horses stopped in a little stream to drink. Bryan decided it was a good place to make camp, and they moved several hundred feet upstream to an open spot where native tribes had camped for hundreds of years.

"You take care of the horses while I set up the tent," Bryan directed.

Except for the ones in the Mescalero encampment, Walter had never seen a tent before coming to work for the railroad. He and his father had always slept underneath their wagons.

Next morning, Walter woke to the smell of bacon frying and coffee cooking on an oak fire. He was rested and still in awe of the depth and beauty of the lush Texas hills, a love that would last Walter the rest of his life.

The two young men picked up as they had left off months before, sketching and surveying. Now, however, they were alone, enjoying the Texas wilderness halfway across the state from where Walter lived. The pair worked twelve to fourteen hours each day.

The weather was, for the most part, as beautiful as the countryside, except for the fierce thunderstorms that sometimes rolled through at night. The work was far easier than what Walter was used to in springtime on the Little Hatchet.

Had Walter known what a vacation was, he would have called that spring one. In fact, throughout his life, Walter looked back to that year when he turned seventeen years old as one of the most pleasant of his life.

In a month, Bryan and Walter had surveyed all the way to the site that had been selected for the bridge across the Guadalupe River. They moved on to the other side of the river and resumed mapping the course for the path of the San Antonio and Aransas Pass line toward Kerrville.

Eight miles east of Kerrville, the two surveyors had exhausted most of their provisions. Bryan and Walter rode into town to replenish their food.

"I've been wondering when you would show up," the owner called to Bryan the moment the pair walked through the door of his little country store.

"I've been holding a letter here for you for a week," he explained.

It was an urgent message from Mr. Easterly, asking Bryan and Walter to get back to San Antonio as soon as possible.

CHAPTER EIGHTEEN

Bryan and Walter's return trip to the city consumed two days.

"We left as soon as we got your letter," Bryan explained, facing Mr. Easterly, who sat behind his desk.

"Thanks for coming, quickly," the railroad executive said.

"I've got big trouble out west and I need to get people out there, pronto. Bryan, the bosses in San Francisco have decided we need another bridge across the Pecos and they want every available engineer out there. I'll be along myself in a week or ten days.

"Walter, I think I remember your father told me that you're a pretty good carpenter. Is that right?" Mr. Easterly posed.

"Well, yes sir, I suppose I'm all right. I helped him build most everything on our ranch," the ever-modest Walter confirmed.

"That's what I thought I remembered," Mr. Easterly responded.

"You see, we've got another kind of mess in Del Rio. We're trying to build pens for cattle and sheep, a depot just for freight and a hotel.

"It seems like every rancher in West Texas and half the stockmen in Mexico have heard about the railroad and have driven their cattle to Del Rio to ship back east.

"They've got cows strung out on both sides of the Rio Grande for fifteen miles in all directions, and I don't know if we're ever going to get all that livestock out of there.

"Walter, I want you on this afternoon's westbound with Bryan. You get off at Del Rio and see Frank Granger. He's the railroad's construction supervisor. He has an office in this building, but the people in California had me send him out to Del Rio a couple of weeks ago.

"Granger sent me a wire the other day, saying it looked like he would be there all summer.

"I need your help on this, Walter," Mr. Easterly told his young protégé. "I'm wiring a message to your father in El Paso to let him know that I'm putting you on the payroll as a full carpenter on our construction crew, that I'm going to be wiring your pay to the bank account he set up for you in El Paso and that I'll have you home in New Mexico for Christmas. Is that all right with you?" he asked, clearly expecting a strongly confident response.

Walter was in shock. He stood silently until he felt Bryan kick the side of his foot.

"Yes sir," Walter said firmly.

"Good," Mr. Easterly smiled, shaking Walter's right hand and pressing a piece of cardboard into Walter's other hand.

"This is a full pass on the railroad. It allows you and any member of your family traveling with you to ride anywhere on the Southern Pacific system, any time."

Walter continued shaking Mr. Easterly's hand for quite a while after his boss had finished speaking. Walter's astonishment had deepened. He couldn't believe what was happening.

"Thank you," he heard himself say.

"You're welcome," Mr. Easterly responded.

"Now, you two need to get a move on. The train leaves in less than three hours and you will want to stop over at the hotel and get cleaned up."

When Walter felt the warm air of the San Antonio afternoon hit his face, he realized he was outside. Once again, Walter was charging down the street with Bryan, headed for the same hotel where they had eaten chili a month earlier.

It didn't seem as if Walter would ever see San Antonio. Every time he entered town, someone was hurrying him to catch a train for somewhere else.

The next morning, the train stopped in Del Rio. Bryan got off with Walter to help him get his horse and to make sure she was taken care of at the railroad's stable. There was no cavernous barn like the railroad owned in San Antonio, only some corrals with a covering on one end for the horses to get out of the weather. Walter left his mare, but the man who ran the stable told Walter to take his saddle back to the stationmaster's office for safekeeping.

"Many things here walk across the river. Your saddle would be gone before lunch," he explained.

With the arrangements complete, it was time for Bryan to make his way back to the train and Walter needed to find Mr. Granger.

"I'll see you soon," Bryan said.

"Yeah," Walter managed, struggling to maintain his composure.

Anxiously, he watched his best friend climb aboard the train. Then Walter walked into the station to inquire about Mr. Granger. Quickly, Walter spotted a man who was just slightly taller than Walter and had a big smile.

"Are you Mr. Granger?" Walter inquired.

"Depends on what you want?" he chuckled.

"I'm Walter Oakley. Mr. Easterly sent me," Walter replied.

"Glad to meet you, Mr. Oakley," Frank Granger said, extending his hand for a greeting.

"I hear you can carpenter and you're not afraid of hard work. Is that right?"

"Yes sir," Walter confirmed.

"Well, you seem a mite young to me, but Bill Easterly's been building railroads longer than I have. He says you're all right, and that's good enough for me. I don't suppose you have tools?" Granger asked.

"No sir, I was helping on a survey," Walter explained, surprising himself with his own confidence.

"Not that important. We can fix that. Walk with me for a minute and we'll get you fixed up with a toolbox, so you can start building a home for some of these cows.

"You ever seen so many cows?"

"No sir," Walter admitted.

"Me neither," Granger agreed.

In less than a minute, Walter and Frank Granger came to a tool shed near where Walter had stabled his horse a few minutes earlier.

"Benito, this young fella is Mr. Oakley," Granger announced.

"I got kids older than him in San Antone, but Mr. Easterly says he's a carpenter. So he needs some tools. Give him one of those short boxes we've been handing out to the men working on the pens."

In a minute, Walter had a wooden toolbox in his hands.

"Look it over and see if it'll do you," Frank Granger suggested.

Walter looked inside. The box contained a handsaw, hammer, small level, square, three chisels of different sizes and a cloth tape measure.

"Anything else you need?" Mr. Granger asked.

"Well, sir, a plumb line and a file might be handy," Walter replied.

"Well, Benito, this boy might really be a carpenter," Mr. Granger said with an approving smile.

Benito slipped the requested items into Walter's new toolbox. Then Frank Granger led Walter back toward the station to a spot where four or five men were sitting under a tree, conversing in Spanish.

Mr. Granger motioned for one of them to come over.

"How are you called?" Mr. Granger asked the man in Spanish.

"Armando," he responded.

"Armando, this is Walter Oakley," Mr. Granger said in English, as Walter stepped forward to shake hands.

"Armando is a carpenter's helper, and he doesn't speak English. Do you speak any Spanish?"

"No," Walter answered, puzzled by the question and wondering who Mr. Granger thought might have taught him to speak Spanish.

"I don't understand how people who grow up across a river from Mexico can't communicate with the folks they've spent their whole life around," Mr. Granger observed.

He was not really upset. As Walter would soon learn, Frank Granger was a man who left few thoughts generated by his mind unspoken. Walter would also discover that Mr. Granger meant no harm with his spontaneous remarks. At any rate, Mr. Granger didn't really know enough about Walter to understand that the Little Hatchet ranch wasn't across a river from Mexico.

To get to the border, Walter would have had to go down the mountains on the south end and cross twelve of the most barren desert miles anywhere in the United States. As he would later return to the conversation to further consider Mr. Granger's words, Walter hit upon a painfully obvious answer. Miguel or one of his family members could have taught Walter to speak Spanish. Technically, that would have been possible, but for one additional, obvious fact. Miguel, Walter, and everyone else in their little world along Little Hatchet Creek were all too busy for language lessons. Later, Walter had learned that Frank Granger had studied Spanish in college, another place Walter had not been.

"Well, that's not important. You're no different than almost every other gringo around here," Frank Granger had continued, apparently not including himself in that category.

"What's important is to build some pens to put those cows in. So if you two gentlemen will follow me, maybe we can get some stockades built?"

Walter and Armando walked closely behind Mr. Granger. Walter listened carefully as Mr. Granger explained where the lumber and nails were and described the pattern in which he wanted the rails constructed. He paused for a second by a completed pen to show Walter what he wanted him to build.

"Do you see what I mean?" he asked, pointing to the way the rails came together.

"Yes sir," Walter responded, assuredly.

Mr. Granger looked skeptical, but didn't say anything, choosing just to lead the two workers to a stack of western yellow pine that the Southern Pacific had hauled in from California. It was beautiful timber, and Walter had never seen anything like it. It was stacked four feet high and seemed to stretch for a quarter mile. Mr. Granger moved on to show Walter and Armando the nails but paused after a few steps when he noticed Walter had not followed.

"What's the matter, son? You look like you've never seen lumber before."

Walter suddenly noticed that Mr. Granger was waiting on him and hurried to catch up.

"These are your nails and here are some aprons to put them in," he informed the pair, tossing an apron to Walter, then another to Armando.

Mr. Granger was just about to put his new team to work, but thought back to how Walter looked, staring at the lumber.

"Son, you have seen lumber before, haven't you?" he asked.

"No sir, not like that."

"Now, what kind of trick is this? How can you be a carpenter and tell me you have never seen lumber?" Mr. Granger asked, suspecting that maybe his old friend Easterly was playing some kind of practical joke on him by sending this boy to Del Rio.

"Well, sir, I do know a little about building things with wood. But on the Little Hatchet Creek, Papa and I had to make all our lumber from the trees that grew up on the ridge," Walter explained.

Granger didn't know whether to laugh or cry.

"Well, we don't have time for that here," he said. "We've got most of the cows in Texas and half the ones in Mexico, standing around out here, running over people's flowers, while these bovines wait for a train. Now, do you think you can build me some cow pens or not, son?"

"Absolutely, sir," Walter answered confidently, uncertain whether Mr. Granger was angry.

"I can build cow pens exactly like the one you showed me."

"Well then, why don't you get started over there?" Mr. Granger said, pointing about two hundred feet away, where one wall of a pen stood, one third completed.

"I'll be by to check on you in an hour or so and see how you're doing," Mr. Granger said as he turned to walk away.

However, after about five steps, he spun around so quickly that Walter was afraid Mr. Granger was going to fire him on the spot.

"And son," he called in a loud voice.

"Since you don't speak Spanish, just point at whatever you want Armando to do. He's used to it. None of the other Texan carpenters speaks Spanish, either."

This time, Mr. Granger really was on his way back to the station, leaving Walter and Armando to get to work. Armando did not wait for instruction. He put two hands full of nails into his apron, then placed six of the one by eight-inch rails onto his shoulder and headed toward the unfinished pen. Walter rushed to do the same.

In less than five minutes, the two were busily nailing the first rail in place on the posts that had been set for them. Walter saw at once that Armando was an excellent carpenter and wondered why he was a helper and not a carpenter. Armando, who appeared to be a man of twenty-six or twenty-eight, also noticed, to his great surprise, that Walter knew what he was doing.

Armando had not understood why Mr. Granger had brought such a boy to supervise his fence building. In less than thirty minutes, the rest of Armando's doubts had been erased as the two reached the end of the pen and turned the corner with the rails.

"Very good," Armando said to Walter in Spanish.

"*Gracias*," Walter replied, just about exhausting his Spanish vocabulary.

Armando smiled, and the two kept carrying and nailing rails. Walter wished he could communicate with Armando but didn't know how to go about it. Instead, the two simply built the fencing as quickly as they could. In another thirty minutes, absorbed in their work, Walter and Armando startled at the sound of Mr. Granger's voice.

"Well, son, for a boy who's never seen lumber before, you do all right," Frank Granger offered.

This time, Walter could tell by the tone of Mr. Granger's voice and the broad smile lighting his face that he was genuinely pleased.

"Thanks," Walter beamed.

"But it's mostly Armando. He's a real good carpenter, sir."

"Is that right?" Mr. Granger mused.

There was something else Frank Granger seemed about to say, but he didn't say it. He turned and started on his way. This time, he took ten steps before he turned around.

"Do you mind if I watch you work for a minute, son?" he asked.

"No sir," Walter agreed, casually.

Walter and Armando resumed work, while Frank Granger looked on. After they had completed putting up their third rail, the railroad executive spoke again.

"Walter, if I got Armando a helper, could he build a pen on his own?" Mr. Granger asked.

"Sure, he's a fine carpenter," Walter replied.

Mr. Granger thought for a minute. He had worked for the railroad a long time and he had seen all kinds of labor trouble caused when Mexican or Chinese workers were given too much responsibility. After Walter and Armando had nailed up two more rails, they heard Frank Granger's voice again.

"What the heck?" spilled out through Walter's boss' lips.

"I don't see how we could get much further behind than we are. And most of these Texans that call themselves carpenters were just cowboys last month anyway," the supervising engineer remarked as he turned to face Armando.

"Armando, are you really a carpenter?" Mr. Granger asked him in Spanish.

"Yes sir," he answered.

"If I got you a helper, could you build a pen, just the two of you, working by yourselves?" Mr. Granger asked.

"Yes sir," Armando affirmed.

"You know, if I make you a carpenter, I can't pay you as much as I pay the gringos. You understand that don't you?"

"Yes sir," Armando responded.

"You fellas get back to work. I'll be back in a few minutes," Mr. Granger directed.

In about ten minutes, Mr. Granger returned with two of the men Walter had seen sitting under the tree earlier. Jesús was introduced to Walter as his new helper. Walter and Jesús went to work, and Mr. Granger led Armando and the other man to the next pen. Mr. Granger watched to see Armando start the pen to make sure that he really did know what he was doing. Another hour passed. Mr. Granger came back from the station to check Armando's work, then Walter's.

"Well, this beats all," he announced, shaking his head in disbelief.

"Easterly sends me a wet behind the ears kid and I hire a Mexican and this is the most work I've gotten done in a given morning, since I started this cake walk. This beats all," Frank Granger repeated.

About that time, there was a loud clanging on a bell.

"That's the signal for lunch, son," Mr. Granger explained to Walter.

CHAPTER NINETEEN

A s the five of them began walking to where the cooks had set up tables for lunch under some shade trees on the courthouse lawn, Mr. Granger asked Walter to hold back from the others for a minute.

"I don't suppose Jesús is a carpenter, too, huh, son?" Mr. Granger asked.

"Yes sir, he is," Walter replied.

"This is going to cause trouble," Mr. Granger warned, seemingly to no one in particular.

Walter did not know what his new boss meant, but he decided not to ask. This had been a confusing morning, and Walter realized for the first time that he was tired. He had ridden the train all night to get to Del Rio and been working hard in the sun.

Lunch did not help Walter's exhaustion. The meal was pinto beans, cornbread, and canned peaches. Walter was starved and ate way too much. When the cooks rang the big iron triangle they used for a dinner bell, signaling the end of the meal break, Walter felt sluggish and sleepy. He had worked for about two hours before the drowsiness began wearing off.

By the end of the afternoon, Walter and Jesús had finished the second pen. Armando and his helper had also built one complete pen and started another.

"I've never seen anything like it," Mr. Granger announced, as darkness crept over the river town.

"This is going to cause trouble," he added, repeating his earlier prediction.

Walter still didn't know what Mr. Granger meant, but he was too tired to care.

As soon as supper was over, Walter was ready for bed. Walter had failed to notice; but Armando, Jesús, and the other Mexicans had not been fed supper. Ordinarily, as soon as they finished work, these laborers crossed the river into Mexico as a group and went to their homes there. However, on this night, they lingered on the Texas side. One of the helpers understood enough English to be concerned about something he had overheard.

Some of the Texan carpenters were unhappy about Armando being promoted to carpenter. The helper also thought he understood the Texans blamed Walter for Armando's elevation. So the Mexicans waited behind the big barn that had been cleaned up a bit for use as a bunkhouse for the carpenters.

Mr. Granger didn't sleep in the bunkhouse. He had a room in a boarding house across from the station and an office in the station, which is where Jesús found him.

"Come quickly, Mr. Granger," Jesús yelled to him in Spanish.

"What's the matter, Jesús?" Mr. Granger asked urgently, as he grabbed his hat off the rack and began to follow.

"And what are you still doing in Del Rio?" he quizzed.

"Hurry please, Mr. Granger," Jesús urged.

"It's the cowboys. They have Mr. Walter," he explained in Spanish.

"Walter? What do they want with Walter?"

"I knew there was going to be trouble," Mr. Granger spoke, answering his own question.

When the two men reached the barn, it turned out that Jesús had not been precisely accurate. The Texans did not have Walter. They had an entire group of Mexican workers who had surrounded Walter in a corner of the barn. The biggest of the cowboys, Luke, had a piece of stove wood in his hand. He was waving it at Antonio, the largest and strongest of the Mexicans, who had taken a position at the front of the circle.

"Back off, Luke!" Mr. Granger commanded, as soon as he saw the seething throng that was threatening to ignite this tense standoff into a race riot, perhaps even a lynching.

"Back off or draw your wages right now!"

Luke lowered the lumber but stood his ground. Frank Granger waded through the Texans, moving them back until he got to Luke.

"Drop it Luke and calm down," he ordered.

"It ain't right, Mr. Granger," Luke protested.

"Drop the lumber, Luke, right now, or you're fired," Mr. Granger warned.

The timber fell to the ground and Walter breathed a sigh of relief, remembering how he had gotten into a fight his first night on the trail with the survey crew.

"It ain't right," Luke repeated.

"What ain't right?" Mr. Granger asked.

"Hiring Mexicans as carpenters," Luke said.

"You mean Armando?" he asked.

"Yeah, that Mexican over there," Luke scowled, pointing at Armando.

"When you answer me, it would be better if you said, 'yes sir' instead of, 'yeah,'" Mr. Granger told Luke.

"As for Armando, I watched him work today. He built a whole pen and part of another without bending a nail or ruining a board. How many pens did you build today, Luke?"

The big cowboy looked sheepish, but he wasn't finished.

"That ain't got nothing to do with it," Luke proclaimed forcefully, reasserting his role as leader of the mob.

"You bring a kid in this morning at full wages. Then by dinnertime, we got Mexican carpenters. It ain't right."

"You're through, Luke," Mr. Granger had listened to all he was going to.

"Get your stuff and go up to my office and I'll pay you off. Any of the rest of you think Luke's got the right idea about how I should be running this railroad can clear out with him. Everyone understand?"

No one else moved, and no one said anything. Luke kicked his boots in the dirt and walked over to the side of the barn to collect his belongings.

"Everybody else who wants to stay around here and collect railroad pay had better understand that the Southern Pacific railroad will decide who it wants to hire and what it wants them to do," Mr. Granger said.

"Starting tomorrow, Mr. Oakley will be the new foreman. When he speaks to you, he's talking for the railroad. And if you don't want to listen, that means you don't want your twelve dollars a week.

"He may be young, but he knows a lot more about carpentering than any of the rest of you. We knew you were cowboys when we hired you, but you were the best we could get.

"The money's good here. If you want to keep getting it, you won't cause any more trouble. If you do, I'll get rid of the whole lot of you. Is that clear to everybody?" he challenged.

No one spoke, and the Texans drifted toward their bedrolls. Mr. Granger looked at the Mexican workers.

"You men get on across the river to your homes. There's work to be done in the morning," he told them.

"Walter," Mr. Granger called out.

"If you're going to be foreman, you sleep at the boarding house. Get your stuff and come with me."

The walk from the barn to the station was one of the few times in Walter's dealings with Frank Granger that the older man was not talking.

Mr. Granger had Walter sit in the office as he paid off Luke. Then Walter and his boss walked over to the boarding house, where Mr. Granger spoke with the owner.

There were no more rooms, but the landlady agreed to let Walter sleep on the back porch, where she had moved her own two boys to make room for more railroad men.

The next morning, as Walter sat by Mr. Granger for breakfast, Frank Granger had more news.

"We're going to have to start building some houses, Walter. The stationmaster wants to bring his family here and the crews need a place to sleep while they lay over and wait for trains. We've got to get on that."

"Yes sir," Walter agreed, trying not to reveal that he was more confused than ever.

Yesterday, Mr. Granger had the young Walter building pens for cattle. And less than twenty-four hours later, he wanted houses for railroad workers. Things were moving too fast to sort out, but Walter would soon see that the speed of changing responsibilities and events had only accelerated. In two weeks, the pens were all being built by Mexican carpenters, supervised by Antonio. Walter had the best of the Texans and a few selected Mexicans building houses for the stationmaster, for train crews and for the yardmaster who had not even arrived from San Antonio. There was also a huge gang of Chinese workers camped along the river. The railroad brought them in to build a switchyard, its most intense and body-destroying labor.

In two more weeks, Mr. Granger had stopped supervising carpentry altogether, because he was spending all his time drawing plans for a new hotel. By the end of the summer, Walter was finishing the hotel and supervising the carpenters, who were building more houses and a freight station. Soon after, the railroad sent Frank Granger to a site near the Pecos River to build wooden trestles across gorges. Mr. Granger's new duties led to Walter being assigned the responsibility for all the railroad's construction work in Del Rio. The weekly payroll for Walter's operation became so big that the Southern Pacific sent the money in a special train coach guarded by armed security men.

The engineers in San Francisco were under constant pressure to make the route followed by the track through West Texas shorter. Walter's whole life had become a whirlwind, and he had no idea where it would end.

The furious pace of the young supervisor's daily schedule didn't lessen. But a week before Christmas, there was a break. A conductor found Walter at the freight depot and handed him a big packet from Mr. Easterly. The first thing that Walter encountered when he opened the packet was a note from Mr. Easterly, congratulating him on all his fine work. The paper also directed Walter to take the rest of the contents of the package home with him to New Mexico. Walter was to use his railroad pass and to hand the conductor of the train he rode a second note.

That paper authorized the train to make a special stop fifteen miles east of Lordsburg to let Walter and his horse off the train. The note also informed Walter that the eastbound *Sunset Limited* would stop at the same spot on January second for Walter and his horse, if his father would let Walter come back to San Antonio.

Walter stayed in Del Rio two more days, seeing to the completion of the freight depot, then caught the westbound for New Mexico. He rode off the ridge and down to the Little Hatchet, an hour after sunrise on Christmas Eve. Secured to the back of his horse was a huge bundle of presents: one for each brother and sister, plus special presents for Little Matt and his mother.

Walter had wired a list of things he wanted as presents to Mr. Robertson at his store in El Paso. He had also sent a telegram asking the bank to pay Mr. Robertson from Walter's account. The bundle was waiting for Walter at the station in El Paso when his train pulled in.

The day after Christmas, when lunch was over, James asked Walter to walk with him down to the barn. When they got there, James leaned up against a wagon and pulled a letter out of his coat from Mr. Easterly.

"You know, son, it had always been my dream for you that you become an engineer," Walter's father began, then paused for a few seconds before continuing.

"As I've thought about it these past two days, I have come to realize that maybe it wasn't my dream for you, so much as it was that my own dream to be an engineer got interrupted. I'm not sure, but you being an engineer is something I have had in my mind since your first day.

"You not becoming an engineer is something I would have to get used to," James conceded.

"I don't want to do anything to make you unhappy, Papa," Walter said.

"And if you think I need to go to school to be an engineer, then that's what I'll do."

"Thanks, Walter," James said.

"You've been the best son a man could have, and I know you'll do what I ask you to. But I guess what we need to get to is: what do you want to do?"

"No Papa. If you think I should go to college, that's what I want, too," Walter said, speaking firmly.

"But you see, son, that's just it. You being an engineer is something I've always wanted for you, but maybe I have just wanted you to become an engineer because the war kept me from doing it myself. And now I've come to realize that being an engineer may not be what you want for yourself. It may not be the best course for you at all. This is your life we're talking about. You should make your own choice," James explained.

This time, Walter said nothing.

"And what Mr. Easterly says in this letter makes a lot of sense," James continued. "He says you're one of the best carpenters that anybody at the Southern Pacific railroad has ever seen. He says you are supervising men twice your age and that you've seen to the construction of a hotel, houses, stockyards, and a freight depot in a place called Del Rio. Are all of those things true?"

"Yes sir," Walter confirmed.

"He says that since you left here, you have made enough money to more than pay for your first year in engineering school if that's where you choose to go. Is that right?"

"I don't know. They never told me how much they were paying me. They just sent it to the bank in El Paso. Anyway, I don't know how much engineering school costs," Walter smiled.

"Well, Mr. Easterly sent along a statement to me of how much they have paid you and when they gave you raises and bonuses. And I'd say from what I have been able to gather, that you have enough money on your own to make a fine start at any engineering college in the country, maybe even enough to pay for the whole thing.

"Have you given any thought to where you might like to attend college?" James posed.

"Well, sir, I suppose if I could, I would like to go to Cornell," Walter replied.

"From everything I've heard, that's a fine school," James concurred.

"What made you think you might want to go there?" Walter's father asked.

"That's where Bryan went to college, sir," Walter replied.

"I guess that would be this Bryan Whittaker Mr. Easterly writes about?" James asked.

"Yes sir," Walter acknowledged.

"Mr. Easterly also tells me something else," James continued.

"He says that you are the most talented natural construction project foreman he has ever run into. And he says that even without becoming an engineer, in a year or two you'll be making as much money as most of the engineers who work for the railroad.

"He also says that, if you want to break away from the railroad after a while and become a private contractor, that there's no way to tell how much money you could eventually make. This is a pretty sobering letter, and it makes me very proud to be your father," James told his eldest child, revealing the pride he almost never addressed directly with words spoken aloud.

Walter did not know what to say; so there was silence, while both Oakleys composed their thoughts. Finally, James spoke.

"Here are the facts. It's not right for me to decide your future. It's your decision and only yours. If you want to go to college and become an engineer or a doctor or a lawyer or anything else, that's your right and I'll see to it that you have the money. And if you want to go back to the railroad and make a career out of that, then that's your right, too.

"I'm really proud of you and I'll be just as proud one way as the other. And your mother feels the same way, too. We've talked about it."

Walter was dumbfounded. He had never heard his father talk like that before. Walter had always assumed that he would become an engineer. However, before he went to work for the railroad, what he had really wanted to do with his life was stay right there on the Little Hatchet, which he had always thought of as the most wonderful place on earth. Walter was confused by these new possibilities, and his confusion led to a long period of silence.

"Well, you don't have to make your mind up right now; and you can talk to your mother, if you want. I think she might like that. As a matter of fact, I am sure she would," James told his son.

Walter did not feel that he could talk about these things any more with anyone. He agonized over the decision for the rest of his stay at home. Several times, he started to talk with Katie, but he could never get the words out. He even thought about talking with Harry, but that didn't happen, either.

Finally, the day before the New Year Walter, wrote his mother and father a letter announcing his decision. After lunch on New Year's Day, he saddled up and rode to the spot on the tracks where he had gotten off the train ten days and a lifetime earlier. In two days, he was standing in Mr. Easterly's office in San Antonio.

"Glad you're back," his boss proclaimed, welcoming the young man he considered the most outstanding protégé of William Easterly's long career with the railroad.

"You made a wise decision," he told Walter.

Walter wrote his father several times during the winter and spring offering to go to Cornell in the fall. Each time his father wrote back to tell Walter he was proud of him, but the decision on whether to go to college belonged to Walter alone.

Walter never became an engineer.

CHAPTER TWENTY

I t was a year later than he had hoped, but Walter finally got to see San Antonio, which became the site of the Southern Pacific's winter construction crisis. Building a locomotive shop and car barn to service Texas had become the railroad's most urgent priority. As the number of trains increased, the need for maintenance had become critical. The railroad brought Walter in to supervise a crew of sixteen carpenters and their helpers. It was astounding how quickly the railroad was growing and how fast it was changing Texas, California, and all the points along its route from New Orleans to San Francisco.

Walter moved into the boardinghouse Mr. Easterly had promised the year before, though he seldom got to his new home before nine o'clock at night and was always gone by or before five o'clock every morning but Sunday. He wrote to his mother and father that there was a Presbyterian church in San Antonio and that he was attending both Sunday school and church. It was a nice place, and several of the church families had invited Walter for Sunday dinner.

Walter was becoming quite skillful at entertaining his colleagues at the Southern Pacific with stories about Peyote and the Little Hatchet. Some of the shyness Bryan had seen when the two first met was fading, at least when he was around men he worked with. In that sense, the long hours Walter worked were a blessing. When he was working, Walter forgot the terror he felt when he was alone with the daughters of one of the families at church.

At Sunday lunch with the McGill family, Walter was fine, perhaps even comfortable, when Mr. McGill asked him about the progress of the work at the locomotive shop. He answered with little trouble, even though Lucinda never stopped looking at him for even a second when he spoke.

Walter thought his answers made sense when Mrs. McGill had asked questions about his family. However, when he was alone after lunch with Lucinda, he could not answer even her simplest questions. It was not that he did not know what to say. It was worse. He couldn't talk at all. Not that his muteness discouraged her: she went right on talking to him, as if nothing were wrong. She apparently could not see in his face the stark fear Walter felt inside when Lucinda waited for Walter to answer her.

Walter's agony got worse when his mother would ask in one of her letters whether her son had met any young ladies in San Antonio that he found attractive.

Despite his misery, the invitations continued and Walter kept accepting them. After lunch with the Burkes, the family went for a walk along the river. Walter and Clara walked at a distance behind the rest of the family.

"It's a beautiful day," Clara observed, with a smile as bright as the sunshine.

Walter could not speak.

"Papa says that you are the most promising young man at the Southern Pacific. He told us that everyone says that," she continued.

Walter's lips were welded shut.

If he had been told, Walter would never have believed that Lucinda and Clara were delighted to sit or walk with him. They considered him handsome and San Antonio's most desirable prospective husband. They knew from the minister that Walter came from a good family and the stories they had heard about his courage added to his attractiveness. But Walter couldn't get over being terrified.

On Palm Sunday, he wanted to avoid church, but he had promised his mother. Walter had never broken a promise to his mother. So he washed, combed his hair, put on his good clothes from Vernel Robertson's store in El Paso and walked up the avenue to church.

His worst fear became reality on the steps of the Presbyterian church right after the Palm Sunday sermon. Mrs. Wilmont and her daughter Rachel, who Walter thought was the prettiest girl in the congregation, walked up to Walter.

"Hello, Walter," Mrs. Wilmont said, smiling brightly, while not allowing even a second to pass for Walter to make a response.

"Mr. Wilmont and I would like to invite you to join our family for Easter dinner next Sunday, and Rachel would like you to be her guest for lunch at the church picnic on the Sunday after. Now, don't think of saying no," Rachel Wilmont's mother insisted. "Because we won't even consider any answer but yes."

Rachel was standing beside her mother, smiling. She had beautiful dark curls and deep brown eyes. She was as pretty as any girl Walter had ever seen. And, of course, Walter had never spoken a single word to her, not so much as hello. He had been too terrified to even return her smiles, probing his shoes with his eyes, instead.

Walter stood, struggling for any word, any kind of excuse, but his mouth would not open. Mrs. Wilmont was cagey. Before Walter could get any words out at all, Mrs. Wilmont and Rachel had wrapped up the conversation with a chorus.

"See you next Sunday, then," they both said in unison.

With that, they turned and walked down the steps to Mr. Wilmont, who had witnessed Walter's entire painful ordeal from the sidewalk. Walter remained on the steps, speechless. He had heard about the church picnic. The young ladies prepared special lunches for the eligible young gentlemen of the congregation and the couples would eat these lunches apart from the main gathering, their blankets or quilts spread out under the shade of live oaks on the church grounds.

How would Walter be able to sit through an entire luncheon of fried chicken, potato salad, beans, rolls, and apple pie without speaking a single word? More to the point, how would he get out of the trap in which Mrs. Wilmont and Rachel had so skillfully captured him? Walter was so distraught that he skipped Sunday lunch at Mrs. Schmidt's boarding house that afternoon.

Sometimes on Sundays after lunch, Walter took White Cloud on long rides into the Hill Country. She seldom got exercise during Walter's long work weeks in San Antonio, and Sundays were his only chance to see his prized mare.

Walter needed to think. So he walked to the stable, saddled his horse and rode off toward Fredericksburg. The mare was glad to see Walter, and Walter was relieved to be out in the fresh air of a beautiful spring afternoon.

He rode fifteen miles out of the city, thinking about his dilemma as he went. He could go see Mr. Wilmont and explain that Rachel was the prettiest girl he had ever seen, and he would love to be able to carry on a conversation with her, but he just couldn't.

No, Walter thought. That wouldn't work. He could write a letter, explaining. Explaining what? That he became a complete mute when faced with the possibility of spending an hour with a beautiful girl? The fact was, Walter couldn't explain it to the Wilmonts if he couldn't explain his predicament, his failings, to himself. He just could not speak when he was paired with a girl, any girl at all. He didn't know of anyone else who was like that. He had never heard of anything like it, and he didn't know whom to ask.

Walter dismounted from his mare, two hundred yards west of the road, where a creek widened into a pool. The bottom was solid limestone. The water was less than two feet deep, but it was sparkling and clear. Walter allowed the mare to pull some fresh green grass beside the creek as he lay on the bank trying to resolve his problem.

He had been lost in thought about the Wilmonts' invitation for perhaps thirty minutes when he heard something thump into the ground right beside him. Before he had time to figure out what had made the noise, Walter heard a scream and saw a horse rush past White Cloud.

That was when Walter realized an arrow had struck the ground beside him and that the same arrow had been responsible for making the sound that had puzzled him. Walter turned his head and saw a small, shockingly thin Comanche brave, perhaps sixteen years old, chasing after White Cloud, his beautiful mare.

"White Cloud!" Walter screamed.

The little quarter horse made an abrupt stop, the way she had been trained to do when working cattle. The brave sailed past the pony, missing her reins by a few inches.

Walter heard more hooves beat the ground nearby. He looked up to see a second Comanche, no bigger than the first, leaning off his horse to the side. He was coming full out, directly at Walter, with a stone war ax raised and poised to strike.

Precisely when the brave was on top of him, Walter grabbed the young Comanche's wrist. Leaning off the horse toward Walter, the attacker was already very much off balance. Walter had learned from his first fight how valuable it was to stop an opponent right away, and whenever possible, use an opponent's own weight against him. Mr. Easterly had explained to Walter that having the breath knocked out of a person was completely disabling. Mr. Easterly had also shown Walter where the solar plexus was, in the center of the chest at the bottom of the rib cage.

All this information melded into Walter's strategy. Counting on the Comanche's position, Walter had easily removed the brave from his horse and his attacker hit the ground very hard. Walter rolled quickly on top of him and punched him once, forcefully and directly in his solar plexus. He'd taken the second Comanche out of the fight just as quickly as he had Ezra Johnson.

Walter had not fully focused on the attempt to steal his horse yet, but he was aware enough of the Comanches' efforts to be furious. Without considering that there could be more than two attackers, Walter picked up the ax he had dislodged from the Comanche and scrambled to his feet. He checked to make certain the second of the braves he had seen would not attack his back.

"This horse stealing has got to stop!" Walter shouted at the young man, who had shot the arrow at him, raising the Comanche ax to emphasize his point.

This caused the brave to stop chasing White Cloud. To Walter's astonishment, the mounted Comanche drew an arrow and aimed it at him. Walter grabbed for the disabled brave's horse, and, using it as a shield, he began advancing toward the archer. Walter was no more accomplished as a fighter than he had been when he had skirmished with Ezra Johnson. His actions were being controlled solely by his own intense anger.

"The Apaches got my first horse and you fellas aren't going to steal this one," Walter yelled at the menacing Comanche, who continued to point the arrow in Walter's direction.

Walter's skilled horsemanship shocked the young Comanche. He could not imagine any white man having such expertise. The very young brave still had not shot, apparently fearing that he would hit his companion's horse. Walter kept the horse turned sideways between them and continued advancing. As Walter closed to within ten feet, the Comanche shot the second arrow, aiming at Walter's legs, but the arrow missed by three feet. As soon as the arrow struck the ground, Walter ducked underneath the pony and rushed straight for the brave who had just shot. He struck the Comanche's horse smack in the head with the flat part of the ax, causing the horse to stumble and fall.

When the horse went down, Walter was on top of the undernourished young brave in a flash. The Comanche was much smaller than Walter. Instinctively, Walter pinned his attacker's shoulders to the ground by placing one knee on each of the Comanche's upper arms and he pressed the handle of the ax against the brave's throat to deprive him of air. When his assailant lost consciousness, Walter pulled back the ax handle and stood up.

Fearing that the other brave might recover, Walter went quickly back to him to discover that he was still flat on his back. Working swiftly, Walter cut a leather strap from the rein on that brave's horse. He had bound the Comanche's hands tightly behind him just as he had learned to do with the hogs on the Little Hatchet. In a few more seconds, Walter was back to the horse, where he cut the second rein. He led the horse to where the brave lay on the ground. Using the strap he had tied around the Comanche's wrists, Walter jerked the young man to his feet and boosted him onto his horse. The stunned brave did not resist. Walter used the second strap to tie his ankles beneath the horse.

In less than a minute, Walter had completed the same process with the Comanche who had shot the arrows at him. He turned both horses to the west; and using the bow that Walter had captured as a whip, Walter slapped each animal strongly on its rump. The horses trotted off, carrying the Comanches away from the road and away from San Antonio.

"No more horse stealing!" Walter called after them in his loudest voice, as the two horses carried the two Comanches west, completely dazed from their encounter with Walter. The young railroader dusted off his clothes and rode back to town. When he reached the stable, it was well past dark. Walter brushed White Cloud down and watched as the stable attendant led her off to be watered and fed.

The next morning, Walter was up an extra thirty minutes early, so he could go by Mr. Easterly's office with the bow and ax. He related the incident to Mr. Easterly in just a few sentences. Mr. Easterly listened in stunned silence, as his young foreman told how he had taken on two Comanche braves. Walter told his story with unembellished words, as if he were describing an everyday activity.

"Well, by looking at this hatchet, I'm pretty sure that they were Comanches," Mr. Easterly offered.

"Most of them have been moved up above the Red River into Indian Territory, but there are a few strays still around. Occasionally, someone spots them.

"From what you tell me, the two you ran into weren't big enough to pose any serious threat, but I suppose we ought to send word to the Rangers that you saw them, anyway," Mr. Easterly said.

Before noon, the story of Walter and the Comanches was all over San Antonio. After lunch, a Texas Ranger Captain stopped by the engine barn to talk with Walter and make sure that he had the information right. At supper, railroad men crowded around Walter looking for details of how he had single-handedly whipped a whole band of angry Comanches. Walter laughed.

"There were only two, and they were barely more than boys," he corrected.

However, the stories continued to spread and grew more outlandishly inaccurate with each telling. When Walter went to his room at Mrs. Schmidt's that night, there was a note from Mrs. Wilmont. She asked Walter to let her family know he was all right. Everyone was talking about his battle with the Comanches, and she offered to treat any injuries. She also reminded Walter that the Wilmonts expected him for Easter dinner.

Until the note, Walter had forgotten about his problem with the Wilmonts. Now, with the whole town talking about Walter, as if he were a legendary Indian fighter, his circumstances had grown worse. He might not be afraid of two armed Comanches, but Walter was more terrified than ever at the thought of having to face Rachel Wilmont alone.

CHAPTER TWENTY-ONE

As the weekend approached, Walter worried endlessly about Rachel. There appeared to be no way out; but on Good Friday, a train wrecked near Langtry, the site of a railroad camp between Del Rio and Sanderson. Before sundown, Mr. Easterly had every man he could find, including Walter, on a special train headed to the Pecos River crash site. Walter was spared.

The late afternoon sunshine revealed only a trace of the West Texas thunderstorm that had produced the flash flood which had washed out the trestle. There was no water flowing through the gully where the derailment occurred, but the soil was still muddy from the heavy rain.

The big freight locomotive had traveled for a distance in the air before it plowed into the bluff on the east side of the wash. The nose of the engine had lodged itself four or five feet into the wet embankment. Then it had sunk down another two to three feet into the mud. It seemed doubtful that the crew on the locomotive would have survived the crash under the best of circumstances. However, the freight cars loaded with lumber slammed into the wash on top of the engine, ending any hope of the crew getting through the wreck alive.

By the time the special work train from San Antonio arrived, the portion of the wrecked train that stayed on the tracks had been pulled back to Sierra Blanca. A switch engine had also been brought in from the west. The engine and mules worked together to tow the derailed freight cars out of the way. A Chinese section gang was already building a temporary track around the wreckage. Walter's crew would put in a trestle for the temporary track, then help replace the permanent trestle the flood had washed away.

Walter was amazed by the organizational skill driving back the chaos created by the accident. Late Easter Sunday night, the first train passed slowly over Walter's temporary trestle. Frank Granger had a good start on a new permanent trestle even before the crane arrived to remove the derailed locomotive from the gully.

Mr. Granger simply went thirty feet back from the existing rim of the wash on both sides and set new footings for a much stronger trestle. His new structure was designed to prevent a recurrence of the Good Friday wreck.

When Walter's crew had finished with the replacement track, they moved over to help Mr. Granger's men work. Just after midnight Wednesday morning, thunderstorms began pounding the railroad workers. The wind blew fifty or sixty miles an hour; then the hail started. Horses and mules panicked, and the railroad men chased after the runaways. The section gang huddled under flatcars and the other men, who were not chasing horses and mules, took shelter in boxcars. The hailstones almost beat Walter and Bryan senseless, but they would not let the frenzied animals run off or get hurt, falling into a ravine. The hail changed to a driving rain and Bryan and Walter discovered they were wading through mud that was ankle deep as they searched for the livestock.

"Bryan, Walter!" Frank Granger called.

"Y'all can find the rest of the animals after daybreak."

The two young men looked at one another. Neither wanted to quit.

"He's right," Bryan agreed, still out of breath from the hard work the roundup was demanding.

"We're not going to find any more runaways in the dark."

Bryan vaulted into the boxcar, where Frank Granger had taken shelter and Walter followed. Mr. Granger offered the young men some water.

"Thanks. We'll get the rest in the morning. I hope this rain doesn't wash out the new footings," Frank Granger added after a pause.

When he heard no response from the young men, Mr. Granger looked over. Walter and Bryan had fallen asleep, their backs propped against the sides of the rail car. The rain poured steadily for another hour and a half. No one was measuring, but it was likely that more than three inches had fallen during that storm.

Just before the rain from the first group of clouds stopped, vicious lightning tore the sky ten miles to the southwest. The winds roared again, soon gusting up to sixty miles an hour. The second system lacked hail, but the rain was even heavier than the first storm had produced. It fell at a rate of five or six inches an hour, and the desert on both sides of the ravine turned into a lake. The wash itself was now a roaring torrent. Frank Granger kept thinking that he needed to check on the new footings for the trestle, but the rain was so dense he could not see the ground outside the boxcar door. Remarkably, Bryan and Walter slept through the entire storm.

"I need to go check the footings," he informed them.

Frank smiled to himself when he saw the young men still sleeping, then he eased himself to the ground. It was difficult walking in the deep mud. Even though the rain was light, the wind blew in erratic gusts, making it close to impossible to keep the lantern lit. The holes for the new foundation were flooded and some of the timber had washed completely away. Frank Granger was startled by a noise and spun around.

"Oh it's you, Joe," Frank realized, somewhat relieved.

Then he bowed slightly to the Chinese crew boss. There were four other workers standing with him.

"Pretty much ruined, I'd say, Big Boss," Joe declared as he inspected the interrupted work.

"I suppose you're right, Joe. But we won't be able to see how bad it is for sure 'till morning," Frank surmised.

Joe pointed and issued some directions in a Chinese dialect. Joe's instructions sent his men scurrying down the side of the embankment.

"Careful, it's slick and the bank may not be stable," Frank cautioned.

The words were still hanging in the air when the man nearest the top began sliding. He reached for one of the foundation timbers that was mostly buried in the mud to help him stop. It held, and the worker called up to Joe that he was all right. Joe frowned, and the worker began using the timber to help upright himself. As the worker tugged repeatedly with all his strength, the huge piece of lumber came free, sending the man tumbling toward the bottom of the wash. The momentum of the worker's fall pushed all four men into the water. Joe and Frank Granger peered over the edge, but the light was so dim that they could not see the bottom. Joe called to the workers in Chinese, asking if they were all right. They answered they were okay, but Frank and Joe could hear them thrashing in the water.

Before Joe could speak, there was another low rumble that sounded almost like a gusting wind, followed by the sound of something big and heavy hitting the water. Lightning flashed and Frank Granger looked in disbelief. A section of the bank twelve feet thick and at least a hundred feet long had crashed into the normally dry creek bed. There was no sign of the workers. Frank and Joe both slid down the side of the wash together and were buried in mud up to their waists.

"We've got to get them out from under this mud before they suffocate!" Frank exclaimed, as the two men began clawing at the mud with their hands.

They had likely been digging for ten or twelve minutes before exhaustion forced them to rest.

"Men dead, Big Boss," Joe announced, solemnly.

"They probably are, Joe. Let's rest for just a minute, then we'll go get some help to dig them out," Frank Granger said haltingly as he struggled to catch his breath.

The railroad engineer buried his face in his muddy hands. A distant roar interrupted his grief. Frank's head snapped up so he could listen more carefully.

"Flash flood!" he screamed, as he scrambled for the bank.

Frank turned and saw Joe's legs had become stuck in soft mud. Frank rushed back, reached his arms around the old man, locked his fingers on Joe's chest just under his arms, and pulled. In seconds, Frank and Joe were buried beneath a mountain of roaring floodwater.

Everyone gathered for breakfast, but no one was eating when Walter and Bryan walked up.

"Where's Mr. Granger?" Bryan asked the cook.

"Haven't seen him," the cook replied.

"Why isn't anyone eating?" Bryan asked.

"Can't say. The Chinese are upset about something," the cook answered.

Bryan and Walter walked to where the Chinese workers stood. A murmur hung over the group, and many of the men bobbed their heads and moved their hands as they talked.

"Where's Boss Joe?" Bryan asked loudly, in a tone designed to get the men's attention.

Several of the workers walked toward Bryan and pleaded with him in Chinese. Bryan and Walter looked at one another. The workers were extremely distressed, but that was all they could decipher from the conversation. Joe was the only man among the Chinese workers who spoke English, and none of the Texans spoke Chinese. It was ten minutes before Walter found someone who had seen Frank Granger and the Chinese leave the railroad cars.

"Bryan, better come over here. This man saw something, but he's telling me mostly in Spanish and I can't figure out what he's saying," Walter called out from across the camp.

As soon as Bryan had translated the story, he and Walter headed for the trestle site at a trot. Walter was the first to spot something in the mud. When he got to the bottom of the wash, what Walter had seen turned out to be the hand of one of the Chinese workers. It took nearly fifteen minutes to dig the four bodies out of the mud and another hour before Bryan and Walter agreed that Frank Granger and Joe were not among the bodies they had recovered.

Neither Bryan nor Walter felt like eating after what they had seen and done. So, following a brief rest, the two rode out searching for Frank Granger. They were more than a mile down the creek bed when Walter spotted the two bodies. Both were entangled in brush about a hundred feet apart. Rocks and debris carried by the flood had battered the men almost beyond recognition. Bryan and Walter sat on their horses, looking at the bodies. There was no use running to the creek. Both men were clearly dead. All Walter could think of was how strange a vibrant human being looks, after life is gone from his body.

Frank Granger had been a friend and one of several substitute parents who had looked after Walter since he had left his home in New Mexico. He was a little bigger than most men when he was alive. But in its current state, Frank's body looked small and fragile, as if life had never existed inside it. Bryan was concerned about Walter, wondering whether the corpses of Frank Granger and the workers were the first he had ever seen. Being with Walter, it was hard to keep in mind how young he was. Bryan felt foolish. He was not doing too well with this experience himself.

"It's hard looking at a friend like that. Last night, we were trying to save our work from a storm, and now Frank is gone. This will be a hard thing to get over," Bryan pronounced solemnly.

Walter did not respond. Bryan's words summarized much of what he had been thinking, but Walter was concerned with other things. He had been remembering the first time he had met Frank Granger and how long ago that seemed. Walter imagined how terrible Mrs. Granger and her children would feel when they heard. Who would tell them?

Not me, he thought. Please don't let it be me who has to tell them.

Bryan was speaking again, but Walter had not been listening when his friend had started talking. Walter was overwhelmed and struggling to appear composed. He was also focused on his effort to control an almost irresistible urge to vomit.

"Is this the first time you've ever seen dead people?" Bryan asked a second time, after realizing Walter had apparently not heard his original question.

Walter swallowed hard and took a deep breath before answering.

"No," he managed to answer weakly.

"I saw Peyote after he died."

"It's tough," Bryan observed.

"I don't see how men get used to dealing with this sort of thing. I hope I don't have to do too much more of it in my life."

Walter swayed from side to side with the movement of the car as the special train chugged toward San Antonio. He was numb from the day's experiences. None of it seemed real. He could not believe that he got through the entire ordeal without giving in to the constant nausea. He was surprised that he had not thrown up. Not becoming visibly ill did not seem like much of an accomplishment, but those were his thoughts. In snippets along the way to San Antonio, Walter had thought back on what had happened. Removing the bodies from the brush in the creek had been the hardest part.

Walter prayed he would never see another friend or anyone else he loved look like that again. But his thoughts wondered off into the future. Would he have to take care of his wife's body when she died? What could be worse? Would he have to deal with the body of a dead child, even one of his own children? Please, no, God, he thought!

The arrangements had been made in a series of telegraph messages back and forth with San Antonio. Mr. Easterly had located a mail car in Del Rio. A funeral director there had sent the coffin Frank Granger's body was riding in, and the bier it was resting on. Walter looked at it. How strange. Why not just put the coffin on the floor of the car? This arrangement was more respectful, he guessed. Frank Granger was a special man. William Easterly was an extraordinary person with a matchless sense of loyalty, and this was his way of showing his respect for an exceptional friend. Frank Granger's value in life would be honored in death by his colleagues and by the Southern Pacific Railroad.

Walter fell asleep, pondering these values: honor and respect. He knew from the frequency of the whistling that the train was pulling into San Antonio. The doors of the car had been left partially open, allowing Walter to see it was dark outside. He stood and straightened his clothes, which were the cleanest he had.

He had washed as well as he could before the special train arrived, but there was still creek mud caked under his fingernails. As the train pulled up to the platform, Walter tried to make himself somewhat presentable by combing his hair with his fingers. When the doors opened, he saw Mr. Easterly, Mrs. Granger and all her children standing beside the track. They were somber in their black clothes. A funeral coach was parked behind them.

This time, Walter was incapable of holding back his tears. He stumbled from the car into Mrs. Granger's arms, unable to stop crying and having lost the capacity to speak. I'm so sorry, he wanted to say, but the words would not come.

"Thank you for taking care of my husband. He loved you like one of his own sons," Mrs. Granger told Walter, as she held the young railroad man.

Having spoken those words, Mrs. Granger began weeping as well, while Mr. Easterly moved to comfort the children who had been brave, until they saw their mother's tears. Ten minutes passed before the coffin could be transferred from the car to the hearse. Mrs. Granger rode alone in the funeral coach with Frank's body. Mr. Easterly, Walter and the Granger children rode behind in a carriage. They took the body to the Grangers' home, where a place for it stood ready in the living room. Mrs. Granger could not bear to have the body wait for burial at the funeral parlor. Walter did his best to comfort himself, Mrs. Granger, and her children over the next three days.

"Grief has to wear off. Only time fixes it," Mr. Easterly had told him.

On the train back west, Walter was still numb. He wished there had been something he could have done to help. He had felt useless. Mrs. Granger had made such a fuss over him. Walter should have been comforting her, but it had been the widow providing the support for Walter. Walter felt that he had messed up this whole thing. Mrs. Granger's words, as they had stood on the platform in San Antonio saying goodbye, still echoed in Walter's mind.

"Thank you so much for being with us, Walter. I couldn't have gotten through this without you," she had told him.

Bryan was waiting as Walter stepped down from the caboose. There was a handshake instead of a hug. It was time for normal life to resume.

"You got a lot of work done," Walter remarked, as the two friends looked at the nearly completed new trestle.

"Railroad sent a new boss for the Chinese crew from San Francisco. The workers don't like him, but none of us could speak Chinese. It was mostly pointing anyway. Joe had trained these men well. They know what they're doing. The new boss just got here yesterday," Bryan explained.

The emergency group that had rushed to the wreck Easter Sunday finished the rest of the repairs in ten more days. Bryan moved farther west to erect a new steel bridge over the river.

After finishing the locomotive shop and car barn in San Antonio, Walter took his crew to Del Rio to build additional houses for railroad supervisors and a dormitory for train crews. He spent Christmas in New

Mexico. Walter and Bryan wrote one another occasionally; but their paths remained separate for some time and Walter badly missed his friend.

When he thought of Frank Granger, Walter did his best to remember him as he had been when they met on Walter's first day in Del Rio. Gradually, the picture in his mind of Frank and Joe draped over the brush in the creek bed faded just as William Easterly had told him it would.

CHAPTER TWENTY-TWO

The Pedernales water sparkles like sunlight bouncing off quartz, as it rushes through the Texas hills near Fredericksburg. The water in its sister rivers, the San Antonio and Guadalupe, is green, a color they acquire from algae stirred up along their paths. But the Pedernales flows too swiftly to collect anything as it passes.

In March, the Pedernales' water was ice cold, so cold that it seemed unlikely to Walter that the hillsides could be spectacularly green, so cold that the blindingly bright bluebonnets would be too fragile to endure the chill. Just the same, there they were, a panoramic canvas of spring blue and green on the edge of an almost endless desert, stretching west more than a thousand miles to the Pacific Ocean.

Walter had already begun to think of these Texas hills as his home. But he was not prepared for what he saw on his first trip to Fredericksburg, even with what Bryan had previewed for him.

Walter and his men spotted their first German farms at the end of the tracks. The farmhouses were stone and the fences made of cedar posts with stone corners. Flowers grew profusely in boxes built underneath the windows of the houses. The meadows were lush green, the rows of crops neat and well-tended. Each farm had a windmill, and the barns were freshly and brightly painted.

The town was even neater. The buildings, whether stone or frame, were as clean as the bluebonnets that grew in the fields. The main buildings had walks, and the streets weren't as dusty or muddy as most Texas towns. Fredericksburg was a morsel of Europe, transported five thousand miles across an ocean. The people spoke German, just as Bryan had said. They knew English, but among themselves they preferred communicating in German.

The tracks stopped fifteen miles from town. So, Walter rode White Cloud into town and the crew traveled the rest of the way in a wagon. The Southern Pacific wanted to have facilities ready in each new town when the first trains arrived. Walter's group was sent in advance to build a small depot, a house for the stationmaster and a boarding house for train crews who would stay over in Fredericksburg.

The town was proud of its public school and there was a school at St. Mary's Catholic Church, as well. Zion Lutheran Church was almost as large as St. Mary's and a small Methodist church stood nearby. Walter stopped by all three to introduce himself, just as Mr. Easterly had instructed. He also visited in all the offices at the courthouse.

Most of the railroad men had gotten used to how young this construction supervisor was, but his age shocked the leaders of Fredericksburg. Even so, they were all grateful to see him, because they knew the railroad would ensure their town would continue to grow. Texas communities courted railroads shamelessly. Those that succeeded flourished. The ones that failed to attract a railroad withered. Any representative of the Southern Pacific railroad was immediately important to the leadership of Fredericksburg.

After church on his first Sunday in Fredericksburg, Walter dined with the mayor and his family. The next week, he was the guest of the county judge. And on the third Sunday, he picnicked with the parishioners at St. Mary's after Mass.

The townspeople took immense pride in the new railroad station that Walter's men were building. Their delight was on full display when the lumber for the peak of the roof was tacked into place. That same night, violent Texas spring weather blew the timbers down to the top of the walls. Nearby, Walter's crew slept in their tents and endured the full fury of the thunderstorms, which collapsed the canvas roofs of the tents onto the heads of the railroad men and scattered the company's livestock all over town and beyond.

Down the street, a tornado took the roof off the courthouse. So before the Southern Pacific men went back to work on the depot, they pitched in to help the people repair the county's governmental building. It was May before work resumed on the depot; and by then, the tracks were only three miles from town.

The first Sunday in May, most of the people in town and lots of farm families turned out for a picnic on the courthouse lawn to thank Walter and his crew. There was a speech from the county judge to mark the historic impact Southern Pacific rail service would have on Fredericksburg.

After he spoke, the county's leader called each of the railroad workers forward to be recognized by name for his contribution to the community. As the construction foreman, Walter came up last and received the most applause.

James Alsobrook, who farmed along the Pedernales, eleven miles east of town, brought his family to the picnic. James had come to Texas from Arkansas, following the Civil War. He bought his farm from a German family, who decided that they would return to Europe.

Growing peaches was something James Alsobrook had learned in Arkansas, but he turned it into an art at his farm on the banks of the Pedernales. He also built a mill to grind flour and cornmeal. James prospered in Texas, but it was his family that brought him joy, especially his remarkably beautiful daughter, Ada.

Ada was the one who had insisted the family come to the picnic. She loved her family's farm on the Pedernales, but she longed for excitement and she wanted to meet new people. She dreamed of meeting a man who would take her to elegant places in Galveston or San Antonio.

No one who lived along the Pedernales seemed likely to help Ada realize her dreams. So the railroad men interested her, particularly the youngest one, Walter Oakley.

He was handsome and strong and unlike any young man Ada had ever seen. She was determined to meet him. After lunch, Ada and her mother went over to Reverend and Mrs. Robert Thompson. He was the pastor of the First Methodist Church of Fredericksburg.

"Yes, we know Walter. He attends our services," Mrs. Thompson told the Alsobrooks.

In a few moments, Walter walked over in the company of Judge Knecht. After hellos, Reverend Thompson introduced the young railroad supervisor.

"Mrs. Alsobrook, may I present Walter Oakley, the construction foreman for the Southern Pacific," the pastor said.

"Walter, this is Mrs. James Alsobrook and her daughter, Ada."

Walter was stricken. He had thought that Rachel Wilmont was the most beautiful girl he had ever seen, even if he had been terrified of being close to her. Ada's beauty, however, was entirely different.

Her hair was nearly blonde. Her skin was lighter. She was stronger and seemed more mature, even though she was a year or two younger than Rachel. Ada looked very much like the German girls she lived among, but she was not German. Ada's ancestors had been English and Irish. Walter was amazed. He looked intently at Ada during the introduction and discovered that he could speak to her easily and confidently.

"How are you?" he had asked with no sense of fear.

"Fine, thank you," Ada answered with a warm and extremely confident smile.

Both young people felt their lives immediately changing. Both thought of the meeting the rest of the day and night, and through the week that followed.

The next Sunday, the entire Alsobrook family rode back into Fredericksburg for eleven o'clock services at the First Methodist Church. After church, they were guests for lunch at the Thompsons. Walter had also been invited.

There were so many people that the Thompson's house could not hold them all, so most of the Alsobrook children ate outside. Walter and Ada ate with the Alsobrooks and Thompsons inside. After lunch, Reverend Thompson led his guests on a walking tour of Fredericksburg.

Walter and Ada walked behind the others. The young ladies in San Antonio had mostly made small talk when they had walked with Walter, but Ada's first question was blunt and serious.

"So what kind of man are you, Walter Oakley?" she posed, as the distance separating Ada and Walter from her parents and the Thompsons became respectable.

"Well, I suppose I'm all right," Walter replied, pleased with his answer, but more pleased with the confident tone he heard in his voice.

"Well now, I suppose you do think you're all right. As a matter of fact, I suppose you think quite a lot of yourself," Ada challenged.

Walter was shocked.

"Now, what's that supposed to mean?" he asked, surprised at the boldness of this clearly no-nonsense lady.

"Just that you think you're some kind of big shot," Ada responded.

Walter looked at her and saw a slight smile appear on her face. He could tell that she was not ready for war, but she wanted him to understand that she could see right through him, get right to his core.

"Well, I'm not a big shot," Walter responded, calmly in a tone and cadence which sounded more like his father, when James was explaining something to a family member.

"I'm Walter Oakley from Little Hatchet Creek in New Mexico, and I'm just a carpenter for the Southern Pacific Railroad."

He did not speak the next words out loud. But the impression he meant to convey with his tone of voice was, "and I would never want anyone to think I'm acting like a big shot."

"Well, it seems to me from the way Judge Knecht talked about you last Sunday and the way folks talked to you at lunch today that you are a lot more than just a carpenter," Ada stated.

What she had not said explicitly, but what she had clearly meant to imply was that she would never consider marrying someone who was just a carpenter. Walter hoped that his conversation with Ada was about to get back on an even keel.

"That's what I do. I build things for the railroad," Walter explained quietly, waiting for Ada's response.

Her silence surprised him. She walked beside him past an entire block of store windows, saying nothing. Walter wondered whether the fear that had tormented him the previous spring in San Antonio would again destroy his ability to speak. Instinctively, he knew that if that happened, Walter would lose his chance to attract this fiery young lady, who had completely captivated him. He walked another half block in silence, then recovered his confidence.

"My father wanted me to be an engineer," he spoke quietly, waiting for another pointed question.

"I see," Ada noted, with what amounted to a verbal nod.

This was more challenging than Walter had suspected. Ada was tougher than a Comanche raiding party. Walter needed a deep breath, but he worried taking one would reveal his anxiety. That could threaten his chances of meeting Ada's expectations.

"It was a difficult decision," Walter resumed, this time not waiting for prodding from Ada.

"I think my father had wanted to be an engineer, but the war took that dream away from him. All my life, he talked to me about becoming an engineer.

"When we sat by the fire studying algebra and trigonometry late at night, he would tell me that's why he was teaching me math, so I could go east to school and become an engineer."

Walter paused, but still heard nothing from Ada. He had glanced over and observed that she was listening intently to what he was saying.

"After I went to be an apprentice with Mr. Easterly at the railroad, Papa and I talked about his offer very seriously. Mr. Easterly wrote Papa a letter suggesting that I might do as well, or even better, by taking a permanent job with the railroad now, instead of going to college to study engineering.

"Papa left it all up to me. It was the hardest thing I ever had to decide, but I wanted to work for the railroad and Papa understood," Walter concluded.

"So you did what you wanted, instead of what your father wanted you to?" Ada asked gently.

"Yes," Walter acknowledged.

"You love your father very much, don't you?" Ada observed.

Walter and James did not use those specific words when they talked, so her question sounded strange. But Walter responded at once.

"Yes."

Walter had never had a conversation like this one, not even with Bryan. He wanted to talk all day; but as he looked up, the gate in front of the

Thompson's small frame house was only a few feet away. The conversation was over, and Mr. Alsobrook took the lead.

"Mrs. Thompson, that was certainly a fine lunch," James announced.

Everyone agreed, and Ada's mother began gathering the rest of the family. After they rounded up a couple of stragglers, the Alsobrooks were all seated in the wagon and James coaxed his horses into motion with a slight movement of the reins.

"Hope we'll see you in church again soon," Reverend Thompson called to the departing family. "It's not that far, you know."

"I expect so," Mr. Alsobrook responded, as the wagon rolled away down the street.

Walter felt choked by emotion. The ending of the visit had been so abrupt. When would he see Ada again? Walter's distressed thoughts were interrupted as he felt a comforting arm slip around his shoulder and heard Mrs. Thompson's warm, encouraging voice.

"Isn't she beautiful?" she asked softly, displaying a sympathetic smile to Walter, who obviously was enraptured by Miss Ada Alsobrook.

"Yes ma'am," Walter agreed.

The Thompsons had sensed Walter's isolation and uncertainty.

"It must be hard for you sometimes, being so far from your family," Mrs. Thompson continued.

"Yes ma'am," Walter confirmed, relaxing a bit.

"You're always welcome here, Walter," Reverend Thompson said, joining his wife's efforts to soothe their young guest's uneasiness.

"Thank you, sir," Walter responded.

"I wonder, mother, if Walter would mind taking me over to his depot to see how it's coming along," Reverend Thompson asked.

Walter, of course, complied. As the two walked back through Fredericksburg, they made small talk and discussed the progress of Walter's construction project.

When they arrived at the station, Walter walked through each corner of the building, talking about the progress of the work. The waiting room was still open to the sky, thanks to the sudden nastiness of the Texas weather.

"I think she likes you very much, Walter," Reverend Thompson observed, diverting discussion away from the building project.

"I'm not sure I want to talk about this," Walter responded candidly.

"That's only natural, but don't let the uncertainty of things torment you unduly," Reverend Thompson suggested.

"If you want to talk to someone, anytime, day or night, just come on by the house," he offered.

Walter felt better. He wished he had known Reverend Thompson last year in San Antonio. That's when he had really needed someone to talk with. Before saying goodbye, Reverend Thompson told Walter that he expected to see him in church on Sunday. The two shook hands and parted with the Methodist minister heading back home and Walter walking toward the stable. There was no one about at the barn, so Walter saddled White Cloud, then rode east along the Pedernales. He had ridden halfway to Johnson City before dark. He hoped he had ridden past the Alsobrook homestead, but all Walter knew about the location of the farm was that it was along the Pedernales, east of the city. When Walter returned White Cloud to the stable, it was almost ten o'clock.

CHAPTER TWENTY-THREE

A t work the next morning, Walter's mind was still on Ada. Was Reverend Thompson right? Did she really like him, or was he hoping for something that could never happen? Walter vacillated all day. His station was far from complete, and the tracks were almost within eyesight of Fredericksburg. The delays caused by the weather were not Walter's responsibility, but he still felt that he was letting someone down, if not the railroad, then Mr. Easterly or himself. Walter wanted the depot to be complete when the first train arrived.

Sunday, Walter was at the First Methodist Church for Sunday school and church, but the Alsobrooks were not. The pastor's wife invited Walter to the Thompson home to join their family for Sunday lunch, but Walter's answer was an obvious evasion. He said he had reports that had to be finished and sent to San Antonio, but that was always the case. There was never a time when he didn't have paperwork due.

Walter almost never lied, even about small things; and he felt horrible about the excuse he made to Mrs. Thompson. He knew she was only trying to cheer him up. However, he just could not force himself to be with other people that particular Sunday, especially people who knew how obsessed he was with Ada.

Walter went by the railroad camp, where the workers were having lunch. He wrapped some rolls and a pork chop in a napkin and headed for the stable. Soon, he was riding White Cloud along the Pedernales again.

This time, he rode all the way to Johnson City. He still didn't know where Ada lived, but the lovesick Walter hoped that somehow he might catch a glimpse of her.

Walter had no way of knowing; but at that very time, things at the Alsobrook farm were in a rare state of turmoil. Ada and Jim had fought for the first time in her life.

Ada had told her father on Friday morning, before he went out to work in the orchard, that she wanted to go to church in Fredericksburg on Sunday. James had not answered her directly. On Saturday, when Ada still had no reply from her father, she asked him again.

"Please take us to church in town tomorrow?" she pressed.

"I think this needs to wait," he responded.

"Wait for what?" Ada all but demanded.

"Things just need time, daughter. You don't have to rush this business with that young man," he replied.

"I'm not rushing anything, Papa. I just want to see him again. This is very important to me," Ada explained, not believing her father had refused her request.

"He's not going anywhere," James asserted.

Ada's face turned red, but she didn't say anything else. She went into the house and begged her mother to talk with him. After everyone else had gone to bed, Naomi spoke to Jim.

"It would not hurt to go to church in Fredericksburg," she said, hoping her husband had come to his senses.

"I think this thing needs to cool, mother," he replied.

"It does, or you do?" the perceptive Naomi probed.

"I don't know," Jim admitted.

The next morning, there was an ugly scene between Jim and his daughter. The family went off to the little church at the crossroads without Ada.

She stayed home and considered riding into Fredericksburg on her own. That would have been scandalous. She would not have gotten there in time for church. Even as mad as she was at her father, she had no intention of chasing after any boy, not even Walter Oakley.

So Ada concentrated her anger on her father. She did not speak to him all week, and she did not repeat her request that he take the family to church in Fredericksburg. That Friday, most of the town and farmers from throughout the area turned out to celebrate when the first train pulled into Fredericksburg. The depot was far from finished, but at least a roof covered it.

Walter was glad that Mr. Easterly had not ridden on the first train, because the young foreman was not eager to show off his uncompleted railway station.

Sunday came again, and Walter went to church, but Ada was not there. As soon as he could politely free himself, Walter rode out to inspect a bridge at Comfort.

After a second week of not speaking to her father, Ada had gone with her family to the crossroads church near their farm. Naomi had all but stopped speaking to James as well. The family had never experienced such discord.

Following Sunday lunch, Ada helped her mother and sisters with the dishes. Hurting and feeling isolated, Ada walked down to the river, where she sat alone until sunset, contemplating another long week. She began to believe that she would have no future with Walter.

Deep disappointment had also enveloped Walter. Even so, he would not give up on Ada. He was determined that, if the Alsobrooks did not show up at church in Fredericksburg the next Sunday, he would learn the specific location of their farm, ride out there and ask permission from James to talk with his daughter.

When Walter entered the sanctuary at First Methodist Church the next Sunday, his heart soared to uncharted heights. The Alsobrook family was seated conspicuously near the front of the church. After worship, when Mrs. Alsobrook invited Walter to dinner at their home on the following Sunday, Walter was ecstatic. But of course, there was a dilemma.

Walter could not break his promise to his mother. He had told her he would unfailingly attend church every Sunday. So, he thought of a solution. But the plan Water had formulated risked the possibility that his actions might embarrass the Alsobrook family, and perhaps even humiliate Ada. Discretely, Walter got directions and went forward with the precarious plan. As he hitched his horse to the rail outside, Walter drew a deep breath, then anxiously began walking toward the door. After another brief pause to breathe, he turned the knob and entered.

Walter's arrival at the little church at the crossroads caused quite a stir. The small congregation rarely had visitors, and almost everyone knew at once that the handsome young stranger who had just entered their church was Ada's suitor. Secrets were nonexistent among the families who farmed along the Pedernales.

Everyone greeted Walter warmly after church. As he rode along behind the Alsobrooks to their farm for lunch, Walter was pleased by how friendly the members of the congregation had been. Once inside the spacious Alsobrook home, however, Walter felt self-conscious, even with the more than cordial treatment he received from Naomi and James.

The younger children just couldn't help staring at Walter, who was sitting next to their big sister at lunch. The kids giggled and kicked each other under the table so frequently that Naomi had to threaten several of her children with banishment from the dining room.

The meal went well, and the food was amazingly delicious. Mr. Alsobrook and Walter walked through Jim's prized peach orchard while the dishes were being washed and the kitchen was put back in order. James Alsobrook felt comfortable as the two walked among the trees. He genuinely admired Walter, despite the threat the young man so painfully represented inside Ada's father's mind.

"Do you like farming?" Jim asked Walter, with no attempt at subtlety.

The doting father had no experience that prepared him for this conversation.

"Yes sir, very much," Walter told him candidly and politely.

"Do you like it better than working for the railroad?" he continued.

Walter thought for a minute.

"I'm not sure. I lived on a farm all my life until I went to work for the railroad. I love our farm. I enjoyed the work, and I especially liked working with my father every day. I miss that part quite a bit," he answered.

The conversation was easy for Walter. He was confident in his dealings with older men. Walter had success, and he expected the positive results he worked hard for in life to continue, perhaps even increase.

"I suppose what I'm getting at is that when it comes time for you to settle down, do you want to go on working for the railroad? Or do you want to farm?" James asked his guest.

"As we were talking about at lunch, Papa wanted me to become an engineer. So I sort of went with the railroad, instead of being an engineer. I think Papa kind of has in his mind that Harry and Ike and maybe some of the younger kids will stay with him at the farm on Little Hatchet Creek," Walter concluded.

"Well, that's not the only place you could farm. There's still some good land to be had right here along the Pedernales," Jim suggested.

"Yes sir. It's certainly as pretty as any place I've ever been. I guess I'd have to give it some thought, but I like it around here very much."

Walter could not be more candid, under the circumstances. However, if he could have been, he would have told James that he would gladly quit the railroad and farm along the Pedernales, if that meant he could marry Ada. Walter couldn't devise an appropriate way to say those things, so he changed the subject.

"I guess one thing that could make a difference that I hadn't really thought about before is that I have saved almost all the money I have made working for the railroad. It doesn't cost me much to live, and the railroad pays for a lot of things for me. So I suppose if I did want to buy some land, I've got enough money in the bank back in El Paso to make a good start," Walter explained.

Jim really liked what he was hearing and felt more comfortable with Walter. James Alsobrook didn't want to lose Ada. However, as the two walked between the rows of peach trees, the notion of Ada marrying Walter sounded less ominous to Jim than it had seemed during the past several weeks. As soon as the men were back inside, Naomi took charge.

"Ada, I think Walter might like it, if you took him down to your special spot on the river," Ada's mother suggested.

Naomi glared at her husband to make sure he did not interfere. Jim knew the glare, knew the trouble he had been in around his house and stayed quiet. The couple walked without talking until they had moved a safe distance from the house.

"Well, you certainly were bold enough, strutting into church like that," Ada proclaimed.

"I promised my mother I would attend church every Sunday that I was in a town," Walter replied quietly, again sounding like his father at his most patient and controlled.

"And you always keep your promises?" Ada shot back.

"Yes," Walter asserted.

"And you never lie?" she pursued.

"No, I lied to Mrs. Thompson," Walter confessed.

"Whatever for?" Ada asked, caught completely off guard.

"After church two weeks ago, she invited me for lunch. I told her I had to write some reports because I wanted to ride out here and look for you," he responded.

Ada felt a wave of elation wash over her. Her soul was in flight. She wanted to shout and run. She didn't shout. Instead, she grabbed Walter's hand. Together, they ran the rest of the way to the little section of rapids along the Pedernales, where Ada so often sat. Both were exhilarated, and neither could speak for some time after they reached the river. Ada told herself that she had to regain control. So she did not speak for some time, even after she felt she could talk without breathing hard.

"And what did you and Papa talk about on that long walk through the orchard? Peaches, I suppose?" she quizzed.

"No," Walter replied.

"What then?" Ada asked.

Walter's face grew red. He knew he had to answer, but he was terribly afraid of making a big mistake, of going too fast.

"Well, it kind of seems like he was asking me if I'd like to farm around here instead of working for the railroad."

Ada's anger with her father rose quickly, her cheeks glowing crimson.

"Well, I hope you told him no," she said, holding back as much anger as she could.

Walter was swept by confusion.

"I didn't know exactly what to tell him, so I didn't shut the door," he explained.

A chill seemed to fall on the young couple, getting acquainted as they sat together on the bank of the Pedernales River.

Apparently, Ada was upset with Walter, as well as her father. Here was a man she had thought knew how to stand up for himself. Here was a man who had probably never lied about anything serious before in his entire life, who had told a lie, hoping it would help him get to see Ada. Now, Ada was furious because she felt Walter had not faced up to her father.

"Well, I certainly don't intend to marry any farmer around here," Ada blurted out, no longer caring whether she controlled the conversation.

Walter was sheepish.

"I thought you liked it here. I thought you told me that this river was your favorite place on earth," Walter offered, looking for a way to prevent the conversation from turning into a disagreement.

"It is," Ada conceded, her cheeks still red.

"But that doesn't mean that I want to spend the rest of my life here."

She finished her sentence, combining a sigh with a large expulsion of breath. Walter sensed an opening.

"Well then, where do you want to spend the rest of your life?" he challenged with newfound confidence.

Ada was immediately back in control. She knew the answer to his question. She also knew it was a trap. Who did Walter think he was dealing with?

"I'd have to think about that," she countered, giving not the slightest hint that she intended to discuss her wishes at all.

"I would have just thought that someone, whom everyone seems to believe is so important, would know more about dealing with people," she added, her voice now very measured and confident, as she plunged masterfully on with her rebuke.

"This morning you barreled into our church, shocking the dickens out of everybody. And this afternoon you take one walk around the peach orchard with my father and let him completely buffalo you. I wonder about you, Walter," she concluded.

Where was his control now? Walter had thought that he was going to direct the conversation, but now this headstrong young lady he was sitting with beside the river had just finished calling him an idiot. He felt like an idiot, too.

Walter sulked, but Ada did not give in. If they were going to have a relationship, Walter was going to have to learn right away that he had to pull his own weight. Ada wanted someone she could look up to, not someone she had to carry along. If a man could not be stronger than she was, Ada did not want him.

Of course, she wanted Walter desperately, but he was going to have to live up to her idea of what a man should be. He was going to have to outdo her father or she would just stay on the Pedernales and marry a German farm boy. Or maybe she wouldn't get married at all.

"It's time to go," she announced, standing up quickly.

Walter jumped to his feet, but his eyes stayed focused on his shoes. He thought about how hopeful he had been an hour or so earlier, when Ada had grabbed his hand and run with him to the rapids. Now she felt he was a fool. How lightning fast things changed.

On the silent walk back to the house, Walter began resolving himself to the probability that he would not win Ada's heart. He had really messed things up.

As they approached the house, Walter could see Naomi and Jim sitting on the porch. Ada walked up the steps immediately, as Walter stood abandoned on the ground.

"Thank you, Mrs. Alsobrook. It was a delicious lunch," Walter called.

Naomi was about to respond, when she heard her daughter's pointed and calculated pronouncement, a decree, really, Naomi thought.

"Yes mother, it was a wonderful lunch," Ada proclaimed.

"I hope you will invite Walter back for next Sunday," she added confidently.

"And I hope then that Papa will not take up all of our guest's time with another walk through the orchard," James Alsobrook's petulant daughter concluded.

Ada looked directly at her mother and straight past her father as she spoke. Before anyone responded, she had passed through the door and into the house.

Walter was so happy he could scream. Jim was in shock. While Naomi wanted to discipline her daughter for the haughtiness and rude manners, she was quietly glad for the way Ada had put her father in his place.

"Well, of course, Walter, I think it would be delightful if you could join us for lunch again next Sunday."

Then, with only the slightest pause, Naomi continued.

"And I'm afraid you'll have to excuse Ada's lack of manners. Sometimes she is a bit headstrong, a trait I'm afraid she acquired from her father. But that's neither here nor there. Please come for lunch and join us for church. I know that it is quite impossible for you to attend services in town and ride all the way out here in time for lunch."

Walter decided Ada's headstrong qualities could easily have come from either parent. He knew he was supposed to respond, but Naomi was moving right on, directing Jim to walk Walter out to get his horse. Ada's mother did not say it in so many words, but it seemed to Walter that Jim was also being put on notice to not say anything else that could get him in trouble. However, Jim could not resist giving in to his sense of humor. He was chuckling when he spoke.

"Well, Naomi, I'm not sure that, between you two ladies, you've given the boy much of a chance to say what he wants. I hope he didn't have any other offers, because the two of you would have scared 'em right out of him."

Walter and Naomi both laughed, but Walter jumped in quickly.

"No ma'am, I don't have any other offers and I'd love to come back next week. And if you don't mind, I would like to join you for church. You see, I promised my mother that I would go every week, when I was in a town. That's the reason I had to burst in on you this morning," Walter explained.

"Think nothing of it, and think nothing about Ada's carrying on, nor Jim's either. There are just too many chiefs around this farm," she remarked, as once again everyone laughed.

"I take it Ada gave you a little going over about our talk, huh?" Jim asked when he and Walter had gotten out of hearing distance of Naomi.

"Yes sir," Walter admitted.

"Well, she's certainly got her own way of doing things. And I guess she's also right about me getting too mixed up in her business. But if you haven't already guessed, that girl is the apple of just about everyone's eye around here. And we, or at least I, kind of feel obligated to look out after her."

"Yes sir," Walter agreed.

"But you're a good boy. You've got a lot better head on your shoulders than most men your age, certainly better than I had when I was as young as you. So, we'll all be glad to see you again next week," Jim confirmed, his voice turning mischievous again.

"Except maybe for Ada. She may have taken up with the Comanches by then."

Ada's father laughed and Walter laughed with him.

CHAPTER TWENTY-FOUR

T hat week, Walter and his men finished the depot and began framing two houses. It was raining Sunday morning, as he rode beside the Pedernales toward the crossroads church. Walter was excited about seeing Ada again, but he knew that his time in Fredericksburg was nearly over.

Jim didn't quiz Walter at lunch. After the meal, the rain cleared, and Walter and Jim went to the barn for a look at Jim's animals. Walter loved horses and enjoyed talking about them. Around the time that Walter presumed the kitchen cleanup should be concluding, Jim shocked his young guest.

"I expect if you can handle a wagon full of bacon, you can manage a little rig like that one, huh, son?" Jim suggested, pointing to a small one-horse carriage in the corner of his barn.

"Yes, sir, I can," Walter replied, a puzzled tone in his voice.

"Then why don't I hitch old Buttermilk to the rig, and you and Ada can go for a little drive?" Jim proposed.

Walter was at a loss for words. He and Mr. Alsobrook had been getting along well that day, but the offer of his buggy and horse was much more than Walter had anticipated.

"That would be very nice, Mr. Alsobrook," Walter agreed cautiously.

Soon, Buttermilk was trotting down the road toward Johnson City with Ada and Walter in tow.

"And did my father behave himself better this afternoon?" Ada questioned.

"You mean did he try to get me to buy a farm next door?" Walter teased.

Ada laughed. She and her mother had talked during the week. Ada, who did not find it easy to understand another person's view of her actions, realized that she had perhaps been too intense with Walter.

"I just want to make sure that he's right, that he's strong enough," Ada had told her mother, in conversations during the week since Walter's first visit to the Alsobrook farm.

"I know, but you can't find out everything about someone in one or two afternoons," Naomi had attempted to explain.

They had also talked about Ada's father and how hard he was taking the possibility that he might lose his daughter.

"He only wants good things for you," Ada's mother had said.

"No he doesn't. He wants me to stay around here with some dull farmer," Ada had protested.

"No honey, he just knows how badly he's going to miss you after you're gone. Anyway, what would be wrong with Walter buying a farm around here, if you and he eventually agreed to get married and if you decided you wanted to stay in the county?" Naomi had tried to reassure her daughter.

"Walter should have stood up to him," Ada had protested, becoming more animated at that point in their conversation.

"No darling, Walter knew that he had to be polite to have a chance at winning our favor," her mother had said, attempting to help her daughter understand.

She had spoken evenly to Ada without making any progress, it seemed. Naomi thought for a minute before she had decided to be more forceful.

"It seemed to me that you did quite enough standing up for both of you. What if you had gone to Walter's parents' house and acted like that? Do you think they would have been more approving of you?" Naomi had asked.

"No ma'am," Ada had replied.

"Then what makes you think that we would have been more impressed with Walter if he had carried on the way you did?" her mother had challenged.

Ada had seen some light. And a few minutes before she came downstairs to go for the ride, Ada paused to refresh her mind, recalling that portion of the conversation. As a result, Walter was caught off guard with the less intense, calmer version of Ada who emerged for their ride in her father's buggy. He was anxious and wished to avoid another slip up. After they had ridden a mile or so, Walter began to relax. For a time, the conversation between the couple was lighthearted. Eventually, though, it was Walter who turned the dialogue from banter into a more serious exchange.

"You know, it won't be but a few weeks until my work here is finished and the railroad will send me somewhere else," Walter began.

"I know, and I've been thinking about that. I suppose having thoughts about our impending separation is at least part of the reason I got so impatient with you and Papa last week," Ada confided.

"I need to ask you some things. Last week, you said that you didn't want to stay here all your life. It would help if you would tell me what you want to do," Walter resumed.

"I want to live in a city, like Austin or Galveston or San Antonio," Ada replied, with an enthusiasm, revealing her desire for adventure and perhaps even for some glamorous experiences.

"And you wouldn't miss the farm and your river?" Walter posed.

"Yes, I would, but I don't think I'll ever be happy until I've seen more of the world. Maybe someday, I'll want to come back here. But maybe after I've been in the city for a while, I won't want to leave. I don't think I'll know how I feel until I've tried," she explained.

"Don't you love living in San Antonio?" Ada prompted.

"Well, I suppose. But to be honest with you, I don't think I've spent more than three or four weeks in San Antonio during the whole time I've been working for the Southern Pacific," Walter revealed.

"Then you're gone from there most of the time?" Ada questioned, clearly surprised by the reality Walter was presenting.

"So far," Walter conceded.

"I'm not sure I would like that. I mean, moving off to the city and getting married and then being by myself in a strange place all the time. That sounds very difficult," Ada candidly admitted.

"It's something to consider. and I think I should be honest and tell you that I don't have any hesitation about living on a farm. I've done it most all my life and I like it a lot," Walter continued.

"But you didn't go to work for the railroad or give up going to college to become an engineer so that you could farm, did you? If that had been what you really wanted in life, wouldn't you have just stayed home?" Ada said. Walter agreed.

"You see, there are things I want to do, experiences I want to have, but I can't go away to college or go to work for a railroad. I'm a woman, so I can't do those things. But I would never want what I desire for myself to stop someone I care about from doing what they wanted to do. Can you see things that way?" Ada asked.

"Of course, but please understand that I wouldn't mind being a farmer, if that would make you happy," Walter offered.

"It wouldn't make me happy because it wouldn't be right. You are an exceptional man with special gifts and skills. People admire you and look up to you. Walter Oakley is a young man already doing what most people could only dream about being able to do at some distant point in their lives, if ever. It wouldn't be right for you to waste all those gifts and grow old raising peaches along the Pedernales River," Ada concluded.

The young couple was reaching toward the future. The next two Sundays, they talked the same way. Walter and Ada talked about their dreams, what kind of house they would like to live in. They discussed children, conversations that were quite serious. The fourth Sunday, the Alsobrooks rode into Fredericksburg for church. They brought a huge picnic lunch with them. After church, they took Walter a short distance away from town to a magnificent clearing that perfectly framed the hills to the west. When they finished lunch, the family stayed at the picnic ground while Walter and Ada drove over to the depot so Walter could show Ada what he had built. She shared how pleased she was with what he had achieved, openly praising Walter lovingly and beaming with pride. Ada and Walter had grown to feel that each was part of the other, that they were forever together.

Knowing that Walter and his men were almost finished and would soon leave for San Antonio, Ada finally asked the question she had been dreading, all day.

"When will I see you again?"

"I'm not sure, but I will come see you as soon as I can," Walter replied.

"Where will you go next?" she asked.

"I don't know. I guess I'll find out when I get back to San Antonio. If my new work assignment keeps me in San Antonio for a few weeks, you and your parents could come for a visit. I could get you passes to ride the train," Walter added.

That's almost exactly what happened. Jim would not accept the passes. He insisted on buying his family's tickets.

CHAPTER TWENTY-FIVE

Three weeks after Walter left Fredericksburg, Jim, Naomi, and Ada boarded the Thursday train and arrived in San Antonio, just before nightfall. Walter took off work early, so he could bathe, rent a carriage and meet the train. He had needed the bath desperately. He and his men had been building more cow pens, terrible work in San Antonio's brutal July heat. Walter was fresh, clean, and eager, as he stood on the platform, waiting for the train from Fredericksburg.

The Alsobrooks were excited, if somewhat rumpled from their long ride. None had ever been on a train before, so they were electrified by the experience. For Ada, the girl from the Pedernales with such big dreams, this was a romantic adventure. Ada was giddy as she stepped from the train. She was dying to run over and hug Walter, but resisted. Naomi seemed happy to be on firm ground. She had been excited by the train ride and had enjoyed watching the scenery of the Hill Country whiz by. But the motion of the cars swaying back and forth had been frightening, and she had been apprehensive, zipping along so fast.

Because it was miserably hot, all the windows on the train were open, leaving the passengers wind blown and sooty. But no amount of physical discomfort could lessen the thrill of being in San Antonio, overwhelming the small town and completely inexperienced travelers from the remote

Hill Country of Texas. The Alsobrooks were surprised to see Walter waiting at the station. Jim and Naomi were concerned because Ada's suitor had taken off work to meet their train, but that was momentary. Soon they were captivated by the delicious big city sights unfolding all around them, as Walter stylishly conveyed them to the hotel. Naomi scolded Walter for renting a carriage to carry them such a short distance.

"I hired the horse and rig to use during your whole visit," Walter explained.

All three of the Alsobrooks were too poised to hang out of the surrey and gawk, but they wanted to. They had never seen so many large, splendid buildings. San Antonio was grand, just perfect, Ada decided. The real shock came when they entered the hotel lobby.

"It's so elegant," Ada gasped as she looked in at the marble floors, crystal chandelier, sculptured trim, and molding.

"Are you sure we can afford to stay here?" Naomi whispered to Jim, unable to keep from gawking at the stuffed chairs and finely polished marble tables scattered throughout the lobby.

Jim lovingly shushed her. Walter had someone bring the luggage from the carriage and led the Alsobrooks to the registration desk. This was the life Ada had seen in her dreams and she was swept away.

"Oh, Walter, it's so fabulous," she proclaimed.

"And they have a restaurant right here in the hotel."

"They sure do, but I'd advise you not to eat the chili," he laughed, recalling his first experience in the hotel with Bryan.

"If it's all right, Mr. Alsobrook, we'll call for you at seven," Walter suggested, as a member of the hotel staff was preparing to lead the Alsobrooks to their rooms.

"Mr. Easterly would like to come by and meet you and he has arranged to take us to a restaurant for dinner," Walter told his special visitors.

At seven, Walter and Mr. Easterly were back in the hotel lobby, where they found the Alsobrooks refreshed, dressed in their finest clothes and eagerly anticipating the coming adventure. As soon as everyone had been introduced, Ada grabbed Walter's sleeve and pulled him away from the crowd.

"Walter, there is a bathtub right in our room and they bring you all the hot water you want. This is the most splendid place!" she whispered ecstatically.

The restaurant was only three blocks from the hotel. But the walk took almost twenty minutes, because Ada and Naomi had to stop at every window with a dress, linens, or dishes to admire and comment.

Jim was concerned that Mr. Easterly would lose patience. To the contrary, Walter's gracious boss was tremendously enjoying watching Ada's and Naomi's excitement. Walter had only seen his boss laugh two or three times before, when James Oakley had told him a story about something funny that had happened on their Little Hatchet farm. But on this evening, San Antonio was filled with Bill Easterly's laughter.

Walter was quite at ease around Mr. Easterly. There was a special relationship between them, and it was obvious to the Alsobrooks. After the group was seated inside the restaurant, it was Mr. Easterly who spoke first.

"I am so pleased that you accepted my invitation for dinner. My wife died some years ago, before I came to Texas. We never had any children. So when Walter told me he had guests coming from out of town, I asked if I could impose and entertain them. Walter's family is so far away, so I promised his father, if he would let him come to San ..." he was telling the Alsobrooks, when Mr. Easterly noticed a waiter standing beside him holding a bottle of wine.

"Sorry to interrupt, Mr. Easterly," the immaculately dressed and groomed server apologized.

Mr. Easterly looked at the waiter.

"Mrs. Alsobrook is a Christian woman, and we wouldn't want to do anything to offend," the railroad executive announced, then turned to face Ada's mother.

"Mrs. Alsobrook," Mr. Easterly addressed Naomi.

"It is customary in a restaurant like this to have wine with dinner, but we wouldn't ..." but Naomi spoke before Walter's boss could finish his explanation.

"Certainly, Mr. Easterly. You men go ahead. Of course, it's not an appropriate thing for ladies," Naomi added quickly.

"Of course," Mr. Easterly agreed with a deferential smile.

"That's quite nice," Mr. Easterly said, once again speaking to the waiter, who was holding a bottle of excellent Bordeaux.

"But I seem to remember that you had that same vineyard in a '72," Walter's boss hinted.

"Oh yes, Mr. Easterly," the waiter beamed, before quickly disappearing to retrieve the requested vintage.

"Well, as I was saying, I promised James, Walter's father, that I would look after Walter like my own son and that's turned out to be a delight. In all the years I've been building railroads, and that's a long time now, I've never seen anyone like him," Mr. Easterly proclaimed, glancing at Walter, whose face had turned completely red.

Again, it was Naomi who spoke.

"We also think Walter is a very fine young man," she concurred.

By that time, the wine had arrived. Mr. Easterly tasted it.

"Excellent," he remarked to the waiter, who began pouring for the men, including Walter, who had never tasted wine before.

After his second sip, Walter began to feel hot, just as he might have had he been working at the cattle pens. He pushed his glass back slightly, deciding to go very easy. The wine made him feel lightheaded, and Walter didn't want anything to spoil his special and critically important evening with Ada.

Jim and Mr. Easterly struck up a conversation and the rest of the table listened attentively, as the two men explored with each other how they had gotten to Texas, what they had done during the Civil War, and all the big expectations they had for Texas in the future.

Walter was amazed to learn that Mr. Easterly had been a colonel in charge of a Union Army engineering brigade. To Walter's great surprise, the revelation didn't seem to bother Jim at all, and the conversation continued without a hitch.

Everyone in the restaurant seemed to know and like Mr. Easterly. For his guests, the dinner was unlike any experience they had known. If Mr. Easterly had meant to impress Ada on Walter's behalf, he had certainly succeeded. Walter tried two more tiny sips of the wine, then gave it up entirely. Mr. Easterly noticed, smiled, but said nothing.

After dinner, Mr. Easterly led his party on a walk along San Antonio's beautiful river. Walter and Ada at last could talk. She went on and on about dinner and the hotel, so Walter listened. She seemed mildly disappointed when Walter admitted he had never stayed in the hotel, only eaten chili there once; but she was as happy as she had ever been and willingly gave Walter credit for her joy.

Walter should have been content, but he found something to be cautious about.

"You know, I'm glad to see you so happy, but life in San Antonio isn't always like this. Mostly, Mr. Easterly and I just work. I've never been to that restaurant before," Walter admitted.

Ada laughed.

"But don't you have dreams?" she prodded.

"I suppose, but I never dreamed of eating a supper like that," Walter confessed.

Ada's laughter became uncontrollable for several minutes. While she worked to recover her composure, Ada took Walter's hand as they strolled along the riverbank.

"It has been the most wonderful evening of my life, but I don't expect all our nights to be like this," Ada told him, but then, mischief got the better of her.

She just couldn't resist teasing her wide-eyed companion.

"Maybe Papa is right. Maybe you should buy a farm on the Pedernales." Ada laughed, squeezing Walter's hand.

He didn't mind the teasing at all. He was walking beside the river with the most beautiful woman in San Antonio, and she was holding his hand. Nothing could have been more special. Things continued at a dizzying pace for the young couple. Walter worked Friday; but Friday night, the four of them enjoyed another excellent dinner at the Alsobrooks' hotel.

Following the meal, they walked past every store window in San Antonio, so the ladies could see absolutely all the city's delights. After their window-shopping marathon, they found a place to sit and talk in a park a few blocks from the hotel.

Naomi and Jim kept a discreet distance from the young couple. Ada's parents were enjoying themselves in a special way. They had courted during harsh times following the Civil War and they'd never had the opportunity to enjoy something as exhilarating as their San Antonio adventure.

Perhaps things were going too well. When Walter woke Saturday morning, a note was waiting, asking him to come to Mr. Easterly's office. Walter worried there might be a train wreck or other emergency that would take him out of San Antonio. Or, even worse, that he had done something to displease Mr. Easterly.

Walter almost ran to the office. When he arrived, he was relieved to find his boss with a broad grin on his face. Walter was not used to seeing Mr. Easterly like that.

"What's wrong?" Walter asked as soon as he entered the office.

"Sit down, please Walter, and thank you for coming," Mr. Easterly began.

"Ada is a delightful young lady, and the Alsobrooks are fine people. I can't recall when I had a better time than at dinner Thursday night."

"Thank you very much for arranging the dinner," Walter interjected.

"It was a great experience for all of us."

"It was nothing, son, and it brought me great pleasure," Mr. Easterly said.

"Now, the reason I asked you to stop by before work is to request your permission to meddle in your business a little bit further.

"What I'm about to say has nothing to do with work, and if you want to tell me to butt out, just do it and nothing else will ever be said of it. Do you understand?" Mr. Easterly asked.

"Yes sir," Walter replied, feeling a little nervous about the conversation, because Mr. Easterly sounded so serious.

"If you don't mind my asking, Mr. Alsobrook seems more than a little concerned about the prospect of losing his daughter to you in marriage. Do I have that right? And remember, you can tell me it's none of my business, if you want," Walter's boss proceeded, cautiously.

"I don't mind answering at all. At first, I thought it was me. But after a while, it seemed like Mr. Alsobrook just doesn't think much of the idea of anybody marrying his daughter," Walter responded.

"Well, you see, that's my point," Mr. Easterly picked up.

"If you had grown up down the road from the Alsobrooks, then he would not only have known you all your life, he would have had dealings with your father. He would have known your family and certainly would have held them in high regard.

"In a case like yours, Jim would probably have gone to your father, and they could have talked about things, but your father is too far away to make that practical.

"So if I have your permission, I propose to call on Mr. Alsobrook, take him to lunch and have a talk with him about you and what I think your future is. I believe it could help, but feel completely free to tell me no," Mr. Easterly said.

"I think it's a great idea," Walter agreed quickly and enthusiastically.

"Mr. Alsobrook seemed to really enjoy talking with you. He didn't even get mad when you told him you had been a Yankee ... I mean Union officer," Walter corrected himself, feeling completely embarrassed by his mistake, an error that produced a burst of laughter from his boss.

"All right then, I'll send word over to his hotel that I'd like to see him for lunch before they get out and about for the day. It might give Ada and her mother some time to go shopping.

"Do you think I should include a couple of suggestions of places to shop in my note?" he asked Walter.

"Yes sir. I think they would appreciate that, even though I have already walked them by every store in town two or three times," Walter said, bringing more laughter from Bill Easterly.

"And Walter, I don't think it would hurt you to take off a couple of hours early today, so you can spend more time with them," Walter's boss explained.

"No sir. I don't think that would be a good idea. They were pretty sure you were going to fire me for taking off early, when I met their train."

Once again, Mr. Easterly was chuckling.

"Well, I could explain to them that it was my idea," he tried.

"No sir. I believe they're pretty much like my family. On the farm, we just figure, if the sun is up, you should be working," Walter stated flatly.

"I'll accept your judgment on that, but you're sure you don't mind if I talk with Mr. Alsobrook?" Mr. Easterly asked, just to make certain.

"I believe it's a terrific idea," Walter reassured his boss.

CHAPTER TWENTY-SIX

T he two men met for lunch and had a great talk. Before Walter left work, he received another note from Mr. Easterly, asking him to come by the office before he went to his boarding house. Walter did as he was asked, afraid that this time Mr. Easterly had bad news about his meeting with Jim.

"What's wrong?" Walter asked as soon as he entered the office.

"Nothing at all. We had a fine visit at lunch. Mr. Alsobrook thinks the world of you. But in the end, he told me that he would not even think of allowing his daughter to marry someone whose family he had not met," Mr. Easterly responded, displaying a smile meant to convey reassurance.

"What did you say to that?" Walter asked nervously.

"I assured him that your father was as fine a man as I've ever met. And judging by your manners and the way you behave, I believe your mother to be even nicer. I also suggested that when he got ready, I could send rail passes to your mother and father and everyone could meet in San Antonio," Walter's boss explained.

"How did he react?" Walter asked.

"He said he wouldn't hear of putting them out like that, and he could not accept a gift of that magnitude," Mr. Easterly answered.

"I know. He wouldn't even let me provide passes for them to ride to San Antonio. So, what can be done?" Walter asked, clearly discouraged.

"We talked things over some more and we discussed the idea of Jim going to New Mexico sometime, if you didn't object."

"Of course, I wouldn't object. But what will Ada say? I haven't even asked for her hand or anything," Walter explained.

"I see. And I wouldn't rush that, if I were you. Jim hasn't gotten used to the idea of losing his daughter, not to you or anyone else," Mr. Easterly responded, in a thoughtful tone.

"There was one other thing," Mr. Easterly continued.

Walter's heart sank, certain this was bad news.

"Jim would feel better, unless you have an objection, if I wrote your parents about our visit and gave them my impressions of Ada and her family. Have you written to your family about Ada?" Mr. Easterly asked.

"No sir. They don't get mail until Papa goes into El Paso for the first time in the fall," Walter answered.

"I think they should read your letter before they get one from me. That is, if you don't mind my writing them," Mr. Easterly said.

"No, I would like for you to write. But I'm not sure Ada is going to like any of this," Walter added.

"Jim felt the same way, but I don't think he's going to give in. If you two decide you want to get married and you want his blessing, I'm convinced you're going to have to do things his way," Mr. Easterly submitted.

"That's fine with me, but I don't think Ada is going to care for it," Walter remarked.

"I'll let you work on that part. I hope I didn't cause you any problems," Mr. Easterly told Walter.

"No sir. I appreciate your help. I just don't know what to do about Ada and her father," Walter admitted.

"Well, good luck. And now, I would guess that you had better get ready," Mr. Easterly suggested, as he stood up.

Walter went quickly home, bathed and changed into his suit. He worried constantly until he reached the hotel. As soon as Ada and her mother walked down the stairs, Walter forgot the concerns he had taken away from his conversations with his boss.

Ada was absolutely devastating in the new dress she and her mother had spent the afternoon picking out. When Walter looked at her, he couldn't speak. He could hardly breathe.

They had another mystical evening, topped with a second walk along the San Antonio River. By bedtime, Walter had all but forgotten his conversations with Mr. Easterly and lost track of Jim's misgivings. He could think of nothing but Ada.

The lingering excitement of the evening kept Walter awake; but when he did finally nod off, he slept more deeply than usual. He was awakened by a knock on his door from Mrs. Schmidt. Walter had never, during his entire stay in her home, slept late, and his landlady was concerned.

"Walter, you had better get going. I saved you some breakfast," Mrs. Schmidt called through the closed door.

"I'm sorry, Mrs. Schmidt," he apologized, noticing from the clock on the buffet cabinet that it was after eight when Walter walked into the dining room.

"I know. I think it's because you were probably too excited to sleep last night. You came in very late," she added with a broad smile, her words and expressions bringing a blush to Walter's face.

"I saved you some sausage and biscuits and I'll fix you some eggs," Mrs. Schmidt said, in her noticeable German accent.

It was Mrs. Schmidt, who had suggested the plans for Walter's last day in San Antonio with the Alsobrooks. When Walter returned to the dining room dressed for church, the huge picnic basket she had promised was waiting on the table covered with a linen cloth.

"Hurry, or you will be late for church," she cautioned.

Walter sat a proper distance to the left of Ada during worship. He permitted himself an internal chuckle as he looked around the congregation at the young ladies he had been afraid to speak to when he had visited their families for lunch.

When church ended, Walter hoped for a fast escape; but Jim lingered to talk with the minister, missing no chance to investigate his potential future son-in-law's background.

Jim's unconcealed interview of the genial and cooperative clergyman gave Mrs. Wilmont an opportunity to squeeze onto the steps and introduce herself and Rachel. Looking directly at Ada, she told the Alsobrooks that Walter had been invited to the Wilmont home for Sunday dinner several times.

Ada could hardly keep from laughing aloud, as Walter's face bloomed redder with each word Mrs. Wilmont spoke. Finally, the minister stepped in front of Mrs. Wilmont and freed Walter and the Alsobrooks.

As soon as the family took their seats and Walter put the surrey in motion, Ada burst into laughter.

"Mother, Rachel is quite handsome, don't you think?" Ada teased.

During an earlier conversation in Fredericksburg, Walter had confessed to Ada how Mrs. Wilmont had pursued him, and how he had been terrified to speak to Rachel when the two of them had been alone. To Walter's surprise, it was Jim who came to his rescue.

"Well, you're right about that daughter. She is a beautiful young lady," and Jim emphasized the word beautiful.

"But her mother could have talked our Savior right down from the cross."

Uncontrollable laughter flashed through the carriage, taking Walter off the hook.

Walter selected a shady spot outside the gates of the *Mission de San José*. Several dozen groups were scattered in clusters under the oaks with their picnics spread about. The chatter was lighthearted as everyone enjoyed the stroll through the old mission.

Driving back to town, Walter circled the spreading city so his guests could see some of the extravagant new homes.

"These places are so big! No one could possibly need so much room," Naomi exclaimed in total disbelief.

CHAPTER TWENTY-SEVEN

That evening's walk led the Alsobrooks and Walter back to the park they had enjoyed so much, two nights earlier. The San Antonio adventure would end soon. Walter and Ada needed time to make plans and Walter knew he must tell Ada about his conversations with Mr. Easterly.

"I'm so glad you have enjoyed yourself on the visit," Walter began.

"Oh I have, so very much. It's been the best time of my life and I wish it could go on forever," Ada proclaimed, squeezing both of Walter's hands to emphasize her feelings, as tiny tears of joy formed in her eyes and threatened to flow onto her cheeks.

"Then you must promise me something," Walter said, observing as Ada's face tightened.

"Promise?" he repeated, gently.

"Oh, all right," she gave in, permitting a slight smile to show.

"You must promise that you won't get angry with me. There are some things that I have to tell you. You won't like what I'm going to pass along, but we have to talk about these things, and I need your promise that you won't get mad," Walter continued.

Ada pouted for a second or two, but relented.

"Yes, I promise. But, if this is something else my father has done, I may have to scream," she hedged.

"You can't do that. We have to work our way through these things. I don't want your father to feel bitter toward me. So, you have to help me find the right way to handle things, even if you don't get what you want," Walter cautioned.

Ada clearly did not like what she was hearing. Walter began, speaking calmly, but firmly.

"Mr. Easterly has been talking with your father and there are a couple of things your father wants to do. He wants Mr. Easterly to write a letter to my parents, telling them how he feels about us and giving them his impressions of you and your family," Walter explained.

Ada remembered her promise and spoke evenly, almost whispering.

"Walter, I think you should do that," she said.

"I will, but your father will feel better, if Mr. Easterly writes as well," Walter explained, then paused to allow Ada time to become comfortable with the first request, before he continued.

"Your father also wants to go to New Mexico to meet my folks," Walter said, ready for an explosion.

Ada sat silent as a stone. A promise was a promise, but Walter could see blood rushing into Ada's face, even in the dark. More than a minute passed, before she was composed enough to speak.

"And you agreed to this?" she asked.

"Mr. Easterly is convinced, that we will never obtain your father's approval in any other way," Walter explained.

"And how will your folks feel with my father going all the way out there and barging in on them?" Ada challenged, struggling to keep her anger from boiling over.

"They won't mind at all. As a matter of fact, I think they are likely to feel better about things, if they meet him. This is the way good parents feel about their children," Walter offered.

"I'm not a child, and Papa should quit trying to tell me what's best for me," Ada asserted.

They sat quietly for a long time. Walter was worried that he had mishandled things, but he could find nothing else to say. After a long silence, Ada posed a question that traumatized her young suitor.

"Do you think I'm prettier than Rachel Wilmont?" she asked.

"Yes," Walter answered.

"Do you think I'm prettier, because of how I look? Or do you think I'm prettier, because you love me?"

Walter was in shock, certain that he could not speak; but he knew he must.

"Ada, you are the prettiest woman I have ever seen." he managed, surprised to hear his own voice.

"I'm glad, but you didn't answer my question. I want to know," Ada confided warmly, while simultaneously revealing a vulnerability Walter had never seen in her before.

"Know what?" Walter stumbled, stalling for time.

"If you didn't love me would you still think I am prettier than Rachel?" she repeated, patiently.

"Yes," Walter acknowledged, his voice breaking as he spoke.

"Then you do love me?" Ada continued.

Walter hesitated for as long as he could.

"Yes," he managed finally, but his voice was barely a whisper.

"Is that so frightening, then?" she asked.

"Yes," he whispered, again.

"Are you afraid of me?" she asked.

"No," he replied, his voice slightly stronger.

"Then you must be afraid of being in love with me?" Ada suggested.

"I guess," Walter agreed, not knowing what else to say, speaking quietly, and only because he knew he must answer.

"Can you tell me that you love me?" she asked gently.

Walter could not sit still, could not run and he was certain he could not speak.

"I don't think so," he managed finally, in his weakest whisper of the night.

"But I thought that you were not afraid of anything," Ada asked.

Walter was silent for a long time, as Ada waited for his courage to take control of his voice. When he did not speak after several minutes, Ada resumed.

"My father told me some stories yesterday that Mr. Easterly told him at lunch," she began.

"He told me that you had chased a band of Apache warriors, who stole your little brother, that you kept chasing them even, after they shot you, that you chased them until you got him back.

"He said that last year, you tied up two Comanches, who attacked you and tried to steal your horse. And he said that you whipped a grown man five years older than you with one move, when he jumped on you, when you were just sixteen.

"Are these things true?" Ada inquired.

Walter's entire face was covered with perspiration. He was overwhelmed by a feeling that he was not going to be able to breathe much longer, and he was desperate.

"Yes," he managed to say, exhausting what little air remained in his lungs.

"You are not afraid of Comanches, but you are afraid to tell me you love me?" she asked.

Noticing how dreadful Walter looked, Ada put her right arm around his neck and used her left hand on his cheek to lay his head on her shoulder.

"You poor dear," Ada said. "You must love me, very deeply."

"I do, more than anything," Walter told her, shocked that his voice had returned.

"I do love you," he was able to announce.

"I love you, too. I love you very much," Ada told her wonderful young man.

"And if you ever get up enough nerve to ask me, I would be very proud to be your wife."

Walter wanted to scream for joy. He wanted to run around the square and shout. He wanted to sing, even though he never sang, not even on the trail sitting around the campfire. He wanted to tell everyone he could find how much he loved this completely beautiful young woman. Then he opened his eyes and realized the cloth of Ada's sleeve was in his eyes. He started to jerk his head up but held back. He took her forearm in his hand, easing the too tight grip she had on his head. Silence returned. Eventually, it was Ada who again spoke first.

"How come you didn't tell me about the Indians?" she asked.

Walter had relaxed and could speak almost normally.

"I don't know. I wouldn't have wanted you to think I had made it up, I

LITTLE HATCHET • 185

guess. And I wouldn't want you to think I was a braggart," he answered, truthfully.

"I thought I had you all figured out, but I guess that's one of the things I've learned this weekend. You are more complicated than I thought," Ada said, smiling, her face reflecting calmness and warm admiration.

"I've learned that, and I've learned that you really are shy. I thought that was just an act, but it's not. You are very, very shy," Ada admitted.

Walter didn't think of himself as shy. Because in his mind, he was like everyone else in his family. For the Oakleys, it wasn't uncommon for the entire household to go for long periods without conversation. Walter had to admit to himself, that he still knew very little about the world, even three years after he had left the Little Hatchet.

"You are so very beautiful. I can't believe how lucky I am to have found you," Walter told Ada.

Suddenly, he seemed to possess abundant boldness. For the first time since he had known her, Walter took Ada's right hand and held it tenderly in both of his. He looked directly into her eyes and a tiny tear rolled down Ada's cheek. This time it was she who could not speak. When they looked up, Jim and Naomi were standing by them.

"Come on children, it's late," Naomi said, softly.

"Walter, we have had such a wonderful time here. I never imagined anything like this, and I hope that you will find some way to convey to Mr. Easterly how much we appreciate everything he has done for us," Naomi said, as the four began walking back to the hotel.

"I will, and I think he has enjoyed this as much as we have. Like I told Ada the other night, all he and I have ever done, until this weekend, is work. I haven't seen him laugh as much in three years, as he has in the three days you have spent with him," Walter offered.

They walked in silence until they reached the hotel door. That was when Jim spoke up to close out the evening.

"Thank you, Walter. Like mother said, we'd never imagined we could have such a time as this."

"I have had a wonderful time, too. Thank you so much for bringing Ada to visit," Walter said, beginning to turn for his walk home, then hesitating, stopping, and turning to face the Alsobrooks.

"I'll pick you up for the train in the morning. Mr. Easterly absolutely insisted and I want very much to do it, as well," he added, anticipating Mr. and Mrs. Alsobrooks' protest.

"Goodnight," they all called out, more or less in unison.

The next morning, Walter delivered the Alsobrooks to the train. He wouldn't see Ada in Fredericksburg again until September. Following that amazing visit, Walter wrote his letter to his parents as soon as he returned to San Antonio, telling them about Ada and spelling out the sequence of events that would follow. Mr. Easterly waited a month, then sent his own letter. After an extremely busy fall, Walter could finally pay a visit to the Alsobrook farm in December.

"I have written my parents and Mr. Easterly sent his letter a month later. I want your permission to ask your father for your hand in marriage," Walter informed Ada the first moment they were alone.

Ada waited in complete silence until Walter finally spoke again. This time his voice was less controlled, but he did not fall into the whisper that had afflicted him in San Antonio, when they had, at long last, gotten to the word love.

"I love you with all my heart and soul and I want more than anything for you to be my wife," he told her.

Ada erupted in tears and began hugging him tightly. She was gasping for breath and still streaming tears when she began to speak.

"Oh, Walter! Of course, I will marry you!"

For once, it was Ada who needed time to regain her composure. It took almost five minutes.

"You know when you left in September without asking me, I was afraid maybe you weren't sure any more," Ada finally managed

"I've been sure since the first moment I saw you," Walter pronounced, his eyes dancing with joy and his cheeks red, as emotion raced through him in a way he had never experienced before.

"Papa's so busy finishing the harvest, that I think we should wait until tonight for you to ask him," Ada advised.

They spent an anxious day talking over the best way to approach Jim. Finally, that night, Walter asked James Alsobrook for his permission to marry his daughter. He told Ada's father that Mr. Easterly had sent his letter, then continued, bravely.

"If you have no objection, I would like to arrange for you to visit my parents. I could work out the details with them when I go home for Christmas," Walter suggested.

Jim agreed, telling Ada and Walter, that if all went well in New Mexico, the radiantly happy couple could begin making plans for a wedding in the spring. Jim stayed in the living room for a few minutes, then walked outside. He needed time away from everyone and remained in the cooling night air outdoors for almost an hour. No matter what words or logic Jim used in his numerous attempts to convince himself, he could not accept that it was the proper time for Ada to marry, even though he enthusiastically approved his daughter's choice of Walter as her husband. Someday, just not yet, Jim's subconscious kept repeating.

CHAPTER TWENTY-EIGHT

I t was their third night back together, before Bryan asked his friend Walter about Ada.

"When did you think you might get around to telling me that you're getting married?" Bryan teased.

A red glow seemed to surround Walter's face. But Bryan couldn't decide whether the campfire was responsible for the color, or if instead, his friend was blushing. During his Christmas visit with his family, Walter had had the same problem that he was now experiencing with Bryan. He had found it difficult to talk about his impending marriage with his parents, even though he had made the long trip to New Mexico specifically for that purpose. Walter had also made the journey to prepare his parents for Ada's father's coming visit. James and Rebecca had had to drag most of the information from their son, one small bit at a time. Walter had volunteered almost nothing.

"Well, I would think, if I were about to marry one of the most beautiful girls in Texas, I'd have something to say about it," Bryan prodded.

Bryan could see his friend was smiling, something Walter always did when he thought about Ada—and he thought about her a lot. However, when anyone asked him about Ada, Walter became emotionally jumbled. He felt something between ecstasy and terror.

"I don't know why, but I have trouble talking about her. I feel sort of embarrassed, even though I know I shouldn't be. She's wonderful. I never dreamed I would meet anyone like her. And she is, like you say, very beautiful," Walter replied after a noticeable silence.

Walter looked up, as if he were hoping to communicate something like, "I just don't know what I'm supposed to say."

"Well, Mr. Easterly spent most of the holidays telling me about her visit to San Antonio. He said you seemed to have plenty to say to her then," Bryan laughed.

"Ada says I'm shy," Walter offered.

"Now that's a real discovery," Bryan said, his laughter intensifying.

The banter continued for a few more minutes, but Bryan learned little else about Ada and his friend's wedding plans.

Everyone on the survey crew was tired. Walter made a final check on the stock; and soon, all the men were sleeping soundly. Just after midnight, Bryan woke to discover Walter, kneeling beside him and whispering. His friend's lips were just an inch or so from his ear.

"Something's after the animals," Walter informed Bryan.

"I don't hear anything," Bryan responded, coming quickly awake.

"Are you sure?"

"Yes, and it's most likely people, because the horses were very quiet, and I am almost certain that I heard one or two of the mules running away," Walter answered.

Both men quietly picked up their rifles and began moving toward where the horses had been hobbled to graze. They crept silently in a crouch. All the animals were definitely gone.

"They're gone all right," Bryan confirmed, standing erect and speaking in a low voice, instead of a whisper.

Walter was scanning the ground, looking for tracks. There was no moon, but he could faintly detect a trail of packed down grass, indicating the pathway, created when the animals had been taken away. In a few seconds, Walter returned with a lantern.

"They led the horses, and at least two of the mules, straight over that ridge," Walter announced.

"Indians?" Bryan asked.

"*Banditos*," a third voice answered.

"They're wearing boots," Antonio explained.

Bryan and Walter now noticed that Antonio was standing beside them. Neither of them had heard Antonio approach. Walter stepped forward with the lantern and walked a few steps, far enough to determine that there was a clear pattern of footprints. The toes were sharply pointed, and the heels narrow and tall. The tracks had been made by the kind of boots Mexican cowboys wore.

"I'm afraid our horses have gone to Mexico," Antonio added.

"Well they're damn sure coming back to Texas," Walter pledged, with an edge in his voice Bryan had never heard before.

In seconds, Walter had stalked off nearly a hundred yards.

"Where are you going?" Bryan shouted.

"To find those two mules that ran away from the bandits," Walter called back, his voice still hard and determined.

Ten minutes later, Walter was leading the balky mules back to the fire Bryan and Antonio had built up. He said nothing, but began immediately gathering things into a blanket. Bryan and Antonio watched in silence, as Walter tied the material expertly and compactly into the blanket. In continuous sequence, the obsessed young railroader stunned the bigger mule, stuffing a bit into his mouth. When Walter threw his saddle blanket on the animal's back, the mule kicked Walter's leg.

Just as quickly, Walter retaliated, booting the mule in the leg. Then he jerked the animal's head down to his face and stared into its eyes. When the saddle went on, the mule stirred, but did not kick Walter again.

"You coming?" Walter asked, looking at Bryan.

"We should get the sheriff," Bryan suggested.

"No sheriff is going into Mexico," Walter answered, putting his foot into the stirrup and swinging himself onto the mule.

"I'm not sure I can saddle this mule without help," Bryan admitted.

Walter expertly dismounted from his mule and quickly began saddling the second animal, as Bryan gave instructions to Antonio.

"Take enough supplies for two or three days, just in case you have to walk the men all the way back to Fort Hancock

"Try to flag down a freight train when you get back to the tracks. My guess is they won't stop, but it's worth a try. When you reach Fort Hancock, get someone to help you send a telegram to Mr. Easterly. Tell

LITTLE HATCHET • 191

him I've gone off to Mexico to try and keep this pig-headed young fool alive," he directed.

Bryan wanted to write a message for Antonio to send, but Walter had finished saddling the mule and Bryan could tell he would not wait. Bryan hurriedly gathered his blankets, a rifle, some food, and water, and threw them behind the saddle Walter had put on the mule. Antonio had not moved, and his expression signaled to Bryan that there was a problem.

"What's the matter?" Bryan asked, impatiently.

"I cannot let you go into Mexico alone, *Señor* Whittaker. You will get killed!" Antonio replied.

Bryan looked at Walter with a sense of satisfaction. He wanted to say something like, "see, I told you so." But he could tell immediately that Walter was unmoved by Antonio's warning. Walter turned his mule toward the river and the animal started to walk. Bryan looked back and forth between Antonio and the departing Walter.

"What is it you propose to do, Antonio?" Bryan asked, his voice revealing the fear he was feeling at a situation that appeared to be rapidly unraveling.

Bryan gauged Walter had already moved a hundred yards away.

"Walter, would you hold up long enough for us to work this out?" Bryan pleaded.

Walter stopped his mule but did not turn to face his distressed friend. In a few minutes, Antonio had wakened one of the other workers, passed on Bryan's instructions to return to Fort Hancock and was back with a rolled blanket slung over his shoulder. The aging man moved ahead of Walter's mule at a trot, picked up the trail of the fleeing bandits and led the way toward Mexico. An hour later, the trio splashed across a trickle of a river and out of the United States. They paused briefly, to allow the mules to drink, then rode on. It was the first time either Bryan or Walter had left the country.

"I would have thought the Rio Grande would be a little bigger than that," Bryan remarked.

Walter did not answer, and Antonio was too far out front to hear. They rode for hours through the Chihuahuan Desert without seeing anyone. Around two in the afternoon, they came within sight of a small village called El Porvenir. Antonio held up his hand, signaling for Walter and Bryan to stop.

"Is that one of our horses tied to the hitching post in the village?" Antonio asked Walter.

Walter leaned forward in his saddle and concentrated his eyes on the middle of three horses.

"I think you're right, Antonio," he decided, after painstakingly studying the horses.

"Then I think we should go to that house over there, instead of riding into the village," Antonio suggested.

"How come?" Bryan asked, wiping sweat from his forehead.

"If the *banditos* spot two Anglos riding mules, it could mean trouble. For sure, it would be much harder to find where they have hidden the rest of the horses."

In a few minutes, Antonio signaled for another stop, about a hundred yards in front of the door of the adobe farmhouse.

"*Buenos tardes,*" Antonio called, standing about halfway between the two mules with riders and the house.

"Is anyone home?" he asked in Spanish.

In less than a minute, a tiny man walked warily out of his house. He was about thirty years old and wore a *serape* and a straw hat with a broad brim and a tall crown. The man had been asleep. He stopped about ten feet outside his door. He did not speak, but looked suspiciously at Bryan and Walter.

"We would like to water our animals. And with your permission, I would like for my friends to wait outside your home, while I walk into the village," Antonio explained to the man in Spanish.

"We will gladly pay," Antonio added, after a moment of silence.

The man seemed to consider the offer. Antonio decided it might help to show him some money. So, he pulled a bandana from his pocket and opened it, revealing some copper and silver coins. The man stared at Bryan and Walter for a moment, then walked nearer to Antonio so he could see the coins up close.

"Twenty cents American," he said softly, apparently hoping that Bryan and Walter could not hear.

Bryan thought he had understood what the little man had said.

"Give him a quarter," Bryan called to Antonio, startling the man and causing him to jump back.

Antonio handed over a quarter. When the man took it, Antonio displayed a second quarter.

"I would also like to borrow your *serape* and *sombrero* for my trip into town. I will give them back to you, when I return," Antonio explained.

The man accepted the second quarter. He took off his hat and blanket and handed them over to Antonio, who put them on. The man walked behind his house, returning in a minute or so with two wooden buckets of water. He put them down in front of Antonio and motioned for Bryan and Walter to follow him. The man picked up the buckets again and led the two remaining railroad men to a simple, small, well-made shelter behind the house.

Bryan and Walter dismounted from the mules, drank some water and began stretching their legs. They saw Antonio turning onto the road for El Porvenir. While Antonio was away, the man brought some tortillas and beans in a clay pot. He refused the money Bryan offered, explaining that they had paid too much already.

"It was *siesta,* so I had to wait for people to wake up. That's why it took so long," Antonio explained, when he returned.

"I think the *banditos* have the rest of the horses hidden in a ravine about six miles from town," Antonio reported.

"But I will have to follow the *bandito* in the *cantina* when he leaves. After it's fully dark, you can come closer to the village. When you see me trail after the *bandito,* wait ten minutes, then follow about a half mile behind me."

"It might help if I had some money to buy a bottle of tequila," Antonio concluded, looking directly at Bryan.

"How much?" Bryan asked.

Antonio remained silent. Bryan thought for a moment and remembered that he had not reimbursed Antonio for the two quarters, he had given to the farmer. Bryan handed over two silver dollars. Antonio's plan worked perfectly. Bryan and Walter laughed vociferously, as they watched from a safe distance. Antonio stumbled into the outlaws' camp with the giant bottle of tequila. His performance was perfect. Eventually, Bryan and

Walter laughed so loudly, that they had to bury their faces in their hands to keep from being heard.

The long day of watching turned into a very late night of more watching. It seemed as if the bandits would never get drunk enough to pass out, no matter how much tequila they guzzled. Walter guessed it was after two o'clock, when the last of the bandits began snoring, uncontrollably. Antonio waited for another half hour, before he led the tethered horses to the ridge where Bryan and Walter waited.

"Most of those aren't our horses!" Walter whispered angrily to Antonio after he had led the animals to where Bryan and Walter waited.

"Untie the horses that don't belong to us!" he commanded.

Bryan was ready to reinforce Walter's orders, when Antonio spoke.

"No, *Señor* Walter. The bullets fired by drunk men kill you just as dead. These may not be our horses, but they aren't the *banditos'* horses either. And I have no intention of allowing those drunk men to chase after us on horses that I left behind for them to ride," Antonio explained.

Walter hated he was stealing horses, but he knew immediately that Antonio was right.

"We'll turn them loose when we get to that farm on the other side of El Porvenir," Walter said, as the trio of railroad men began leading the horses away from the bandits' camp.

They walked the horses for a mile and a half before Walter stopped to remove the saddle from his mule and transfer it to one of the railroad horses. Bryan used the second saddle and Antonio rode bareback. Bryan had something to tell Walter, but he approached the subject gently. His young friend remained upset about leading horses that didn't belong to him.

"I've got something I want you to consider, Walter," Bryan began. "These other horses probably were stolen in Texas just like ours. Why don't you give some thought to taking them to the sheriff in Sierra Blanca?" Bryan suggested.

"Let me think about it," Walter answered, after a lengthy and reflective pause.

Antonio led them around El Porvenir. There was no reason to make it easier for the horse thieves to find them. Walter figured the farm where they had spent the previous afternoon was a mile away when he spoke again.

"How do we know the other horses weren't stolen in Mexico? Why shouldn't we turn them into the law down here?" he asked.

"I don't know whether there is any law down here," Bryan responded.

"Antonio?" he invited, turning to their guide for help.

"It's not that simple," Antonio began.

"On this border, things kind of move back and forth. *Banditos* cross the river and steal from the ranchers. Ranchers come to Mexico and steal their own animals back and sometimes take whatever strays they find as well.

"Those strays usually belong to Mexican ranchers who go back across the river and so on.

"As for the law, I wouldn't count too much on that on either side of the river. If we could find some Mexican soldiers, they would take all our animals. And, if they did not shoot us or rob us, they would surely put us in jail.

"The way they see it: we have no business in their country, or at least you two don't," Antonio said, looking at Bryan and Walter.

Walter pondered this amazing account of life along the border, as he rode in silence for a few minutes.

"I guess we'll take all the horses to Texas," he said finally, but he still had grave misgivings.

CHAPTER TWENTY-NINE

The ride to the border seemed endless and bone numbing. For Bryan, the January heat was unbelievable; but for Walter and Antonio, who had spent their entire lives along the border, it seemed perfectly normal. Antonio managed to doze as he rode.

As soon as he saw the soldiers, Walter was certain he had been right. They should have left the other horses behind.

Three mounted men blocked the river crossing directly in front of Bryan, Walter, and Antonio. As soon as the railroaders rode past the collection of shabby adobe buildings which served as an occasional outpost, four additional uniformed men with rifles closed in from each flank and the rear.

"*Buenos tardes*, gentlemen. You have some papers to prove your ownership of the animals, perhaps?" a well-dressed young man in the middle of the mounted soldiers called as Bryan's men stopped their horses.

Both Bryan and Walter were studying the other side of the river, looking for any sign of life at Fort Hancock. The makeshift military camp had been built for the U.S. Army to wage war against the Comanches, Apaches, and other native peoples. It had also been intended to provide American soldiers a base to use when they were called on to assist in matters such as the one Bryan and Walter now faced. Unfortunately for the three representatives of the Southern Pacific Railroad, Fort Hancock was in pathetic disrepair and showed no sign of human activity.

Walter could see the Southern Pacific water tower farther inside the United States, but no one was stirring there, either. *Siesta* was observed equally on both sides of the Rio Grande. That probably had a lot to do with the lack of activity the Texans were observing. Antonio was inconspicuously evaluating a ridge downstream, that might provide some cover for a quick escape. However, it was more than a quarter mile away. Any attempt to flee in that direction would be hopeless.

"I am afraid not. We're a survey crew for the Southern Pacific railroad," Bryan answered pleasantly, pointing toward the water tower across the river in Fort Hancock.

"Unfortunately, our horses wandered across the river a couple of nights ago and we had to chase them down. You can see how they are branded," Bryan finished, knowing immediately that he had made what was probably a catastrophic mistake.

The young soldier in charge edged his horse toward those of the railroad men and began looking at the SP brands on the animals. When he had ridden around the herd, he pulled his horse to a halt directly in front of Bryan.

"I see that six of the horses and the two mules are branded just as you say, but six more horses have different brands or no brands at all. And maybe you can tell me why your *Mexicano* friend has no saddle?" he asked.

His voice was still polite, but the smile that had been on the soldier's face, when he had greeted the trio, was now gone. Antonio sensed the situation was out of hand and decided to explain things to the soldier before events moved beyond hope of fixing.

"*El Teniente*," Antonio began in Spanish.

But before he could speak another word, the largest of the other mounted soldiers flashed toward Antonio. In a single motion, he stopped his horse at the precise spot for the best angle and slapped the barrel of his rifle squarely across the right side of Antonio's face, knocking him from his horse. Bryan looked in horror at Antonio, who was lying unconscious in the dirt.

"Walter!" Bryan screamed, but his attempted warning was too late.

Before the words were completely out of Bryan's mouth, Walter had grabbed the rifle the big soldier was holding and used the weapon as a handle to jerk the soldier to the ground. Walter's arms were raised above his head, and he was preparing to dive on top of the soldier, who was now lying in the dust beside Antonio. A blow from another mounted soldier's rifle struck Walter's back and the rear of his head, sending him sprawling to the ground. The big soldier had regained his feet and kicked Walter twice in the ribs. The larger man used all his strength, and Walter's unconscious body moved several inches with each blow.

Three of the foot soldiers had advanced, pulling Bryan from his horse and pinning him to the ground. He felt a series of kicks and punches, as the small men struggled to pull his arms behind his back. In less than a minute, they had tied Bryan's hands behind him and stood him in front of the young soldier's horse.

"I think we have a big problem here," the soldier announced.

Walter began shaking his head and trying to get to his feet. He could not stand, but he managed to sit up on the ground, about the same time as he heard a splashing sound. He shook his head again and began wiping his eyes, which were resisting Walter's efforts to force them into focus. The man was speaking in Spanish, so Walter only recognized two words; but he was immediately overwhelmed by feelings of both relief and embarrassment.

"Lieutenant, I am Colonel William Easterly, United States Army, Retired," Mr. Easterly was telling the young Mexican officer in Spanish.

"I received this telegram from my section foreman for the Southern Pacific railroad at my office in San Antonio, yesterday morning, telling me that some of the railroad's horses had been stolen and that these three men had ridden off into Mexico to retrieve them. It looks to me like I got here precisely in time, just before someone made a terrible mistake."

Walter was no longer trying to stand. He was watching mesmerized, as his boss was attempting to single-handedly face down a detachment of Mexican soldiers who were apparently prepared to do just what Antonio had predicted—kill all three of the railroad men.

"I apologize for the lack of papers for these horses. I have the records proving ownership back in San Antonio. Our people don't ordinarily carry the bills of sale with them in the field. But as you can see, the animals are clearly branded as the property of the Southern Pacific railroad."

Walter noted that Mr. Easterly was not looking at the horses, but straight into the eyes of the young lieutenant. Walter was certain from observing the young officer's face, that whatever they had been discussing, Mr. Easterly had clearly won the poker game. However, when the lieutenant answered in English, Walter's heart sank.

"Ah, but colonel, if you will look more closely, you will see that only half the horses carry your brand," the lieutenant responded.

"How can I tell that the other six animals belong to your railroad, as well?"

Mr. Easterly looked hard into the eyes of the young man with an overwhelming intensity, an act clearly meant to stop any debate, before it could start.

"Because sir, you have my word as an officer and a gentleman."

Mr. Easterly's tone was defiant and stone cold as he spoke. At least a minute passed before anyone said anything else. The young lieutenant was staring at the ground. Perhaps he was looking for a way out, for a solution that would not cause a loss of face for his men and his country. Mr. Easterly sensed what was going on in the man's head and he knew how to fix it.

"I know border duty can be a lonely command. It's hard to know, whom you can trust, when you're young and so far from home. I felt the same way when I was just out of West Point. In a situation like this, you start to realize how lonely command really is. So if I may make a suggestion, lieutenant?"

"Of course, colonel," the young officer replied, deferentially.

"I'm going to have the papers for these horses brought out to you on the next train from San Antonio. The railroad has a telegraph right over there," Mr. Easterly said, pointing to a shack beside the water tower.

"We'll wire 'em this afternoon and the papers will be here by noon tomorrow. That will clear this mess up and let you get back to your responsibilities. In the meantime, I'm prepared to post a hundred dollars cash bond in gold to support the railroad's claim in this matter," Mr. Easterly continued, removing two fifty-dollar gold coins from his vest pocket and holding them so all the soldiers could see them.

After pausing the appropriate amount of time, Mr. Easterly handed the coins to the lieutenant, as the soldiers crowded in for a closer look.

Walter's mouth fell open in complete astonishment. The lieutenant looked at the coins for a minute, then slipped them into his jacket.

"*Hombres, vamanos,*" the lieutenant ordered.

"Lieutenant, one minute, please?" Mr. Easterly called.

"Would you be kind enough to cut Mr. Whittaker's restraints and to help Walter and Antonio onto their horses, please?"

The young lieutenant gave some quick orders. Before he had time to see if he could stand on his own, Walter felt two soldiers jerk him to his feet and vault him onto his horse. Antonio was still out cold, so it took four soldiers to lift him. They contemptuously draped Antonio over the back of his horse. They gently and quickly cut the leather straps binding Bryan's hands, and a soldier helped him onto his horse. Bryan moved instantly to Antonio's horse and took its reins in his hand. Walter gathered the leads of three horses and two mules with railroad brands and began leading them toward the river.

"I'll take those, Walter," Mr. Easterly said in a loud voice, though when he spoke Walter was directly beside him to his right.

Mr. Easterly then spoke quietly so only Walter could hear.

"Walter, I gave that Mexican officer my word that all these horses belonged to the railroad. Get the others please and I'll take these," he whispered.

Walter handed over the reins, then turned back to get the rest of the horses. If he had any doubts whether the soldiers had ever been concerned about who owned the horses, those doubts were erased at that point. Before Walter had reached the first horse, the soldiers had all turned and moved quickly away. Those on foot were already at least a hundred yards behind the mounted men. None of them saw Walter gather up the horses the Southern Pacific did not own.

When they were safely across the Rio Grande, Walter spoke.

"But Mr. Easterly, these are not our horses. We only brought them along to keep the bandits from chasing us on them," Walter told his boss.

"They may not have been our horses a few minutes ago, Walter. But they are now," Mr. Easterly explained.

Later, after everyone's wounds had been tended and the men had eaten their first food of the long day, Mr. Easterly agreed Walter could take the six horses without Southern Pacific brands to the sheriff in Sierra Blanca.

Walter finally understood that all of Mr. Easterly's actions at the river had been nothing but a show to make the bribe he had given the Mexican lieutenant appear honorable. It had been a hard lesson for Walter, but it was not over. Bryan and Walter went to a lot of trouble to arrange for an empty stock car to take the stray horses the forty-three miles from Fort Hancock to the sheriff in Sierra Blanca. When they arrived, they found the sheriff passed out on a filthy cot in his only jail cell. The entire sheriff's office stank of whiskey and stale beer. Three makeshift spittoons, half full of tobacco juice, were placed around the small office, but there was as much brown stain surrounding the spittoons on the floor as there was tobacco spittle in them. Both men tried clearing their throats, but the sheriff continued snoring.

"Sheriff, I'm Bryan Whittaker, the chief surveyor for the Southern Pacific Railroad," Bryan announced loudly.

When the sheriff continued to sleep, Walter walked over to his cot and nudged his shoulder. Walter tried poking the sheriff's ribs with his finger, but still the drunken snoring continued. When Walter shook the sheriff's arm and shoulder forcefully, the reaction was violent. Walter stepped away to avoid the slap that was aimed in his general direction, then moved quickly back in to keep the sheriff from rolling off the cot.

"What do you want?" the sheriff managed to ask finally, one bloodshot eye partially open.

"I'm Bryan Whittaker, chief surveyor for the Southern Pacific railroad," Bryan said a second time.

"Some of our horses were stolen and taken to Mexico, while we were surveying about twenty miles west of Fort Hancock," Bryan explained, then paused to make certain the sheriff was still awake.

"When we found our horses, we also discovered six other animals that we suspect were stolen in Texas and taken to Mexico. We've brought those horses to you, hoping that maybe you will be able to get them back to their rightful owners," he concluded.

The sheriff said nothing at first, but finally gave Bryan an irritated response.

"You can put them in the pen behind the jail. I'll have the deputy take care of 'em."

When neither Bryan nor Walter moved to go, the sheriff raised his head slightly.

"Anything else?" he asked, still fogged by residual effects of the previous night's whiskey.

"I guess that's it," Bryan said.

Bryan and Walter turned to leave, and the sheriff rolled over on his other side, turning his back to the two railroad men.

"Hope you remembered to hang them horse thieves," the slovenly drunk, who represented himself as the sheriff, grumped.

"I get tired of chasing down into Mexico after 'em."

When they closed the door to the jail, Bryan and Walter heard the alcohol fueled snoring from inside resume. A few months later, Walter heard the sheriff and his deputy had sold the horses to Wallace Peterson in El Paso. When he first heard the story, Walter hoped the money from the sale had at least gone to the county. However, he learned later that the two men had spent all the money they had gotten for the horses that Walter had risked his life for. They had drunk and gambled it all away, before they had left El Paso.

Walter admitted to himself that Antonio had been right. There was no law on either side of the Rio Grande. It was a bitter lesson. As the years passed for Walter, he would see that lawlessness was just part of life along the border between Texas and Mexico. Neighbors, who were less optimistic than Walter, would say that border life had always been that way and always would be.

CHAPTER 30

The first Saturday afternoon in June, the little crossroads church was covered with flowers. The Reverend and Mrs. Thompson led the group from Fredericksburg. Walter rode in a carriage with Mr. Easterly and Bryan, who had come to represent Walter's family. Judge Hecht, the mayor and all the families, who worked for the Southern Pacific came, as well.

They arrived shortly after two o'clock. The families from the church and their German neighbors were already gathering. Ada and her family arrived at two-thirty. The church elders waited with Walter and Bryan behind the church so Walter would not see her go in.

At that very moment, Ada was the most beautiful she had ever been in her entire life. Her face reflected the rich and abundant happiness and love she felt inside. Ada's gown had been sewn in San Francisco, a special wedding present from Bill Easterly. The dress was perfect, but no more stunning than the bouquet of fresh flowers she held. Jim had grown them especially for her wedding. Ada couldn't have dreamed anything better than the reality of that precise instant. It was five minutes before three. Ada was led outdoors and around to the side of the church, while Walter, Mr. Easterly, and Bryan circled the church in the opposite direction and entered through the front door. Walter took his place at the front of the church. Naomi was escorted to the head of the gathering, followed by her other children.

The building was so small, that most of the guests stood outside. Because there was no piano or organ in the church, a string quartet from Fredericksburg performed the music. As the elderly Germans played, Ada's sister Annie, escorted by Bryan, and Ada's best friend Carolyn, paired with Ada's brother Sid, processed to the front of the church. When the attendants were arranged properly with Reverend Thompson, the musicians paused, then began a wedding march.

As Jim led Ada into the tiny church, Walter gasped. Beginning with their first meeting, Walter had believed Ada was the most beautiful woman he had ever seen. But the way she looked on that Saturday afternoon, overwhelmed him. Walter used all of his willpower to keep tears from his eyes. He had never been so happy.

The time came to say the wedding vows, and Walter was so engulfed by the towering wave of emotion that he could barely speak. People standing very close to Walter heard him recite his promises to love and care for Ada. But Walter did not hear himself; nor did he hear what Reverend Thompson said; nor Ada. It was as if he were somehow detached from his body. In an ethereal state, Walter felt he was watching the ceremony from high in the back of the church. Seemingly, he could view himself standing beside Ada in front of Reverend Thompson. He felt detached from the wedding taking place in the front of the church. But at the same moment, in his trance, Walter could see Ada's radiant face. It was startlingly close, and Walter looked deeply into Ada's mesmerizing eyes.

Snap! The ceremony was over. Walter felt the touch of Ada's lips against his in a fleeting kiss. His mouth was as dry, as if he had gone days without water; and he had no ability to speak aloud, absolutely none. Walter slowly concluded he had not been dreaming at all, that he had not witnessed someone else's wedding. What he had earlier believed that he had observed from a distance was a real wedding, Walter's own marriage to Ada.

Returning to the reality of the moment, Walter noted musicians were playing spiritedly. Ada and her new husband were walking through the crowded church, then to the door, where Ada turned toward Carolyn and threw her bouquet. Walter could see dozens of people, adults up front and neatly dressed children, closer to the door, moving about excitedly. He looked to his right and found Ada was still with him, holding his hand.

Suddenly Walter, who had been unable to speak above a whisper when he said his wedding vows to Ada, startled the entire crowd by bursting out with a giant war whoop. Having shocked himself with his momentary loss of composure, Walter quickly turned beet red with embarrassment. Everyone around him laughed robustly. But no one laughed harder than Ada. She loved the outburst of emotion from her shy young man, her hero.

With Mrs. Thompson's help, the wedding party and the quartet moved away from the entrance of the church and into a shady area, allowing everyone to escape from the stifling chapel.

Outside, a pleasant breeze cooled the wedding party. Under the shade of the trees in the grove near the church, tables of food stood waiting, covered with linen. Neighbors had decorated the churchyard with flowers and hung paper lanterns from the branches of the pecan and live oak trees. After most of the food had been devoured and the children had run out some of their energy playing games, Ada asked that everyone gather under a giant oak tree. When the crowd was still and happy with anticipation, Ada read a poem that Walter's sister Katie had written for the newlyweds and mailed to Ada.

The people of the Pedernales celebrated with the young couple until sunset. Several miles from the little church on the Funderburgh farm, a charming, but unpretentious cabin, built very near to the river by an early homesteader, remained. The homesteader had moved on long ago. Naomi and Mrs. Funderburgh had spent two weeks cleaning the cabin and Jim had brought a bed over from his own house so the young couple would have a nice place to spend their wedding night. All this effort and dusty work was a special gift from the loving parents of a daughter treasured by her family.

Just before the party was finished, Naomi packed a basket with food for the night, plus bread, cheese, and fruit for the next morning's breakfast. After the wedding guests were gone, the family exchanged hugs. Tears of joy and anxiousness glistened on the cheeks of Naomi and her eldest daughter. Finally, Walter and Ada climbed into the carriage Walter had rented in Fredericksburg and the newlyweds headed for the little cabin by the river. All went well until midnight.

Walter and Ada did not hear the cabin door open. The first sign of the intruder was the big thud the couple felt on top of them. Ada screamed and Walter flew from the bed, prepared to battle the intruder. The room was pitch dark, as Walter waited for the attack to continue. Ada lay dead still, paralyzed with fear. Walter's mind raced, trying to determine what he could use for a weapon and how he might reach it in the dark.

Walter had no gun, so he finally settled on a piece of firewood he found stacked by the hearth. He stood poised, alert to any sign of movement; but the cabin was silent. After a minute had passed with no suggestion of violent aggression, Walter found the lantern and lit it. When the couple saw the big red dog in the middle of their bed, their fear changed to uproarious laughter. It was almost five minutes before Walter could compose himself enough to shoo the animal out of the cabin.

No one had told them, that a big dog kept by the Funderburghs made a habit of sleeping in the cabin. When he had completed his rounds on the farm that night, Jake, a giant cur with red fur, thick as a grizzly bear, had strolled to the cabin, nudged the door open, discovered the big bed and jumped in. Fifteen minutes after the couple went back to sleep Jake was pawing at the door. Walter ran him off again and Jake came back a third time.

As soon as Walter left the bed to push Jake outside, the dog sneaked past and eased into the space at the head of the bed Walter had left. Ada scurried out of the bed, searching for Walter in the dark. Again, Walter lit the lantern. This time he carried the dog outside and dropped him, hoping rude treatment would make Jake understand he was not wanted. Jake shook himself and trotted off.

Walter put the trunk containing Ada's wedding dress in front of the door to keep Jake from coming back. The fourth time Jake woke them up, Walter convinced Ada that the only way they would get any sleep, would be to let the dog stay in the cabin. Walter made a place for Jake, beside the fireplace.

However, at sunrise, Jake, smelling like he had spent a month in the hog pens, was snuggled contentedly among the newlyweds' feet. When Jake saw Ada raise her head and stare at him, he stood up in the bed, enjoyed a long and vigorous shake, moved up to Ada and began licking her in the face.

"Walter!" Ada screamed.

"Do something with this dog!"

Walter shoved Jake out of the bed, then out of the cabin. With the sun peeking over the hills in the east, Jake had work to do at the chicken house. So, he stretched and trotted off, feeling content, well rested and pleased that he had made two new friends. Ada, Walter, and everything else in the cabin smelled just like Jake, leaving the newlyweds with a slightly different view of their relationship with their honeymoon cottage's permanent resident.

Ada and Walter slipped off to the river for a bath in the icy waters of the Pedernales. The cold water quickly revived the young couple, rinsing away Jake's smell and the night's ordeal. Walter playfully pushed Ada out into the running river. At first, he thought her screams were just responses to his teasing. Once Walter realized Ada was spine chillingly panicked, he grabbed her, pulled her back and cradled her head in one of his arms, while placing his other arm under her knees.

"What's the matter?" Walter asked, frantically.

Ada was so terrified that she couldn't answer, right away. Her arms were desperately wrapped around Walter's neck. Walter began moving her, first to the left then to the right, causing her to hold on even tighter. Walter was searching the surface of the water, afraid that a snake or perhaps a swimming animal might have bitten Ada.

"What's wrong?" he tried again.

"I can't swim and I'm afraid to death of drowning," his new wife finally managed to whisper.

How odd, Walter mused, as he comforted his bride. Ada had lived her whole life on the banks of the Pedernales. It was her favorite place to sit and dream, but she was desperately afraid of drowning in it. He filed the information away, resolving never to repeat that morning's mistake.

Walter moved Ada to San Antonio, where Mrs. Schmidt arranged for the young couple to have a larger room than Walter had occupied. It sat at one end of the house by itself. During the summer, Walter was not away from San Antonio for more than three or four days at a time. When fall came, the railroad assigned Walter to work on a new line the Southern Pacific was building that would run east from San Antonio to the Gulf of Mexico. Ada didn't want to stay in San Antonio, while Walter was away, and Walter decided to talk with Mr. Easterly, trusting his boss and friend to find a wise solution.

They agreed that Walter and Ada would live in the first of the houses that Walter would build for railroad families in the town of Yoakum. Throughout the fall and winter, Walter and his men built the station, several trestles, and finally the rest of the houses.

In the spring, the rails moved north to Flatonia, and it was time for Walter and Ada to move with them. As he had done in Yoakum, Walter built one house for Ada and him first, then began the other construction.

Ada looked on the moves as adventures. She and Walter made friends in Yoakum, folks they were sad to leave. Then, they made new friends in Flatonia. It was not the romantic life in San Antonio or Galveston Ada had dreamed about, but it was exciting. Walter worked with his men when there was daylight and, very often, had to work on construction plans until late at night. Ada made lunch for Walter every day and that became their special time together.

When Walter needed to go to San Antonio, Ada went along, and they stayed in the big hotel. It was a grand part of their lives. Although it was different than what she had dreamed, Ada enjoyed her real life even more than the fantasy she had conjured for her future before their marriage. But everything changed in a town called West Point, when the Oakleys moved into their third home, along the route of the new rail line. A month after they moved to West Point, Ada learned she was pregnant. Ralph was born on time and without complication. Maryon and Glenn were born in Skidmore. Jimmie and Edythe began life in Alice. Ralph started school in Skidmore and Maryon began her education in Alice.

CHAPTER THIRTY

Something else happened, while Walter was living in Alice. Mr. Easterly retired from the railroad. Saying goodbye was extremely difficult for Walter. The way Walter looked at things, he had never really worked for the Southern Pacific. He had worked for Bill Easterly. Mr. Easterly was moving to California to spend his retirement years, secluded in the Sierra Nevada.

Before he left San Antonio, Mr. Easterly wrote to the railroad's headquarters in San Francisco, suggesting that Walter was a logical choice to replace him in Texas. Perhaps his letter had been too good. Walter was summoned to California and told that Mr. Easterly had recommended him as his replacement. But the men who ran the Southern Pacific believed that the expansion that would make their railroad great would happen in California. Instead of offering Walter Mr. Easterly's job, the Southern Pacific wanted Walter to coordinate all its construction in California. Walter needed to talk to his father, but it would take days after the wire reached Deming for someone to ride down to the Little Hatchet and bring James to the telegraph office. So, Walter would have to decide alone.

San Francisco was the most beautiful city he had ever imagined. Walter loved the buildings. He walked through as many as he could during the light. At night, as he pondered the railroad's offer, he explored the squares and savored the city's exciting sights, sounds, and aromas for hours. The experience was way beyond anything he had ever dreamed existed.

Walter's answer, when he finally reached it, was simple. He told the men who ran the Southern Pacific, that he would build anything the railroad wanted built in Texas, but he could not move to California. At heart Walter was in love with the life he had known from his first memories working with his father beside the Little Hatchet Creek.

He rode the *Limited* back to Lordsburg, rented a horse and rode to the Little Hatchet.

"Did I do the right thing, Papa?" he asked James.

"Son, you're thirty-three years old. I'm sure you've always known what was right, and I know you're right about this," James Oakley replied.

"I think it's time for my family to stop moving every six or eight months," Walter told his father.

"We'd love to have you here, but I don't think that's what you have in mind. Would you like to settle near Ada's folks?" James asked his amazingly successful son.

"I don't know. For fifteen years, all I've done is build one thing after another for the railroad. At first, I didn't think it would last. Then, it got to where I didn't think it would end. Now that it has, I don't guess I've had time to think of what I would do if I weren't building things for the Southern Pacific."

Walter felt better talking with his father, but it didn't settle anything. There was a wire waiting in Lordsburg asking Walter to go to the Southern Pacific office in El Paso and contact San Francisco. When he stepped off the train, Walter decided to stop by the bank before going to the Southern Pacific office. In fifteen years, he had spent little of what he had been paid. Walter was shocked to learn that he had slightly more than sixty thousand dollars in his bank account. From the bank, he walked over to the railroad's new office. There was an envelope waiting for him there, containing a cashier's check for five thousand dollars and a contract to build eight hotels for the railroad in Texas.

Walter wired his acceptance of the offer and deposited the check in his bank. In his wire, Walter also asked the railroad for two months to move his family before he began the hotels. Walter rode the eastbound *Limited* to Junction. He hired a horse and looked for a place to settle his family.

Perhaps providentially, he found a farm four miles north of Telegraph on the South Llano River. Immediately, Walter knew it was perfect, his and Ada's equivalent to James and Rebecca's farm on Little Hatchet Creek. Walter paid the owner in cash for his farm, sent Ada a wire, and began making the farmhouse ready for his growing family. Working eighteen-hour days, often by lantern light, he completely rebuilt the house and added three new bedrooms.

Walter also wired his father asking for six Little Hatchet hogs, two boars and four sows. The hogs came with a surprise: Joaquín Velasquez, Miguel's grandson. Joaquín also brought his wife and three daughters to the South Llano.

"What on earth are you doing here?" a completely astounded Walter asked Joaquín.

"*Señor* James said you would not have time to raise the pigs," he answered, flashing a warm smile that would light up the banks of the South Llano River for decades to come.

"So he sent you along to raise them?" Walter asked.

"Yes sir," Joaquín replied in Spanish.

Walter thought for a minute, held his anger in check, then asked Joaquín a question.

"How much do you want to be paid for running my farm?"

"I don't know, sir. My family has been raising pigs and making bacon on the Little Hatchet, since I was born. It's just what we do. Your father, I guess, has taken good care of us. And I guess you will, too," Joaquín Velazquez responded.

"There aren't any other Mexican families near here, and I doubt that people around here like Mexicans very much," Walter told Joaquín.

"That's fine with me. I am an American. I was born in New Mexico Territory," Joaquín smiled.

Walter's laughter roared.

"I don't think it's that easy. But, I guess, if you're anything like your grandfather, there isn't much I can say that would change your mind."

"Yes, sir. My mother says I am exactly like my grandfather. She says I have the hard head," Joaquín contributed.

Walter laughed again.

"Do you know how to build a house?" Walter asked.

"Yes I do, but you already have a beautiful house," Joaquín said.

"Thank you, but you don't. And I think those girls are going to need some place to live. I would stay and build it for you, but I have a contract with the railroad to build some hotels. I think they are tired of waiting for me to start building," Walter explained.

"Don't worry for me, sir," Joaquín said.

"I will take care of my girls. They are beautiful young princesses, just like their mother."

"I'm sure you will provide excellent care for them. But, it might make things go faster for you, if I have the supply yard in Junction bring out enough lumber for your house.

"After you're finished with it, I will have the folks at the lumber yard see to it that you have what you need to build pens, barns, and a smoke-house," Walter told his new farm manager.

"Thank you very, very much, sir," Joaquín responded in Spanish.

The next morning, Walter rode White Cloud to Junction. He found a stable for her, arranged for the lumber to be delivered to his farm, and caught the train for San Antonio.

When he checked in at the Southern Pacific office, Mr. Easterly's replacement gave him an envelope from San Francisco. It had a draft to cover the cost of the materials for the first hotel in Kerrville, plans for the hotel and a new lifetime pass for Walter and Ada on the Southern Pacific.

If Walter was no longer an employee of the railroad, it had not forgotten him, either. Walter worked for a month on the new hotel before returning to his farm for a two-day visit.

He was astounded how much progress Joaquín had made on the farm. Joaquín Velazquez was using James Oakley's farm as a pattern. He had built enough pens for the first year's hogs. Joaquín had framed and roofed his family's house, which he had sited almost a half mile upstream from the Oakleys' house.

Using scraps from Walter's rebuilding of the main farmhouse and other materials he had found in the farm's original barn, Joaquín had constructed enough temporary walls to keep the wind off his family. This was a lot more progress than Walter had expected.

From Alice, Ada's letters to her husband showed a growing impatience.

· · ·

Dearest Walter,

We have had nothing but rain, rain, rain, all spring. The children are tired of staying inside all the time and I'm tired of mopping up mud. I hope the weather is better in Kerrville, so you can finish the hotel. The children will be out of school for the summer in less than a week. When do you think you can come home to move us to our new farm? Everyone is so anxious they cannot wait another minute!

Of course, the older children think we are moving to the end of the earth and Maryon and Jimmie are certain they will never have another friend in their whole lives. Most everything that can be packed is already in boxes, but the railroad says the rain has everything messed up and they don't know when they will be able to spare part of a boxcar for us. If things don't get better, we may have to move in wagons, and I certainly don't look forward to riding all these kids 250 miles in wagons.

Please tell me you will be home before the end of June. All the children send their love.

Your loving wife

Ada anxiously waited for Walter's reply, as the downpours and flooding continued all over South Texas, throughout the month of June.

CHAPTER THIRTY-ONE

July fifth brought an end to Ada's patience. She went to the Southern Pacific depot in Alice, looking for some answers.

"Mr. Bullard, I hope you can help me," she addressed the stationmaster.

"Well Mrs. Oakley, you know I'm going to do everything I can," he answered, bracing for an unpleasant conversation.

"I haven't had a letter from Walter in over two weeks, and I know, if he'd answered any of the telegrams, you would have had them brought to me," she continued, hoping that the day held some good news from her husband.

"You know I would Mrs. Oakley, but I hear from San Antonio that the telegraph lines are still down around Kerrville. They've had more flash floods over that way. Nobody seems to know when they'll get 'em back in working order. I think the flooding has delayed the mail from out there, too," he suggested.

"I kind of figured that," Ada agreed, continuing to maintain her composure.

"Fact is floods, or no, I've got to get these kids moved, in time for school. It's past time for us to go."

"Well Mrs. Oakley, I told you that I would let you know, as soon as they could turn loose of a boxcar in Houston or San Antonio. We can't move lumber or anything. These terrible storms have just messed up everything.

"Most of the time we can't even get a train out of here with all the bridges under water or washed out. As a matter of fact, I think the railroad may have your husband working on bridges somewhere around San Antonio," the stationmaster explained.

"None of that is very good news, Mr. Bullard. So, I'll tell you what I need for you to do. I need you to find me a couple of wagons and teams and some spare horses, so we can move the most important things to Telegraph.

"You can hold on to the other stuff until the railroad gets back to normal," Ada suggested.

The stationmaster felt the ground slipping from under him. There had been a tone in Ada's voice that gave her words the authority of a directive.

"Who's going to drive the wagons for you, Mrs. Oakley? Every man I've got is out working on bridges or washed-out track. I don't have anybody at all," he explained.

"Mr. Bullard, I'm going to drive one and my son Ralph is going to drive the other," Ada announced, with finality.

"Mrs. Oakley, Mr. Oakley would skin me, if I let you go out of here like that," Mr. Bullard told her.

Ada cut him off.

"Mr. Bullard, I'm going to skin you, if you don't. You leave dealing with Walter to me. I've got to get my children to their new home, and that's all there is to it. I'll be around again at four to see what you've come up with.

"Thank you, Mr. Bullard."

With that, Ada turned and walked away. Thurston Bullard had one of the worst days of his life. He spent most of it frantically trying to find Walter Oakley. True to her word, Ada knocked on his office door exactly at four.

"Good afternoon, Mr. Bullard," Ada began politely.

"Good afternoon, Mrs. Oakley," Mr. Bullard replied.

"I hope you have found me some wagons, Mr. Bullard," Ada asserted.

Mr. Bullard wiped sweat from his forehead.

"I'm sorry, Mrs. Oakley. I couldn't find any and I couldn't find your husband, either," he confessed.

Thurston Bullard's hands shook as he watched the color rise in Ada's face.

"I thought I told you, I would deal with my husband," she began sternly.

"Well, I do have some good news for you, Mrs. Oakley," Mr. Bullard interrupted, hoping to avoid the tirade he felt certain was coming.

Ada paused, then cautiously posed a question.

"What's that?" she asked.

"Since the railroad has been unable to find a boxcar to move your stuff, they are sending out a business car from San Antonio to move you and your children. It should be here by two o'clock in the morning. I've found a man who will help me load your stuff, and if we're lucky, I can have you on your way to San Antonio by four tomorrow afternoon."

"That's very encouraging, Mr. Bullard. I hope I haven't been too much trouble to you, but this has just got to be done," Ada said, affording Thurston Bullard a small measure of relief.

"Now, one thing you said concerns me a little," Ada resumed.

"You said you would have me on my way to San Antonio. I need to make sure this car can take me all the way to Junction. My husband has hired a caretaker for the place and he can bring a wagon to get us, I'm sure."

"I'm still working on that part, Mrs. Oakley," Mr. Bullard responded.

"There are problems with bridges and track west of San Antonio, just like there are around here. But I'm sure I can get you to Junction, if I can get you as far as San Antonio."

Mr. Bullard's prediction turned out to be almost right. A washed-out bridge west of Mountain Home stopped Ada's journey fifty miles short of her destination of Junction, the closest place the railroad came to her new home. The Southern Pacific tried to persuade Ada to return to San Antonio until the bridge could be fixed. The railroad also frantically tried to find Walter, who was, in fact, doing emergency bridge repairs. Neither plan worked.

Ada telegraphed a man in Kerrville that she had heard Walter talk about. Her husband's friend sent two wagons and teams, unaware that

Walter was not traveling with his wife and family. Fortunately the stream that had flooded and washed out the railroad bridge was now barely a trickle. Ralph drove the lead wagon, with his brother Glenn sitting beside him. No sooner had Ada and her girls splashed into the little creek in the second wagon than Maryon and Jimmie began fighting over who would hold Edythe, the baby.

"Let me drive the wagon, Ralph. Mama said I could," Glenn complained loudly, from the lead wagon.

"You're not strong enough. If these horses took off with you holding the reins, we'd both be killed," the older and much bossier brother answered.

"These old nags ain't goin' wild," Glenn retorted.

"We don't say ain't, Glenn," Ada corrected, from her wagon.

"Tomorrow you can ride with me some and drive this wagon. Let Ralph handle those horses for now, son," their mother said, with finality.

Soon, everyone but Ada and Ralph were sleeping in the blistering heat. I'll never understand it, Ada thought. No matter how much or how long it rains around here, it's always hotter than blazes, an hour after it stops. You'd think I would be used to it, living here all my life.

Ada watched proudly, as Ralph drove his team expertly. He was built exactly like Walter, but Ada was sure, that when he finished growing, he would be two or three inches taller than his father. As the years had passed, with Walter gone most of the time, Ada had come to rely on Ralph, as a surrogate head for the family. The girls adored him and Ada was not aware of the ways Ralph dominated his little brother by force and fear. Glenn took the beatings from his brother and never told his mother.

"Why is it so hot, mother?" Maryon whined, on the second morning of the trip.

Ada explained how the humidity caused by the evaporating floodwater made it feel hotter, but Maryon lost interest in the lesson long before Ada finished. Jimmie played noisily with a doll, since Maryon would not let her hold Edythe. Glenn tossed small stones at a cactus beside the road. He seemed to have an endless supply of missiles. The children loved when they made camp. Cooking outside reminded them of being with their father. When he was home, Walter would wake his children early on Sunday and take them to a shady spot beside the river, where he would cook bacon and eggs for them over an open fire. Ada would not allow fishing on Sunday, and they were always home in plenty of time to dress for church. But those outdoor breakfasts were among the most special times in the children's lives.

During this seemingly endless journey, Jimmie liked it best when supper was finished. She got to take care of Edythe, while Maryon helped Ada clean the skillet and wash the dishes. Ralph and Glenn gathered firewood for the night and the next morning. The second night, Glenn scared Jimmie almost to death when he walked into camp holding a live copperhead.

"Glenn! Put that thing down before it bites you!" Ada commanded.

"I know how to hold him," Glenn protested.

Ada's movements were a blur. Before the children realized what was happening, Ada had jerked the snake away from Glenn by its wiggling tail. She swung it quickly over her head and cracked the copperhead like a whip, breaking its neck.

In another nimble flash, Ada hurled the dead snake into the campfire, where it began sizzling and crackling. Before the children could sort out what their mother had done, Ada had resumed methodically washing dishes. When Glenn reached into the fire to retrieve the dead snake, Ada paused long enough to grab the pointed end of a long-handled fork. She cracked Glenn sharply on his forearm with the fork's wooden handle. Glenn dropped the snake back into the fire and Ada washed another plate, glaring at her son, defying him to pick up the snake again. Maryon and Jimmie giggled at their brother's embarrassment but said nothing.

In the middle of the third afternoon, the wagons rolled into Junction. Ada was surprised how small and sparse the town was, compared to Fredericksburg, but she said nothing. Ada did not want the introduction of her children to their new home to begin with an unfavorable impression. A man riding horseback tipped his hat and Ada stopped her wagon. Ralph reined his horses in, as well.

"Can you tell me where the Southern Pacific depot is?" she asked the passing rider.

"Sorry ma'am, but we don't have one. There's just a water tower and a covered platform here. Closest depot is in Kerrville," the man answered.

"Is there a telegraph office, then?" Ada inquired.

"There's a little shack next to the platform, ma'am, but nobody stays there. Someone off the train has to open the shack to use the telegraph. Trains aren't running, anyway. A bridge is out over toward San Antone," he added.

"So there's no way to send a wire until the next train comes, then?" Ada asked.

"I guess that's right, ma'am," the stranger agreed.

The man tipped his hat again, before riding on. Ada told Ralph to guide his wagon toward the water tower. After a conversation with the man who ran the small store and post office, Ada realized there was no place for them to stay in town without imposing on strangers. So after getting directions from the storekeeper, Ada and Ralph headed their wagons south toward Telegraph. The countryside was beautiful, but rugged and dry, even after the heavy rains. Ada hoped Walter knew what he was doing, when he bought their new farm. It seemed too remote and wild for Ada. After the younger kids were asleep, Ada and Ralph sat by the fire.

"I wish we had been able to send someone to get this man your father hired to look after the farm," Ada told her son.

"It's not that far," a confident Ralph, assured his mother.

The first peal of thunder sent the horses scurrying. It startled Ada from her sleep and she bumped her head on the floor of the wagon that she and the children were using for shelter. The floodplain, where Ada had chosen to camp was immediately attacked by dozens of lightning bolts. In seconds, the children were awake and huddled under the middle of the wagon. Ada reached immediately for Edythe and held her tightly to her breast. The older children watched in horror, as the lightning began chasing the horses around the creek bank. The rain fell in torrents. Ralph moved suddenly, positioning himself to dash into the violent superstorm, hoping to rescue the horses from the murderous bolts of lightning.

"No Ralph!" Ada screamed in order to make herself heard above the ear splitting thunder.

Ralph hesitated when he heard his mother's terrifying warning.

"If you go near those horses while the lightning is chasing them, you will be killed," Ada shouted.

"Mother, if I don't do something, they will be killed or run away," he called over the bone rattling thunder.

Ralph pointed as two horses fled up some rocks and away from the exposed ground. Maryon and Jimmie were hugging their mother, and both were crying, terrified by this absolute classic example of a Texas electrical storm.

"Most of the time, the horses survive the lightning. And if they run away, we can find them after the storm," Ada explained, seeking to reassure Ralph and the younger children, as well.

Ada had often comforted her children during severe weather with stories about floods, hail, and colossal thunderstorms she had survived on her family's farm along the Pedernales. She had also spoken to them about her father's horses, about how much he loved them and how skillful their grandfather was with his animals. The collective effect of these years of storytelling gave her enough credibility to calm the children and to dissuade Ralph from risking his life chasing the frantic horses.

The downpour inundated the creek bank for almost three hours, soaking everything and everyone. Thankfully, the lightning lasted for less than ten minutes. When Ada was certain the lightning was gone, she whispered for Ralph to come closer. She spoke softly, so she would not wake the sleeping children.

"Now you can go gather the horses, but be extremely careful. The storm has made them very nervous and they'll be hard to handle," Ada instructed.

Ralph began gathering halters and rope.

"And Ralph, if any horses are missing, don't go after them. We'll find them in the morning," Ada called to her son, just as he was ducking out from under the wagon.

She watched anxiously, as young Ralph skillfully brought all four of the horses back to the wagons and tied them. When Ralph was once again safely under the wagons with the rest of the family, Ada dried him as best she could. Soon, the two drifted into a restless sleep like the others. It was the stirring and neighing of the horses that woke Ralph just before dawn. He reached over and poked Ada's arm.

"Mother, we need to move the wagons. The creek's coming up and the horses are standing in water," Ralph reported.

This time, Ada was careful not to bump her head. The rising water was already under the first wagon, just a few inches from the wagon, where the family was taking shelter.

"Let's be calm. Move the first two horses out of the way, then drive the other wagon to the top of that cut over there. I'll take care of the children, while you work," Ada directed.

CHAPTER THIRTY-TWO

Ralph started moving the horses and wagons, as Ada woke the children. In twenty minutes, the family had moved to higher ground. Morning brought a bit of dull gray light and the rain turned to drizzle. Ada, Ralph, and Glenn rigged the wet ground cloth they had slept on into a crude lean-to between the two wagons. Ada coaxed a few twigs and some wet grass to smolder and finally ignite. Amazingly, she had a fire and was cooking breakfast in only half an hour. The food and fire warmed the children, but the raging creek did not return to its banks until two in the afternoon.

The children were sneezing, and Ada was determined to have them safely in their new home by nightfall, hopefully before their sniffles led to pneumonia. Ralph hitched the wagon while the children finished loading soggy things into them. The horses were still edgy after the terror they had endured during the lightning storm. As the horses gradually calmed down, Ralph and Glenn scouted for a safe place to cross the creek.

"We found one. The water's no more than three feet deep and Ralph has waded it. He says the horses will do fine," Glenn called to his mother.

Ralph was standing beside Glenn by the time his younger brother finished his report. He confirmed with an authoritative nod what the younger Oakley son had told Ada.

"Very well. We'll be very careful crossing the creek," Ada declared, while trying hard to keep her fear of drowning in the raging flood hidden from her children.

In a minute, the two wagons had been driven off the bank and positioned at the edge of the roaring creek. Ada looked at the rushing water with trepidation, determined not to allow fear to get the better of her. Her children needed a dry place to spend the night.

"Go ahead, Ralph," she called, forcing her voice to sound as strong as she could.

Ralph confidently shook the reins, and the horses moved into the water. Ada would wait until Ralph and Glenn were safely across. At midstream, the horses stopped and pushed back against the wagon.

"Git on!" Ralph shouted to the horses, popping the reins hard against their backs.

The animals did not budge. In a second, Ralph was in water deeper than his waist. Standing in front of the horses, he grabbed the rein on the left side of the lead animal very close to the bit. He pulled hard on the strap, while slapping the right side of the horse's neck.

"Let's go!" Ralph commanded.

The horse took a step, then hesitated.

"Come on girl," Ralph urged, and the wagon began to move.

The team paused again, and Ralph clicked his tongue. The horses jerked forward and burst out of the creek as Glenn held on for dear life. Across the creek, Maryon and Jimmie applauded and screamed their approval. Glenn sat in stunned silence on the wagon bench.

"All right, mother," Ralph called to Ada.

"If your horses stop, I'll wade out to help."

Ada was frozen with fear and considered whether she should ask Ralph to drive her wagon across the still angry stream. I must not look at the water, she told herself.

"Gidap!" she commanded and slapped the reins on the horses with too much force.

The horses bolted into the creek. The left horse, still spooked from the lightning, slipped on a rock. As she struggled to keep from falling, panic set in. Ada jerked too hard on the reins and the mare surged left trying to escape from the harness. The wagon moved downstream a few feet and off the flat place Ralph had found to ford the creek. The mare fell in a hole. She struggled even harder to break away. As she fought, the wagon's left front wheel slipped into the hole as well, causing the wagon to dip. Maryon was holding the baby and sitting to Ada's left. She went into the water first, but Ada was right behind her.

"Get Jimmie!" Ralph screamed to Glenn.

Both brothers hit the water at once. Ralph went immediately for Edythe. Maryon was struggling to get to her feet and holding onto the baby with all her strength. In seconds, Ralph had a hold on Maryon and was pulling his two sisters to safety. Glenn was in the seat of the wagon almost as fast to rescue Jimmie. In the melee, trying to regain her balance, Jimmie had grabbed the reins to the horses. The mare found her footing and instinctively Jimmie had guided them out of the hole and managed to get the half-sunk wagon to a stable spot on the bottom of the creek bed. Far from being grateful for Glenn's help, Jimmie held the reins tight with her left hand, while furiously attacking her brother with her right.

"Get away from me, you idiot and find Mama!" Jimmie screamed.

Ralph and Maryon had reached the bank and were checking to make sure Edythe was breathing, when they heard Jimmie's screaming. They looked up to the wagon just as Glenn dived from the wagon into the water. Ada was nowhere in sight. Ralph reached his feet just as Glenn surfaced.

"I can't see anything! It's too muddy," Glenn shouted.

"She's way down there!" Jimmie screamed, standing up in the wagon and pointing a hundred feet downstream.

Ralph began racing down the bank of the creek toward his mother, just as Jimmie fell into the roaring floodwater.

"Get Jimmie!" Ralph alerted Glenn.

Ralph lost sight of his mother as he ran, but he kept his eyes tightly focused on the spot where he had seen her. Ralph plunged into the creek again and went straight for the spot. He vainly searched the creek bottom for Ada. When he could hold his breath no longer, he surfaced for a quick breath of air. For a flash, he saw his mother's head pop out of the water, fifteen feet further downstream.

"Hold on, mother!" Ralph shouted, hoping desperately that she would hear.

Ralph raised his right arm to begin swimming just in time. A huge log struck his shoulder, barely missing his head. Ralph went underwater, gasping for air. He got water instead and came up choking, spitting and frantically trying to breathe. There was no sign of his mother. Ralph used all his effort to swim to where he had seen her surface.

"Mother!" Ralph shrieked, certain that he had lost her and received no response.

Ralph kicked hard with his leg to swim farther down the creek. He could see the log that had knocked him underwater was several feet in front of him. As he kicked again, he felt something brush his leg, then a second later he was being pulled under. Ralph swallowed more muddy water, as his head went under the surface of the stream, again. Ada held Ralph's leg in deathly panic and pushed her head out of the water. She began choking and gasping for life. Several times, as she struggled for the surface, Ada kicked Ralph in the head. He was dazed, drowning quickly and unable to move. Ralph did not comprehend that his mother was standing on top of him. He only knew that he would die if he did not get air.

Ralph planted his feet as firmly as possible on some large rocks lining the creek bed and lurched upward with all his strength. Ada flew into the air, then back into the turbulent stream, as Ralph burst out of the water like a sea mammal. Ralph, gasping for breath, caught sight of Maryon on the bank in front of him. She was thrusting her sister forward and to her right, inadvertently using the baby to point.

"Over there!" she screamed to her big brother.

Through this bizarre process, Maryon managed to communicate where their mother was, as Ada flailed at the water with her arms. She was fighting for her life, using every ounce of strength and determination she possessed. But despite her consuming effort, Ada was going under, again.

Ralph kicked hard to start his swim toward his drowning mother, but struck his foot against a rock, shooting paralyzing pain through his body. There was no more time. Ralph forced himself on, quickly finding another rock and pulling himself to his feet in water that was only knee deep.

He ran as fast as the water would permit, reaching his mother in ten or eleven strides. Ralph jabbed his left arm into the creek and grabbed his mother's hair. He pulled desperately and Ada came toward him. He could not tell if she was alive. Before Ralph knew what was happening,

Ada had locked her arms around his neck and pulled him back into deep water.

This time, Ralph knew what to expect. He used all his strength to break away from her death grip. He quickly found his mother's feet, wildly kicking the water. Ralph placed his feet on the bottom of the creek and bent his knees. When he surged upward, he caught Ada's feet, held them on his shoulders and vaulted her toward the bank.

Ralph quickly ducked to his right and pushed up onto the rock ledge and out of the deep water. He circled behind Ada and grabbed her under the arms. She fought furiously, but Ralph kept his head. In a few seconds, Ada was lying on the bank, safe from the flooding creek.

"My God!" Ralph exclaimed, collapsing on the ground beside his mother.

There was almost no light left in the gray sky, when Joaquín spotted the rider coming off the ridge. He sat on his front porch, squinting at the silhouetted figure. Joaquín was exhausted from a long night and day of rescuing hogs and possessions from the flooding South Llano River. His tired eyes and mind struggled to identify what they were seeing.

"It's *Señor* Walter," Joaquín said finally, speaking in a soft voice, that only he could hear.

I wonder why he has no saddle, he asked himself in Spanish, as the horseman drew nearer. In less than two minutes, the gray twilight faded, and the man and horse were just a shadow. Joaquín stepped off the porch.

"*Señor* Walter," he called.

"I am Ralph Oakley, Walter's son," a voice called from the back of the big mare, a draught horse, if Joaquín's guess was correct.

"You look just like your father," Joaquín answered, still able to see only an outline of the rider against the dark sky.

"I need your help," Ralph stated.

"Mother and the girls are stranded at a creek five or six miles north of here. Mother nearly drowned."

"I will get a wagon at once," Joaquín responded.

"No, just bring a saddle horse. We have two wagons and we'll need your help to get them here. One of the wagons is still stuck in the creek. I couldn't get it out."

"Is your mother all right?" Joaquín asked.

"I think so," Ralph answered.

"Maryon and Glenn are taking care of her. She swallowed a lot of water, but she is breathing well.

"Come. I will get you a saddle horse, too," Joaquín offered.

"No, this one's all right. We'll need her to pull one of the wagons anyway," Ralph responded.

In less than an hour, Ralph and Joaquín were kneeling beside Ada.

"I am Joaquín Velázquez, ma'am. I hope I can help you," Joaquín said.

"Ralph saved my life. I almost drowned him, but he saved my life," Ada spoke in a voice that was weak and shaky.

"Things will be better, when we get you to the house," Joaquín told her.

"Yes they will," Ada agreed, her voice a slightly firmer.

"Help me to my feet, please?" Ada asked Ralph and Joaquín.

"You'd better rest, while we get that wagon out of the creek," Joaquín suggested.

"No, I'll feel better, if I walk around," Ada explained, before looking over at the wagon stuck in the stream.

"That creek's just a trickle, now. It's hard to believe that I nearly drowned in that! Just moments ago, it was a roaring flood," she mused, laughing quietly and rising to her feet, as Ralph supported one arm and Joaquín the other.

"It was quite a flood, all right. I have been up since three this morning, trying to save the hogs," Joaquín told Ada and Ralph.

"You must be very tired," Ada observed, still precariously perched on her unsteady feet.

"Can you stand on your own?" Joaquín asked.

"Glenn, please come over here and help me, while Ralph and Mr. Velasquez take a look at the wagon," Ada called.

"I'm Mrs. Oakley. I'm afraid I forgot my manners. Please forgive me," Ada said to Joaquín.

"We'll have a long time to get to know each other. Right now, I'd better see about getting you home," Joaquín suggested.

"Let's have a look at that wagon. Joaquín proposed, turning his attention to Ralph.

The axle was broken, but Joaquín and the two Oakley boys got the wagon out of the stream using the power of all four horses.

"We'll come get it tomorrow, Mrs. Oakley. It's time to get everyone up to the house," Joaquín said, once they had the wagon on dry land.

When Ada woke the next morning, Maria Velasquez was cooking breakfast in Ada's new kitchen.

Another three days passed, as Walter finished the emergency flood repairs that put the railroad back in operation. Only then did Walter learn that Ada had moved their family to the farm on the South Llano. When he reached Junction, Walter learned that Ada and the children had not been heard from since the wagons had been delivered to her at Mountain Home. He rode out of Junction at a gallop, anxious to find his missing family.

CHAPTER THIRTY-THREE

A ir burst from Walter's lungs, when he caught sight of his new farmhouse. He had never been more relieved. Smoke billowed from the stovepipe above the kitchen. He saw two unfamiliar wagons parked beside the barn. And the best sight of all, a small army of children played in the shade of a grove of live oaks near his front porch. There appeared to be equal numbers of Velasquez and Oakley children in the group.

The reunion lasted only three days. Walter had work to finish in Kerrville. Walter completed the hotel and wrapped up the rest of the projects called for in that contract. By mid-November, Walter returned to his farm.

Ada's appearance shocked him when he first arrived. Looking at his wife, Walter thought of how tired his own mother had looked years before on the day that Walter had left home to work for the railroad. There were lines in Ada's face he had never seen before. Her skin was dull, and even Ada's beautiful hair seemed somehow to have lost its luster.

Walter was maturing. He resisted the impulse to blurt out a ridiculous question, such as, "Are you all right?" The answer was undeniably obvious. The responsibility of rearing her children as an only parent had made Ada weary deep down into her bones, erasing all traces of her youth.

The long absent Walter encountered both Ralph and Joaquín before he entered the house.

"Joaquín seems to be taking good care of the farm," Walter remarked, after failing to devise a satisfactory way to address his concerns for Ada's health.

"From what I can tell, he has grown plenty of food for the hogs. It looks like we have enough vegetables for the winter and milk for both families. He told me he's been able to sell the extra milk and some eggs and chickens, too," Walter added.

When Ada made no response, Walter didn't know what to do or say next. He also was worried about Ralph, whom he thought seemed sullen and perhaps resentful.

"What is wrong with Ralph?" Walter asked too hastily and without sufficiently considering how to approach the subject.

The expression on Ada's face immediately reflected defensiveness. Ralph was a great help to her, and she felt as if she were being asked to testify against her son. Walter, alarmed, quickly tried to discharge some of the tension he had carried with him into this homecoming.

"My father and I worked so closely together. But today, I could hardly get Ralph to speak to me at all."

"Walter, this is not comfortable for me to talk about. But I believe that you and your father spent ten or twelve hours a day working together. Is that right?"

"Well yes, but what does that have to do with Ralph being upset with me?" a perplexed Walter responded.

Ada shook her head. She wanted her explanation to be as gentle as she could make it.

"Don't you see? You and Ralph don't spend as much time with each other in a month as you and your father used to spend working together in just one day.

"Ralph's a fine boy and I couldn't manage things without him. You would be so impressed if you could see all the things he's accomplished, things that I have seen and been part of," she explained.

Walter became intensely sad. He had worked so hard to make a good life for his family. But now he realized that a cavernous gap had developed between Walter and his eldest son. That night, as he thought instead of sleeping, Walter realized that there were so many things about his children he did not know. Before he finally nodded off, Walter decided to honor his contract with the railroad. However, when he finished the hotels, Walter intended to return to his farm for good. He was missing too much.

His resolution to fix his problems with Ralph made Walter feel better for a time. But when Walter came home for the Christmas holidays to spend ten days with his family, the crisis between father and son quickly boiled over. Christmas Eve morning, Walter spotted Ralph on the porch as he rode back from touring the farm. He dismounted and held the reins out.

"Would you mind taking this old girl to the barn for me, son?" Walter asked, smiling at Ralph.

"I'm not the hired help around here," Ralph protested before stepping off the porch.

Walter rested the horse's reins on the porch rail and followed his son, who had walked to the well behind the house. He was leaning moodily and defiantly against it when Walter approached.

"That's no way to talk to your father. If I'd ever spoken to my father like that ..." Walter began sternly, then paused, hoping to steer the conversation onto a more positive track.

"Maybe I didn't like the way you talked to me. And I don't care at all how you talked to your father," Ralph shot back.

Ralph's sentence was interrupted by a loud crack and blood gushed from his lips as the force from the back of his father's hand settled in. Ralph ran to the barn and slammed the big door behind him. Walter was now horrified at how he had lost his temper with his son. He looked to the back porch, where Ada stood, crying uncontrollably.

"How could I have done something so unforgivable, so completely horrible?" Walter asked his wife, in a voice accentuating how totally distraught he was.

"What came over me? I have never done anything so stupid in all my life."

In a few moments, Walter walked to the barn and apologized to Ralph through the barred door.

"I am so sorry, my son. I have never done a worse thing in my whole life. Please forgive me," he called through the thick door.

Walter tried his best to ensure that his tone conveyed his deep remorse, while making sure he spoke loudly enough for his son to hear his apology. But Ralph did not answer. It was three hours before he returned to the house, going immediately to his room and closing the door. Glenn spent the night sleeping on the couch in the living room, terrified of what his brother would do to him, if he tried to enter the room shared by Glenn and Ralph.

The day after Christmas, Walter knocked on Joaquín's door.

"I wonder if I could talk with you a minute?" he asked.

Joaquín invited him in, but Walter preferred Joaquín step outside to talk.

"Do you think you could find someone for me?" Walter inquired.

"Sure, *Señor* Walter," Joaquín responded, without hesitation.

"Have you ever been to Del Rio?" Walter inquired.

"No sir," Joaquín answered.

"Well, I would like for you to ride to Junction, take the train to Del Rio, then cross over into Mexico. The man I want you to find is a carpenter named Armando Henriquez. When you find him, tell him I need his help," Walter directed.

Five days later, Armando and Joaquín rode up to the house. Walter had finally realized that he was trying to do too much. Walter told Armando he wanted Armando to be the construction foreman for all of Walter's railroad projects. This move was a vital element in Walter's plan to move home to the farm and live with his family.

When the two men arrived in Seguin, Walter's best intentions blew up, instantly. As he introduced Armando as the new foreman, a carpenter named Red Berry stepped forward. His beard was stained from the tobacco juice that constantly drooled out of his mouth.

"I ain't working for him," Red proclaimed insolently.

The incident reminded Walter of his first day in Del Rio, working for Frank Granger and how quickly racial trouble had developed on that occasion. Walter looked at Red. He had been a troublemaker from his first day on the job, but Walter hated firing people.

After the outburst, Walter momentarily considered reasoning with Red, then accepted that it would be a waste of time. He had never wanted this despicable man to work for him in the first place.

"Well, I'm sorry, Red," Walter told him, reaching into his pocket and counting out money for one day's pay.

"You haven't been here long enough to do any work today, but here's your day's pay, anyway," Walter said, as he handed him the money.

None of the rest of the men said anything, but by lunchtime, they had done almost no work. Instead of telling the men it was time for lunch, Walter called them to the front of the hotel. He wordlessly paid each of them for a day, and they all walked away.

For nearly ten minutes, Walter and Armando sat silently on the porch of the hotel. With a good crew, the hotel could be finished in three weeks.

"Do you have any ideas?" Walter asked Armando.

Armando's English was not good, and Walter had never learned more than a few Spanish words, so communication between them was slow.

"If I could go back to my village on the river, there are plenty men," Armando suggested.

Walter thought for a minute. That would take at least a week.

"Too far," Walter responded.

They fell silent and Walter thought for another twenty minutes.

"Let's catch the three o'clock train for San Antonio," Walter said to Armando.

They closed up the hotel and walked to the train station. In San Antonio, Walter checked into the hotel. Armando could not stay there because he was Hispanic. He told Walter he would find a place to stay, and they would meet in the morning.

Armando was waiting outside the hotel at six-thirty, when Walter came out.

"Good morning, my friend. I have some good news for you, I think," Armando announced.

Walter was jovial, despite his troubles.

"Well, I could use some good news," he responded.

"Can you walk just a little ways with me, sir?"

Walter followed Armando around the corner to an alley behind the hotel. Armando had assembled twelve men. As Walter watched, Armando introduced each of the men, and in hesitant English, explained his skill. A big smile came across Walter's face. He led the group to the store, where he always purchased supplies. Walter bought two large tents like the railroad crews used, tarps, blankets, and some large pots to cook in.

"I think you had better find us a cook, too," he suggested to Armando.

By midafternoon, the new construction crew was in Seguin. As the day passed, town's people walked slowly by the hotel to watch the workers. The crew was housed and fed on railroad property, just outside of town. Walter slept in the unfinished hotel at night.

The stationmaster offered to loan him his shotgun, but Walter declined. No one ever actually attempted to carry out any of the threats that were made against either the hotel or the workers, and the job was completed on time.

Walter and Armando rode together as far as Junction, where Walter left the train. Before Armando rode on to Del Rio, the two men agreed to meet in Junction, two weeks later.

CHAPTER THIRTY-FOUR

Walter felt his problems at home were more serious, than those he had faced in Seguin. For his first two days home, Walter carefully avoided any confrontation with Ralph and Ralph did his best to avoid his father, altogether. At the end of the second day, Walter invited Ralph to go fishing with him, the next morning.

"I'm sorry. I promised to help Joaquín finish some new hog pens," the young man declined, showing no emotion.

After breakfast, Ralph went to work. Walter allowed him a five-minute head start and followed, taking along his tools.

"Good morning," Walter called to Joaquín.

"Can you use an extra hand?"

A broad smile crossed Joaquín's face.

"Sure, *Señor* Walter," he answered.

There was no doubt who had taught Joaquín carpentry. Walter worked as easily with Joaquín, as he had with James. He noticed quickly that Joaquín had passed the skill along to Ralph. Walter was filled with pride.

"That's fine work," Walter said to his son.

There was a deadly silence. While he worked beside Joaquín and Ralph, Walter prayed for Ralph to end the stillness that kept them apart, but not a single word was spoken. After lunch, Walter excused himself.

"I need to ride into town and talk with some of the school board members," he explained.

Ralph and Joaquín continued their work without him. The sadness infecting Walter grew worse. Ada did not know what to do, but she tried to work things out, beginning with Ralph.

"I want you to promise me you will make an effort to talk with your father when he comes home again," she told him.

"I will, mother," Ralph agreed.

Maybe in Ralph's eyes, he kept his promise, but the two grew further apart. Nearly a year passed, and Walter knew he had to try again.

"I know I've been gone a lot, but I think it's important we try to get closer. It would mean a lot to me," Walter began, as the two walked to the river, together.

Ralph did not respond.

"You are an excellent carpenter," Walter told Ralph.

"You don't realize it, but we had the same teacher. I could tell from watching Joaquín that my father had taught him to build, just as he taught me. And I can tell from watching you that Joaquín taught you just as your grandfather would have if he had lived closer to us," a desperate father explained to his son, trying to build a bond with a son who slipped farther away each day.

Ralph's eyes were watery, and Walter thought he might be reaching him.

"When school is out, I'd like for you to ride the train to Columbus and help me build my last hotel for the railroad. I'll pay you the same as I pay the other carpenters and you can do whatever you like with the money.

"When that hotel is finished, I am quitting the Southern Pacific and moving home for good. Too much has slipped away from me in the years I've been gone," Ralph's father confessed.

Walter's eldest son was choked with emotion and could not speak, but he took a letter from his pocket and handed it to his father. It was from Ada's brother Amos, inviting Ralph to St. Louis in the summer to work in his drugstore.

"I see. Have you and your mother talked this over?" Walter asked, his voice cracking slightly.

Ralph shook his head, still unable to talk.

"I'm your father, and I am very proud of you. I want to help you every way I can. And of course, if you want to spend the summer in St. Louis, that's what I want you to do."

Walter also had a thought he left unspoken. And if you changed your mind and wanted to come to Columbus with me, nothing could make me happier. That was the thought Walter kept to himself.

When summer came, Ralph went to St. Louis, and he returned there the following summer. The second fall, with Amos' help, Ralph won a football scholarship to Sewanee Institute in Tennessee. Walter moved home to Telegraph, having learned a hard lesson. There were more important things in life than building buildings for other people. He was determined not to repeat with Glenn and the younger children the mistake he had made with Ralph.

In Telegraph, Walter's days were filled with children. If Ada did not look any younger, at least some of the strain and tiredness were gone from her face.

The farm prospered. Joaquín slaughtered fifty hogs during Walter's first fall in his new home. Joaquín built a smokehouse, hired help to process the hogs, make the sausage and smoke the hams. By that point in their lives, he and Maria had seven children.

When measured by the standards of his fellow Tejanos, Joaquín was becoming a wealthy man. In exchange for Joaquín's excellent work building up the farm, Walter gave him the title to two-fifths of the farm's land, including the portion where the Velasquez house stood. His farm manager protested, but Walter insisted.

Armando kept in touch with Walter as well. He provided crews for dozens of Southern Pacific construction projects. Glenn loved spending time with his father. They fished and Glenn was happy to help Walter build things on the farm. He also went with Armando to work on railroad construction projects when school was out.

Unlike Ralph, Glenn showed few skills as a carpenter and failed to distinguish himself in school. Ralph was outstanding. Glenn enjoyed his life and his family but showed few serious interests.

Maryon was like her mother and just as beautiful. She was not estranged from her father because of absence or rivalry. However, in Walter's absence, she had become a young lady. Jimmie was brilliant, but as wild as the wind. Edythe was quiet and bright. The baby, Brooks, captivated the entire household.

In October, Naomi came to Telegraph for two weeks, while Walter and Ada went to Tennessee to see Ralph play football. Ada could not watch the boys bang furiously into one another, but Walter thoroughly enjoyed the game.

Ralph was Sewanee's star player and Walter cheered loudly during the entire contest. The game was played on Saturday. After it was over, Ada and Walter ate with the boys at the school. They went with them to church the next morning and were, along with Ralph, the special guests of the headmaster for lunch on Sunday.

While they ate, Walter and the headmaster took turns praising Ralph's accomplishments on the football field and in the classroom. After the meal, the headmaster led the luncheon guests on a walking tour of the campus.

"Ralph is one of the most exceptional young men we have had during my time at Sewanee, Headmaster Roberts told Walter as they walked.

"His mother and I could not be more pleased," Walter replied without attempting to hide his pride or beaming smile.

"And watching them play football yesterday, why that was one of the proudest moments of my life."

Ralph knew how hard his father was trying to show his pride and how deeply he cared for his son. But even knowing these things, Ralph could not reach across the void that separated father and son.

The next fall, Walter and Ada came to the last football game of the year. Once again, Ralph was the star for Sewanee. During this visit, Walter and Ralph had a serious conversation. Europe was at war and talk was strong that Americans would be in the conflict soon. At Sewanee, some of the young men who had graduated the spring before had joined the British forces fighting in France.

"I've never had much to do with politicians," Walter told Ralph.

"But working for the railroad, I've met most of them. Given what you've done here at Sewanee and with the help of Headmaster Roberts, I think the chances are pretty good that you can go to West Point. I don't think it will be hard to get our Congressman Blanton or one of our senators to support you, especially the way you play football," Walter explained.

"I don't know, father. A lot of the boys are going to England and joining the army to fight against the Germans. And almost everyone thinks we'll be in it by next year," Ralph hesitated.

"Well, I certainly don't object to your being in the army. Your grandfather was. But think of it, son," Walter urged. "You can go to West Point and become an officer. And when the war is over, starting as an engineer, schooled at the military academy, will be a tremendous advantage."

"I'll think about it," Ralph promised.

Ada and Walter returned in the spring for graduation. Finishing second in his class, Ralph spoke at the ceremony. Ada cried, and Walter had never been prouder. After the graduation, Walter showed Ralph a letter from Congressman Blanton, agreeing to sponsor Ralph for an appointment to West Point.

"I appreciate what you've done, but Uncle Amos has made arrangements for me to go to pharmacy school. He'll pay for it. It won't cost you anything. And when I get out, I'll pay him back by working in his drugstore," Ralph told his father.

After he graduated, Ralph didn't come back to Texas, but spent the summer with Amos, working in his drug store. However, in the fall, instead of going to pharmacy school, Ralph continued working in the store.

Walter accompanied Ada to St. Louis for another visit with Ralph, Amos, and Amos' family. During the long trip home, Walter had plenty of time to be disappointed that Ralph didn't want to apply for West Point.

"I would give anything if I could fix what is wrong between Ralph and me," Walter told his wife.

"I know," Ada acknowledged, taking her husband's hand.

CHAPTER THIRTY-FIVE

Walter forgot his disappointment when he stepped off the train in San Antonio. Armando was waiting for Walter on the platform at the station, and the expression on Armando's face told Ada and Walter something was wrong.

"What's the matter?" an extremely worried Ada burst out.

"It's *Señor* Glenn. He's in jail," Armando answered.

"Whatever for?" Walter roared.

"The sheriff, a very bad man, says he stole a horse," Armando told him.

"Stole a horse?" Walter echoed.

"Why that's crazy. What's gotten into Noel Johnson?"

"No, sir. It's not Mr. Johnson. *Señor* Glenn is in jail in Del Rio," Armando explained.

Walter's confusion grew with each answer.

"What in the Sam Hill was he doing there?" Walter thundered.

"Have you forgot, *Señor* Walter? You gave him permission to travel to my village with me after we finished our job in Uvalde."

That memory came back to Walter.

"Now I remember, but how did Glenn wind up in jail?" Walter asked, as the initial shock brought on by Armando's greeting subsided a bit.

"Well, as I said, the sheriff, he is very bad. I went to him and tried to give him two-hundred dollars to let *Señor* Glenn out of the jail, but he would not take it. The bad sheriff, he said I must have stolen the money, and he wasn't going to get in trouble with the Rangers, taking stolen money from a Mexican over a drunken boy," Armando explained.

"Drunken boy!" Walter exploded.

"How did Glenn get drunk?"

"When I was sleeping, I think he snuck away to the *cantina,* and I think maybe that he might have been drunk when he took the horse. He probably just borrowed the horse, I think, and maybe got lost."

"Anyway, the Texan, he got his horse back, and he told the sheriff to forget it. But, *Señor* Glenn, he is still in jail."

Walter was devastated, and Ada could hardly breathe.

"How long has he been there?" Walter asked.

"Three days, *Señor.*"

Walter turned to face Ada.

"I'll get someone to take you home when we get to Junction. Then Armando and I will go on to Del Rio for Glenn," Walter said, attempting to comfort his still distraught wife.

No one spoke during the ride to Junction. Ada got off, and a friend drove her to the farm. The train arrived in Del Rio the next morning around eleven, and Armando led the way to the jail. Sheriff Brennan was sitting at his desk with his feet propped on it. He looked up when he heard the door open and recognized Armando.

"What can I do for you?" he asked, quickly taking his feet off the desk, when he spotted the well dressed, distinguished Anglo with him. But he remained in his chair.

"I'm Walter Oakley from Telegraph. You've got my boy in jail. Could I see him, please?" Walter requested, displaying earnest authority.

"Well Mr. Oakley, I don't think that would be a good idea right now. Why don't you come back after the prisoners have had their lunch, and I'll see what I can do?" the sheriff offered.

"Sheriff, either I see my boy right now, or I'm going back to San Antonio for the Rangers," Walter warned.

The slovenly excuse for an officer of the law didn't hesitate.

"Roger!" the sheriff snarled.

In a few seconds, a man with a four-day growth of beard, stinking clothes and a deputy sheriff's badge appeared from the hall behind the sheriff's desk.

"Roger, get Mr. Oakley's boy and bring him out here," Sheriff Brennan ordered.

Glenn looked terrible. He was glad his father had come for him, but he was too embarrassed to look him in the eye. His clothes were torn and stained where he had thrown up on them several days earlier. He smelled even worse than the deputy and had no color in his face at all.

"Are you all right, son?" his father asked him gently.

"Yes sir," Glenn replied.

"Sheriff," Walter said, turning his head slightly to the despicable creature seated at the desk.

"Armando told me something about two-hundred dollars. Is that his bond or a fine?"

"I don't guess we need that," the sheriff interrupted, an impudence Walter tolerated only because he was focused on getting his son away from the horrible place where Glenn had been locked up.

"I suppose your boy just had too much to drink. I suspect he's learned his lesson and we can just call this a misunderstanding," Sheriff Brennan pronounced in a tone that Walter might have described as smirky.

Brennan paused for a minute.

"But I guess you can see that I'd just soon not have him back in my jail for stealing horses a second time," the sheriff said, looking over at Glenn.

"You can go, son. But if you come back to Del Rio, don't do anything that will land you back in here," Sheriff Brennan warned, then turned to his deputy.

"Did he have anything with him when he came in, Roger?" he asked.

"No sir," Roger answered.

"Take your boy on home, Mr. Oakley," the sheriff said.

Walter motioned for Glenn to step forward, then Walter walked from the sheriff's office right behind his son and construction foreman without speaking.

"He is a very bad sheriff," Armando reiterated with a soft, but angry voice, and in Spanish, when the three were outside of the courthouse.

Walter did not respond. Instead, he took ten dollars from his pocket and turned toward his friend and business associate.

"Armando, would you mind going over to Bottoms' store and getting some new clothes for Glenn? I'm going to take him over to the hotel for a bath. Would you bring the clothes over there, please?" Walter asked his friend.

Walter and Glenn walked to the hotel in silence. Walter rented a room and arranged for a bath for his son. He asked the desk clerk to send Armando up with the clothes when he got there. Two hours later, Walter and Glenn were on the train bound for Junction, and Armando went back across the river to his brother's house.

About an hour before the train reached Junction, Glenn began sobbing. A few minutes later, he spoke through his tears.

"Dad, what am I going to tell Mama?" he choked, before breaking down entirely.

When Glenn's crying subsided enough so he could hear, Walter answered his question.

"I suppose you would have been better off, if you had thought of that, before you went to that saloon," Walter replied, then paused for another burst of sobs from his son.

"There's no way to take back what you've done, so you need to try to make things right. Tell her you're sorry. Promise her you will never do anything like this again and ask her to forgive you."

Glenn cried quite a while longer before speaking again.

"I am sorry, Dad, and thank you for coming to get me," he said quietly.

"You're welcome, son," Walter responded, using all the willpower he could find to keep from crying himself.

For the next few minutes, as the train rolled through the Hill Country, Walter contemplated how much pain he had felt for his children, Ralph and Glenn. If he had not experienced those feelings, Walter would have never believed that anyone could hurt so badly.

Ada's reunion with Glenn was painful; but like Walter, she was extremely glad to have him safely home. Walter's concerns about Glenn churned inside him, along with the guilt he carried from the mistakes he had made with Ralph.

"Sometimes when I'm completely without an answer, I turn to the Bible," he told Ada.

She tried hard to remember whether her husband had ever started a conversation with words like those before, hoping to find a hint about what would come next.

"While Glenn slept on the train, I prayed a whole lot. But if the Lord answered, I never heard what he said," Walter smiled.

Ada did not smile, but she was sympathetic. She had prayed almost continuously from the time she had gotten the bad news about Glenn at the station in San Antonio until she received Walter's telegram telling her that Glenn was safe.

"Most of the way to Junction, an old lady sat across the aisle from us on the train. One time while Glenn was asleep, I was staring out the window when I heard her clear her throat. The old lady had spent most of her time on the trip reading her Bible. When I looked at her, she passed the Bible over to me.

"Maybe this will help some," she suggested quietly.

"When I looked down, I saw a marker in the Bible. I opened it and began reading where she had marked a passage, the story of the prodigal son."

Ada watched Walter's face, carefully. He was holding back tears.

"I remember a minister in San Antonio one time preached on that story," Walter resumed.

"He said it was the essence of the whole Bible. He said all of God's teachings were summed up by that one parable."

Ada guessed at what was coming next.

"So you're asking my permission not to punish Glenn?" she asked.

Walter nodded, still fighting against tears.

"You think four days in that dirty jail are enough punishment?" she continued.

Walter nodded again.

"You think the woman handing you that Bible with the story about the runaway son was God's answer to your prayers, don't you?" Ada asked, and Walter responded with a slight nod of affirmation.

Ada was silent for a long time.

"I know you believe it, Walter. I don't know what I believe right now. I never imagined children could cause so much pain and hurt. One thing I still believe in for sure, though, is you, Walter. You handle this the way you think best," she told him, rising to her feet.

She crossed the room and kissed her husband lightly on the lips. Ada put her left arm around the back of his neck and pulled his head to her, holding him tight for a long while.

"I love you so much, Walter," Ada said, then left the room, dabbing a handkerchief in the corner of her eye.

The next morning, she woke to her husband's whistling, coming from the back of the house. He was walking from the barn, carrying fishing poles.

Ada smiled. Seeing the joy on his face made her feel good. As he passed the well, Ada remembered how hurt he had been on the day he had struck Ralph for talking back. Ada would much rather see her husband happy, the way he was now. She stuck her head out the window and called to Walter.

"Remember what the preacher said to Glenn?" she called.

"You can stay here in the church, boy, but that whistling will have to go."

"Good morning," Walter responded after a hearty laugh.

The story about Glenn whistling in church, when he was a small boy had been repeated often in the Oakley household, and it always produced laughter. In a moment, Ada heard her husband enter Glenn's room.

"Get up, son. We're goin' fishing."

When a letter contained particularly good news, or when it had something in it that worried her, Ada carried it in her apron pocket, sometimes for days. During private moments, she would take the letter out, read it and pause to think about what it said. In October, there was a letter so disturbing that she had carried it in her pocket for ten days. Amos was concerned about Ralph.

"I have had several conversations with him about starting pharmacy school," Ada's brother wrote.

"He says he is still planning on going. He just doesn't know when he will be ready.

"He is still working in the drugstore, but he does not seem to be enjoying it, the way he did at first," the letter continued.

After worrying about the letter for another week, Ada finally showed it to Walter.

"Why don't you write Ralph and ask him if he would rather go to college and study something other than pharmacy?" Walter suggested.

Ada wrote to both Amos and Ralph, but only Amos answered.

"Ralph wants to wait a while before deciding whether he wants to be a pharmacist. For now, he wants more independence and more money, than I can afford to pay him at the store.

"The St. Louis and Southwestern Railroad is hiring clerks in their bookkeeping department, and Ralph should be able to get a job there easily with Walter's help. He also wants to get a room of his own," Amos' letter concluded.

Ada was furious with Ralph. She was so angry that as she sat writing the letter, Walter could physically feel her agitation from his armchair all the way across the room.

"What's wrong?" he asked.

Ada did not reply. Walter rarely saw her upset, and he tried to coax the information out of her.

"Don't ignore me, please Ada. I want to know what's bothering you," Walter pressed.

"It's Ralph," she admitted.

"What about him?" Walter asked.

"He wants you to do something for him, and he didn't even bother to ask you. He got Amos to write me instead," Ada exhaled loudly, venting her frustration.

"What does he want me to do?" Walter continued.

"He wants you to get him a job in the bookkeeping department with the Cotton Belt in St. Louis," Ada replied.

"What's wrong with that?" Walter responded.

"If he wants me to help him get a railroad job, I'll be pleased to do it."

"Yes, but he should ask you. You're his father," Ada snapped.

"Well, he's never been comfortable asking me for anything. And it's not only because of the way things are between us, currently. But I'm his father, and if he needs my help, he's going to get it. This is nothing new here. And it's certainly nothing for you to get upset about. Now tear up that letter you're writing, please. Tomorrow, I'll go into San Antonio, talk to John Smiley, and see what I can do."

The next letter Ralph wrote to his mother was filled with details of his new job and his new rooming house. He passed on a greeting from a railroad executive in St. Louis to his father, but he did not say thank you.

Things were also going better with Glenn. He and Walter spent lots of time together, working on projects around the farm after school. Walter was the contractor for a new building for the bank in Junction and he had talked with several people in Junction about building houses for them.

Ada wrote Ralph with unusual sternness.

"I expect you home for Christmas. You have never seen your new brother, Ray."

She did not get an answer and Ralph stayed in St. Louis during the Christmas holidays. Walter was not pleased that Ralph had ignored his mother's suggestion, but Ralph was grown and there was really little he could do.

Ada was not so easily daunted. She wrote Ralph a letter expressing her displeasure. He replied with a brief note saying he was sorry, but he had been busy at the railroad.

Spring was approaching, and Maryon was excited. She was preparing to graduate from high school and planned to attend Baylor University in Waco in the fall. Ray was taking most of Ada's time. He had been sick almost continuously since birth. The doctor had been called out from Junction three times since November. Brooks was walking, and Armando produced a record crop of hogs. Life was very busy along the South Llano River.

CHAPTER THIRTY-SIX

Two weeks before Easter, Ada woke Walter on Sunday at four in the morning. She had been up most of the night with Ray, who was suffering with colic. An enormous thunderstorm was rattling the house, so Ada had checked on the children.

"Walter, wake up," she urged as she shook him.

"What's wrong? Do you need me to sit up with Ray?" he asked.

"No," she answered, struggling to remain composed.

"I can't find Glenn!"

"What do you mean?" Walter asked groggily, swinging his legs out of bed and sitting up.

"I've looked all over the house. He's not here," Ada told her husband, concern reflecting off her face in the frequent lightning.

Walter pulled on his pants and boots and walked through the entire house with Ada. Glenn's only roommate was Brooks, a toddler who was into everything, but his vocabulary comprised a few cute words and no sentences. Walter stepped outside the big house, where the wind from the back side of a thunderstorm was still whipping the trees furiously.

"Glenn!" he yelled, as loudly as he could.

"Glenn!" he tried a second time, after there had been no response to his first call.

Still nothing. Walter went inside and told Ada he was going to the Velasquez house and look there. Walter knocked at the door and woke Joaquín.

"I have not seen him but let me get my clothes and I will help you look," Joaquín said in answer to Walter's question.

The men began searching, starting at the river.

"Maybe *Señor* Glenn went outside during the thunderstorm? Maybe he went to check on some damage and ran into some high water?" Joaquín suggested.

They walked the entire length of the river through the farm, calling Glenn's name, but found nothing. They searched the hog pens and smoke-house, also without result.

"We'd better get some horses and ask some of the neighbors to help," Walter proposed.

When the men entered the barn, Joaquín spotted an unfamiliar horse.

"Look over there, *Señor* Walter," he said, pointing at the horse still saddled with a rein looped over one of the stall rails.

Walter picked up a lantern and struck a match. The lamp was out of fuel. He found a second lantern and lit it. When he shined the light around the horse, he saw Glenn and Jimmy Barnes lying next to one another in the hay near a stall. Between them was an almost empty quart bottle of clear, homemade whiskey.

"Glenn," Walter called, but his son did not answer.

Walter knelt next to him and shook Glenn, but still got no response.

"Glenn, wake up!" he said in a much louder voice.

Nothing happened, so Walter shook him harder. Glenn's eyes opened briefly, and he vomited. Walter sat him up, but his son's eyes were closed again. Walter took his handkerchief and wiped the regurgitation from Glenn's face. The young man was dead drunk but otherwise all right.

Walter then checked Jimmy Barnes. His pulse and breathing were fine, so he let the boys sleep.

"They're all right, just drunk. Thanks for helping me search. I'm sorry I had to wake you," Walter apologized to Joaquín.

Joaquín looked sadly at Walter but said nothing. He walked out the door and back to his house. As soon as he was sure Joaquín was gone, Walter put his face in his hands and sobbed for fifteen minutes. When he felt strong enough, he went inside to tell Ada. Once Ada could control her crying, Walter made a large pot of coffee and took it to the barn.

"Jimmy," Walter called, nudging Jimmy Barnes with his boot.

"Huh?" he responded, while cautiously sitting up.

Jimmy accepted the cup of coffee Walter offered. Soon, Glenn was awake and throwing up again. Walter bent down to his son, supporting him with his hand on the back of Glenn's neck. Glenn took several swallows of the coffee but couldn't hold it down. When he had expelled the last drop of coffee, dry heaves shook the pale young man.

"Glenn, you stay here while I take Mr. Barnes home," Walter instructed.

"Oh, I can get home by myself," Jimmy Barnes said, offering a smile.

"When I want to hear from you, I'll let you know. Otherwise, you keep quiet," Walter declared sternly.

Walter saddled his horse, and he and Jimmy Barnes rode toward Junction. When they had ridden five miles, Walter asked a question.

"Why did you decide to come to our farm to drink last night?" he asked the young man, who still appeared relatively cheerful.

"Glenn paid for the whiskey," Jimmy Barnes replied.

Walter decided to save the rest of his questions for Glenn. During the rest of the ride, Walter planned what he would say to Jimmy Barnes' father.

They rode up to the ramshackle house where Jimmy Barnes and his father lived. Walter got down from his horse and knocked on the door. When there was no answer, he knocked again.

"Pa is probably drunk," Jimmy Barnes offered.

"When he's drunk, you can't wake him up. It's best not to, anyway."

Walter swung open the door of the one-room house and saw Mr. Barnes passed out on a bed against the far wall. An empty whiskey bottle—identical to the one Walter had seen in his own barn—was overturned next to the bed.

Saddened even more, Glenn's distraught father withdrew from the house and plodded back to his horse, forgetting all the things he was going to say to Mr. Barnes. As he swung up onto the horse, Walter looked at Jimmy Barnes with pleading eyes.

"Please stay away from Glenn," he begged.

"And don't come back to my farm."

"Gosh, Mr. Oakley, Glenn's the only friend I've got," Jimmy Barnes replied, appearing genuinely hurt.

"Jimmy, Glenn can't afford a friend like you," Walter said, gently.

Tears formed in Jimmy Barnes' eyes. Walter turned his horse onto the road and began the solemn ride back to his farm. The sting of a peach switch against the bare leg of one of the Oakley children was not unusual. Ada reinforced lessons that way, but serious corporal punishment was rare. Only a few times had Walter disciplined with a razor strap. What was delivered to Glenn in the Oakley barn that Sunday would be more accurately described as a beating.

For the first time anyone could remember, Sunday came without the Oakleys going to church. There was no elaborate Sunday dinner. Ada served only cold corn bread and leftover biscuits with buttermilk, but the dreadful day was not over.

At three o'clock, Walter went out to the barn and told Glenn to get cleaned up and go inside. Ada had left him some biscuits and buttermilk on the table, but she was upstairs with Ray, who now had a terrible cough and was running a high fever. The baby's color turned flaming red with each coughing spell. Walter rode to Junction for the doctor. It took more than an hour for Walter to bring Doc Wimberly. The physician examined Ray for a few moments, then turned to Ada and Walter.

"Whooping cough," he pronounced.

Monday, when Dr. Wimberly returned, Ray seemed very close to death. Tuesday, the doctor did not come until after dark.

"I sent to San Antonio for something new," he explained.

Dr. Wimberly opened a smelly jar of ointment with a label that said *Vick's Magic Croup Salve*. He rubbed some on Ray's chest and put smaller amounts in the baby's nostrils. In a few minutes, the coughs eased. Dr. Wimberly stayed with Ray all night and tried several times to persuade Ada to rest, but she sat with them. By ten o'clock, Ray was sleeping comfortably. At daybreak, when Doc Wimberly left, Ray was much better. Ada continued the salve treatment. In a week, Ray was back to normal. Except for castor oil, *Vick's Salve* was the first miracle drug any of the Oakleys had ever seen.

Before the end of school, Ada and Walter found out about two more drinking episodes that Glenn had been involved in, and they suspected there were others. It seemed the punishment, no matter how severe, would not stop Glenn from drinking. The day after school was out, Walter and Glenn boarded a train for New Mexico. Harry met their train at Deming.

Glenn fell immediately in love with the Little Hatchet. Walter stayed in New Mexico for two weeks, leaving after it became clear his son was much better and staying away from alcohol. Glenn worked the whole summer on the farm, returning to Telegraph just in time to start school in the fall.

The third Monday of the new academic year, Glenn went to school with the other children but disappeared at recess. When he did not return the next morning, Walter went to Mr. Barnes' house and learned that Glenn and Jimmy Barnes had gone to San Antonio.

Walter asked a friend to ride to the farm and tell Ada that Walter was going to San Antonio to look for the boys. Walter searched the city for two hours before finding Glenn and Jimmy. He took them to Armando's house to sleep off their drunk. And the next morning, Walter and the two boys were on the westbound train. Jimmy Barnes finished his journey in Junction. Walter got off the train there just long enough to write and send a note to Ada. He explained he had Glenn, that their son was fine, and that Walter was taking him back to New Mexico.

CHAPTER THIRTY-SEVEN

At first, Glenn was glad to be back on the Little Hatchet. But after the first week passed, Glenn became bored. In ten days, he couldn't stand it any longer. And at the end of the second week, he left. Glenn wrote his Uncle Harry a note.

"Thank you for taking me in. I really like it here, but I guess I need some adventure. Please don't worry about me. I can take care of myself. Tell Mama I love her, and I'll be fine and please ask Papa not to come looking for me."

Walter went to San Antonio an hour after he read the telegram informing him of his son's disappearance. He quickly learned where Glenn and Jimmy Barnes had gone together after Glenn had left the Oakley ranch in New Mexico. However, their trail went cold in San Antonio. Walter left word everywhere he could think of, including with his friend Captain Carl Parker of the Texas Rangers, asking to be contacted with any word about Glenn.

Ada was completely heartbroken. She stayed in her room for two days and came out then, only because Ray was sick. Life moved on without Glenn, as a whirlwind of changes swept through the Oakleys' lives. Walter was shocked when Judge Willi Rheinhardt and a group of his neighbors came to visit.

"Walter, I've decided to retire," Judge Rheinhardt began.

"I've been justice of the peace around here for even longer than I can remember."

Walter joined the men's laughter.

"Everybody who came with me today believes you should be the one to replace me, and we're all prepared to support you in the June Democratic Primary."

"Judge, I'm honored, but I've never even thought about running for anything. I wouldn't begin to know how to go about it. Come to think about it, I'm not completely sure what a justice of the peace does," Walter admitted.

"Walter, the justice of the peace runs a small court that handles minor civil matters and misdemeanor crimes. Texas justices of the peace have the power of arrest and are considered in some ways to be law enforcement officers, as well as judges."

"Well, Judge, I'm not a lawyer, and I don't know anything about being a policeman. I wouldn't know the first thing about how to arrest anyone or what to do with 'em after I got them arrested," Walter confessed.

The other men laughed, and Walter joined them.

"You don't need to be a lawyer to be a J.P. I'm not and most other justices of the peace aren't, either. The J.P. association puts out a book that tells you most of the law you need to know, even has a section on how to perform a wedding and how much to charge for one," Judge Rheinhardt winked, then continued his pitch after the laughter died down.

"Walter, you've got just what this office needs: common sense and fairness. There is no one around here that people trust more than you. That's what they need to help them settle their disputes, a man who is fair and someone they can trust.

"If you want to learn how to arrest someone, Sheriff Wilson can teach you in about fifteen minutes. I've always found it better to talk sense to people myself. You could use the small office I have kept next to the feed store on the south side of Junction, or you could even open your office in Telegraph, if you want. That would be up to you.

"I won't say no right away," Walter told the men after several more had spoken.

"Out of respect for you fellas, I'll talk with Ada, but I guarantee you that she'll be against it. She hates politics. And Judge, with no offense to you, she hates politicians, too."

Ada objected less than Walter had predicted. She knew it would keep him closer to home. Walter had several more conversations before he agreed to run. When he announced, the other men considering the office decided not to become candidates, leaving Walter unopposed in the June voting.

Judge Rheinhardt died in September, and the county commissioners appointed Walter to fill out his term. He inherited Judge Rheinhardt's small office, next to the feed store, and the people of the county began calling Walter, Judge.

When one of Captain Parker's Rangers finally located Glenn in Laredo, the telegram notifying Walter was sent to Judge M. Walter Oakley, Telegraph, Texas. It was that telegram that Walter handed to the federal police captain across the river in Mexico, where Glenn and Jimmy Barnes had gone to escape the Texas Rangers.

"Good morning," Walter said, passing the yellow paper to the officer.

The captain spoke extremely poor English, but he could read the language somewhat better. When he saw the title judge attached to Walter's name on the telegram, he immediately sent one of his men to bring the two boys from a nearby *cantina*. Glenn was contrite and apologized for his behavior, but this time, something was different.

"Dad, I asked Uncle Harry to tell you not to come and get me," Glenn told his father.

"Son, your mother is just about to die of a broken heart, worrying over you," Walter explained.

"If you make me go home with you, I'll just run away again," Glenn told his father.

The Mexican police captain excused himself from his own office, while this Texas judge and his son talked. Walter thought for a few minutes, then came up with a compromise.

"How about this?" Walter asked. "You come with me to San Antonio. I'll get you a job with the railroad and a decent place to stay, and I won't bother you anymore. How's that?" he asked.

"What about Jimmy?" Glenn responded.

"Jimmy's welcome to come along, but I don't think I can get the railroad to hire him," Walter said.

Both boys were thrilled to stay in San Antonio. The railroad job appeared to be good for Glenn. He wrote to his mother once a month, and Walter kept in contact through his friend John Smiley at the Southern Pacific.

Ray continued to be ill for longer periods of time than he was well. Doc Wimberly visited the Oakley farm at least once a week. Ada's dealings with Ralph remained strained.

Across America, most people were preoccupied with the war in Europe as America sent its sons to fight in France and Belgium. Glenn wanted to go, but he was too young to enlist without his parents' permission.

"It might be what he needs to get straightened out, but I would never forgive myself if he got hit with mustard gas. So many awful things are happening to our men over there, and I'm not even sure we should be in a war for the sake of Europeans. I don't see why they can't settle their problems without us," Walter told friends at the courthouse.

Ironically, Walter felt differently about Ralph. He could be an officer if he chose to go. Perhaps Walter felt that officers were not as likely to be attacked with gas. Or maybe he just felt Glenn was more vulnerable and needed his father's protection.

No matter what Walter thought, Ralph had lost all interest in the military and the war. He had become obsessed with getting rich. Each of these rapid-fire crises was punctuated by another illness for Ray. Life along the South Llano kept a dizzying pace all spring. But early in May, Glenn shocked the family again by suddenly moving home.

At first, he said nothing was wrong. But after several days, he told Maryon that Jimmy Barnes had been arrested for robbing a bank. Glenn had been at work when the robbery occurred, so he hadn't fallen under suspicion. Jimmy pleaded guilty and was sent to the state penitentiary in Huntsville. Possibly because he might have been scared by his friend's misfortune, Glenn seemed to be calmer, more comfortable with his life. He talked with Walter about moving to New Mexico. They also discussed the possibility that Glenn would go back to work for the railroad, but nothing quite jelled.

Eventually, John Smiley came up with an answer. The railroad desperately needed men in the Rio Grande Valley. Glenn was rehired and went to work on a construction crew down there, as the tracks progressed steadily toward Brownsville.

The Model T Ford was becoming a common sight in San Antonio and in much of the rest of Texas. Doc Wimberly bought the first one to be seen in Junction and the car caused a lot of commotion in the rural community. It was noisy, backfired and scared the horses. But unlike his older, less adventuresome neighbors, Walter was fascinated by the new automobile.

"I think I should get one of those things, don't you, Doc?" he teased Dr. Wimberly.

Doc Wimberly laughed. He could not believe his friend was serious. But late the next day, Walter came sputtering down the hill in his new Ford, sending all his farm animals into a panic. The kids ran outside to greet Doc Wimberly, who had the only car any of them had ever seen. The younger Oakleys were amazed to see their father driving the machine. Walter was all bundled up in the completely open car, attempting to protect himself from the cold weather that had moved in the night before.

The Model T proudly displayed a shiny, luxuriously deep, black finish when it left San Antonio. By the time the new Ford arrived in Telegraph, its coat had become dull gray from dust and mud. The children jumped and screamed.

"Take us for a ride?" they begged their father.

"You'll have to wait your turn, kids. My best girl gets the first ride in this new car," Walter teased.

To Walter's amazed disappointment, Ada turned him down flat.

"I'm afraid of automobiles, Walter. They make too much noise," his wife, who had been so ready for adventure, as a young lady along the Pedernales, protested.

"Take me, Daddy?" each of the children shouted.

Driving up the hill for the first time, Walter killed the motor twice. He was having trouble getting used to the clutch. However, once he got the car onto the road, it only took fifteen minutes to get to Telegraph. The speed was frightening.

When the little Ford chugged down the hill the second time, all the Velasquez children were waiting excitedly for a ride. It had become completely dark by then, so Walter just rode them around the yard for a few seconds and promised them a longer drive the next day.

The car made Walter's trip to his office in Junction easier. Before spring, Walter had bought a truck for Joaquín to use on the farm. Even after weeks had passed, and the animals on the farm no longer took notice of the comings and goings of the Model T, Ada remained unnerved by the new automobile. Walter could not get over the change in Ada. Her sparkle and curiosity seemed had given way to worry and fear of the future.

In June, Walter drove up to his office in Junction. Brooks sat on his father's lap, pretending to steer the car and laughing because he was having so much fun.

"There you are, Judge," Sam announced, as he prepared to swing his leg over his new bicycle. "I just delivered an urgent telegram to you from John Smiley in San Antonio. No one was there, so I left it on your desk."

The wire contained bad news. Glenn had vanished, again. Walter rode the train to Falfurrias, which was still the end of the line for the Southern Pacific. No one at the railroad camp had heard Glenn talk about leaving, and no one had noticed anything unusual.

"I went drinking with him about three nights ago. He seemed all right when we parted, came back to work, the next morning. Then he just disappeared," a worker told Walter.

Walter sent a series of telegrams, including wires to Captain Parker and the state prison at Huntsville. Walter learned that Jimmy Barnes had been released after serving less than two years of his sentence. The early release came mostly because of his very young age.

At the end of the second week, when Walter was just about to give up hope of finding his lost son, he heard from Captain Parker. One of his men in Brownsville had been told by a Mexican policeman that Jimmy Barnes and Glenn were in Veracruz. Walter went to Port Isabel and sailed on a steamer that traveled between the two ports. He found the two young men. They had no interest in returning and nothing Walter said to them changed their minds. He spent several days trying to persuade them. But in the end, Walter went home alone to give Ada more bad news about Glenn. She sent Glenn an urgent letter.

"Mama, I love you very much, but I have to live my life my own way," her son wrote back.

Two weeks later, a letter from Captain Parker sent Walter and Ada into complete despair.

"I'm sorry that I have to tell you that your son Glenn and his friend Jimmy Barnes are the chief suspects in a bank robbery in Edinburg, Texas," the Ranger wrote. "We believe them to be hiding out, probably in Northern Mexico, perhaps in Matamoros. My men have instructions to arrest Glenn and Barnes if they find them, but they cannot go into Mexico after them.

"Please tell us if you should hear from your son. These men are fugitives and it would be better for them if they turn themselves in," Captain Parker's letter ended.

Ada was desperate, but she understood Walter was right when he told her that, even if he found Glenn, there was nothing he could do to fix the mess he was in. Ada was frustrated. Being a woman, she could not go to Mexico and search for her son. After anguishing for two weeks, she wrote Ralph and begged him to find Glenn. Ralph asked the railroad for time off and headed for Matamoros.

CHAPTER THIRTY-EIGHT

Glenn and Jimmy Barnes were easy to find. Their home was a brothel, less than a mile outside Matamoros. Ralph saw Glenn slumped against a wall a few feet from the bar. He grabbed his younger brother, who was in a stupor, and slapped him very hard. Glenn didn't recognize Ralph and took a wild swing at him.

As Glenn fell toward his brother, Ralph landed a solid blow on Glenn's chin, knocking his brother unconscious. Ralph picked his little brother off the floor and carried him over his shoulder to a horse-drawn taxi waiting outside. Twelve hours passed before Glenn regained consciousness in Ralph's hotel room.

"Ralph, is that you?" Glenn asked, in utter disbelief.

"Well, of course, it's me," Ralph replied, peevishly.

"What are you doing here?" was Glenn's second question.

"Mama sent me to take you home," Ralph responded.

"Why? I can't go back to Texas. They'll put me in jail. Jimmy and me robbed a bank, up in Edinburg." Glenn told his brother, speaking in an indifferent tone of voice.

"Well, you can't stay here either," Ralph told his brother.

"Of course we can. We gave the police commandant half the money from the bank, and we can stay as long as we want," Glenn replied.

"That won't stop the Rangers from coming after you. You should know that," Ralph asserted.

"They haven't come so far. Anyway, the commandant says that the Ranger in Brownsville told him that since Dad was friends with his captain they probably wouldn't try to grab us in Mexico," Glenn countered.

"This is a mess," Ralph snarled, nearly biting his cigar in two.

"What am I supposed to tell Mama? That her son's a bank robber?"

"Just tell her you found me and I'm all right. You did your job," Glenn suggested.

Ralph turned and walked out of the hotel room to think for a minute.

"What are you going to do when the money runs out?" he barked at Glenn after he returned to the room.

"The Rangers might let you alone, if you robbed one bank. But if you go back to Texas and rob another one, they won't let the Mexican police stop them from taking you. It's likely they'll kill you," Ralph warned.

"That's what the commandant said, too," Glenn agreed.

"Jimmy and I have a business. We're buying girls," he told his brother.

"You're what?" Ralph screamed.

"We're buying girls. You know, for the fancy whorehouses in Galveston and New Orleans. About every two weeks, we hire a taxicab and ride out into the country. We give the girl's father or a madam fifty dollars in gold. We bring the girls back to Matamoros. Ortiz gives us two hundred and fifty dollars. We give the commandant a hundred and we make a hundred dollars profit. A hundred dollars buys a lot, in Mexico. We're living like kings down here," Glenn rationalized.

Ralph slammed the door and stomped down to the street, jumped into a cab, and ordered the driver to take him to Brownsville. He waited until the train stopped in Houston before he wired his mother. In the end, Ralph told her what Glenn had suggested. There was nothing else to say.

Walter wrote, asking to know details of his visit, but Ralph didn't answer. Captain Parker finally was the one who eventually told Walter the truth about Glenn. As Walter rode the train back from his meeting with the Ranger in San Antonio, he tried to think of a way to tell Ada. There was no way. So when she asked him, Walter lied.

"Captain Parker didn't know anything," Walter said.

Ada knew her husband was lying. Both parents feared the tragic ending coming for Glenn. Their sense of being powerless to stop the looming tragedy only deepened their sadness.

"I didn't expect to see you down here again," Glenn said when his older brother returned to Mexico.

"I didn't expect to be back. But I never thought the prohibitionists would take over, either," Ralph conceded.

Ralph stood opposite Glenn inside a posh hotel bar in Matamoros. He hardly recognized his brother. Hard drinking had taken a distressing toll, making Glenn look like a man of thirty-five. He wore a silk vest and expensive clothes. He sat at a table, his hair in disarray and his eyes bloodshot and wild.

"So that's why you're here, huh? You want to make some easy money running whiskey?" Glenn laughed drunkenly.

A year and a half had passed since Ralph's first visit. Glenn's face tightened before he spoke again.

"Well, big brother, any money you make working for me won't be easy money," he warned.

Ralph had enough of Glenn's tough guy routine. He moved toward his brother, intending to jerk him out of his chair.

"That's close enough right there," Glenn told him, lowering the pitch of his voice and sounding ominous, even dangerous.

Ralph looked down and saw his brother pointing an old long-barreled Colt .45 revolver directly at Ralph's abdomen.

"This is a tough country, big brother. Prohibition has made it even tougher. Right after you left last time, I got tired of big guys like you messing up my face. So I decided to let my friend, Mr. Colt, help me out. Tough hombres don't seem to need a fight, as bad as they thought they did, when Mr. Colt is around," Glenn asserted, before turning his head toward the bar.

"Jimmy, bring my brother a drink!" Glenn ordered.

The Mexican bartender started over with a glass of Canadian whiskey, but Glenn waved the pistol toward the bar for a moment, then pointed it back at his brother.

"I said for Jimmy to do it," Glenn told the bartender, keeping his eye fixed firmly on Ralph.

Jimmy Barnes took the glass of whiskey from the bartender, brought it to the table, and set it in front of Ralph.

"Jimmy, you remember my brother Ralph, don't you? Glenn asked.

"Sure, how you doing, Ralph?" Jimmy Barnes said.

"Fine," Ralph replied tersely, wishing his little brother would put that pistol down so he could give him a good beating.

"Have a seat, Ralph," Glenn directed.

"And we'll talk some business. That is why you came, right? I don't suppose Mama would ask you to waste time on a second trip to bring me home," Glenn speculated, with another drunken laugh.

"I did come for business, but I should have known it would be a waste of time dealing with a drunk," Ralph said.

"You're wrong again, big brother. This business is about drunks," Glenn explained.

This time, when Glenn started laughing, Jimmy Barnes laughed, too. Ralph thought for a second and joined the laughter. Ralph sat down and took a sip of the expensive liquor.

"I'm not really a bootlegger, if that's what you've heard. I guess I sort of help with arrangements. Maybe you could say I'm kind of a politician," Ralph's younger brother continued.

Glenn thought for a minute, then chuckled again.

"Yeah, that's it. Me and Dad, we're both politicians, now. But politics is a little more open down here than it is back in Texas. When you give a politician money here, he's not afraid to take it on top of the table. It's more honest. Don't you think?

"So I guess your next question is, when am I going to introduce you to Fernando Ortiz? Is that right?" Glenn asked.

Ralph nodded. Glenn laid the pistol down on the table in front of his glass. It was no longer pointed at Ralph, but it was within easy reach.

"And then next you want to know how soon you can get a boat and a load of whiskey or rum and have a run at the sheriff up in Galveston. Am I right again, big brother?

"You see, I know you're smarter than me. But what you don't know yet is that you're going to be paying me for my experience. For example, you don't know that if I give you the envelope that the money goes in for that sheriff, he's going to take your money and tell you a place to take your whiskey. If you were to try and do it on your own, old Sheriff Woods would steal your money and your whiskey and slap you in jail. You didn't know that, did you, big brother?" Glenn challenged. "You thought I was just a stupid drunk who didn't have any more sense than to rob banks in Texas."

Ralph still didn't like the way Glenn was talking to him, but he was listening carefully now.

"I guess you thought a bunch of Italians or Irishmen from Chicago were the only people who had sense enough to organize the whiskey rackets. Well, if that's what you thought, you thought wrong.

"Isn't that right, Jimmy?" Glenn asked.

"That's right, Glenn," Jimmy Barnes chimed in, providing enthusiastic support to his friend and boss' oration.

Glenn turned his head so he could stare intensely into Ralph's eyes.

"Be back here at ten o'clock tonight, and we'll see if you can be of any use to us," Glenn concluded.

Ralph found a hotel and went to his room. Before he had been there long enough to open his suitcase, Ralph heard a knock on his door. Wishing he had brought a gun, Ralph stood to the side of the door.

"Who is it?" he called.

"It's me, Jimmy, Jimmy Barnes," the voice said.

Ralph opened the door cautiously. After making sure no one else was outside, he stepped back so Jimmy could come in.

"I'm sorry Glenn treated you that way," Jimmy Barnes apologized. "But he didn't like how you roughed him up the last time you were down here. He said, when y'all were kids, you were always beating him up and he was tired of it.

"Anyway, I think he's just gone crazy. For a while, we had things real good down here. About every two weeks we'd go out in the country and buy some girls and sell them to Mr. Ortiz. And we had all the money we needed. Then bootlegging got up a full head of steam, and Glenn wanted more and more money," Jimmy said.

Ralph was listening carefully. Jimmy was telling Ralph that the brothers had something in common Ralph had not known about.

"When did he start carrying that gun?" Ralph asked.

"Not long after you left," Jimmy Barnes said.

"A big Texas Ranger came down here from McAllen. He beat and stomped Glenn real bad. That's when Glenn got the pistol. A couple of weeks later, we were in a whorehouse up near Reynosa when a big Mexican jumped on him. He bloodied Glenn's nose and knocked him down. He raised his foot and was getting ready to stomp on Glenn when Glenn shot him. Killed him dead, right there.

"We jumped in the car and ran straight back to Matamoros. *Commandante* Cisneros had to go to Reynosa to straighten things out.

"Since we got into rum running, I've heard Glenn shot two or three other people that tried to steal money from Mr. Ortiz. I didn't see the shootings myself, but that's what everybody says. One of them was supposed to have been a deputy sheriff up on South Padre, where we're going tonight.

"Don't mess with him. You may be his brother, but Glenn's way crazy. I think he'd shoot you," Jimmy Barnes advised, then paused for a minute.

"I'm his best friend, and I know he'd shoot me," Jimmy finished.

Ralph was strong and smart, but not perceptive. He listened to Jimmy Barnes' warning, but rejected the idea that Glenn could hurt or kill him. He did believe that Glenn would shoot Jimmy Barnes, however.

Ralph also refused to believe that his little brother had skills intelligent people would pay a lot of money for. Ralph concentrated on one unknown fact he had gotten from Jimmy Barnes. Glenn was as greedy as Ralph.

CHAPTER THIRTY-NINE

They stepped onto the yacht, just before eleven o'clock.

"Welcome aboard, Mr. Oakley," Fernando Ortiz said, after he had been introduced to Ralph.

"What can we get you to drink?" he asked, solicitously, as the yacht motored into the bay.

Glenn and Jimmy Barnes seemed quite comfortable on the luxurious boat. Ralph had never been on any boat other than a ferry in St. Louis.

"I suppose some Canadian Club," Ralph answered, trying to take in everything around him.

"Water or soda?" Ortiz asked graciously.

"Doesn't matter," Ralph replied.

"I don't drink much," he continued, his eyes moving to his brother Glenn.

Ralph hoped to communicate with his expression that Glenn drank more than enough for both Oakley brothers. Glenn had the pistol he called Mr. Colt tucked in his belt. Ralph also noticed that Glenn carried a war surplus Thompson submachine gun when he walked aboard the vessel.

"I have heard many stories about your career as a football player," Ortiz remarked, after the steward returned with the drinks.

Ralph sipped his drink and puffed his cigar, waiting for a few moments alone with *Señor* Ortiz. He planned to convince the Cuban smuggler to reorganize his operations, making Ralph, the smarter of the Oakley brothers, his second in command. Ralph made a lot of plans. None of those plans included taking orders from Glenn. Nor did they include being seasick. Twenty minutes into the voyage the *Corpus Christi* was rolling in six-foot swells.

"I'm sorry the sea is a little heavy tonight," *Señor* Ortiz apologized.

"Mr. Oakley, if you will excuse me, I need to talk to the captain for a moment."

First, Ralph felt uncomfortable; then he threw his cigar into the water. In a matter of minutes, Ralph was leaning against the rail throwing up over the side. Ralph looked up to see Jimmy Barnes standing beside him, offering a wet towel.

"I don't think Glenn ever got seasick because he stays too drunk," Jimmy reported.

Then he thought for a moment and reconsidered.

"Of course, I stay drunker than Glenn, and I got sick the first four or five times we came out here. Put this on the back of your neck. It might help," Jimmy suggested.

Sick or not, Ralph despised Jimmy Barnes, and would have told him so if he had not been so busy heaving the contents of his stomach into the turbulent water. Ralph had some choice things to say to Jimmy Barnes, but he couldn't get the words out of his mouth for all the constant gagging and vomiting. Three hours went by, and the boat never stopped rolling. Finally, Ralph felt the engine pull back, as the *Corpus Christi* came about to face the swells roiling the Gulf of Mexico. Ralph was helped into a launch, containing *Señor* Ortiz, Jimmy Barnes, Glenn, and two other men with guns.

The little boat swung wildly as it was lowered into the water. It heaved mercilessly while it rode the swells. A gasoline engine started just as a giant wave washed over the small boat. The water from a swell killed the motor, and it was four or five minutes before Ralph heard the trill of the engine again.

Even with the launch under power, the surf did more to push the little boat than the engine. Ten or twelve minutes after the launch was put into the water, the two gunmen Ralph did not recognize were wading in the surf, pulling the small boat onto the beach. As they dug in and held the craft on shore with taut lines, the rest of the party stepped from the boat and onto the beach.

Ralph was the next-to-last person to leave the launch. He stepped onto the sand at the same time a giant wave was crashing onto the beach. Ralph's face landed in the sand and he felt the pull of retreating water drag him into the gulf. As soon as the water withdrew, Ralph scrambled onto the beach, soaked by the gulf's water and covered with wet sand. As the party stood on the beach, and names were being exchanged, suddenly Ralph heard *Señor* Ortiz say.

"Sheriff Schertz, this is Glenn's brother, Ralph Oakley."

Ralph, still busy wiping sand off his face, paused for a moment, then stuck out his hand to shake Sheriff Schertz's hand.

"Glad to meet you, sheriff," Ralph sputtered.

"Don't go to sea much, do you, son?" the sheriff laughed.

Everyone but Ralph laughed; then, Ortiz spoke again.

"I'm sorry about that nasty business with your deputy," he apologized to the lawman.

"Who, Shultz? He got greedy," the sheriff noted dismissively.

"He put a gun to my head," Glenn interjected.

"Think nothing of it, son," the sheriff said to Glenn, then turned to Ortiz.

"Did you bring the rent, my friend?" he asked in Spanish.

"Of course," Ortiz replied, handing over a fat brown envelope.

"You see," Ortiz said, looking directly at Ralph.

"That's where a lot of our competitors go wrong. They try to dodge the police. We find things work much easier if we call the cops in advance. That way, they can give us an escort," Ortiz laughed.

"Yeah, we have a strong pro-business disposition here in Willacy County," Sheriff Schertz said.

The sheriff's comment produced more laughter. Ortiz shook hands with Sheriff Schertz and his rum runners turned and headed for the launch.

"Keep a lookout for the Coast Guard," the sheriff called.

"They've had a boat down here from Corpus the past couple of nights."

"We will," Ortiz acknowledged.

Ralph still felt awful as he stood on the beach, waiting to board the launch. But as soon as the little boat was pushed into the surf and began climbing the waves and falling into their troughs, Ralph was again overcome by dry heaves. He had thrown up everything in his stomach several hours previously. By the time the launch was hauled up to the yacht, Ralph could barely stand on the pitching deck of the bigger boat. He had never been so sick.

As the captain prepared to get the yacht underway, a huge light flooded the deck, and the wail of a loud siren overwhelmed every other source of sound on the boat. In less than a minute, Ortiz's men heard a voice shouting through a megaphone.

"You there, on the *Corpus Christi*, this is the Coast Guard. We're coming aboard to search for contraband," the voice proclaimed.

The loud roar of the Coast Guard boat's engines could be heard as the young guardsman maneuvered his vessel to a point immediately beside the yacht. A few seconds later, lines were thrown onto the deck of the *Corpus Christi*. Two men caught the lines and tied them off.

On the deck of the patrol boat, Ralph could see the shadowy outlines of two men pointing submachine guns at the people onboard the *Corpus Christi*. The weapons looked like the gun Glenn had carried onto the yacht.

Apparently, Glenn had hidden his Tommy gun before the men went to the beach. As the Coast Guard men scrambled onto the deck of the *Corpus Christi*, another command boomed from the man with the bullhorn.

"Raise your hands while we search you for weapons."

The guardsmen patted each of the Ortiz men down, but they did not find any weapons. Jimmy Barnes told Ralph later that Glenn and the other two gunmen had thrown their pistols into large vents on deck as soon as they saw the light from the patrol boat.

When the guardsmen finished their search, a young ensign stepped up to Ortiz.

"Are you the captain?" the Coastguardsmen asked.

"No, I am the owner, Fernando Ortiz," he replied politely.

"Are you a U.S. citizen?" the officer asked.

"No sir, I am a citizen of Cuba," Ortiz answered.

"May I see your passport, please?" the officer asked.

"Of course, but it's in my cabin," Ortiz informed his inquisitor.

"I'm afraid that I'll have to go with you," the officer informed Ortiz.

"That is not a problem at all," the Cuban smiled.

Ortiz led the young officer off the deck and into his cabin. In a few minutes, they were back topside, and the officer seemed satisfied.

"Mr. Ortiz, we stopped your vessel to search for illegal liquor. Do you have any liquor on board?" the Coast Guardsman asked,

"Only what is in the bar in there," Ortiz explained, pointing into the main cabin.

"I'm afraid we'll have to seize that as contraband," the officer told Ortiz.

"Liquor is illegal in the United States."

"Take it with my compliments," Ortiz responded, still displaying his elegant smile.

"We sailed up from Mexico last night. I'm afraid I forgot about your rather unusual law. You call it prohibition, I believe?"

"Yes sir, that's right," the officer confirmed, motioning to one of his men, who began collecting the bottles from behind the bar.

"We need to search the rest of your vessel," the man told Ortiz.

"Of course," Ortiz agreed, casually.

For forty-five minutes, Coast Guardsmen pored carefully over the boat. There was no liquor on board for them to find. The guns discarded by Ortiz's men went undiscovered, and the cash had already been taken ashore. The ensign knew he was dealing with bootleggers, but he also knew that he had no evidence.

"May I ask the purpose of your visit to the beach?" he questioned.

"We went looking for flounder, but the water was too muddy and turbulent," Ortiz answered.

"If I were to make a suggestion?" the officer posed.

"Of course," Ortiz replied.

"The next time you go for flounder, take some lanterns and gigs. You're likely to have much better luck," he recommended.

Ortiz laughed aloud.

"I would offer you a drink, *Señor.* But of course, that is not possible. Your men took all our refreshments," Ortiz teased the young man.

"Enjoy the rest of your voyage. I bid you good morning, Mr. Ortiz," the officer said.

"*Buenos dias,*" Ortiz responded.

With that, the Coast Guard party was over the side and back on the patrol boat. The boat's gasoline engines roared, and the two vessels began to separate. In a moment, the patrol boat sped north, and the *Corpus Christi* sailed back to Mexico. When the Coast Guardsmen were well away, Jimmy Barnes swore.

"What's the matter, my young friend?" Ortiz asked him.

"We can't even have a drink. They took all our whiskey," Jimmy Barnes answered.

"Don't worry. Follow me," Ortiz chuckled.

He led Jimmy Barnes down into the engine room. Ortiz pointed to a five-gallon can with a Texaco star on its side. Printed lettering indicated the container was filled with motor oil, and the can was machine sealed. Ortiz handed Jimmy Barnes an oversized can opener.

"Open that up, my friend," he directed Jimmy.

It was a long way around the rim of the can. But in less than ten minutes, Jimmy Barnes had the lid off. Carefully wrapped inside the can were bottles of Canadian, Irish, and Scotch whiskey, rum and gin. Excelsior stuffed in the container provided extra cushioning for the liquor.

"Perhaps you would like to take these up on deck?" Ortiz suggested.

"I'll be," Jimmy Barnes pronounced, astonished.

In less than a minute, Jimmy had the liquor up in the main cabin. Within five minutes, everyone was laughing and drinking, everyone but Ralph and Glenn. Ralph was too sick to do anything, laugh or drink. Glenn was morose as he drank. For Glenn, there was no longer any pleasure at all in life, even from whiskey.

The sun was coming up. About forty-five minutes after the Coast Guard left, the cook was carrying skillets into the main cabin filled with *chorizo*, eggs, and beans. There were also lots of steaming tortillas and hot sauce. Everyone ate heartily, except for Ralph and Glenn. Ralph was too sick to eat, and Glenn never ate when he was drinking. Possibly, that explained why Glenn only weighed one hundred thirty-five pounds.

CHAPTER FORTY

At nine in the morning, the *Corpus Christi* crossed back into the calm bay waters. Everyone was asleep, except for the captain, Ralph, who was still sick, and Glenn, who stood watch on the foredeck, submachine gun ready.

Two young men waited at the dock as the captain brought the yacht alongside in one effortless motion. He reversed the engines and the two men on the dock scurried aboard with lines to secure the vessel to the pier.

Once the engines were shut down and secured, the captain found his way to his bunk. Around noon, Glenn woke one of the other gunmen to stand watch. Just before he found a place to lie down, he turned to Ralph.

"Get some sleep. It might make you feel better," he told his brother.

Ralph found an empty bunk and slept. At four o'clock, everyone on the boat was stirring. The cook had coffee and sandwiches. Ralph tried a few sips of coffee, but was not ready to face a sandwich.

That night, Ortiz hosted an enormous meal for his gang of smugglers at his villa. Ralph had never seen such opulence. He was able to eat; but several times during the dinner, Ralph felt queasy, and was afraid he would have to dash from the table.

Ortiz had brandy served on the terrace. By then, Ralph's legs felt stronger. Ortiz pulled the two Oakleys off to the side of the main group.

"Ralph, your brother feels you are overly ambitious and he has warned me that you are likely to try to horn in too much on what we do here," Ortiz asserted.

"Now before you say anything, let me tell you that I have never known a man whose services I value more than Glenn's," Ortiz continued.

"If he were to ask you to leave, I'm afraid I would have to get along without you. Glenn also says that you are very bright and determined. That's the part I want to hire. What do you say?" the Cuban asked.

Ralph understood he was expected to be deferential to his new boss, and to affirm the assessment Ortiz had made.

"I think I may have underestimated my brother," Ralph said, without exposing the condescension he felt churning within him.

"I have already seen that there is a lot I can learn from you. You clearly are a man who knows how to make money," Ralph added.

Ortiz laughed.

"You have a way of cutting through things," he observed.

"What you say is good enough for me but let me give you a final caution. Don't offend your brother if you expect to stay with us. He is indispensable to me."

What Ortiz told him amazed Ralph, but he had no intention of giving up a chance to be wealthy, just to win a fight with Glenn.

His mother and his Uncle Amos were the only two people Ralph genuinely loved. Glenn had never been more to him than a minor annoyance. He was weak, and not too bright. If Ortiz believed he needed Glenn, that was fine with Ralph. It was Ortiz's money Ralph wanted, not his friendship.

"Can you shoot?" Ortiz asked.

"Yes," Ralph responded, coldly.

"Have you ever shot a man?" Ortiz asked, then immediately answered his own question without giving Ralph a chance to respond.

"Of course not. It is one thing to shoot a target, or even a deer. It is very different to shoot a man. It is even more difficult to a shoot a man who is trying to kill you, but I am not hiring you to shoot people.

"I am hiring you because you are bold and because you are a leader. I have friends in Cuba and Canada who can provide more whiskey than we can get into your country.

"I hope, after you learn something about our business and gain some experience, you can help change that," Ortiz stated.

Ralph's appetite was whetted. He was ready to get started, ready to make money.

"There's one other thing, my friend," Ortiz said to Ralph.

"This may not be a respectable profession, but you do not steal from me," Ortiz paused for effect, then added a last word.

"Ever."

"Your brother sees to that," he said after another pause to add emphasis.

Ortiz turned quickly away from Ralph and walked into his house, Glenn by his side. Ralph stood alone for two or three minutes before hearing Jimmy Barnes' voice.

"I'm glad you're going to be with us." he told Ralph.

"I was with Glenn and *Señor* Ortiz this afternoon. Glenn wasn't real happy about things. Sometimes, I think, even *Señor* Ortiz is scared of Glenn. But after a while Glenn, he said it was all right with him," Jimmy recounted.

Ralph despised Jimmy Barnes. Instinctively, he wanted to hit him in the mouth, to make him be quiet. But Ralph understood he was on trial, so he turned quietly and walked into the garden alone.

Twenty minutes later, excitement rippled through the house as a dozen ladies from *Señora* Castillo's arrived at the party. Jimmy Barnes was the first to choose.

"That one's mine," Glenn announced, immediately preempting his friend's choice.

Ralph watched from a distance. He regarded drinking as a character flaw, but he viewed the need for sex as a sign of extreme weakness. As each of the other men paired with a woman and disappeared, Ralph looked on. When the number of prostitutes dwindled to six, Ralph slipped back into dark shadows and put distance between himself and the party. He waited to make sure he had not been missed, then left the gathering and returned to his hotel.

The next morning, he woke early and walked back to the villa. As people came down for breakfast, Ralph casually merged into the group. He was refreshed and confident, while most of the others were hungover and sluggish.

Ortiz watched carefully. He knew Ralph had disappeared, and he knew the elder Oakley brother had returned to the gathering, believing that no one had noticed. When eight of his gang of smugglers had gathered in the dining room, Ortiz entered.

"So Ralph, you do not care for the young ladies?" he remarked, as giggles rippled through the breakfast party.

"I came for business," Ralph responded.

"Ah, but *Señor*, this is Mexico, and in Mexico, we mix business with pleasure," Ortiz offered.

"Business is pleasure for me," Ralph stated.

"Spoken like an American capitalist," Ortiz answered.

"Come, let us have some breakfast," Ortiz announced pleasantly.

When they had finished eating, Ortiz took Glenn and Ralph for a walk and spoke deferentially to Glenn, his words offered as a request for advice rather than a directive.

"I would like for your brother to lead next week's procession of trucks into Texas," Ortiz began.

"Fine with me," Glenn said flatly, his body language asserting that Ralph was no threat to Glenn and Mr. Colt.

The following Tuesday, fourteen trucks rolled up to the international bridge in Matamoros. The trucks varied in size, and all were covered with tarps. *Commandante* Cisneros was waiting at the bridge. He halted the trucks in Mexico.

"Wait here," the police commander advised Glenn, before Cisneros drove across to the Texas side.

"It's all taken care of," he told Glenn, when he returned to the Mexican side of the river.

The convoy started across the bridge with Ralph riding in the passenger seat of the lead truck. There was a single U.S. Customs agent at the American end of the bridge.

"You can go on. You're all right," he told the driver without even a pretense of a search.

Then he motioned for all the trucks to keep moving. At the first opportunity, the trucks veered to the west through rows of rundown adobe houses. After bypassing most of Brownsville, the smugglers found dirt roads leading north into Willacy County. There, the convoy turned east toward the coast and followed the main highway.

"The liquor arrived on a ship from Cuba last night," Glenn explained.

Ralph observed how completely alert for danger his brother was. At ten o'clock, the motorboats began running the cases in to the beach. Ortiz had arranged a makeshift ferry— a single barge lashed to a small towboat—for crossing the Laguna Madre.

"We take the trucks across the lagoon, two at a time," Glenn told his brother, as the first two vehicles rolled onto the improvised ferry.

The loading process, including ferrying the trucks back and forth across the lagoon, took less than an hour. When all fourteen trucks were on the mainland, the tarps were removed. For the first time, Ralph could see that he was leading a fleet of delivery trucks. Four of the trucks had *Foremost Dairies* painted on them. Several others said, *The Texas Company,* and had the familiar Texaco star displayed on both sides.

The remaining trucks were painted red and had *National Laundry* lettered on them. Ralph was admiring the thoroughness of the operation when he heard his brother again.

"Here they come, right on time," Glenn observed.

Three marked patrol cars, each containing two of Sheriff Schertz's men, silently joined the convoy as they began the drive north toward Houston.

"The deputies will arrest all of us and seize the load, if federal or state cops show up," Glenn explained with a chuckle.

"Will the feds know what they're up to?" Ralph asked.

"Doesn't matter if they do or don't. These guys are the law. They'll have handcuffs on us and they'll even lock us in cells, till the G-Men disappear, if they have to go that far to make their act convincing," Glenn tutored.

Sheriff Schertz's escort continued through Willacy County.

"We'll get new escorts in Kenedy and Kleberg counties," Glenn continued.

A mile before Highway 77 entered Nueces County, the deputies led the trucks off the road and into a giant barn filled with bales of hay.

"What's happening now?" Ralph asked anxiously.

"We're going to be on our own for a while," Glenn answered.

"Watch and you'll see how it works."

One of the deputies drove north without the convoy.

"I checked as far as Robstown," the deputy told Glenn, when he returned to the barn in about an hour.

"You're all clear."

"Driver knows what to do. We'll meet near Missouri City," Glenn told Ralph.

"Get going," Glenn ordered, turning to the driver.

Ten minutes later, the second truck rolled out of the barn. Fifteen minutes passed before the third truck drove on. Eventually, the whole convoy was well spaced along the highway. Eight of the trucks went to Galveston, six to Houston. Each truck carried a shipment for a designated club or restaurant. The rendezvous took place at a cotton farm between Sugar Land and Missouri City.

"Everything go all right in Galveston?" Glenn asked Ralph when his truck was parked at a loading dock extending out from a giant barn. Each of the trucks was being loaded with dry goods.

"Fine. Everything was smooth," Ralph answered.

"What are we doing now?" he asked.

"These goods are scarce in Mexico. We'll take them to Brownsville and *Commandante* Cisneros' men will see they get to Matamoros and Reynosa," Glenn explained.

When Ralph delivered the money to Ortiz, Glenn stood beside Ortiz with his Tommy gun. Ralph wanted to brag about his success, but the sight of his younger brother's finger on the trigger dampened his ego. Even for Ortiz, the way Glenn stood watch created a feeling of tension, an atmosphere very like being in a room where a bomb is being defused.

Instead of praising Ralph's work, Ortiz quietly took the money.

"Join us for breakfast and we'll talk," he invited.

Ralph led the run to Galveston the next week and supervised two convoys the third week. By the fourth week, he oversaw forty-two trucks. Every second or third run, Glenn rode in a truck directly behind his brother, the submachine gun in his lap to ensure Ralph never entertained any thoughts of stealing.

CHAPTER FORTY-ONE

After his third trip, Ralph understood Glenn's value to Ortiz, and Ralph no longer doubted Glenn would shoot him. He also came around to Jimmy Barnes' view that even Ortiz was afraid of Glenn. Ralph changed his mind about something else as well. Glenn was not as greedy for money as Ralph had believed. He took his share of the money, but what Glenn really sought was the power he experienced in seeing other men terrified of him. Glenn felt positively triumphant that he, the little brother, could produce in Ralph a fear that was totally and undeniably paralyzing.

When Glenn was escorting either Ortiz or his liquor, he was completely alert. Most of the rest of the time, he was in a stupor. Ralph continued to drink very little and infrequently. Ralph was not actually concerned about Glenn because they were family, but he found Glenn's behavior difficult to understand. Because he could not talk with Glenn directly, Ralph went to Jimmy Barnes.

"What's got into Glenn?" Ralph asked his brother's friend during an encounter in the driveway outside Ortiz's house.

"Lower your voice," Jimmy Barnes urged.

Glenn was inside with Ortiz, at least a hundred yards away.

"He can't hear us," Ralph blustered, not concealing his aggravation and disdain with this pathetic little man.

"He's right inside the house. He hears everything," Jimmy Barnes warned, clearly believing what he was telling Ralph.

"He thinks people are talking about him all the time. Two nights ago, he killed two Mexicans who laughed at him because he fell down in the street," Jimmy Barnes continued in a barely audible whisper.

"He don't want nobody talking about him."

Ralph wanted to believe that Jimmy Barnes was lying or exaggerating, but he was virtually certain that his brother's friend was telling the truth.

"But he's gotten worse! I didn't think that drinking could make anybody as crazy as it makes Glenn," Ralph declared.

"It ain't the drinking. It's the opium," Jimmy Barnes said, finally coming clean with Ralph about his contention that Glenn was getting worse.

"Opium?" Ralph almost shouted.

"I told you. Keep your voice down," Jimmy urged, clearly terrified, his alert spoken in an urgent whisper.

"He'll come out here and kill us both. He's just looking for an excuse to kill you, anyway. When he gets crazy, he mumbles about killing you all the time, talking about how you used to box him around when y'all were kids."

"Where does he get it?" Ralph asked, this time in a voice no louder than Jimmy was using.

"The opium?" Jimmy Barnes asked.

Ralph nodded.

"He gets it from Chinese sailors. He started smoking it, right after you came down here. That's why we got that house we're living in. None of the madams wanted us around with that stuff. They were afraid their girls would get into it and it would make them all crazy.

"Now, whenever we want some women, I've got to go someplace and bring them back to the house. Course, none of the madams charge us anything. They're too scared of Glenn.

"Several times, when I was too slow getting back home for him, he came over to the house I was at, waving that machine gun around, threatening to shoot me and everyone in the place.

"He's gotten real bad," Jimmy finished, trembling uncontrollably.

No trace of color remained in Ralph's face. He did not love Glenn the way one brother is expected to love another, but he could not believe that alcohol and opium had changed his once cheerful little brother into a homicidal maniac. Ralph wanted to go home and tell his father what had happened to Glenn; but the truth was that there was no one to tell. There was nothing Ralph, or anyone else, could do. Glenn was what he had become; and not even Walter's love, nor Ada's enormous will, could change that. Before Ralph spoke again, he heard someone whistling happily and fast footsteps moving toward him. He turned to see Glenn, nattily dressed in a new yellow suit. He was wearing white spats and a highly polished new pair of shoes. Glenn tossed some keys at Ralph.

"Come on, big brother," he invited.

"We're going home. We're going to drive that new Packard to Telegraph."

Ralph looked closely at the middle of his brother's body. He saw no gun and no bulge in his clothes to indicate that the big Colt was tucked in his belt under his vest.

"Come on, Jimmy. You want to see your daddy, don't you?" Glenn called cheerily.

Ralph opened the door and slid behind the wheel of Glenn's new car. Glenn took a seat in front and Jimmy Barnes jumped in the back, just as Ralph started the big Packard rolling.

"Ortiz had it made special, just for me," Glenn announced in praise of his new automobile, his face still covered with a broad smile.

"When we get into Texas, I'll really show you something," Glenn bragged.

In a few minutes, the big roadster stopped at the international border. Glenn motioned for the Mexican customs agent.

Glenn never traveled into Texas, except on business. The Rangers had made it clear that he was not safe in their state. Glenn handed the customs man a hundred-dollar bill for him to keep. He also passed along ten ten-dollar bills as bribes for the other men on the Mexican side and five twenty-dollar bills for the customs men on the American side.

In less than five minutes, the Mexican customs officer had returned to Glenn's Packard. He stood on the running board of the car and grabbed the door.

"Drive on," he told Ralph.

One hundred yards inside the United States, he jumped from the running board and was picked up by a car one of his men had driven across from Mexico. In less than a minute, the agent was back in Mexico.

"You know where McCluskey's Icehouse is, don't you, Ralph?" Glenn asked his brother.

"Drive over there and stop."

When the Packard eased to a stop in front of the icehouse, a young Tejano scrambled to the car. In seconds he had loaded two cases of premium Canadian beer into the icebox between the driver's seat and the passenger's seat. As soon as the last bottle was in place, two other young men covered the bottles with ice.

"Pretty neat, huh?" Glenn beamed.

The custom beer box was made of stainless steel, with a latch that pulled the lid tight on the cooler. The ice box would keep the beer the young men put in it in Brownsville cold for several days. Ralph was surprised that no liquor was loaded into the car.

As Ralph drove northwest along the river, avoiding the main highway, Glenn and Jimmy Barnes swigged beer and threw the empty bottles from the car. Glenn remained cheerful and sober for the entire trip.

"I want you to stop in Cotulla," Glenn told Ralph.

A San Antonio taxicab met them there and took them quietly to San Antonio for the night.

"I've got us a three-bedroom suite," Glenn announced, when the cab pulled into an alley behind the St. Anthony Hotel.

The manager, who greeted them, escorted the three young men through a back door and up to their rooms.

"I apologize for using the freight elevator," he told them cheerfully.

"I have asked the chef to prepare quail for your dinner. I hope that will make up for the inconvenience."

After supper, six young ladies arrived from a local brothel.

"Here," Ralph said to the two young ladies who came to his room. He handed them each a two-dollar bill. "This is for your trouble."

As they left the suite, he shut the door behind them. The next morning, Ralph looked for a taxicab as the manager led them into the alley. Instead, a big black limousine belonging to the Mexican Consul was waiting for them. Breakfast was served on the ride back to Cotulla, and Glenn and Jimmy Barnes had several eye openers to clear their heads.

Before ten, Ralph was guiding the big Packard along back roads around San Antonio. At midafternoon, Ralph turned the car off the road, then down the drive to the South Llano River. Ada nearly died of fright when she saw her two sons step from the car.

"I can't believe it!" she exclaimed, while Edythe, Brooks, Ray, and the Velasquez children quickly mobbed the car.

They had never seen anything like Glenn's brand-new Packard. By the time Ada reached her front porch, the children covered the car. Ada wiped tears from the corners of her eyes with her apron, then called to her sons.

"I can't believe it!" she shouted again.

Glenn and Ralph had dropped Jimmy Barnes off in Junction to stay with his father.

"I'll get Dad," Brooks called out, as the other children continued crawling over the car.

Brooks ran to the barn, jumped on a horse, and rode to the river at a gallop. Walter knew a lot about the lives that Ralph and Glenn led along the border. Ada suspected. But for the next day and a half, the Oakley family pretended they had never been apart, that Glenn and Ralph were not bootleggers, and that Glenn was not a hunted criminal. No one wanted things to be any other way. Before supper on the second night, Walter asked Ralph to walk with him past the barn, where no one else could hear.

"Something went wrong between you and me, a long time back," Walter began. "I know you don't care much for my advice, but I have to tell you something. It's too late for your brother, but you can come back. No one's ever charged you with a crime. If you'll stop now, you can go back to St. Louis. You can get your old job back, and it will be like nothing has ever happened."

Ralph said nothing. He looked at the ground and thought hard about what his father was saying and about what he had seen his brother become.

"You don't have to answer right now," Walter offered. "Just please, think about what I'm saying. Your mother's heart is broken. She doesn't want to see both her sons dead."

Ralph had never respected his father. For reasons he could not explain, even to himself, he looked upon his father as weak. Everyone who knew the Oakleys looked up to Walter, holding him in a position above most people they knew or had ever known. They thought of him as an Indian fighter, a railroader, a pioneer, and an honest leader and role model.

Ralph knew at once that what his father had suggested was right. Since his first trip to Matamoros, Ralph believed Glenn would be killed. For more than a month, Ralph had feared that Glenn would kill him. Ralph was afraid, and he knew that ignoring Walter's counsel would be a big mistake.

Had Ada been the one who had talked with Ralph instead of Walter, Ralph might have let Glenn and Jimmy Barnes go back to Mexico without him. But in the end, it was the emotional estrangement of Ralph from his father that prevented him from taking Walter's sound advice.

For a few days, Ralph and Glenn enjoyed something they had missed having all of their lives. For a brief time, they were brothers who enjoyed their family and each other's company. Glenn kept the warm glow from the trip for several weeks, after returning to Mexico. He was happy, stayed mostly sober, and kept away from opium.

CHAPTER FORTY-TWO

Ralph was leading a convoy of liquor to Houston and Galveston without his brother. In Matamoros, everyone inside Ortiz's house was asleep. Jimmy Barnes was lying on a couch at the foot of the stairs when an intruder bumped into a piano. Jimmy looked up to see five or six shadows moving through the dark room.

He scrambled from the sofa and up the stairs to get Glenn. One of the bandits started shooting at the noise Jimmy made as he ran. Wounded in the leg, he stumbled past Glenn at the top of the stairs just as Glenn opened fire with the Thompson.

The noise from the gunfight was hellish. Glenn stood alone at the head of the staircase, raining bullets on the bandits below. Less than thirty seconds after he started shooting, the intruders stopped firing and began scrambling in panic.

"Let's get out of here," one bandit screamed in Spanish.

By then, three of the would-be robbers lay dead in the living room. Three others crept to the front door, then ran toward Glenn's Packard.

"Come on, Jimmy. They're getting away," Glenn said, when he heard the bandits flee.

Glenn charged athletically down the stairs and onto the porch. He spotted the three who had fled the house and saw two others climbing into his Packard.

"Not this time," Glenn screamed.

Again, fire spewed from his submachine gun. He raked the car back and forth until the magazine was empty. The night air was still and silent for thirty or forty seconds when Glenn felt, or perhaps heard, breathing beside him.

He looked to his right and saw Ortiz standing next to him holding a twelve-gauge shotgun, a box of shells and Glenn's Colt. Glenn dropped the Thompson and took the weapons from Ortiz. He tucked the Colt in his belt and walked to his car. It was filled with bandits and their blood was dripping from the car's floorboard onto the ground.

Glenn walked to the first robber, who was slumped over the steering wheel. He placed the shotgun to the driver's head and fired. Glenn shot each of the dead bandits in the head with the shotgun, went into the house, turned on the lights, and shot a round of buckshot into the heads of each of the dead men in the living room.

When he was finished, he walked to the bar, found an unbroken bottle of Canadian whiskey, sat on the couch, and began gulping the liquor. Ortiz sat beside Glenn and took Glenn's left hand in both of his.

"Thank you," Ortiz whispered.

"Holy Mother of God," *Commandante* Cisneros exclaimed, when he stepped from his car outside Ortiz's house a few moments later.

"I have seen a lot of gore. But in all my years as a policeman, I have never seen such carnage as this."

"Are you all right, my friend?" *Commandante* Cisneros called to Ortiz, when he entered the big living room.

Ortiz had moved to the bar to pour himself a drink. Glenn, still sitting on the couch, had drunk half the whiskey. Seeing the policemen, Ortiz half filled five glasses with whiskey: one for each of the policemen and one for himself.

"Maybe this will help," he said, handing glasses first to Cisneros, then to his men.

"Mother of God," the *commandante* repeated.

Everyone drank silently for a time. Then, after a few minutes, Ortiz spoke quietly to *Commandante* Cisneros.

"I don't like publicity, ordinarily, but maybe some pictures will deter anyone else who wants to steal from me," he said.

"I agree," the police commander nodded.

Cisneros sent one of his men to get newspaper photographers from Matamoros and Brownsville. Glenn finished the bottle of whiskey before the photographers arrived. He rummaged through the broken glass to find a third bottle. He pulled the stopper out and took a big gulp.

"Come on. I need a driver," he told one of Cisneros' men.

Commandante Cisneros nodded, and the two men pushed through the broken glass and dead bodies to a police car. Glenn told the policeman where to take him, a gathering place for Chinese sailors who smoked and sold opium. Another of Cisneros' men was sent to Brownsville for an American doctor to remove the bullet from Jimmy Barnes' leg.

"You need to go to the hospital in Brownsville, where I can properly treat your wound," the doctor told Jimmy Barnes.

"The Rangers would be waiting for me as soon as I cross the river into Texas," Jimmy Barnes responded.

"You'd better take the bullet out right here."

By the time Glenn and the Mexican policeman found a sailor with some opium, Glenn could barely walk.

"I cannot sell opium to you," the Chinese man told Glenn, glancing at the lawman standing next to him.

"He works for us," Glenn mumbled drunkenly, and pulled the Colt from his belt.

Glenn pulled the trigger, but Cisneros' man bumped Glenn just as he fired. The bullet whizzed past the running sailor, who dropped the opium as he fled. The policeman scrambled to his knees to pick up the opium for Glenn. Glenn was sitting on the curb, pointing the pistol at the cop. Glenn intended to shoot the officer, who had stopped him from killing the vanished Chinese sailor, but the policeman acted fast.

"Let me help you," Cisneros' man said, as he helped Glenn prepare the opium for smoking. The policeman's quick thinking probably saved his life.

In five minutes, Glenn was lying in the street, unconscious. The officer dragged Glenn into the back seat of his car and drove him home. An hour or so later, another of the Cisneros men arrived with Jimmy Barnes, who had received surgery on Ortiz's couch. Within a week, the pictures had been published in most of the major papers in Texas and Mexico. Ada had a folded copy of the *San Antonio Light* with her as she sat down in front of Sheriff Wilson's desk.

"Bill, I know you've seen this," she said, as she opened the paper containing a photo of the massacre for the sheriff to see.

The story that accompanied the picture mentioned Jimmy Barnes and Glenn Oakley, son of Kimble County Justice of the Peace Walter Oakley but not Ralph.

"You know that Ralph is with his brother," Ada stated.

"I'm so sorry," Bill Wilson offered, sincerely and sympathetically.

"I need your help. I need you to talk to the Rangers down there and get Ralph's address for me," Ada continued.

"It'll take a couple of hours," the sheriff answered.

He was subdued and overwhelmed by the hurt he saw in Ada's face.

"I'll come back," Ada said, rose silently and left.

When Ralph arrived at Ortiz's late in the afternoon the day after the shootout, Cisneros' men, armed with rifles, were everywhere. A dozen Mexican workers were cleaning up and repairing the damage from the night's shooting.

"What happened?" Ralph urgently asked the first policeman he recognized.

Ralph listened to the answer for about thirty seconds, before concluding it was time to get out of Mexico. If I don't, I'm dead, he thought. Two long days passed before Ralph could see his brother. Glenn looked like a corpse. The drinking, drugs, and killing had left Glenn without normal human feelings. Hate, self-loathing, and exhaustion were all that were left inside of Glenn. The young man staring back at Ralph was almost in hell, waiting only for death to complete his journey.

Ralph's thoughts raced back to the recent trip the brothers and Jimmy Barnes had made to Telegraph. The face Ralph was looking at did not seem like it belonged to the same person he had traveled to Telegraph with. And certainly, the face Ralph saw before him bore no resemblance to the face of his little brother.

Glenn didn't speak but reached into his pocket and pulled out a roll of bills. Ralph extended his hand. Ralph wanted to say thank you, but he could see that there were tears in the corners of his brother's eyes. So he took the money, squeezed Glenn's hand and walked away. He just told me goodbye, Ralph concluded, as he sat alone in his room counting the money, twenty thousand-dollar bills. Two mornings later, at five o'clock, Ralph was awakened by a knock on his door. Terrified, he stood beside the door, holding a loaded pistol.

"It's open," he called, attempting to make his voice sound calm and, as if it were coming from the bed.

"*Señor* Ralph?" *Commandante* Cisneros announced tentatively as he entered the empty room.

Ralph stepped quietly from behind the open door. He had lowered the pistol to his side, and relief showed clearly on his face. *Commandante* Cisneros held out a package for Ralph. It looked smaller than a shirt and was wrapped in brown paper.

"A Texas Ranger brought this for you ten minutes ago," Cisneros said, passing the package to Ralph.

"Let me know if you need my help," he offered before he turned and left the room.

When the door closed, Ralph placed the pistol on the nightstand and sat in the chair beside his bed. He carefully opened the package and read a letter from his mother.

Dear Son,

Run for your life! It is too late for your brother, but I could not bear to have both my sons die in the horrible mess you are in. I was wrong to send you after Glenn and I will never stop blaming myself for that mistake, but you have to leave today! Surely, you know your brother will be killed, and you must not die with him.

Sheriff Wilson helped me get this letter to you. He says that there are no criminal charges against you in Texas. Even though the Rangers know you are a bootlegger, they have no proof. It's Glenn and Jimmy Barnes and that horrible man Ortiz they want, and the sheriff says the Rangers will kill them on sight. (That's so terrible I cannot even think about it—that my wonderful little boy will be shot like a mad dog.)

The picture of the shootings at that man Ortiz's house has been in all the newspapers and the papers say that Glenn killed those men. I know that can't be true, but the

*Rangers believe it and I know they will kill Glenn and they will kill you too, if you
are with him.*

Get out today and come home!
I love you and I am sorry for what I asked you to do.
Love,
Mama

Ralph disappeared. He left without saying goodbye to his brother or Ortiz.
He paid a man to row him across the river to a little town in Texas called
Los Indios. At sunup, he paid another man to drive him to Harlingen.
Using cash, Ralph bought a new Chevrolet and drove north.

Life went on in Matamoros, even as the chaos continued to swirl
around the Ortiz smuggling organization.

Veronica was astoundingly beautiful. She had blonde hair, big blue eyes,
and a sleepy look that stayed with her even when she was not tired.
Everyone who knew Veronica and Jimmy was mystified by her obsession
with the strange little criminal, who had been an accomplice to so many
murders, if not a willing participant in them.

She had just shown up in Matamoros, intent on marrying Jimmy. They
had lived together in San Antonio before Jimmy began robbing banks and
had been forced to flee. For reasons known only to her, Veronica had
decided that now, of all times, presented the proper occasion for Jimmy
and her to get married.

Glenn had been disoriented and disconnected. He could not account
for the weeks between the shootout at Ortiz's compound and Jimmy
Barnes' wedding. Opium and alcohol had taken away any feeling of orderli-
ness and any sense of the sequence of time.

Father Enrique and Ortiz were the only Catholics present for Jimmy
Barnes' and Veronica Scholtz' marriage, but the church blessed their union
just the same. Ortiz gave the couple five thousand dollars as a wedding
present, and so did Glenn.

Jimmy and Veronica Barnes spent five blissful days away from the Ortiz
bootlegging business; but the Sunday after the wedding, Glenn
interrupted.

"It's time to go back to work," Glenn told Jimmy.

CHAPTER FORTY-THREE

In Junction, Sheriff Bill Wilson told Walter that he had helped Ada get a letter to Ralph.

"I hope he's all right," Walter said, as the two sat on a bench under a shade tree on the courthouse lawn.

"We haven't heard from him."

"Captain Parker said he wasn't in Matamoros, anymore, but Glenn and Jimmy Barnes are still there. Barnes married some girl from San Antonio, after that whole shooting business," Sheriff Wilson related.

"I blame every bit of this on Jimmy Barnes. But in reality, I know better. I tried everything to keep those two from drinking. I tried as hard as I knew how to keep them apart, but I guess I just didn't do enough," Walter told his dear friend.

"It's easy to look back on this thing, and blame yourself, Judge. But the fact is, everyone around here knows that no two boys ever had more done for them than Glenn and Ralph. I don't know what it was that got into them, but it wasn't anything they learned from you or from Ada," the sheriff concluded.

"I wish you were right, Bill. But what happened to Ralph was my fault, plain as day. I remember once that I complained to Ada that Ralph wouldn't listen to me, didn't respect me. She told me that my father and I spent more time together in one day than Ralph and I did in a whole month. What she said hurt, but it was right. I didn't raise him. She did, and without my being around to help much," Walter countered.

"Glenn was pretty much the same. I spent too much time taking care of the railroad and not enough time taking care of my family."

"You're being too hard on yourself," Bill cautioned.

"Ralph finished first in his class. You got him an appointment to West Point. He was the one who wouldn't take it. Maybe you were gone a lot, when Glenn was real little, but the first sign of trouble, you were right there with him. I never knew any pair that spent more time fishing or working together than you and Glenn. And he loved every minute of it," the sheriff offered as a rebuttal.

So did I, Walter thought as he struggled to keep from being overcome by emotion. I loved those times with Glenn so very much.

Walter's second son was still on his mind a few days later when he went riding with his old friend, the sheriff.

"I've been thinking about what you said," he told Bill Wilson, as the two splashed their horses through a shallow spot to cross the South Llano River.

"Sometimes, I want to take off and go to Mexico. I think, maybe if I could find a spot for Glenn and me to go fishing, we could talk. Maybe we could be happy the way we used to be when we fished together. If I could just get him away from this whole liquor business for a few weeks, we could start to work things out for him," Walter yearned.

"I pray you're right," Sheriff Wilson answered.

"But you don't think so. You think I am just trying to fool myself? Is that it?" Walter challenged.

"Who knows? Try it if you think it might work. Try it, even if you think it doesn't have a chance. Maybe then you will be sure that you've done everything you could do," the sheriff suggested.

The two friends dismounted and sat watching the river rush over the rocks.

"I've seen a lot of changes in my lifetime," Walter observed after a long stretch of quiet.

"I'm nearly fifty years old and almost nothing is much like it was when

I was a kid. I wonder if there's ever been a time of faster change than during our lifetime," Walter asked.

"I don't know. I guess I see the change more when I go to San Antonio. The biggest difference I notice around here is the cars," Bill replied.

"People are different. That's the biggest change. The young folks are running off to the city so fast. When we're dead, I doubt there'll be anyone left around here. They'll all be living in San Antonio. Seems like no one wants to work on a farm anymore," Walter said, perhaps being nostalgic and perhaps for no reason at all.

Walter thought, who am I to talk? I went off to work for the railroad, long before I knew anything about living. My father wanted me to go to college, to be an engineer. Did I listen to him? Did I stay on the farm? It was only after my kids started having trouble that I bought this farm.

"Three of my brothers are drinkers," Walter said, breaking a long silence.

"They packed up and headed to Fort Worth, moved to the city, just like most other folks. What am I thinking about that for?" he asked aloud.

"Maybe you're trying to explain things to yourself. Maybe you think if you can find an explanation some of this bad news will be easier to take," Bill proposed.

"I guess I should be old enough to know better, huh?" Walter chuckled.

"I guess, maybe you didn't listen last time we talked. It's not your fault. You didn't do anything to make those boys do what they did. Maybe you're right. Maybe it is the fast times. Lots of other people's kids have gone into bootlegging, not just your two boys," the sheriff said.

"I'm against liquor, Walter. You know that, but this Prohibition is the wrong way of going about it. People are going to drink. What the Anti-Saloon League crowd did was stupid. This business is making criminals out of a lot of people," Sheriff Wilson suggested.

Walter was not listening. He was thinking about his children. It was fine for Bill Wilson to say that their problems were not his responsibility, but Walter believed to his core that they were his problems. He believed that he'd had an obligation, as a father, to protect his children from these evil influences that were threatening their very lives. Walter believed he was a failure as a parent, because he had not properly guided, taught and shielded the children God had given him.

"I just feel so powerless, half my children are caught up in this mess, and there is nothing I can do about it," the clearly distraught father confessed to his friend.

"You're being too hard on yourself, Walter," the sheriff told him, not for the first time.

Walter was desperately sad. He was certain that he had missed something along the way. There must have been something he could have done. There must have been some way that he could have protected his family from all this grief. These doubts and feelings of remorse just played over and over in his mind.

He returned to planning a trip to Mexico. He needed to find a place he could take his son fishing. That would be a first step. Walter prayed he would not be too late.

With Ralph out of the picture, Glenn and Jimmy Barnes took an even greater role in transporting the liquor to Houston, Galveston, and San Antonio. Ortiz never pressed Glenn, but Glenn never gave him reason to. Ralph had been indispensable until he was gone. The whiskey had to move. And after the shootout, Glenn saw to it that the flow continued.

"I don't like us going into Texas, either. But we still have a business to run. And part of running that business means we have to go to Texas," Glenn told Jimmy Barnes.

Glenn might have lost contact with reality in his personal life, but he never let that interfere with his business. In that way, he was just as reliable as his mother or older brother. But of course, Ada's business wasn't criminal.

Ortiz never doubted Glenn. He had courted Ralph, because he knew Glenn needed help, and because he recognized Ralph's ability. However, the cornerstone of Ortiz's enterprise was Glenn's loyalty. Ortiz trusted Glenn with his business, and with his life.

Until the point when he became a killer, Glenn had found it easy to get along with almost everyone. Of course, Jimmy Barnes had been Glenn's special friend. But after the massacre, Ortiz and Jimmy Barnes were Glenn's only friends. Ortiz was probably as afraid of Glenn as he was dependent on him.

But Jimmy Barnes wasn't simply afraid, he was mortally terrified of his friend. Glenn understood Jimmy Barnes' fear, but it was something they never spoke of. Veronica had noticed the fear immediately. She had noticed, but she never brought up the subject, and neither did her husband.

Thirteen days after their wedding, Veronica slept with Glenn. Jimmy Barnes had passed out and his wife had been in a drunken stupor.

"I can't believe it!" Jimmy exclaimed the next morning when he woke and saw his best friend and his wife in bed together. Veronica and Glenn slept on without responding.

After a few days, Glenn had lost interest in Veronica, but he kept her with him, anyway. When six weeks had passed Glenn, forced Jimmy to move out of the house. Sometimes when Jimmy Barnes saw Glenn and Veronica together, Veronica would have a black eye. Ortiz saw what was happening but chose not to interfere. He was afraid that Glenn might turn on him. Veronica and Jimmy Barnes meant absolutely nothing to Ortiz.

There wasn't anything Jimmy Barnes could do to get his wife back. And each day, his friend continued to taunt Jimmy about Veronica. Jimmy Barnes had never had any self-respect, and he had no experience that might help him deal with this latest humiliation. Jimmy had always felt powerless and worthless.

But the more Jimmy Barnes ignored the mistreatment of his wife by his best friend, the worse Glenn abused Veronica. Several times, he struck her when Jimmy was present. Glenn took Veronica to a brothel and ripped all her clothes off in front of Jimmy, the patrons, and the prostitutes. Three days later, at a party at Ortiz's house, Glenn publicly raped Veronica as people watched in horror.

The next morning, when he stepped onto a streetcar, Glenn heard someone shout his name.

"Glenn!"

As Glenn turned to face his best friend, a bullet fired from a .38 caliber pistol in Jimmy Barnes' hand thumped into Glenn's temple. He fell to the street, dead. He was twenty-seven years old.

Jimmy and Veronica Barnes disappeared, and Ortiz decided to return to Cuba. Ortiz left Mexico two hours after his protector was murdered.

When the news of Glenn's death reached Walter and Ada, they didn't know where Ralph was. As they buried Glenn on their farm in Telegraph, the couple was paralyzed by a fear that their oldest son may also have been killed.

Sheriff Bill Wilson had heard reports that Ralph, after leaving Matamoros, had continued his life as a bootlegger somewhere outside of Texas.

Two days after Glenn's funeral, his father wrote this prayer.

A Prayer for my Son

Loving and wonderful God,

I will never know why my beautiful son had to die.

Truly, Your ways are not our ways.

In time, Father, please give me peace from these questions that threaten to destroy me. I will never know what made Glenn drink or take opium. I will never know why he turned to violence—or why he became a killer.

Your plans for us are not easy to understand.

Today my grief is unbearable; but with your love, the sun will rise tomorrow. Tomorrow Father, may I remember my son Glenn as he was when we fished happily by the South Llano River.

Loving God, please give me the strength to help my family cope with this loss and to go on, sure in the knowledge that you have not abandoned us.

You have been with me every day of my life, God.

You have given me these children, and now you have taken my son away. Keep him with you, my God.

Glenn was not what he became at the end of his life. He was a boy whose smiles and whistles were a delight to his mother, to me and to You.

Hold him in Your arms for me, Father, as I shall long to do every day for the rest of my life.

Walter Oakley
Telegraph, Texas
June 22, 1928

ABOUT THE AUTHOR

Phil Oakley is a writer, educator, film-maker, journalist and executive. He is the author of eight novels. He began working on his first one in the spring of 1964, while a freshman at The University of Texas at Austin. That book finally reached publication fifty years later in 2014. In addition to writing, Phil currently works as a paraprofessional educator at Kennedale High School.

Previously, he served as Director of the Louisiana Film Commission, was a regional executive of The Walt Disney Company, supervising coverage for ABC News in the southwestern United States and Latin America. He also was an

Photo by Brooks Oakley

editor/producer for *The Dallas Morning News*. As a journalist, Phil won national awards from Columbia University, the Radio-Television News Directors' Association and a National Headliners Award. He covered presidents and presidential campaigns, beginning with Lyndon Johnson and extending through the terms of George W. Bush. Phil was born in Austin during the last days of World War II. He lives in Arlington, Texas with his wife, the former Nancy Matens of Baton Rouge. Both are graduates of Louisiana State University. They have two sons and one granddaughter.

THE OAKLEYS WILL RETURN

Look for the next installments in the series:
Runners and ***Longhorn***
Coming soon from

Stoney Creek Publishing

A Member of the Texas Book Consortium

We publish the stories you've been waiting to read

Check out our other titles, including audio books, at
StoneyCreekPublishing.com.

For author book signings, speaking engagements, or other events, please
contact us at info@stoneycreekpublishing.com

Printed in the USA
CPSIA information can be obtained
at www.ICGtesting.com
JSHW021226070324
58661JS00002B/4